1776/66

This is a work of fiction. The characters, organizations, and events portrayed in this novel are either products of the author's imagination or are used fictionally. None should be construed as real.

1776/66

S. A. Scoggin.

Paiutech Media Group
Boston, Massachusetts

June 17, 1775
Charlestown, Massachusetts Colony

"You will oblige me," Major Chartington said casually, "by marching your Grenadiers to the west and joining the assault on the redoubt."

Lieutenant Pryce turned from observing his company. It was his now because Captain Mallory was being carried unconscious back to the boats. Chartington had clamped his left hand hard about his right arm just above the elbow. Crimson oozed glistening between his white bloodless fingers. His lapels and facings were splattered with what appeared to be brains, the late possession of some unfortunate who had been standing near.

"Yes, sir," Pryce responded, then more loudly he called, "Sergeant Kilkins, form the company when the men are ready."

The 63rd Grenadiers were allowed finally to loose their packs and stack them on the edge of the narrow beach. The day had started warm and was now hot, but the company had been ordered to take the hill bearing their full marching load as well as ammunition and rations for three days. Someone higher up now apparently realized the day's task was not going to be as simple as first thought. The appraisal of their opponents brought down from General Howe's staff – that the untrained and unseasoned rabble would turn and scamper back to Cambridge when faced with a serious display of professional soldiering – had been slightly off the mark.

The earthworks appeared in the night. When the sun rising over Boston Harbor lit up Breed's Hill, the astounded British command saw colonial spadework had transformed an innocuous sheep pasture into a creditable fortress. A large redoubt had been sunk at the top of the hill. Displaced soil, layered in bulwarks, protected the defenders. The stronghold was secured on its western flank by the buildings of Charlestown and on the east by a reinforced rail fence running down to the Atlantic.

Only hours before, Pryce and Mallory had breakfasted together in their Boston lodgings and gazed out over the channel at the new fortifications. Mallory predicted two of the smaller Navy ships could easily interdict traffic along the narrow spit of land connecting the rebel construction with Cambridge. In two or three days, he had stated confidently, the defenders would consume their rations and clean the nearby town out of water and food. They would then have to choose to either sneak back to Cambridge and run the deadly gauntlet of the King's cannon, or surrender outright.

General Howe apparently had no patience for starving out his opponent. He agreed with his aides – a vigorous and immediate application of shining steel and drums would flush the shaking colonials like so many quail. General Howe had been wrong, yet he was sipping brandy on his ship while Captain Mallory choked to death convulsing in a longboat.

The rebels might be farmers and shopkeepers, but they had not run. They fought their simple wood and dirt fortification with rapid and accurate musket fire that had twice repelled the British. The first repulse was a surprise, and it angered and shamed the British troops. They regrouped, reformed their lines, and pushed with determination, but again a relentless mass of lead beating on them from the redoubt made them first pause, then falter, and finally break. They retreated once more, ignoring the screaming threats of their officers and sergeants.

Finally the command had come up from the beach to form into columns instead of lines and to concentrate on taking the redoubt. Pryce watched as his sergeants prodded the men into their places. He did not assume to know the business of his generals but still wondered how many of the inert red forms scattered on the grassy slope would be on their feet if those giving the orders cared just a bit less about their personal pride and reputations. Attacking in glorious line had cost them dearly, and in the end they were resorting to the safer if far less magnificent tactic of an assault in column.

What breeze there was turned and carried billowing smoke from Charlestown over the surviving troops, many so exhausted they did not have energy to cover their faces. Pryce held his breath, as it was unseemly for an officer to flinch at any natural inconvenience, and silently damned his General for ordering the town set alight. It was tactical canon, of course, to occupy or destroy any possible refuge from where the enemy might put balls into your flank, and the British lines had on both climbs passed within range of the nearest buildings of the town. Cracks and snaps that might possibly have been musket fire led to reports of snipers, and now the heat of the inferno rolled across the slope and compounded the general discomfort.

Lieutenant Isaac Stark held out the powder bag. It was sewn from a gay blue cloth, which he thought somewhat incongruous, as its function was to deliver death. This bag was a smallish cannon charge. He had knifed it open and examined the coarse black granules. It was not the proper stuff to use in a musket, but that was the least of his concern now. It would burn.

"There is enough for every man to make two shots," he said. "If you have balls, share them out."

Stark's company had marched all the previous day to reach Cambridge, then picked up spades and mattocks from a haphazard pile donated by the townspeople and continued on without a rest over Charlestown Neck to present themselves to Colonel Prescott. Immediately that harried officer pointed to stakes driven into the hilltop and set them to digging. Though spent from the day's journey, they realized whatever barrier they were able to put up in the moonlight would be their only protection from cannonball and musket shot come daybreak. They moved earth with vigor, then came the sun and the British and the taxing work of firing and reloading heavy muskets. Stark watched as one man after another ran out of powder. The look on the face of the soldier who realized he had finally done all he could do and could now sink to the ground and rest with a clear conscience actually amused the Lieutenant – until he counted the number who were no longer able to fight.

Colonel Prescott could count as well, and he sent for the remaining bags of powder stacked behind the few militia artillery pieces emplaced beside the redoubt.

Stark's men regarded him blankly. Some sat on the firing step, their faces grimed with powder smoke and streaked pink where sweat had washed it down. Some lay on the ground breathing hard. All were exhausted but each reached into the bag, drew out powder, and coaxed it into coffee mugs, into leather pouches, into proper horns. When the bag was empty, Stark tore it into strips and passed these around for wadding.

"I have but one ball," an old private muttered. He showed one lead sphere between two bony fingertips. Others nodded, in the same plight.

"Use rocks," Stark said. "And choose them roundly."

A few managed to laugh. The company was primarily men from Provincetown – where Stark had been born and raised –, Truro, and Wellfleet. Most had taken a living from the ocean in some manner before volunteering for this recreation. Fishermen, whalers, crabbers, oystermen, clam rakers; none had been soldiers except Stark, who had fought in the French and Indian War. This experience had gotten him elected their lieutenant.

They owned no proper uniforms but wore whatever they

deemed comfortable for combat duties. At the moment, most were stripped to breeches and blouses, their coats, knapsacks, and blankets piled in a corner of the large square hole they had constructed. All retained hats against the warm sun. They wielded muskets of varying lengths and calibers, some new, some old, some which would be named medieval blunderbusses by a disgusted armorer. In toto, they looked like what they were – a bunch of ordinary citizens who had snatched up their arms and responded to the call. *In the village of the blind, the one-eyed man is Lieutenant*, Stark thought.

The one man not in his command, or more precisely who had not been in his command until about noon today, still wore his waistcoat, which, being silk, was apparently not a burden to him. It was also mostly clean. He had not spent the night burrowing into the hill with Stark's men. He had shown up midday alongside Prescott, who silently directed him to the part of the wall defended by the Cape men.

"Lieutenant Stark?" The man, ruddy cheeked and plump, had not presented anything like a common soldier in his fine clothing and undented tricorn, but he carried a welcome musket. "I am Joseph Warren. Colonel Prescott desires I join your company for the day."

Stark had not recognized the face, but the name stopped him cold. He knew Warren was a respected Boston physician and a noted Son of Liberty. The man was the President of the Provincial Congress, for Heaven's sake – certainly not the man to be here, within range of the King's muskets and cannon, firing a single inconsequential musket. Stark immediately ordered him to leave and make his way back into Cambridge.

Warren smiled a benevolent smile. "Ah, but you see, Lieutenant, I am a Major General and technically your superior. I shall not leave."

"Then," Stark had insisted, "you must take command from me."

The Doctor shook his head. "Thank you, no. I shall fight under you."

The situation stumped Stark. He had never heard of such

a thing, and the logical absurdity of it had set the nearest men to guffawing, though they tried their best to stifle this hilarity and maintain their martial dignity. Stark had looked about him and just shrugged, defeated.

Warren then opened his bag and produced several kinds of cheeses and sausage and instantly became the most popular man on Breed's Hill.

Any suspicion they harbored the dandy would be a liability had been drowned in the first two exchanges. Warren fired and reloaded, while not as quickly as the more seasoned men to his left and right, as calmly as any veteran. Stark had been sure the newcomer would leave his ramrod in the barrel and launch it at the enemy, giving an excuse to order his withdrawal. But Warren remained collected and did not lose his ramrod. Neither did he load several balls atop one another or break his flint or any of the other mistakes men made in the confusion and panic of battle. Soon Stark had ignored him, concluding the doctor's steel had no doubt been honed in bloody operating theaters sawing off the limbs of screaming patients and cutting stones from living flesh.

Now Stark's attention returned to this volunteer. Warren sat cross-legged on the packed dirt floor shaking the last of his tiny allocation of powder into an engraved silver powder horn. Only two of the company had been wounded thus far. The stout walls they had built in the night were more than protection enough against British fire, but one man had been shot in the jaw and another through the shoulder. Warren the soldier had temporarily set his weapon aside those times that Warren the doctor might treat them. Such luck could not hold, not with the powder at an end. Retreating, especially under close enemy fire and pursuit, was a chancy enterprise. Not a few of the men at ease in front of Stark would likely lie on this hill when the day was over.

Isaac Stark nursed no mooning love for a distant King he had never seen, but he had once faithfully worn the royal colors. He had stood next to other men who had fought and died in other battles against that same King's enemies. Today when he peered down the hill on the red-coated lines he imagined he might have ended up on that side but for the chances of birthplace and time. Instead, fate had put him here, shepherding the good Doctor Warren, a Major General by decree but green recruit in reality. Stark's transition from accepting the hard coin of the Royal Exchequer to the flimsy scrip of the Provincial Congress had been guided by self-education in the arguments of the day. He read all the pamphlets that made the hand-to-hand trip to the tip of Cape Cod. He sat up long hours in the Right Whale Tavern listening to political arguments and gossip. Finally he had decided his course and marched off with his townsmen.

So it was he realized – perhaps more clearly than any man in the redoubt – what the patriot movement owed this rather bland fellow in the filthy jacket who sat on the dirt carefully making sure every minute grain of powder made it into his beautiful horn. He was just one more tired volunteer in the shouting haze, but this one had recently captured the varied outrages of all New England and fixed them into the Suffolk Resolves. He had sent Dawes and Revere on their rides which saved Adams and Hancock from arrest. The gentleman seemed to have his hand in every action. His immediate commander thought if an impromptu shooting party of farmers and fishermen had the slightest chance in this improbable contest against the mightiest Empire the world had ever seen – and not just this morning, but until the issue was determined – the Doctor would have to keep up the remarkable pace he had set so far.

Stark stood on the firing step for a while, watching the British forming columns to his right, behind the banks of smoke wafting from the burning town. This time they were coming for the redoubt. Before their force had been divided, fixated on taking the fence running down to the water, but the stretch was defended by New Hampshiremen who knew how to handle their rifles. He turned and saw Colonel Prescott waving at him, making the signs: *Fire and Retreat in Order.* Stark nodded.

He jumped down and motioned for the attention of his unit. "Gentlemen, this time the Redcoats are coming for us in earnest. Without powder, we will not be able to dissuade them, and I do not propose to make their intimate acquaintance. They have bayonets, which most of us do not." Stark pointed at Warren, who was directly in front of him. "All to my right are first, and all to my left are second." He gave them the plan of retreat – the first group would load and fall back to the far wall of the redoubt. The second group would fire on the enemy when they were in range, then proceed back through the sally port and out of the redoubt, there to pause and reload. The first group would mimic that procedure and fire on the enemy as they appeared over the walls, then retreat to a position behind the second unit, there themselves to make ready to fire. "By falling back in turns and supporting the others, we will stifle the ambitions of the King's men and give them no chance to make mischief with the bayonet."

A young private, who could not have been more than 16, jumped up excitedly. "What... if I have no more powder?"

"Then you run like hell for Cambridge Neck," Stark said. "Doctor Warren, my men have practiced this maneuver before and you have not, so please stay beside me and fire as you can."

Warren nodded gravely. His eyes no longer shone with excitement. Stark wondered if the slaughter of a man one meant to kill with a ball was more trying to the soul than the death of a patient one was trying to save with a scalpel. If so, all their spirits were in need of rehabilitation, for the slope in front of them was carpeted in corpses wearing red. He climbed wearily back up on the firing step. The column starting up from the beach was aimed straight for him.

Pryce noticed to his right a group of officers gathered around a civilian. The man was dressed inappropriately for the Boston summer – long black coat, black breeches above stockings which might have been white this morning but were now browned by dust and debris from walking on the weedy, overgrown hill. He had a black tricorn upon his head, no wig, and yet Pryce could not detect a jot of sweat on what little of his face was visible.

Although civilians on the battlefield were out of the ordinary, they were not unknown. Pryce assumed it was some government functionary with a quill and account book come to see why it took so many guineas worth of musket balls to kill an enemy of the King. *If he stays that tall,* Pryce thought, *he shall certainly see how the goddamned colonists feed their families.*

Massed fire of muskets from the redoubt raking the British lines had broken the first two assaults, but it had been the long accuracy of rebel rifles from the fence that killed most of the English officers. By setting foot on the ground this stranger was making himself a tempting prize for some sharp-eyed farmer.

The Devil take him, Pryce concluded. The pitiful groans, screams, and entreaties of the wounded mixed with the crackle and smoke of the burning houses of Charlestown to make a rendition of Hell that might overwhelm the most experienced soldier. This civilian would soon find some excuse to run vomiting back to a longboat.

This time the Grenadiers were far away from the rifles, but there was still the point-blank fire of the redoubt to endure. His men held their own muskets up, their long bayonets toward the enemy. Just the sight of such bristling steel was often enough to make any opponent to a Redcoat force edge backwards. Today it did not seem so fearsome, and the only retreating had been done by an embarrassed British Army.

The column started up the hill slowly. The troops were tired and hungry and uncommon listless, but as they were compelled to step over the scattered remains of their comrades, the body seemed to become more and more angry. The pace quickened even beyond the frenzied cadence of their sergeants. They chilled in anticipation of shot whirring past, then as it did not come, they filled with an unwarranted optimism and excitement. Soon they were almost running into the redoubt's shadow. The top of the wall disappeared in a bank of smoke as rebel muskets coughed, but the volume of fire was noticeably diminished this time. As the sergeants automatically shouted "Close up! Close up!" to fill gaps left by the fallen, Pryce screamed instead. "Over the wall!"

He heard other officers yelling encouragements, and the sergeants began to push their men up the earthen obstacle. Pryce rushed for the barrier and put his boot into the soft soil.

The British were coming too fast. Stark had underestimated them, realizing too late they were animated by unleashed rage and fueled by their sufferings at the hands of the men in the redoubt. The Redcoats came over the top like a crashing crimson wave in the midst of a nor'easter and enveloped the men reloading on the firing step before the group covering them could fire. Stark's men who had stepped back stood with muskets up and shouldered but did not dare shoot into the mix of enemy and friend.

"At them!" Stark bellowed, and he rushed forward with his sword raised. The line behind him roared and charged into the melee, chopping with the butts of their muskets. Some cleared space enough to aim into the British still negotiating their way over the top of the redoubt wall. The renewed fire slowed the Redcoats and allowed the defenders precious time. Stark slashed and punched, grabbing his men as he could reach them and tugging them back, screaming at them to make for the sally port.

Lieutenant Pryce slipped on a flat stone just as he was about to gain the pinnacle of the redoubt wall. That misstep saved his life, as close over his ducking head a barrage of musketry crashed, so close he felt a hot gust as the balls passed. Fiery snatches of wadding smacked into his cheek, burning the flesh. He wiped these away and scrambled up the slope.

Inside, the defenders were slipping out of hidden exits. Some had stood and fought, using their muskets as clubs. Some were swinging swords and rapiers and short knives, but against these the British troops pressed forward with their long bayonets. Many colonials lay bleeding in the bottom of their fort.

Pryce parried and lunged with his sword and advanced until he was at the back of the structure and could see where the enemy was escaping.

"This way!" he called, but he could see that the useful enthusiasm of his troops for this assault was spent. The moment there was no rebel in front of them, men sagged. Too many had stabbed their bayonets into the soft ground and were leaning undisciplined on their muskets, breathing hard the horrible air thick with smoke and sweat and the iron stench of blood.

Pryce continued through the sally port with an ensign and two privates. Behind he heard his sergeants shrieking obscenities at their men, trying to get them to chase the fleeing enemy and finish them off. Pryce stepped out of the redoubt, his sword at the ready, but there was no resistance. The rebels were retreating in good order, covering each other with enough fire to make the scattered British pursuit reconsider that course.

To his left he saw once again the mysterious civilian, this time leading an officer, a captain whose name Pryce could not recall. They must have filtered around the side of the slope, past the abandoned rebel cannons. The civilian pointed toward the enemy, and Pryce had a sudden icy feeling the man was singling out one specific individual to the captain's attention. Pryce shook this off, a battlefield fancy, and held his sword out to his side, stopping his men from going farther. If the rebels were competent – and every indication this day had been that they were – they would have stationed artillery to cover the spit connecting this peninsula to Cambridge. Pryce had no desire to see any more of his men on the ground.

The Cape men slowed under their Lieutenant's entreaties and turned to cover the withdrawal of the militia still sheltering behind the fence. Those riflemen had maintained a deadly enfilade fire onto the Redcoats scaling the redoubt walls and had sustained their barrage to discourage the enemy from marching in force around the of the earthworks to harry the retreat. Now, with ball and powder depleted, the defenders at the fence were in peril.

Stark formed his men into line and commanded those who still could to pepper the British troops milling in front of the fence. It appeared though the colonial withdrawal was evident to all, the King's representatives had no desire to hop over the now-welcome rails which shielded them from fire.

A stray ball came from some distance and struck one of his men in the knee. Stark heard the bone crack, and the man fell down yelping in pain. The Lieutenant grabbed the man's musket and with the aid of two others hauled him up.

"Fall back to the Neck," Stark ordered. "Cover and cross!" He glanced back toward the redoubt and cursed. Warren had somehow fallen behind in the confusion. He had tossed his expensive but useless musket down and was hacking at two enemy privates with a long gleaming saber, parrying their attempts to stick bayonets into a man crawling away from them.

Stark hefted the musket and ran toward the skirmish.

It was no business of Pryce's. If the officer had been less than a captain, Pryce would have loudly demanded the man leave off, but he could by rights only hold his tongue and watch. The civilian and the captain strode to a small cluster of fighting – two British privates who were engaged in a contest of steel with a wounded rebel and a pale round fellow wearing a uniform more fit for a dinner party than a bloody battle. The dandy was giving a good account, however. With skill and energy he held the two privates off from his fellow, who scuttled from the bayonet lunges like a giant beetle, bleeding copiously from one thigh.

The civilian walked rapidly to them, again pointing. The captain, close behind, raised his arm and aimed a pistol.

Stark saw the weapon directed at Warren and shouted a warning. He broke into a run and raised up the musket, praying it was loaded. It fired, but he was still holding his sword and could not properly bring the stock to his cheek. This and the jolting of his sprint slewed the barrel. Still, the ball caught one of the Redcoats in the hand. The man spun around and dropped screaming to his knees.

Stark tossed the gun aside and raised his sword. Warren had broken off the fight, the crawling man now some distance away. The doctor turned to Stark in triumph. Then the dark figure raised a hand – just an empty hand, fingers splayed. Stark saw something leave Warren's eyes. They glazed and went... slack, as if he were staring into a far distance. Warren turned slowly back to face the enemy, but this time his sword stayed limp at his side.

Stark was just behind the doctor now, and he gathered himself to shoulder the man aside, out of the path of the British officer's pistol. Before he could make the final lunge, Stark heard the clack and crash of the pistol. Warren's head snapped back and in an instant rebounded forward. A geyser of red gore and mist burst from his head and enveloped Stark. The scarlet cloud had no substance, yet stopped the Lieutenant's run as if it had been stone.

The President of the Provincial Congress flopped to the earth, a lifeless rag. Stark wiped the warm splatter from his eyes and stared down at the corpse, then back up at the captain, busy reloading. The British private who had not been wounded gawked in awe at the proceedings.

The civilian surveyed his accomplishment with cold amusement. Stark began to boil with a rage he had not felt in the thickest of the day's battle, and he raised his sword and staggered at the smirking bastard.

"Lieutenant! Come away! Come away!" Hands grabbed him and spun him around. His men had run to fetch him. They snatched up the crawling man, and the three touching Stark had almost to lift him off the ground as they pulled him away from the body of Doctor Warren and made for the safety of the Neck.

July 11, 1244
The Holy Land

Two figures struggled up a steep sandy slope, fighting the scorching earth so awkwardly they appear unaccustomed to using their feet. They were dressed for the desert, at least, in linen robes once probably white but now darkened with soil and sweat. The front of one was decorated with a swath of dried blood. They were unwisely without head coverings and made another grave mistake in this heat by bearing heavy swords in battered scabbards on their red leather belts.

They stopped, crouching as if beneath a low ceiling instead of the endless blue sky. Sweat streamed from under their matted hair and dripped onto the ground as they panted.

One spread a hand in front of his mouth to caution his fellow against speech. His name was Ordulf, and he should have been ashamed of the clumsy way he climbed. He had grown up far from the horizontal in the very southern parts of the County of Ascania, where scraps of level ground were prized inheritances. As a legitimate son, he might have rightfully possessed one of those tiny meadows, and a few hills besides, if ten or so of his elders would only die in the proper order. The odds were against him in that, which is how he had ended up on this desolate hill so unlike the brilliant green mountains of his home.

The other nodded. He had nothing much to say anyway. The only way he could communicate with Ordulf, other than hand gestures, was in Latin, a language not taught in the patch of English mud upon which he had been whelped. The name they had put upon him when it seemed likely he would survive long enough to be worth calling at all was Thomas. If he had been the kind of boy who could hold his tongue at the proper moments he might have taken orders and be kneeling in a cool monastery chapel instead of squatting under the blazing Holy Land sun.

After a moment, they continued up, the top so close they kept to hands and knees. Their scabbards rasped harshly against the occasional rock with alarming loudness, and they paused in alarm. Dropping onto their bellies, they squirmed the last few feet to the top, by which time they were coated in sand and sweat. Ordulf muttered, but Thomas could make out only what sounded like "and we were once knights". No impartial observer would have taken them for the chivalrous Defenders of the Cross they professed to be.

When they peeked over the summit they saw the ridge was higher than they had thought. Just below the western horizon was an azure paint stroke – the sea. Closer was the great depressed bowl of the Holy Land and the skirt of sand upon which they had fled around the long salty lake, itself green as cedar boughs. Then the ranges of upraised earth began, higher and higher, up to the one the two warily glanced over.

To their right, north beyond the lifeless lake, rose a brownish red column, translucent, slowly twisting from the earth in search of Heaven. Jerusalem was burning. Thomas caught Ordulf staring hard at the smoke and remembered Ordulf had taken an Egyptian woman as his wife. Jerusalem was lost. All they had worked for these last years was in flames. Thomas had no one there, but everything he had seemingly ever owned besides what he had managed to grab when the wall had finally been breached was now in the hands of the enemy.

They heard loud echoing exclamations below, which snapped their minds away from the lost city. The valley was sharp and narrow and unremarkable - except for the trickle of a creek that ran in flowing curves along its bottom like the script of the Arabs. Following this mighty stream walked a dozen and a half men on a collection of mounts. The first three rode horses; the next five swayed on camels. The end of the line had been relegated to asses, some so puny the rider's feet almost dragged on the ground. The two knights would have been amused by the parade at almost any other time, but not today. All of the men below wore the strange metal hats of the Khwarezm army, and the last four riders had long bows slung over their shoulders and what seemed like hundreds of those deadly heavy arrows in quivers strapped to the sides of their mounts.

Ordulf rolled onto his back. "They think to follow the stream and deny it to us until we are useless from thirst," he whispered.

Thomas nodded, still looking down at the archers from a slit between two stones. "We will have to fight," he said softly. He considered the terrain down the valley, south to where the slow column was heading. If it narrowed, perhaps an ambush could be laid.

"Four of us against all of them, and they have archers? Not a cheerful prospect."

Thomas said nothing. They had seen the effect of the Khwarezm arrows – long, thick hardwood tipped with metal – which passed through knightly armor as easily as teeth through an overripe apple. And the knights had now not even that protection. They had shed all armor in their first hour of flight in exchange for extra speed.

"Don't worry," Ordulf said, his eyes closed against the sun. "Haven't you wondered yet why they don't have men climbing the other side of this slope trying to spot us?"

"I... have not," Thomas admitted. He put his hand to his sword, imagining an enemy face appearing.

"They don't want to find us. Are they excited at the prospect of stumbling across us?"

Thomas looked again. The riders did seem tired and discouraged – exactly the way he felt.

"Their imaginations are working on the picture of their plundering fellows back in Jerusalem relaxing amid wine and fruit."

Thomas snorted. "You mean spoiled horsemeat and sewer water. Do they fancy we weathered their siege in luxury?"

"They don't know that," Ordulf smiled. "I wager you one night shivering in this desert will turn them around."

One night. Thomas was as faint as if they had been fleeing for a month, but it had only been hours. Shortly after the previous sunset, Persian sappers had managed to undermine a wall, and the screaming horde poured in through the gap. The surprised knights leapt from their beds, hacked their way through a thin spot in the Khwarezm line, and fled the lost city. They rode their mounts hard, guided only by the compass of the heavenly stars in the moonless night. By dawn they were on the hard salt lip of the dead lake. As they climbed the other side of the shallow valley, they saw dust beaten into the still air by a force chasing them. The knights whipped their horses toward the rocky hills, until the exhausted mounts slowed despite all urging and had to be revived with the last of the water from the two skins the knights had snatched up in their exit.

No more to drink. Thomas licked his lips at the temptation of the creek far below, then he turned away. One more chill and arid night lay ahead. More ominously, the horses would be useless tomorrow.

He slid downhill a safe distance and stood. The horses below stood still and spent, not even fidgeting or flicking their tails. Beside them two men shaded the head of another lying on the ground. Thomas held his arms out wide, palms parallel, then pumped one fist into the air a dozen and a half times.

The two below understood, and one bent down to speak into the ear of the figure on the ground. They would have to remount and press on.

Ordulf started down the slope. Thomas put his fists to his hips and bent backwards, stretching stiff riding muscles, so his head came up and his eyes took in the eastern horizon.

He stopped and straightened. "Ordulf! Look!"

The other knight followed Thomas' pointing finger to a solitary peak, an odd column some miles away. It stood tall and alone, strangely flat-topped. And near the top were rectangles.

Dark, regular, and unnatural rectangles.

"A monastery." Ordulf pronounced.

"With a spring."

They squinted down at their leaning mounts and the three other knights, then back at the distant anomaly.

"Can he make it?" Ordulf wondered out loud.

He was the man on the ground, Thomas's liege lord. Geoffrey, the Earl of Emberton, who had plucked Thomas by the scruff of his young neck out of a shite-covered field and made him into a knight. In the first moments of their flight an enemy foot soldier had driven a short curved blade into Geoffrey's side. Thomas sprang between them and slashed the Turk across the face, but the damage had been done. His lord had ridden bravely all night only to collapse and fall out of his saddle just as they had started to climb away from their pursuers. Now he lay on the ground, his bleeding slowed but not stopped.

"Yes," Thomas said. *He must make it.*

The knights did not reach the base until the sun was alarmingly low in the west, as the entrance to the valley of the spire was well concealed. They had ridden out in several aborted probes of the convoluted cliffs before finding the narrow path to the interior. Once inside, they thought to be at the oddity quickly, but the massive scale of the mount confounded their estimations. It was in fact hours before they limped up to it.

The spire thrust up out of a huge expanse of dry hard salt. It was white rock, a form frozen in the middle of gushing, like a fountain captured in ice by some far off winter.

There was no sign of any entrance, no trace of human hand at the base or up as far as they could see. From this angle the windows Thomas and Ordulf had spotted were obscured by outcroppings. Guy of Poitou and Jean de Caux, the two who had not climbed with them, cast sidelong glances of doubt – mostly at him, Thomas was sure.

They eased Geoffrey to the ground and staked his horse

to shade him, which was hardly necessary. The horses were near their end and stood motionless, their dull eyes fixed on the ground. The four had to kick the beasts to induce them to walk around the base of the spire – Thomas and Ordulf to the left, Guy and Jean to the right.

When they dismounted together on the far side of the anomaly, each party shook their heads.

"One wonders how they obtain their supplies," Guy said, this time staring directly at Thomas.

Jean ran his eyes up the pristine whiteness. "I have never known a castle window that had not been shat out of."

The sun was half below the hills, but Thomas was still too hot to take offense. He was frustrated, thirsty, and dead tired.

Ordulf stood up frowning in concentration and scanned to the left and right, then pulled a thread from the frayed bottom of his robe. He picked up a pebble, tied it to one end, and lifted his outstretched arm.

"Note the base," he said, one eye closed as he squinted through the thread at the spire.

The other knights obediently examined where the white thrust of rock met the plain.

"What am I looking for?" said Guy.

Ordulf moved his pendulum a whisker to the right. "If they do not shit out of the windows, then they shit inside. They have drainage. And they avoid flooding."

"Small chance of that," Jean said. "Look around you."

"I have," Ordulf replied. "The rocks are my witnesses."

It was true. Everywhere a stone rose up above the flat basin it was marked with horizontal rings at irregular intervals – crusts of evaporation.

"It rains here," Ordulf continued. "Not very often, but when it does it must come down in cartloads and make this flat into a lake. And how do you get past an overflowing moat when your house has no front door?"

"A tunnel?" Thomas guessed.

Pointing to his left, Ordulf said, "It is a trick of the eye. The spire is tilted just a bit, so the land appears level. But it is high there." He dropped his plumb bob and started for the plain. The others jumped up and followed.

They found the door tucked away in a deep indentation on the side of a small sharp gully. It blended into the rocky earth so seamlessly they might have bypassed it had there not been one clear sandal print in the dirt.

Thomas looked significantly at Guy and Jean. Jean shrugged. Ordulf examined the wall with his fingertips. They saw no latch, no handle, no sign of hinges, but the outline of an opening as tall as a man and as wide as arms outstretched was obvious and unnatural.

"No lock to pick," said Jean. "And we neglected to pack a ram."

"We could always knock," Guy said. "It is good manners." He stepped to the door and slapped it with an open palm.

It made a sharp resonant noise, like a drum with a brittle head. And cracked open.

They froze for an instant, then drew their swords in the same choreographed motion. Guy applied his shoulder to the door, pushed harder and more persistently, and with a ghastly screech the thick panel swung fully open. Beyond was blackness.

The tunnel was high and wide – even bigger than the entrance. The knights were able to stand fully upright and could have advanced three across if they had wished, but instead went single file, free hands tracing the wall, spacing themselves by attending the scraping echoes of their boots on the stone floor.

Thomas tried to keep some sense of where they were by counting his steps. The door had been perhaps two hundred paces from the base of the spire, but he soon found he could not walk in the dark with a man close ahead and behind with the same spacing as across open land, and he gave up. The floor slanted upwards. The knights panted from the exertion of negotiating the incline – compounded by the anticipation of a fight.

Guy stopped. Ordulf, second in line, bumped into him, the contact making just enough noise that Thomas and Jean did not trip over them. Guy began to move again, more slowly, and the others soon realized why. The tunnel wall flared away on either side. They were in a chamber, and the four paused again to reorient themselves.

A brilliant light exploded, as if the top of the mountain had been ripped away to let in the sun. The blinded knights threw their arms up over their eyes, the light a painful stab after the black immersion of the tunnel.

It flickered, Thomas sensed. It was not the sun. He willed one eyelid open. Torches flared high overhead beneath a huge rounded white ceiling. He knew this was a deliberate construct; a killing space at the end of the trap. Anyone attempting entry via the tunnel would be paralyzed and disoriented. But what if intruders carried torches – what if their eyes were not disabled? He blinked again, this time able to see more. High up on the wall was a balcony ringing the whole of the chamber, and on that balcony were many figures in hooded robes.

Pitch. Stones, boiling water, spears. There were any number of ways to kill four intruders trapped in the bottom of this well.

Thomas lowered his sword and grounded the tip loudly into stone. Jean, squinting, realized what was happening. He too eased down his sword.

"Greetings!" Jean sang out. His tone was happy and boisterous, as though he had found long lost friends. "We are traveling knights in need of water."

Silence.

The knights were adjusting to the light. Each counted heads above. Thirteen.

The last supper, thought Thomas. He glanced at Guy, whose robe bore the red cross and prayed their hosts were not some sect of belligerent jinn worshipers.

Sandals scuffed, and a man appeared to their left from a hidden cleft in the wall. He was robed but had turned his hood down to reveal his long white hair and bushy gray beard. He stopped several paces away.

"You are Frankish knights," he said in Latin perfect enough for an Italian Pope.

Guy ostentatiously slid his sword into its scabbard. "We are Knights of Frederick, Emperor of the Holy Roman Empire and King of Jerusalem."

The man regarded each of them at length. He had a beaked nose and obsidian eyes deep set below craggy untrimmed eyebrows.

After a moment he reached down into the neck of his robe and brought up a thick silver chain. Attached to one link was a crucifix.

Jean and Thomas went out with four of the hooded men to carry Geoffrey inside. They found him curled up unconscious under his horse, the reins wrapped around his arm.

As the four silent monks – or whatever they were – began to slide Geoffrey onto a blanket, Jean pointed at the other horses huddled about a withered shrub, gnawing without much apparent relish at its dry bark.

"We have to do something with the horses," he said.

Thomas turned. He had been contemplating the vacant face of his lord and feeling lost.

"There are no stables inside," Jean said, "and if the Khwarezm see them here, they might find the door as well."

"But how will we get to Acre without horses?"

Jean shrugged. "One problem at a time."

So Thomas mounted his reluctant horse and led the others back down the valley and through the narrow convoluted entrance. The horses plodded, heads down. Thomas expected one or all to just fall over at any moment, but they made it out past the guarding cliffs well after the last of the sunlight had faded away.

He slipped off his horse and removed bridles and halters from them all. Maybe the Khwarezm would think they were wild horses. They were certainly well on their way back to a feral state. Already Thomas could see their ribs.

"Sorry, old friend," Thomas said, and he slapped his horse on the rump.

The stallion did not jump, as he would have before this trek. He just turned his big head and looked reprovingly at Thomas, then began a slow hopeless amble toward the open desert.

Thomas sent them all on their way and turned his back, tears in his eyes. The night dropped down frigid, and he gathered his robe tight around him.

July 18, 1244
The Holy Land

The Tower was not completely hollow, the knights found. The inhabitants toured them through three main interior spaces connected by winding stairs. The bottom, where they had entered, was used for storage as well as serving when needed as a ruse against trespassers. Above that were the living quarters, spartan cells arranged about a central eating area. The top was open, without walls or dividers, and allowed them to survey all corners of the compass through huge rectangular windows. Rock outcroppings partially shielded the openings and were thus invisible unless, like Thomas, one happened to be at just the right elevation and looked in the right direction. The living quarters possessed no such view but were surprisingly bright, lit during the day through channels baffled by rock. There were no openings at the bottom level other than the door. Torches were required to navigate that vault.

The knights were each given a cell and fresh robes that made them blend into the existing population. They dined several times a day – dried figs and dates, preserved meats, honey, bread – and took their meals in common with the ones they still referred to as monks, though there was no sign of a chapel or any common vocation such as they had witnessed in other monasteries on their way to the Holy Land.

The monks did not talk much. They had obviously not taken a vow of silence, and they were not unfriendly. They just did not have many tongues in common. A few could get by in Latin, and several spoke what Ordulf claimed was a kind of corrupt Greek. Communication happened mostly by short practical phrases and sign language.

The knights were allowed to explore the whole of the Tower, and in which task they invested several days. They also spent hours sitting by Geoffrey's bed. One of the monks possessed some rudimentary training in medicine and had taken charge of the Earl, cleaning the wound and covering it with an herbal compress. The oldest monk, the one who had greeted them on their entrance, talked long and often with Geoffrey. His name was Sidkijah, and he was an educated man, the only inhabitant they could converse with in depth. He grilled the knights about their religion, their individual histories, and what they knew about the natural world. He wanted to know the organization of the Franks and the Turks and the Persians. He wanted to know who was presently on the thrones of the world. There was nothing the knights brought with them that did not interest him. Thomas thought him like a poor peasant in some village far from any traveled road, starved of news.

By the seventh day, Thomas was rested, rehydrated, and thoroughly bored. He was sitting in his cell in the afternoon sharpening his sword when Jean came in and closed the door behind him. Thomas looked up at Jean, who had tilted his head so his ear pressed against the coarse wood and moved his eyes as if he were listening intently for movement outside. After a moment he stepped away from the door and sat on the lone stool that, besides the bed, furnished Thomas's cell.

"Have you much in the past with monks?" Jean said. He spoke in English, one tongue they had not heard among the fragmentary polyglot of the Tower. Jean was only passable in Thomas's native language, but it was clear what he meant.

Thomas shook his head.

"Nor I – but strange to have no chapel?"

Thomas held out his stone. "I am edging my blade for the third time today. I thought to study the Gospel of Matthew this morning. But there is no Bible."

"You asked?"

Thomas shook his head again. "I cast about. I felt yesterday there was something a-missing – then I realized what it was. Where there are holy orders there should be scriptures."

"You did not ask."

"No. I don't know why. An instinct held my tongue, and I retired here to wear my blade needlessly and think upon it."

Jean put his hands together. "I have not seen pray, even before meals."

"They are not the kind of monks I am familiar with," agreed Thomas, putting his sword into its scabbard, "but they took us in with Christian hospitality. They could have easily let us die in the desert."

"True. The door became not locked." Jean shrugged.

"God willing, we will be gone soon. Luckily, I overheard and made sense of two of our hosts planning. A caravan passes the valley entrance around each full moon – seven days from today. It leaves goods for this place in a cave."

"How they pay?" Jean looked away, suddenly occupied with visions of gold coins secreted nearby.

"I do not know. You and Guy and Ordulf shall meet the caravan and travel with it until you can reach Acre."

"And if Acre fall–"

Thomas frowned. "Geoffrey says Acre will withstand a siege such as the Khwarezm can not sustain. You must go. I will wait here until my Lord is fit to travel, then we will follow."

"Another month of this luxury?"

"Another month," Thomas agreed. "It shall be long enough. He grows stronger every day."

July 19, 1244
The Holy Land

But on the eighth day, Thomas entered the cell of Geoffrey to find him feverish and moaning. The monk they had taken to calling Doctor wiped Geoffrey's forehead with a cloth, and Sidkijah stood at the foot of the bed looking grave.

"The wound has turned foul," the old monk said.

Thomas glanced at his benefactor, then considered Sidkijah more closely. The man had his hood down, and yet Thomas could no more judge his true age now than when the old man's face had been shrouded. His skin, though it sagged a bit at the top of his jaw and showed some wrinkles, seemed to glow from inside, pink as a newborn. And his eyes, catching Thomas's examination, were without any mist or imperfection, just clear gray and pure white.

Geoffrey however looked two decades older than he was – pallid and shivering and coated in a sheen of sweat. The doctor peeled the dressing from the wound, and a putrid smell billowed out. Thomas stepped back, staring at the blackened cavity. Thomas had seen the suppurating pus and odor of battle wounds before, and he had never known the outcome to be other than death. He took one deep breath and walked from the room.

Sidkijah motioned to the doctor, who replaced the bandages and left without speaking. Sidkijah knelt beside the bed and took Geoffrey's hand. For a long time they remained in that pose until at last Geoffrey opened his eyes.

"Tell me..." Geoffrey croaked, then swallowed hard and coughed. "Tell me you are ordained to... take my penance."

"There is no need for that."

Geoffrey's head shook, wobbling. "Then bring me Ordulf. He studied for orders once. He can convey my confession...." His eyelids lowered, and he lay back, his breathing shallow and rapid.

Sidkijah whispered, "I had not often enjoyed learned discourse before you arrived. My brothers are earnest, but they were drivers and plowmen and makers of bricks."

"You will have... to keep your end... of the discussion... alone," the dying man managed.

The monk stood abruptly and made motions in the air over Geoffrey's body. The feverish knight peered up and thought the old man was pantomiming an energetic caress of a woman's breasts. He tried to laugh, but nothing came out.

Four monks entered in silence. Geoffrey felt them grip and lift the bedframe. He gathered his strength and said, "My boots. My sword."

Sidkijah waved the monks to stop. "Do you trust me, my friend?"

Geoffrey nodded and mouthed his assent but again could make no sound. He felt his feet being slid into his boots and the hardness of the scabbard against his side, then he lay back – and the room went dark.

When Geoffrey regained his senses he did not know where he was. Two small torches barely lit a circular chamber perhaps thirty paces across. The ceiling was high, the walls rough.

Geoffrey raised his head, vaguely wondering where he had gotten the strength. Sidkijah stood over him holding a small silver cup. Behind the monk a stout rectangular structure rose in an unbroken line from the floor to dominate the middle of the chamber. A flickering light, blue tinged with green, played on the ceiling. Geoffrey realized slowly the colors came from something inside the stone rectangle.

None of the knights had described anything like this to him, and they were each sure they had thoroughly combed the Tower.

He worked his mouth. It was not dry anymore, but tasted sweet and slick, as if honey and milk and olive oil had been mixed on his tongue.

"Where are we?" His voice – strong and unwavering – surprised him.

Sidkijah smiled. "This is our secret, Lord Geoffrey. This is what we guard." He held the goblet out. "And this."

He moved the goblet toward Geoffrey's mouth. The knight parted his lips and received a few drops. The taste was like what was already in his mouth but more intense. He swallowed and could feel the liquid flowing to his stomach. It burned, but then the heat spread like a comfort throughout his chest. He put a hand to his side, to the wound, and pressed. *No pain.*

The monk bent down and lifted the bandages away. Underneath was flesh black as before, but now the affected area was noticeably smaller. All around it the skin was pink.

"What did you do?" Geoffrey asked, staring at his side.

"I cannot give you the last rites," Sidkijah said, "but I can give you something of more utility." He handed the goblet to Geoffrey, who drank the sweet remnants in one gulp. This time the scorching liquid felt like it penetrated all the way to his toes.

Sidkijah turned and put out a hand toward the structure in the middle of the room. "We protect him. And he sustains us."

Geoffrey gingerly lifted his whole torso, turning and resting on one elbow to better see what the other was talking about. The structure reminded him of a grand sepulcher, the final resting place for some king, more fit for the middle of a cathedral than this roughed out tomb.

"Long ago," Sidkijah continued, "there was a war in Heaven. Angel fought against angel. We cannot begin to imagine the weapons they could wield and the hate and love that drove them to violate that sacred place. Many angels fell, as the book tells us." He looked down at Geoffrey, who was gazing up at the flickering green on the ceiling.

"Revelations," Geoffrey said after a minute.

Sidkijah nodded. "One angel fell to earth, gravely wounded in the service of the Lord. He managed to come into this place, which he fashioned even as he fought against whatever is death to an angel."

Another light dawned on Geoffrey, who tilted his head toward the sepulcher. "Here?"

The old monk smiled. "At the bottom of that well lies a holy being, healing in the water. Before he laid down, he gathered the first brothers and commanded them to live in this Tower and to ensure the water covered him until he was whole."

"Is this some magic spring?" Geoffrey asked, searching his empty goblet for an occult manifestation.

"No, just water from the earth. There is a flow of the purest water–" He pointed into a far, dark corner. "It rises up and covers Him. His power excites it."

So this is what an angel tastes like, thought Geoffrey. "You and your brothers take the water?"

"Yes. One sip – as you have just had – each full moon."

"Do your injuries always heal?" He motioned to the wound – irreversibly mortal only moments before. Now it resembled a modest bruise such as he had often gotten in jousting practices.

"Yes."

"How long has he been in there?"

"I do not know," Sidkijah said. "The first brothers had no knowledge of writing, so we hear only the stories told from older to younger."

Geoffrey sat up and swung his feet to the ground. He rubbed his abdomen, then his ribcage. The agony had disappeared, leaving just an itch. "How came you here?"

"I was traveling with a caravan and fell ill. The master feared it was the plague, so they left me on the sand and moved quickly on. Luckily the brothers found me."

"They gave you the water."

"Yes, like you I was more dead than not."

"But," Geoffrey said, "you stayed here when you were well again. How long ago?"

The other narrowed his eyes, mentally calculating. "I have not calculated the time in a while. I think it was... just over three hundred years."

Geoffrey scowled up at him.

"You do not believe me? Even when the hole gouged

from your belly has closed?"

"I have seen wounds heal quickly before, and I have myself convulsed with fever in the morning and danced with my lady in the evening."

"But you have never met someone as old as I."

The knight said nothing.

The old monk shrugged. He held out his hands as before, and the goblet, which had fallen to the bed, twitched. Then it rose into the air as if blown by a gust of wind and flew to the monk, who plucked it out of the air and laughed like a happy child.

Geoffrey gaped.

"You will see," Sidkijah said gleefully. "You will see all the wonderful power he gives. I could not let you die."

Geoffrey caressed the hilt of his sword as if it was the only real thing left in his world. "How powerful is the water? Is there no insult it cannot heal?"

The old monk shook his head. "Brothers have fallen from the highest windows. His power did nothing for them. And there have been attacks. As far from Christendom as we are, there are still attacks. Brothers have been killed defending the Tower."

"And how do you find new brothers?"

The other smiled. "There are always lost souls who find their way to us."

Geoffrey was on his feet now. He felt no dizziness, no nausea. He felt no bad effect at all from the cut that had nearly taken his life. Instead, he was filled with more energy than he could ever remember, including when he was a young wench-chasing buck.

He pointed at the sepulcher. "Did the angel fashion that as well?"

Sidkijah instinctively turned to look where he was pointing. Geoffrey slid his sword silently from its scabbard and in one long motion swung it backhanded into the old monk's exposed neck.

His arm throbbed with power. The stroke drove the blade

30

clear through the flesh and partly through the spine. The man gurgled as blood filled his throat, then Geoffrey pulled hard on the sword and twisted. Bones cracked and broke, and the steel edge sliced through the rest of the muscles and skin.

Sidkijah's head fell and bounced away. The body collapsed into a ragged pile. Crimson rivulets of steaming blood gathered and ran from the corpse like rapid fingers seeking the murderer.

Geoffrey held his sword before him, panting, but after many long minutes it was apparent there was no miracle happening here. The old monk was well and truly dead. And his angel had not twitched in response.

The Earl stepped one pace back, then froze. He heard a rustling, faint in the dark edges. Were there rats this far into the desert? Possibly – at least it was not the sleeper the unfortunate monk on the floor had described. When that ancient warrior rose, he guessed, it would not be heralded by whispers. He did not hear the sound again, so he wiped the blood from his sword on the bed sheets, walked quietly to the door and cracked it open. Seeing no one outside, he slipped through.

December 14, 1773
London

I wonder where Henry shat, the King of England thought. *Probably high in a parapet – on a stone seat which emptied onto the heads of commoners.*

Then another spasm gripped his bowels, and he bent forward even farther so his forehead was within a royal palm's width of his knees and pushed. Nothing of substance moved.

Here am I, George the Third, by the Grace of God, King of Great Britain, France, and Ireland, Defender of the Faith, and so forth. Impressive titles and honors above the space where the royal imprimatur is delivered by my quill ten thousand bloody times a day. By the same quill below the same awesome curriculum vitae I could summon a thousand men with muskets and two dozen ships of the line. Yet I cannot pass this simple daily harvest of rock hard royal turds.

George the Third did not have to suffer the additional hardship of a cold bum. His seat of ease was not chill stone but a round cushion of red velvet surrounding the drop. His excreta might still plummet onto the heads of commoners – he didn't know. It just went down into the depths of the enameled box, and that was the end of his caring about it.

A sudden contraction, this one a full watch of sailors in Satan's Navy splicing Royal entrails into anchor cable. His Majesty groaned like the most verminous beggar on Old Soho. His manservant, who had been hovering outside and offering encouragement, was silent. In fact, it sounded to the King as if he had abandoned his post altogether. George heard distant voices. One he recognized and one he did not.

I will have their damned heads off.

The voice he recognized, Viscount Barrington – the Secretary at War, came closer to the door. "Your Majesty?"

"What in the devil's name do you want?" George snapped, trying not to gasp. *What did the Army want from him today?*

"Forgive me, your Highness. I have–"

It wasn't revealed what the Viscount had, as the King burst from his most private chamber still doing up his britches. Barrington stopped speaking and bowed. Behind him cowered another man. George recognized him from somewhere, then remembered his name. It was Fanshawe, Mayor of Plymouth, who had recently been his host when the King inspected a first-rater under construction at a shipyard in that town. But this pale and trembling man barely fit the royal recollection. Fanshaw met that day had been cool and composed, the very model of a dignified gentleman with public responsibilities.

Barrington reloaded. "Your Majesty, allow me to name my old and particular friend, Richard Fanshawe."

Fanshawe collected his apparently far-scattered wits enough to bow. It appeared to the King the man almost collapsed at the low point of the movement.

George motioned to Barrington, and the two moved away.

"Are the two of you on some grand piss up?" the King whispered darkly, his eyes still on the sweating Fanshawe. "Dick there does not seem to be able to hold his rum."

Barrington frowned. "I assure you, Your Highness, Richard Fanshawe is the most sober man I have ever had the pleasure to know."

"Then why is he... Oh God! He is about to purge himself!"

The King stepped back toward the Mayor of Plymouth, taking care to approach by an oblique route in case the purge was indeed imminent.

"Mayor Fanshawe," the King said amiably, "shall I call my physician? You may be in need of a bleeding."

Fanshawe shook his head, realized that was impolite, and forced out a response. "No... thank you, Your Majesty, I just...."

"Richard came this morning on an overnight coach," Barrington took up. "He desired to deliver a message to Your Highness but feared he would not be received at once. So he came to my house first."

The King considered Fanshawe. No, the disheveled man certainly would not have been admitted. He would have been lucky not to have been arrested. Then George remembered where the man lived and began to worry. Was one of his first-raters on fire? Were the French invading?

"He sent me to tell you...." Fanshawe began, but failed.

"He who?" the King demanded.

"He said his name was Geoffrey," Barrington said, prompting his friend.

The King backed away slowly from Fanshawe, who had reacted to Barrington's comment with a convulsive spasm. George looked coolly at his Secretary at War, then at the Mayor of Plymouth drooping like an unwatered flower. Barrington drew out his kerchief and blotted sweat from his neck, though the chamber was still cold with the dawn. He must have expected the King to fly into a rage and have them tossed into the street, but His Majesty was indulgent. At least this farce temporarily removed from the Royal mind the ponderous ballast clanking about in his intestines.

Fanshawe was too sunk into his misery to remember his manners. "He wished me to tell you he will call on you this afternoon."

George frowned. "See here, Fanshawe. One does not invite himself into the King's presence." The King thought for a moment. "What made him presume it so?"

Fanshawe looked up finally, so wretched George felt sorry for the man. Perhaps he was having a mental collapse.

Fanshawe croaked. "He was.... He came into the harbor in a black ship. Dead black. Black sails, flying no flag—"

"No flag!" The King exclaimed. "Why did you admit an unflagged ship to the harbor?"

Fanshawe shrugged. "I don't... know. It is just that...." The Mayor hugged himself. "I went out in a skiff with the master of the harbor to investigate and protest when... he reached into my head!" He lifted his chin, pointed several fingers at once toward his brow, and almost shouted. "Into my head!" The air went suddenly out of Fanshawe, and Barrington was forced to take his arm lest he collapse at the royal feet.

George lowered his voice. "Really, Barrington, your friend may be of a weak mind, but I expect a great deal more sobriety from my Secretary at War."

"Yes, Your Majesty," Lord Barrington replied meekly, "but, you see... I cannot disbelieve him."

The King narrowed his eyes. "You wish to tell me some vagabond in a dirty ship has possessed your friend?"

"I do not think that is possible, Your Majesty, but someone has managed to do this—" he inclined his head toward Fanshawe, still in his grip. "You see, Fanshawe served under my late brother John in your Regiment of Foot when they defeated the French force on Guadeloupe. John recommended Richard for honours." Barrington paused, considering the frail husk of a man in his arms. "He led the attack on du Triel's

34

flank which carried the day, though he had a musket ball lodged in his knee and was shaking with the fever."

The King gave the stricken man a reconsidering look, nodded, then spoke aside to his servant. Two butlers appeared and carried Fanshawe gently from the room. "I have summoned the physicians," George said. "We will let the poor fellow rest." He glanced down and saw he had misbuttoned his britches in the excitement. He began to remedy the error. "Send down to Plymouth and have that unflagged ship boarded at once. In the meantime, I am going to Kew this afternoon. Call out a company of the Guard, will you? I shall be shearing my Merinos, and the boys can lend a hand. And if the rascal dares to show his face in London he will answer to me for abusing our man Fanshawe."

At four o'clock the King was sitting by a fire with Christopher Levett, the current owner of the old palace at Kew and its expansive grounds and meadows. They drank port in front of a sputtering and unambitious fire. Levett did not worry the tiny blaze, as the day was unseasonably warm and the King's happy face still glistened from the shearing. The monarch had not been able to resist taking up the experimental shears himself and applying them to several of his ewes under the close tutelage of Mr. Drostan Innes, the Scot who had invented the system. The new shears featured an inch-long series of blunt fingers on the bottom edge. These allowed the sheep to be shorn not to the skin but left with a coat long enough to keep the animal warm in the winter. Innes claimed this innovation allowed the wool to be harvested in those fall and winter months which husbandry had previously forbade. The owner might by this timing take advantage of spikes in the prices paid for raw wool. He also promised cold air on a short coat spurred the growth of thicker and more valuable wool at the next shearing.

The King and Mr. Innes had spent the afternoon clipping sheep and talking wool and the wool business while a dozen resigned privates from the Coldstream Guard fetched sheep and held the animals and stuffed curly product into canvas bags and dared not complain about any of it. Then Innes had gone away with a sizeable purse, and the King had retired to relax with his friend.

Levett picked up a bottle and refilled the King's glass. "It will be Christmas time soon enough," he said, "and the days of going out without a long cloak will be but pleasant memories."

George raised his glass in agreement. "I recall last year on this date there was a rain that chilled us to the bone."

"In anticipation of next year then, I shall construct a shearing shed that we may clip the ewes through Advent and beyond in comfort."

The King smiled. "I am stretching your hospitality to uncommon lengths, dear Levett."

Levett waved a hand to indicate it was nothing to him, then he frowned. "Do you hear that, Your Highness?"

His Highness *was* hearing something. He turned his head to the windows looking out over the long lawn leading down to the Thames. "What the deuce–?"

The two men rose and walked quickly to the windows. Levett threw up one of the big heavy sliders. The sound was low and regular. A chant in a minor key, vaguely like Evensong but more sinister, more parts death than life. The wind began to blow in, cold as the grave, and the weak sun passed behind a bank of fog foaming on the western horizon.

The boatmen on the Thames often sang, to be sure, but this song would have driven potential customers off. The King and his host were on the second floor, so they caught sight of the singer over the low hedges in between the house and the river.

The man stood in the bow of a small wherry moving slowly against the stream. The boatman himself sat with his back hunched, working mechanically and not once looking over his shoulder to navigate. Something about that operation sent a chill of alarm through Levett, who sculled quite often on that same patch of rapid, unpredictable river.

The rower stroked steadily, and the man sang. He wore a

dark purple coat with a black hood. None of his face could be seen, yet the hood bobbed as his mouth opened and closed with the chant.

The prow of the wherry ran up on the bank, and the singer stepped off onto the grass as though it had been practiced many times before. He turned to the big house and began to walk up the slope.

Levett, who had been hypnotically fixated on the scene, hopped. "Raley! Raley!" he called frantically. A butler ran into the room. "Send for the Guard," Levett gasped, pointing out the window. "Arrest that man!"

The butler tore from the room. The King and his host heard him scramble down the stairs, calling bloody murder for the Captain of the Guard. They turned back to the window and froze in shock. The hooded man had stopped, his face turned up toward them. He was smiling. The two men instinctively took a step back.

The man had a square gray beard and black eyes deeply set. His thin pointed nose stuck from the hood, giving him an air of a predator.

The King heard quick footsteps, hard heels pounding on stone, and a column of the Guard came into view, sprinting around the corner of the house straight for the intruder. Levett leaned forward and gasped as it appeared the leading Guardsmen would barrel directly into the figure, but they bypassed him, taking no notice at all, and continued on at a run to the river.

Levett wanted to shout, call them back to detain the man, but he could not speak. They had not seen him. The soldiers had passed within feet of the man, but his presence had not registered. The column of Guard, stopped by the river, shouted at the wherry to come back. The rower ignored them. He continued upstream close against the opposite bank, and none of their calls made him so much as turn his head.

The man below watched the Guard scramble down to the river. He again lifted his face to the window and smiled his enigmatic smile, which induced a shudder in both the horrified observers. He approached the front door.

Levett faced his King. The house was empty, silent as a graveyard, and he knew it was futile to ring for the servants. He had a pair of pistols in a sideboard, but they were not loaded. Something told him brandishing them against this sinister intruder would do no one any good.

They heard footfalls on the stairs. The King walked heavily to his chair and sank into it. Levett followed and stood beside as they waited for the door to open.

He entered almost reverentially, his hooded head bowed, hands folded together before him. When he was within three paces of George, he bowed deeply, then actually sank to his knees.

"Your Majesty is most kind to receive me," he said – without, it seemed to his audience – a trace of sarcasm. "My name is Geoffrey, the Third Earl of Emberton."

George stared aghast at the top of the man's hood. What response did this entity expect? He knelt in front of the temporary throne as if in anticipation of being knighted. "What– what do you want?" the King managed to choke out.

Geoffrey raised his head and looked the King in the eye. Levett thought the man must have been carved out of a kind of fluid wood, ageless and ancient and yet full of the energy of youth.

"I?" he said. "I want nothing, Your Majesty. To the contrary – I have come to convey to Your Highness a unique and precious gift."

The King opened his mouth but could not figure out which question to ask first. After a moment of silence, he said, "Is it your ship which came into Plymouth flying no flag?"

"Yes," Geoffrey said. "We sailed from Brest under a French flag – not the best introduction to Plymouth Harbor."

"You spoke then to the Mayor."

"I had that honor. I assured him we were not any threat to the city."

The King had a grave doubt about that claim. He shifted uncomfortably in his chair and said, "The Mayor came to me this morning, quite agitated."

Geoffrey placed a hand upon his heart. "I am concerned to hear this, Your Majesty. I only begged he announce me."

There seemed nothing to say to that, so the King said nothing. After a moment, Geoffrey reached into his clothes and brought forth a small glass phial, brilliant aquamarine and stoppered with a golden plug. He presented it upon his palm to the King.

George reached out, and Levett quivered. His senses cried for him to spring to the aid of his monarch, his friend. He knew he should slap the bauble to the floor, let it shatter and splash whatever manner of death it represented upon the oak boards before his King might– but it was too late. He could not move, could not protest, and His Royal Highness took the phial, uncapped it, and drank the contents.

Levett gaped. Nothing had been said about drinking the thing. The King acted as if it were the most normal transaction, that everyday after tea he imbibed unknown liquid delivered by mad wizards.

Geoffrey said, "I have been abroad for many years. I and my few friends wish – with your blessing – to make England our home." He rose to his feet but still stayed bowed so as not to loom over the King of England. "Please honor us with your Royal Presence. I will answer all of your questions then. Your Majesty."

The old man began to back out of the Presence. The King roused himself visibly, quivering. "Where are you lodging?" he asked, fearing the answer would be a crypt or a haunted cave or a mist-shrouded bog in the middle of some distant moor.

"I shall be at Mr. Brooks' club in Pall Mall," Geoffrey said, and he continued his recessional until he was out of the room.

The King and Levett, suspended in their astonishment, listened to the recessional – deliberate steps, descending the stairs, diminuendo until silence.

August 5, 1246
The Holy Land

After a long period of silent concentration and composition, Jean de Caux cleared his throat. The composition was a tale he constructed to ease the tedium. The concentration was necessary due to the pass they had just cleared – a slim path with cliff on one hand and several hundred deep feet of nothing on the other. Two month's worth of supplies had just been nursed along the precarious road.

"A man is wandering far from his home," he said loudly.

His companion on this errand, Guy of Poitou, turned his head slightly. He was ahead, and they were separated by the two donkeys tethered behind Guy's horse. He also raised his voice. "Has he been driven from his home by a purge of some sort? Or does an evil duke desire his land and woman?"

They were speaking in the tightly clipped language of the Aquitaine region. This tongue had a wonderful vein of metaphors, which Jean was mining.

"I think he is displaced by war," Jean said. "It does not matter to the tale. He discovers a huge egg–"

"Is it a golden egg?"

"No, just a giant egg."

"What good is a giant egg?" asked Guy.

Jean scanned over his right shoulder, then over his left. They had traveled out of the area where thieves were known to lurk, but until they were safely back in their Tower they would not let their guard down. "What good is a regular-sized egg? It is an egg. You can eat it."

Guy shook his head. "If he is alone, then he can only eat part of the egg. The rest will spoil. It is a tragic tale you are set upon."

"That is my point exactly," Jean cried. "Our hero finds a giant egg. He loves eggs. You would think it the happiest day of his life."

"And it is not?"

"No! He can't enjoy the egg. It is too big."

"Is that the whole story?" asked Guy.

"Well, yes. Of course there will be a maiden and a witch. Also an evil knight. The hero will travel and have other adventures. The whole volume will take a monk half a year to transcribe."

Guy nodded agreeably. *Of course we had a whole Tower full of monks who could have done the inking for you. But we had to chop them into bloody fragments, didn't we?*

They rode quietly for a while. The wind picked up, and they wrapped scarves about their heads to keep the blowing dust out, leaving only slits to see through. They both knew what Jean's story was about. It had been two years since they had taken possession of the Tower. Two hot summers and two unexpectedly cold winters. Two years of taking a healthy draught of the water every new moon.

They had no complaints about the efficacy of the water. None had ever been in finer fettle. Jean's crusty rash, which had often tormented him in the saddle, disappeared. Guy's old thigh injury from a wayward arrow no longer throbbed in poor weather, and the scar itself was almost gone. All five knights were hale and suffused with energy. That was the problem.

The caravans the late brothers had once traded with for some reason ignored the new occupants. The bored men did not mind. It gave them an excuse to ride out for food and other necessaries.

Luckily, there had been an egg – in the inedible but malleable form of gold.

After they had dragged the corpses a distance away from the Tower and left them in a pile for whatever kind of jackal or vulture inhabited this niche of the Holy Land, the knights occupied themselves with doing what they would have done in any conquered citadel. They tore the place apart looking for valuables.

Geoffrey alone seemed then much more confident of discovering some trove. The rest were certain – from the threadbare robes that tore in their hands while the deceased wearer was being dragged across the sand, and the simple foodstuffs of the larder – there could be at most probably no more than some small bag of thin and tarnished silver pieces tucked behind a rock somewhere.

In the end even the Earl was frozen in awe when they opened the door.

Halfway up the dark staircase leading from common cells to the top of the peak, Thomas noticed a crack that might have been native to the rock. But it was uncommon vertical. He considered it for a while, then he tested his sword hilt against it. The wall rang hollow.

Inside, in a space no larger than two of the beds they slept on, were crude shelves piled with gold. Jewelry, cups, coins in piles and spilling leather pouches. Crucifixes, stars, small knives. Nuggets, large flakes, quartz rock shot through with thick veins of the stuff. Statues of men, gods, animals, and unknown forms. Ingots thin and fat, square and round. And every other item made by the hand of man impressed with precious stones in a rainbow of sudden prosperity.

Emotions migrated immediately upon the viewing. The knights who had despaired of discovering anything were rapturous with delight. They invaded the space, crowding in, seizing up idols and false gods and kissing them passionately. They slipped necklaces about their necks, crammed rings onto each finger, kinged one another with crowns, and began to play odd man with the larger coins.

Geoffrey looked on from the stairway, pensive. After some time he stood in the tiny doorway and told them what lay in the base of the Tower and the power of the water that had healed him.

And which had allowed the isolated and lightly-armed monks here to accumulate this treasury many kingdoms of Europe could not match – the thought was unspoken, but the Earl was now regretting he had not interrogated first and slain second.

How had the late owners used the power? Did they slip

out into the world and barter with it? Did they steal by stealth, exact tribute through fear? Had they used the power of the water to cloud men's minds and bend the wealthy to their will?

The victors would never know.

The wind died down. Guy unwound his scarf. "When the man finds this egg, he must guard it, of course."

"Of course. It is too valuable to leave."

"But he must travel," Guy continued. "If he is ever to lie again in the arms of a beautiful woman."

Jean nodded slowly. "He is getting full to bursting with the romantic humours. He would like to abandon the egg on occasion and visit the comely wenches in the nearest kingdom."

"Perhaps he can have some friends to help him."

"But he does not trust anyone with his egg. It is like no other egg ever known."

"Can he hide this egg?"

"How does one hide a giant egg?" Jean said. *How does one hide a Tower? We hauled rubble to the top and blocked up a curtain wall to truly hide the openings there. No one will ever again accidentally stand where we had and see those signs of habitation.*

"I would not care to be your hero," Guy said. "Who knows how many years he will sit there in the shadow of that damned egg waiting for the author to resolve the dilemma?"

The horses walked slowly on as their riders listened to the waning breeze and scanned the horizon for telltale plumes of dust signaling potential trouble. Guy saw a thickening to the east, the direction they were bound, and squinted into the low sky trying to see if blue was contaminated with gray.

"Does the egg have a mother?" he asked Jean.

His companion shrugged. "Our hero is more concerned the egg might hatch when he is not paying attention."

December 16, 1773
London

The King slumped in the corner of a borrowed coach on his way to Pall Mall.

This was madness. He knew that. His personal coachman was in the seat above, the only other member of this conspiracy. He came with no bodyguard, not even one burly footman. Alone to face the only being he had ever met who scared the coronated shite out of him.

Which was an apt analogy, he reflected. Whatever was in that beautiful horrid phial had warmed him more than a flagon of the stiffest brandy. It had gushed from his lips to the Royal Anus with an energy so profoundly intense he had been at first convinced it was some acidic corruption. He had slumped, resigned to the Reaper – then the most wonderful things began to happen. The shoulder dislocated falling from a horse in his youth stopped aching. An odd spidery scale developing on his left calf cleared. The persistent ringing in his ears ceased. Most importantly, half an hour after the odd Earl – if Earl he was – disappeared from the Kew grounds, the King retired in haste to one of Levett's private rooms and ejected a most satisfactory pile of firm yet comfortably yielding turds onto several blue cherubs hovering in a flock at the bottom of a porcelain chamber pot.

Now his Highness had come to Pall Mall as invited, yes, but he was deeply conflicted. He had hardly slept five minutes since the appearance of the stranger. The old man was some sort of alchemist – that was evident enough by the effect of his elixir. But he also had some faculties beyond merely the mixing pots and retorts. The way he had made himself invisible to a whole company of Guards, the way one felt compelled to do what the stranger commanded.

George often complained about the burdens of being the supreme monarch, but he liked the position. He suspected having this old man and the friends to whom he had alluded in England would mean they would suddenly ascend to a position superior to even the Throne. The King viewed himself as the true leader of England, with Parliament and the Prime Minister mere advisors who happened to be elected by his subjects. There was no doubt the wizard could control all of those as well as the Monarch – who would be kept happy, healthy, and compliant by a steady drip from tiny phials. And if George the Third had a problem with the arrangement, then perhaps George the Fourth would see the wisdom of accepting the new order.

The problem seemed simple. Live as a puppet with a regular supply of the violet ampules or somehow chase these strange fellows away and return to the joint pains and brick hard stools whose razor edges scored his insides. In the last few years these and other ailments had multiplied and deepened like a Biblical curse.

The King glanced down. He had gripped the handle of the door so fiercely it was about to come off in his hand. God damn it, he was only thirty-five years old, and he felt like a cripple more days than not.

There was one possible way out, and it lay in the chart rolled up inside his coat. The newcomers would have to be persuaded it was the best course for all – and that made His Royal Highness apprehensive. He was not used to negotiating. He was accustomed to issuing decrees on the matters he administered. Policy he, according to Parliament, deserved little say about he ignored. He did not stoop to politic. But now he would have to put into practice what he had observed of those who did.

The jouncing of the coach stopped, the body bouncing on springs for a moment. After a pause, a knock signaled the Brooks doorman without. George cracked the window and slipped out a card – something else he had never done. The King did not need a calling card. The King appeared when he pleased and vanished when he pleased. Any function started when he arrived and was over when he left. Thus George did not even possess calling cards. He had sent a butler down to Cockspur Street to purchase one. Just one – an ivory-white rectangle of pasteboard, blank, upon which he had inked "HRH G.III".

Another knock; George pulled his cloak around him and drew its hood over his head. He opened the door and stepped down onto the paving stones. Mr. Brooks operated his club in a building that was not a majestic place by London standards, just a modest three-story block of khaki brick. Tonight there was none of the usual laughing banter from gentlemen playing whist, nor lights beaming from the big windows on the ground floor. Even though it was well after midnight, the King had expected to see some members gaming. But all was dark except for flickering lights from the top floor.

Jean de Caux was lining up a shot when Geoffrey came in. Jean, bent low over the billiards table, did not look up. He glared at the ebony sphere, drew the cue back smoothly, and struck. The ball shot down the table, colliding with a red ball and sending it clacking off one of the stiff bumpers and rolling back across the green cloth. It dropped into a leather pocket while the black ball rolled obediently to the center.

Geoffrey reached down and picked up the red ball. He turned it over in his hand. The blood-hued dye accentuated the layers of ivory, a reminder some elephant had given his life for the game. "I hear you have spent the evening lightening the purses of our fellow members."

Jean smiled. "They find the lessons a bargain. Where were you while I conducted my class?"

"Visiting our friends in Whitehall."

"Friends?" Jean said, "If we have friends in government, why draw the attention of the King? He can do us no good, but he can surely do us ill."

"Because we are here, and I am tired of moving in shadows. There is a fine globe downstairs in the library. You should peruse it sometime. Somehow the inhabitants of this tiny speck of an island have managed to lay hands on substantial swaths of every continent."

"You said the same about our friend le Roi-Solei and his

far-flung dominions," Jean said. He closed one eye and inspected the end of his cue, holding it close to his nose. "And that came to naught."

"This time we will do the searching ourselves. We know what to look for."

It was an old topic occasionally brought out to rechew. If there had been a war in Heaven, there must have been more casualties than one. And what if their angel had been a mere foot soldier? What if the five knights could discover the sanctuary of an officer? The water from a general's bath would surely be even more powerful. It was just a minor problem of combing the hidden corners of the wide Earth for other sanctuaries.

Jean shook his head. He had long ago given up hope of finding another. "And when the King tires of our presence? As le Roi did, as Suleiman did...." He did not bother to repeat all the names. Everywhere the knights had tried to live the pattern had repeated. For a while they would partake of the local pleasures in secret, but inevitably rumors would start and grow. Attention would be drawn. Talk of witchcraft and whatever representative of evil the locals endorsed would circulate. The knights had not inconsiderable power over single men but less so over crowds of them. Some meddling hot head would decide to undertake violence against them. The threats were laughable, and easily dispensed with, but the dead would have brothers and fathers and sons. After a while the knights would tire of putting down mobs by slaughter and move quietly on.

"I gave him the water," Geoffrey said.

Jean glared at him. "We agreed never to give the water to anyone. Not even when that cunt Prince Ehrenberg had us trapped in Wurzburg did we use the water for bargaining."

"Perhaps we should have done all along."

"No, no, no!" Jean slammed his cue flat onto the table. "You know what will happen! They will demand the source. We can't defeat armies – they will find us out. Can you imagine that pompous prick Louis possessing the Tower? This King is no different."

"I can control this one," Geoffrey said.

Jean held one thumb up and pressed it to his throat. "I say we keep a sharp blade, just in case."

Geoffrey nodded, then even though there was no sound, they both turned to the windows which showed the dark street.

King George entered the room unannounced and found Geoffrey with his back to the door. The Earl was in conversation with another man, one shorter and stouter with thick brows and hair the color of chimney soot. This man merely glanced in George's direction, and the King stopped as if he had run up against a marble column.

Geoffrey smiled. "Your Majesty, you honor us. My old friend and fellow knight Jean de Caux."

Jean made a bow so perfect the effect was ironic rather than sincere.

George searched for a chair, but what supply this room had was hung upon the wall like decorations. It was clear the meeting was to be on foot. He sighed mentally. Two unarmed men were making him feel like he was surrendering.

"I trust you found the potion to your liking?" Geoffrey asked.

"It was quite rejuvenating. I hope you have a gallon of it somewhere."

Jean directed his blank yet telling visage to Geoffrey, who ignored him.

"I compound it as needed," Geoffrey said. "I look forward to supplying Your Highness regularly."

George just nodded. He had a hundred questions – at least he remembered having them, but he could not recall the gist of a single one. "I shall proclaim you the Royal Supplier of Elixir," he said.

Geoffrey bowed, and this one appeared earnest. "His Majesty is too kind – but we would prefer to be your unnamed friends. You can imagine the... elixir is dear and its components rare. It should be the prerogative of the Crown alone."

Now it was George's turn to bow. He made it miniscule

and said, "I take your point well. I would be surrounded by sobbing applicants begging a drop. It must be added to the long list of secrets kept from the horde of sycophants and bureaucrats." He shook his head. "My dear God, how this country teems with unendurable people." He stepped to the pool table and put a hand onto its green surface. "Will you be taking lodging here?"

"Only for a short time, Your Highness."

"Good," George said approvingly. "I myself spend as little time in the city as possible. The shite bobbing in the Thames sets up a thick stench, even on these cool days. In the summer you will be drawing all windows and sweating rather than breathe that malodorous atmosphere. Perhaps you have a country house in mind?"

"Yes," Geoffrey said. "There is my old home in Emberton."

"Well, I hope you do not mind lepers. I think that is where they are sending them these days. Of course, you could try over in Newbury, as long as you purchase upwind of the knackers' yards. I have friends who swear the soil north of Coventry and east of the zinc tailing piles is still as sweet as it was two hundred years ago – although the trees have died out in that district for some reason."

The two knights exchanged glances, then Geoffrey said, "Is there no place in your kingdom you can recommend?"

George considered them for a moment. "If I had your powers, I would not settle for this overburdened rock." He reached into his jacket and slid out the long chart as if it were a rapier. "You brought me a gift. I am here to return the favor."

He put the chart down on the billiard table and flicked his wrists so it unrolled. Its far edge paralleled Jean's cue, and the King reached across and pulled the stick over the map's curl so the vast brown expanse of North America lay across the table before them.

June 16, 1507
Cairo

The Plague returned to Cairo. It had been absent for so long the inhabitants retained no memory of the last bout. Stories of outbreaks reached them from other cities in other countries, and the people of Cairo congratulated themselves on their good fortune. Over time the city came to believe they had more than luck – it was their piety and devotion to Allah that protected them.

It started as it always had, at the docks. First some of the men who loaded and unloaded cargo began to sweat profusely, only to complain later how cold the afternoon had become. Dhows backed up at the key as workers shuffled along at half-pace with painful swellings of the groin. By that time it was already too late to quarantine new boats. The pestilence visited the families of the dock employees, then their neighbors, then it spread away from the Nile and up the slopes of the crowded city.

After ten days of increasing deaths, the usual burial grounds were overwhelmed. Useless stretches of unirrigated sand upriver were appropriated as graveyards for those not affluent enough to already own a family tomb in the grand Qarafa al-Kubra necropolis. The desert was busy with haggard gravediggers and families burying their dead. More families huddled around shrouded corpses, sobbing and waiting for their shallow rectangle to be dug. Rumors circulated that the authorities planned mass graves to reduce the backlog. This prospect horrified the populace, which took the ceremonies of death quite seriously.

The crisis had loosened normally strict procedures, which was why three red-eyed women squatting next to a small mound were not chastised for being present at a funeral service.

"Laa ilaaha illa-Allah," sobbed one, neighbor to the family of the dead girl.

"There is no true God but Allah," the other two repeated automatically. One was the aunt, the other the bereaved mother. They sat close together, three very similar shapes in black robes and dense veils.

"Allah, make her the light which guides our salvation," the neighbor continued.

"...make her a source of reward and treasure..." the aunt said.

"O God, forgive our living and our dead, those who are present among us and those who are absent, those who are known to us and those who are strangers in our land...." The neighbor raised her head. Beyond and above the new cemetery, on a long knoll connected to the city by an elevated leg of harder earth, loomed a hulking walled compound. The central keep jutted up above the rest, its empty windows like soulless eyes.

The aunt followed her neighbor's gaze and lifted her veil with one forefinger to spit in the direction of the compound. The mother buried her head in her arms, her body shaking with silent sobs.

He was a thick man, heavily muscled, and so had always gotten work as a porter or guard. At present he was the latter, and well compensated by his peculiar but generous employers. Their gold paid for the support of his wife, his remaining children, his aged mother, his wife's sister, and her several children. It secured his full attention, which was why he had not been able to properly bury his beloved daughter. His employers rightly feared the appearance of the plague would spark a general panic quickly coalescing into hatred of the unknown and unfamiliar as the survivors sought a place to concentrate their blame. The guard's continuous attendance at the compound was required. He had only twice found time over the last several days to dash home.

Now he was leaving for work again, silent and unhappy. His sister-in-law followed close behind him while he gathered together his gear. She was arguing heatedly, rapidly, and loudly.

51

As he was about to step out of the front door, he turned back to confront her.

"They are not to blame," he snapped. "They came here before Ramadan. If they brought the death, it would have started then."

"But they are jinns – you said so yourself. And they do not observe." She made the last point as if it were necessary and sufficient to establish their guilt.

"They are men," he said. "Just men. They pray to the God of Abraham, who The Prophet teaches us is Allah."

His sister-in-law averted her eyes. "Two more of our children have the buboes," she said quietly.

He turned away from her so she would not be able to see his face and walked down the street.

He went quickly through empty alleys and along the hump that made a path to his job. On the whole long way he passed but two other men. They nodded to him, making no remark. *Another symptom of the Black Death,* he thought. *Friends are now strangers.*

His coworker this evening was a man who lived two narrow winding streets away from him, a short stout fellow five years or so older than he.

When they met outside the compound, the other put one hand on his shoulder and said, "Surely we belong to Allah and to Him shall we return."

The man nodded. "Allah has willed it. How is your family?"

His partner shrugged. "They have gone downriver to Zaqaziq, where there is no plague, Allah be blessed. But on my street – many, many dead. Very quiet. No one dares come out."

Just after sunset, the two men stood on the elevated walkway that circled inside the wall, built so defenders might drop insults and heavy objects down on attackers. The compound was ancient, the builders long forgotten, but they had obviously been wary of massed onslaught. The two men carried spears and short swords, weapons they had not needed to date. The most ferocious sieges they had encountered on this job were idle, drunken youths curious what lay behind the walls and idle, drunken thieves curious what lay behind the walls. Both were repelled with kicks and punches. The guards had not yet had to draw blood.

As they watched the city, it became obvious the inhabitant's fear of the epidemic had been overcome by their anger. They saw torches flaring to life and congregating in wavering bunches. The people did not know where the death came from or how to treat it, but they knew the surety of fire in sterilizing its sources. The hovering flames were like flowers in a field – and the flowers began to flow.

The man let out a deep sigh of resignation. "Here they come."

The compound gates were thick slabs of old mahogany secured by iron bands and thick rivets, locked and triple-blocked with stout timbers. The walls all around the compound were as high as three men and had no gaps. The place was built to be defended, and though two sentries stood alone, their four employers were inside the main house. Four men with scarred faces and the bearing of warriors, who practiced with heavy swords, swinging them as if they weighed no more than dried sticks, and obviously knew how to kill. Plus, the two guards suspected, they might actually *be* jinns.

The compound could be defended. But both men watched the mob form up outside the city and wondered if it should be. They had friends and family out there. The fires clustered, became somewhat organized, and moved across the sands.

Ordulf picked up his wine and went to the window, opened to admit the slightly cooler air that rolled down from the high land to the river in the early evening. It had also let in the distant sound of agitated voices. He bent and put his head and shoulders out.

"What is that about?" asked Geoffrey, chewing a thick

53

piece of goose.

Ordulf pulled back and took a drink of wine, then answered. "Visitors. They are kindly bringing torches, the day not being sufficiently warm."

Thomas and Jean jumped up and ran to look.

"Where are the guards?" Thomas asked.

Jean pointed to the gate. Two pikes were stuck into the ground. "They have resigned."

Geoffrey raised a flatbread and scrutinized both of its faces. "Thomas, would you run down and make sure the gate is secure?"

Ordulf, regaining his seat, jabbed his fork into a goose leg. "They might at least permit a gentleman to fill his belly."

"I say we kill a few most horribly." Jean said, still gazing into the night. "That will give them pause and allow us to eat in peace."

"The strategy worked well in Mersin." Ordulf said with no sincerity. "All we must do is learn to endure the stench of stacks of rotting corpses. Unless you are volunteering to bury all these good people yourself, in the end we would still have to move – far upwind."

Jean turned to reply, but Geoffrey lifted a bell from the table and rang it loudly. A thin dark man dressed in white appeared.

"Fetch the other servants and leave by the back way," Geoffrey ordered. The man bowed wordlessly and ran. Geoffrey studied Ordulf and Jean. "If you have any women you care about in your rooms, you should pay them and see them safely out."

Ordulf shrugged. Jean smiled mischievously.

Thomas returned, out of breath. "The gate is barred."

Geoffrey rose and tossed his napkin onto his plate.

The mob strode with righteous anger, the truth of their position becoming more self-evident the closer they approached the compound of the foreign devils who had conjured down the plague upon the city. But once at the gate,

54

the crowd milled about, confused and shouting. They had not thought to bring a ram to batter down the heavy doors nor ladders to scale the walls. A delegation was sent back to fetch what could be found as substitutes, and in the meantime the crowd satisfied themselves with hammering ineffectually on the hard wood and pissing on the base of the walls.

After quite a long time timbers appeared, meager pieces splintered by age, along with some abbreviated, rickety ladders. The crowd applied enthusiastic energy in making up the deficits of material, and soon the gates bent inward. Men gripped the top of the rampart and cheered as no guards appeared to challenge them.

By the time the first of the horde had actually entered the compound, the knights were pulling the lever that slid a carved panel in the kitchen to seal their escape tunnel.

"Hold the light," Thomas whispered, shoving the mechanism to make sure it had seated in its lock.

Jean supported a bulging leather sack over one shoulder. He struggled to keep the candle in his other hand steady.

"There," Thomas said, "Go."

The four lugged their loads through the tunnel, which was just high enough for them to stand but too narrow for them to avoid scraping their possessions on the sides. Thomas held back a distance, listening for sounds of pursuit. It was always possible one of their servants – or one of the servants of previous owners of the compound – would know about the tunnel.

His free hand traced the wall, and a tactile spark kindled a long-interred memory: another lightless tunnel, the knights in silent file, apprehensive about what they would find inside a bizarre structure deep in the arid wastes. His recollection was fresh, but it had been two centuries and more.

His fingers lost skin to the coarse rock, but he did not attend. The years crowded about him in the dark. The knights had lived longer than any man since Old Testament times, and they possessed a source of power unmatched since those days. Yet Geoffrey had done no great deeds with the gifts. *Neither have I. It is my fault as well.*

The decades had become one city after another, unremarkable and in Thomas' mind coagulated into a single tiresome campaign. In each new home Geoffrey curried favor with their powers, used them to increase his treasure, employed them like a street magician to intimidate opposition. Yet in every place anger against them swelled, inevitably cresting. In the beginning they had fought back, but that tactic did nothing but create more enemies. Lately the knights just moved on.

The only years Thomas recalled without bitterness were the ones spent in his turn guarding the Tower. In 1303 the cabal landed on the island the Arabs called Serendib, where alchemists, according to Geoffrey's sources, had produced the philosopher's vitreous humour – a necessary precursor to the lapis philosophorum, that fantastic rock which touched to lead transmutes the common metal to pure gold. There Thomas had made friends with a small group who followed the tenets of Sramana, and chief among their teachings was there was no Heaven to praise nor was there a corresponding Hell to fear. The cult advocated living for the moment – and prolonging your one and only shot at existence by actively defending it. Correspondingly, the men were always armed and trained constantly with their weapons. Thomas came upon them one afternoon as he followed the sounds of clashing blades to a shaded back garden.

In exchange for teaching them the English way with the heavy broadsword, they taught him to read.

Thomas returned to the Tower at his next watch carrying trunks full of texts. At first all he understood was Tamil, but luckily writers in that language had produced copius books and scrolls of literature, history, and natural philosophy. He filled his days with hiking the valley and and his nights honing his new ability. In each new city from then on he sought out a teacher of the local tongue and frequented the booksellers.

But millions of words in hundreds of dialects and there was yet no mention of a Tower or a sleeping angel or what to do if a mere human stumbled across such a thing.

His lord's gravely voice echoed down the tunnel, the message garbled. He was talking to Ordulf, something about the currents. No doubt their next home was already purchased and outfitted. Geoffrey was always making plans.

Thomas shook his head, sweeping aside the obstruction of memory. Was there pursuit? He held his breath for a minute but heard nothing behind him, and when he emerged into the moonlight the other three were already tossing boxes and bags into a dhow. There was some light on the sails other than from the moon. Thomas pivoted around and saw eager flames were already climbing up the thatched roof of their former home.

December 16, 1773
Boston, Massachusetts Colony

About the same time the King was scouring the royal possessions for a chart of North America suitably impressive to bolster his presentation, Moses Proctor was walking up the slope of Battery March swinging a fifteen-pound cod by its gills. The cod had been swimming with its school in the icy Atlantic at daybreak when it unwisely bit into a herring which twisted temptingly but unnaturally. The smaller fish was actually stone dead, run through with an iron hook by Moses or one of his father's other three crewmen. Now the sun was setting over the Boston hills, and this cod was all that remained of the catch. Moses and the crew of the schooner Hortense had delivered most of their harvest to the Gloucester docks and offloaded some into a smaller ketch which Moses and Osgood Sanders sailed down Cape Ann into Boston Harbor and up to Gibb's Wharf.

This particular sea creature, silvery, clear-eyed, and smelling only of salt water, was destined to be supper for the two hungry fishermen at the Five Crowns – a fine tavern which boasted an upper floor with beds for rent. It was much too late on this short winter day to contemplate a return to Gloucester, so they would, as they had many times before, deliver the fish to the kitchen, drink cider while it was baked or boiled, then consume as much cod and bread as would fit before hauling their engorged bulks up the stairs.

Osgood and Moses entered the tavern, where the proprietor relieved Moses of his fish and delivered them each a pewter tankard. The tavern was empty but for the two newcomers and an elderly man sitting alone in a dark corner reading a broadsheet by candlelight. Moses drank half of his tankard in two pulls, then went out the door to visit the privy. As he turned the corner of the building, he had a clear view of Rowe's wharf and the harbor. In the middle of the farthest anchorage he saw two ships flying the Union Jack. They rode easily on the small swell of the inner harbor. He could see no activity on their decks but up in the high rigging several sailors worked the sheets. He counted their gun ports, and the total – which might have made any loyal subject of His Majesty warm with pride – instead filled Moses with a cold dread.

When he returned to the tavern, Osgood was talking to the old man, who sat in what had been Moses' chair waving the broadsheet for emphasis. Moses pulled up a new chair in time to catch the end of the man's update on the status of the tea ships.

"...and so the Governor will allow the twenty days to go by, then he will take the tea by force and resell it to Tory merchants." He nodded to Moses and said, "I am John Aplanalp, late of the Gazette–" He again shook the broadsheet in front of him.

Moses returned the nod. "When does the twenty days end?" As all who had been following the drama of the tea knew, this was the period which a ship had to unload its cargo and pay any custom due the Crown – else the port authorities could and would confiscate the cargo and sell it off to settle the bill.

"Today!"

"Then the problem would seem to be taken care of by

morning," said Osgood.

Aplanalp shook his head. "Adams and his gang will never allow the tea to be sold in Massachusetts, and every Tory merchant comprehends it. Not a one will admit a single leaf of yonder tea in his warehouse. His dry, wooden warehouse–" a knowing, conspiratorial wink "–and the Fire Wards all Sons of Liberty."

The fishermen invited their new friend to share the cod with them, and they ate and talked for the better part of an hour about the political situation, then Aplanalp noted the large clock on the fireplace mantle and declared it was his bed time.

"But it's not yet six," Moses observed.

Aplanalp shrugged and stood. Osgood, yawning, said, "I am for bed as well," and started to the stairs.

Aplanalp, watching the fisherman as he departed, said quietly to Moses, "Would you care to take an enlightening walk?"

When the two men left the tavern the night was warmer than it had a right to be so close to Christmas, but the streets were barely visible. The sun was well down, and the moon just the barest crescent. Moses cautiously followed the older man as he headed toward the water. After a few minutes they paused under one of the new whale-oil streetlamps, and Aplanalp pulled a round tin from a breast pocket. He opened it, put two fingers into its dark interior, then smeared black on his cheek. He held the tin out to Moses.

"Should we be Africans?" he asked.

Moses stared stupidly at the tin.

"Some are splashing red on their faces and threading feathers in their hair," the old man said. "I have no children at home to beg Wampanoag garb from, but I do have a coal bin."

Beyond Aplanalp, Moses heard voices, and he could just make out the shape of a horde moving on the next street down. "What is this?" he said.

Aplanalp took another scoop of coal dust. "Mr. Osgood,

when tea cannot come onto the land, and it cannot remain on its ship, there is only one place it can go."

Moses felt he had consumed one too many mugs of ale, because he could not parse this mystery. Even in this dark, his loss showed.

Aplanalp sighed. "Into the harbor! It must go into the water and steep a salty brew which Crown and Parliament shall be able to taste these thousand miles away." He looked at Moses, somewhat sheepishly. "I am so used to composing headlines – sometimes I typeset them out loud. What say you? I am to row out with the savages, but it occurred to me you might not only be a more fit with an oar but also in need of an evening's entertainment."

Moses dipped one fingertip into the dirty powder and rolled it against his thumb. It was as fine as cake flour. "There are men of war standing just beyond the tea ships. What will your savages do if they fire upon you as you row out?"

"Set your mind at ease. The navy wants this matter to go quietly over the horizon as much as we."

Moses smiled. He touched a blackened finger to his forehead and rubbed it in a small circle.

December 9, 1774
London

"I would like to go back inside." The woman was beautiful – pale as frost with raven hair – but she did not know how to dress for the weather. Her neckline had been designed to show off her bosom, not to keep it warm. Her companion, a blonde who had been busy this last hour studiously trying to pretend she was not Irish, nodded even though she was wearing a sensible riding coat trimmed at the neck with rabbit, which she had claimed was fox. Both of them blew out long plumes of steam as if to punctuate how desperately cold it was here on the frozen river.

Geoffrey did not acknowledge them. He was concentrating on the skating demonstration. The sharp scraping of the blades on the brittle ice sent physical shivers through the boot soles of all who stood on that surface. After some time he nodded, and the two women stooped to go back into the tent, where tiny logs flamed inside a blue porcelain stove.

"Here comes the packet from Southend." Ordulf pointed downriver. An ivory road coach pulled by four gray horses entered the line of tents and huts, cheered by the bundled crowd and the jugglers, fire-eaters, puppeteers, and all the sellers of meats and drinks and sweets. The occupants of the coach waved and hulloed while the driver snapped his reins and his seat companion brandished a short gun.

The gala was a spontaneous Frost Fair. Not very large and not destined to be one of the legendary gatherings, but it would serve to alleviate the depression of a hard city winter. The Thames had solidified in the past week upstream of London Bridge, where the river slowed against the damming stone. Thick enough at first for skating and sliding, then strong enough for tents and huts, and finally sound enough for horse races and the packet from Southend to make a glamorous entrance – though the coach had traveled most of the way on actual roads and just ventured carefully onto the ice for the last two hundred yards.

Ordulf sent a boy with some coins to fetch them brandy and cuts from the ox being roasted on a monumental spit close by. While they waited for these treats, they resumed watching the skaters cutting swirling figures into the smooth blue ice.

A cadaverous young man squeezed out of the crowd, a square of oiled cloth bound with ribbon under his arm. "M'Lord?" He doffed his cap and presented his package to Geoffrey, who felt in his coats for suitable currency and exchanged it for the message.

"Mumphrey is late," Geoffrey said to Ordulf. They had contracted to receive their own intelligence from the colonies, including that of a Mr. Mumphrey, who operated a Boston tavern frequented, he claimed, by all the most rabid rebels. Mumphrey dispatched weekly a collection of newspapers, broadsides, flyers, and his own notes and observations.

Geoffrey untied the parcel and flipped through the contents. He withdrew a paper upon which their correspondent had made some scrawling notes in the margins and scanned the content.

"Mumphrey declares this proclamation which the colonists style the Suffolk Resolves is the most inflammatory rhetoric yet heard in Massachusetts colony," Geoffrey said in summary.

Ordulf leaned close and tilted his head to make out the print. They read in silence for a time, then Ordulf snorted. "They apparently are laboring under the impression the King is their friend and Parliament their enemy when it is so clearly the other way round."

Geoffrey hit the paper lightly with the back of one gloved hand. "It is easy to be ignorant of the facts when an ocean intervenes. The scum who wrote these words are not going to be satisfied with firing their broadsides from a printing press once it penetrates into their thick criminal skulls that George detests them."

Ordulf kicked down at the frozen Thames. "These damned resolvers are in competition with us for the continent."

Geoffrey dropped the document back into the open cloth. "Perhaps it is time for you to go cross the gap and determine if *we* are indeed in possession of the necessary facts."

"And if the authors of that rag are sincere?"

"If it is the situation, then do what you can to dissuade them."

"Oh," Ordulf said. "Shall I politely ask them to yield?"

Geoffrey nodded at one of the skaters, a fetching young girl whose skates sent up a sparkling shower of tiny crystals as she stopped. "It costs nothing to be polite."

July 22, 1775
Philadelphia, Pennsylvania Colony

The sun had been still touching the Atlantic when Lieutenant Stark left the inn in New Brunswick. The day began hot and clear, but an hour into his ride on the King's Highway a storm front rolled from the west. First the sun clouded over, then a cool wind kicked up in his horse's face. The initial droplets were quickly chased by a driving rain. The road was lightly traveled, so he was able to keep up a good pace even as the visibility shrank to yards.

His greatcoat became saturated. Rain blew sideways under his cocked hat – though he had turned down the brim and fastened the chinstrap – and seeped into his collar. By the time he saw the granite marker which told him he was five miles from Philadelphia he was soaked to the skin and as unhappy as his horse.

Two hours later he walked his mare up to the door of a decrepit tavern hard by the docks. He was still miserable but no more wet, having reached a steady state of hydration. He looked the building up and down, then side to side. As he had been promised, it was exceedingly wide.

His first stop, the State House, had been deserted. Patrons at a public house near that august structure reported his quarry had muttered something about finding a long interior space. A tipsy local, for the mere price of a pint, directed him to this, the closest building fitting the description, which had once housed a sail loft and rope factory servicing the Delaware Bay trade. Now it was a tavern, and not a reputable one by its exterior. He was tempted to turn around, but the interior promised to be somewhat drier than its yard.

No stable boy ran out to assist. Stark walked his mount to the back of the place and found a barn with its door ajar. He loosened his saddle and dried his horse off as best he could with some scraps of canvas hanging from nails, then found a bucket outside the door overflowing with rainwater and held it up while his horse pushed her soft eager lips into it. He went back into the rain and walked quickly to the front door of the tavern.

Stark was not a handsome man. His face was sharp as an axe; his eyes close set and his mouth set in a natural frown. His skin was dimpled from a youthful bout with the pox. But he was tall and muscular and looked as hard as granite. When he entered, three men drinking at a table sized him with narrowed eyes. Stark glared down his nose at them with such intensity they turned back to their mugs.

A fat man standing behind the bar returned his gaze without blinking. He had one hand on the counter and one below. As Stark approached him, the man brought up a pistol and rested it on the bar.

"I am here for John Adams," Stark said, raising his hands, empty and spread wide, up to chest level.

The man did not seem either surprised or comforted by that statement.

"He may be in the company of Mister Thomas Jefferson," Stark continued.

This time the man sniffed and nodded to his right. Stark turned and saw a staircase. He looked back at the man and thought for a second to inquire whether there were clean towels and perhaps a hot bath available, then sighed and headed for the stairs, praying to God this was not a whorehouse.

The second floor showed truly the history of the building. One lantern burned on a table, and by that meager light Stark saw the space ran straight and unobstructed for tens of yards. Casks, lumber, boxes, and coils of rope had been recently dragged to the sides of the elongated room, their paths marked clean on the dusty floor.

He heard a faint cadence, like a sergeant calling the march in a whisper, and at the very end of the room he saw the backsides of two men. One was tall and dressed in an expensive coat. The other was short, rotund, and shabby.

Maybe it was just the lack of light tricking his eyes. They seemed engaged in some kind of march. They appeared to be stepping in an approximation of tandem, in strides as regular as the taller could constrain and the shorter could expand.

They reached the far wall and turned together and began to come back toward him, still attempting to make their feet fall in concert. Neither one, he saw, was John Adams. Nor was either Samuel Adams. He did not know these gentlemen, though he assumed the taller man was Jefferson of Virginia. This guess was reinforced by the man's accent as he counted off steps under his breath.

The pair passed him without heed, made it to the opposite wall, pirouetted again in harmony, and paced evenly back. A short distance from Stark, they said in chorus and more loudly, "One hundred!" and stopped. Each reached for a mechanism hanging about his waist. They held these together, examining them carefully, seemingly without satisfaction.

"Well," the shorter man said at last, "for a spontaneous experiment, that is about as close as one could wish. Given the obvious inequality of the testing method."

The taller man frowned, then seemed to see Stark for the first time. Stark stiffened as if a major general had entered the room. "Have you a twin?" the man asked.

Stark blinked.

The shorter man raised his eyebrows. "Capital idea!"

The taller man tried again. "Sir, were you born a twin? Delivered with a brother, that is. One of identical measurements? Obviously a fraternal twin would not exactly serve."

"No, sir," Stark managed. "I do not have a twin brother."

The taller man pursed his lips. "Odds against us, I suppose. Still, the hypothesis is compelling. Why can we not build a cart," he began to mold this imaginary vehicle in midair with his two hands – hands which Stark noticed were larger and more muscular and callused than any gentleman's hands of Stark's acquaintance, "which has two matched wheels.... With some kind of hinged structure which would serve as a leg, as far as the workings might detect...." He held up his clock-faced mechanism to illustrate the point.

"Ah!" the shorter man cried. "A parallel implementation of the odometer of Archimedes!"

"Exactly – the old Greek's invention is fit for measuring the distance on any road a cart travels, but not on hillsides or other terrain impassible on foot...." He stopped suddenly and reconsidered Stark. "I apologize, sir. When the mood is upon me, I am not in the same world as my fellow man. Except perhaps for my confederate, Mr. Franklin." The short man bowed.

Stark returned the honor. "I am sorry to interrupt your..." *What were they doing?* "...experiment. I am Lieutenant Isaac Stark of the 8th Massachusetts Regiment."

Mr. Franklin gestured to his coexperimenter. "Mr. Thomas Jefferson. I am the peripatetic Benjamin Franklin, recently returned from Paris with the latest pedometer design. As you can see, Mr. Jefferson has constructed his own instrument. You have observed our feeble effort to compare the two. Are you interested in pedometry?"

"I suppose I should be," Stark said, "but that is not why I am here. I am looking for John Adams."

Jefferson motioned, and a young Negro woman Stark had not noticed stepped out of the shadows. "Caroline, fetch us all some punch," he said. She made an trim curtsy and went down the stairs.

"I am sorry to say you are to be disappointed," said Jefferson. "Mr. Adams has taken himself to New York City, and we do not expect him back before the day after tomorrow. If you are bearing a dispatch, you may with surety leave it with Mr. Hancock, who has the honor to be presently the President of the Congress."

Stark shook his head. "With respect, sir, I will wait for Mr. Adams. I have no official dispatch. I have come to disclose to him the details of the death of his friend Dr. Warren on Breed's Hill."

The interest of his audience sharpened noticeably. "Were

you present at the battle?" Franklin asked.

"I was," said Stark, snapping to automatic attention. He proceeded to tell them the account of the action there and his participation in it. As he was describing the disposition of forces defending the hill before the British attack, Caroline – who Stark took to be Jefferson's – brought rum punch and some dainty cinnamon cakes, which Stark, ravenous from his ride, took up impolitely and bit into without pausing in his narrative, even as he wondered this manner of tavern could be home to any sort of cake.

When he related the events surrounding the shooting of Dr. Warren – how Warren had suddenly stopped in the middle of a safe escape and turned to face his killers with a calm detachment and horrible emptiness in his eyes, disregarding the cries and admonitions of Stark – Franklin and Jefferson exchanged a long look. Stark thought Jefferson's face showed a puzzled sadness; Franklin's a determined resolve.

Stark paused for a moment. It seemed each of them wanted to say something to him, but each considered and then was silent, so Stark finished his account and drained his glass. He felt empty and useless. He had met two of the most learned men in the land, and they had not answered his questions, unstated though they might have been. His account had not provoked them. Perhaps Adams would give him more satisfaction. For now, he needed to go and find a place to dry out and sleep.

They thanked him for his tale and made small talk about the business of the Congress, and when the conversation turned to the weather Stark felt it was time for him to depart. He bid them adieu and walked down the stairs and back out into the storm. The flux of rain had actually increased, something he would have sworn impossible not an hour before. The individual raindrops coalesced into sheets of buffeting water. He fetched his horse, tightened the girth, and mounted. The mare did not want to step out into the deluge, and Stark had to kick her ribs three times to convince the beast he was not fooling.

A hundred yards down the mud-slicked path which led away from the tavern, among the tumbledown buildings lining the banks where the Schuylkill and the Delaware combined, a figure materialized in the aqueous gloom. Stark's horse shied and started to rear, but the figure reached out and gripped the bridle, then turned and led them off the lane. Stark felt he should resist this abduction, but something in the surety of the action stilled his protests.

They went a short distance down an even darker, narrower way and into a small barn pressed round by abandoned shacks. Out of the rain, the figure turned and uncovered. It was Jefferson's girl, Caroline, who motioned Stark to dismount.

He slid to the ground and opened his mouth but stopped when Caroline put up a hand. "Would you like to know what Mr. Jefferson and Mr. Franklin had to say after you left them?"

Stark felt he should answer a gentleman would not receive such confidences, but then he considered that this slave girl was no gentleman, and he was feeling much less than civil himself. He was chilled, soaked, and ravenous, no matter the recent cakes.

She waited for a positive sign from him and eventually took no negative sign as affirmation. "Mr. Jefferson was quite agitated. He asked Mr. Franklin if this might be a manifestation of those dark forces of which they had heard rumors. Mr. Franklin said he did not know about the particular case you had brought them, but he had been approached on the Continent by persons who were obviously interested in what Mr. Franklin had been able to divine about the vital electricity. These persons, he felt, were not concerned with any scientific understanding of the subject."

She paused. Stark had been watching her face closely. She did not here comport herself as any household servant Stark had experience with, much less as a slave. In the presence of her master she had been submissive and silent. Now she looked Stark boldly in the eye as though daring him to object.

Stark shrugged.

"You came a long way to make this report," she said.

"Dr. Warren was a close friend of Mr. Adams. I wanted him to hear the particulars of his death from my lips, lest the story reach him with untruths applied to it."

She studied him for a moment. "You want someone to explain his actions to you. That is why you came. You are an officer with duties, with war in the air and no time for such ordinary courtesies. You could have written Mr. Adams a letter."

Stark did not reply. There was too much right with her observation to protest, and they both knew it.

"What did you feel when Dr. Warren turned to face his enemy?"

"I..." Stark put a hand to his face and tried to wipe away the wetness, not all rain now, not knowing exactly why he was telling her this. "...felt sick." He was feeling some of that again, just recalling Warren, his kind round face, excited as a boy, stopping short, his eyes draining, mouth slack, pivoting toward the black-draped figure who clutched at the air. Stark swallowed, panting suddenly. "I was nauseous – with horror, not in expectation of a ball or a shell – as if I was witness to something much worse than death." He tried to smile, but only succeeded in drawing back his upper lip to expose a bit of his teeth. "As if there was anything more abhorrent than that bloody day...." He saw past the walls of this run down barn, his mind returning to shattered bones and screams of dying men.

She put out a hand and touched his forearm, then said, "There is a thing very much more vile."

He shivered.

"I am come from a small tribe called the Dibele," she said. "We live in the green lands south of the great desert. The Dibele are keepers of knowledge and seekers of justice. We fight against one great evil."

Stark had taken off his hat. He twisted it tightly with both hands as he listened.

"What you saw in Dr. Warren's death was that cabal coming to the New World. For some reason they have chosen to enter into your conflict with the King, and they have taken his side. This is not good news for you."

"Who are they?"

"A small group of men who style themselves as knights. They discovered once a source of powerful magic in your Holy Land," she said. "They have been gathering strength ever since. Evil and the defenders of evil gravitate to them. My people have been tracking them for several hundred years and exposing them as they hide among mortal men. They are named the Giza Mashujaa, which in the language of the desert peoples means Warriors of the Dark."

She saw Stark was wavering. "The one on the hill. What did he do to your Dr. Warren that he could not move to save his own life?"

"I guessed he was a ship's surgeon or some such." Stark closed his eyes. "He was dressed in black. I saw him on the edge of the beach as the Redcoats began their last advance. But men fell around him and he made no notice of them...."

"Did you fire your musket at him?"

Stark opened his eyes and shook his head. "We were out of powder. That is why we had to abandon the redoubt, the fence... the whole of Breed's Hill."

She made a motion with one hand. *It would not have mattered.* "Shot is useless against these men. The one you saw reached out through the battle and took Dr. Warren's will from him."

Stark nodded. Warren had lowered his sword and stood motionless as the British officer aimed his pistol. The Doctor stared at the black-coated stranger even as the ball blew through his brain, exploding the back of his head, his hat tumbling, hair streaming....

He took a deep shuddering breath. "Have you told this to your master?"

She shook her head.

"Why?" He asked angrily. "There may come a day when these men – this cabal – come for him. And for Franklin, and Adams, and all the rest. Why not warn them?"

"The knowledge would only distract them from their task, which is already hard enough. They would be in even more danger if the knights feared exposure by such prominent men. It is for my tribe and our friends to let my master work in ignorance so we may protect them as best as we can."

"But you said—"

Her face, hard and fearless, stopped him. "My master and his correspondents have received whispers, and they share rumors, but that is all. They have more important matters to occupy their deliberations. It is to me and my friends to keep the Giza in the shadows."

Stark felt the unsettling bizarre essence of this new world seep over him like warm tar. The slave girl watching over the master, war waged with magic. And he realized baptism in the liquid brains of the late Doctor signified he was now one of this woman's friends and even more responsible for the safety of men like Jefferson, Franklin, and Adams.

She looked down for the first time and balled her hands into fists. "Many of my people have been killed by this corruption over the years. They think that if they can silence the Dibele they will be able to control all other men. They are powerful, more powerful than we. But we are patient, and determined, and we will never stop."

"What am I to do the next time? If shot cannot hurt them...."

The rain hammered unceasingly on the aged roof. They had maneuvered themselves into one of the few undrenched patches of the old barn. All about them, perfectly vertical streams of water, sparkling in what little light reached into this space, carved out craters and pools on the barn floor, a mix of ancient manure and straw now made into a foul paste. The excess sought the nearby river by joining in low channels and making for one wall. Caroline closed her eyes and took a deep breath, then reached behind her neck and undid the clasp of a necklace. She held it out to Stark.

A small oval pendulum of dark silver swung in the air before him. At the center of the pendant was a tiny window glowing with an internal light, a shade of turquoise edged with some more intense blueness.

"The Giza have acquired many tricks over the years, but this is the original source of their energies. This is one drop of what they call simply...the water."

Stark had started to reach out to touch it, but drew back on hearing this.

She put it on his palm and closed his hand over it with both of hers as if reluctant to let it go. "They may use it for evil, but it is not evil. Can you feel its warmth?"

He nodded. Her manner made him certain this gift was spontaneous and unique to him, and her eyes revealed she was not sure herself about the wisdom of it.

"Few men in the world but the Giza and the Dibele have held the water. It can heal – and it can kill. Use it wisely, Lieutenant Stark."

January 16, 1698
The Holy Land

The little girl opened her eyes. She had not been asleep anyway. Her younger brother had woken her with a dig of his elbow as he rolled over, so she was lying on her back, eyes shut, trying to slip back into the wonderful dream she had been inside. Flying low over the bright desert, flapping her arms like a bird–

"Where are you going?" she demanded in a whisper of her sister, the oldest of the siblings.

"Go back to sleep," the older sister commanded. She continued on her way out of the children's night room, stretching a thick cotton robe over her nightgown.

The younger sister pretended to obey, closing her eyes until her sister tiptoed out of the room, then she slid out from under the blankets. Her snoring brother did not stir as she grabbed her own robe.

Her older sister had slinked outside and was scaling the ladder to the roof of their home. The younger followed, light and silent on the wooden rungs, and flopped down onto the flat roof behind the short wall beside her older sister and waited for her remonstrations.

But the older just smiled in the starlight, so used was she to the little one tagging close behind, and pointed through one of the square holes through which the infrequent rains drained into the cisterns below.

"Look there."

The little sister put her eye to the opening. Down at the end of the row of houses she saw by sputtering torchlight a line of men standing shoulder to shoulder, spears at their sides. "Is that Papa down there?"

"Yes," said the older. "Papa is one of the honored guard. Someday he will be one of the council, as his papa was."

"What are they doing?"

"It is the time of the Giza Mashujaa," the older sister said excitedly. "You are too young to remember the last. Every four years a new Giza goes to the Pillar of Heaven and the old Giza comes out."

The little one gaped up at her sister with eyes wide and round. "I did not know the Giza Mashujaa were real!"

"Of course they are real," the older chided. "Who do you think built our home, and all the other homes, and the oasis, and the well, and all the rest? They did. Long ago they built Daskara Hafiz so that we could live here and guard the Pillar of Heaven."

"Have *you* seen it?"

The older sister gave her a haughty look. "Of course I have seen Burj al Janna – and you will too when you are old enough to ride."

The younger sister started to protest she certainly was – when her older sister, peeking over the top of the wall shushed her. "He is coming!"

The line of men bowed their heads. The sisters heard hoof beats, trotting speed, then a figure moved into sight, barely discernable in the combination of the white starlight and the soft yellow of the several torches. A figure clad in a black robe and black hood on a black horse. The sisters could not see his face, as the Giza did not turn his head to acknowledge his guardians nor slow down the least bit. The horse and rider trotted straight ahead and faded back into the night.

November 5, 1776
Salem, New Jersey

Know all men by these presents that I, Gifford Bullus of the Town of Savannah and State of Georgia, for and in consideration of the sum of fifty pounds sterling to me paid by the undersigned have bargained and sold to the undersigned one Negro male named Ruttee–

The Spaniard looked up from the parchment document. "Ruttee?"

Mr. Teeler, the delivery agent, waved a hand. "That's just the name they gave him at port, sir. To have something Christian to call him, you see. You can change it to anything which pleases you."

The Spaniard, who was not yet the undersigned recipient of said Negro male, lowered the paper and studied the object of his question. Ruttee was taller than either his purchaser or his deliverer. He was thin but seemed strong enough, his thinness perhaps exaggerated by his being dressed in only a linen shirt and too-small britches.

They were making the exchange in a sort of half-tent with walls of rough-sawn timber. A canvas roof, draped from a supporting pole hammered into the ground, filled and drooped with the gusting wind like a giant lung. Outside, the snow whipped sideways. The white men were bundled in coats – the black man shivered.

"The monies have been paid," the Spaniard stated as a fact. Mr. Teeler nodded somewhat reluctantly. He had been hoping for a small gratuity from the customer, although he had already pocketed his fee and commission from this trade. The prospect of any additional coin changing hands seemed slim given the customer's strange lack of enthusiasm at taking possession of such a fine and reasonably priced slave.

Other parts of the protected space were in use by merchants driven from the outside marketplace. The Spaniard walked to one of their tables, borrowed a quill and an inkwell containing half-frozen black slush, and signed the bottom of the document. Mr. Teeler accepted this and gave the Spaniard a smaller receipt. The new owner tucked this away in his jacket, nodded curtly at the agent, and motioned to his new possession to follow him out the door.

On the street waited a small covered cart hitched to a huge brown horse chewing patiently, ignoring the snow. The Spaniard rummaged in the back of the cart until he found a long wool cloak. He handed this to the black man, who shook it out and slipped into it as he climbed with his owner to the seat.

They rode in silence until they had passed well out of the small community of Salem and stopped in front of a weathered inn whose three stories dominated a barn and scattered outbuildings.

"There is a small room at the back of the barn for you," the Spaniard said. "It is not possible in this place for you to stay– " He nodded at the main house.

The slave did not reply. He climbed down from the cart and clasped his new coat around him as he walked to his lodgings.

Some time later the Spaniard sought out his purchase. He found the man sitting on a milking stool in the tiny space the innkeeper had made available, an unused harness closet in which some straw had been piled against one of the walls.

The Spaniard held out a wooden tray bearing a chunk of ham, a small loaf of bread, and a mug. "They claim this is tea."

The other stood and accepted the meal with a slight bow.

"Should I call you Ruttee then?" the Spaniard asked as the

slave examined the ham.

"It will serve as well as any other," Ruttee replied in quite passable Spanish. "My real name would be hard for your mouth and might draw attention."

The Spaniard nodded and continued in his native language. "How much do you know?"

Ruttee, chewing a mouthful of bread, appeared to think this question over as if there were more than one topic of which he had knowledge. Finally he swallowed. "I know you are Junipero de la Serra, formerly of Santander in the north of Spain, on the coast, on the Bay of Biscay. You were a piano maker. Your brother was killed by one of... them, and you have been seeking revenge since. This was in 1765."

Junipero frowned. "How do you know these things? And how did you come to speak in my tongue?"

"There are missionaries everywhere eager to save souls by civilizing them with the beauty of Spanish, thereby to read the Scriptures and be saved."

"No doubt. But the missionaries did not tell you about an unknown piano maker. It was Songay Bin, was it not?"

"Yes. That was the name he had taken at the time. He was traveling as a Turk."

The Spaniard laughed. "No Turk was ever so dark — but in Spain he was just another wayward Moor. Plenty of those lurking about. I never believed him a Turk.... Did he tell you I almost killed him?"

The look on Ruttee's face told him this had been left out of the account.

"I had tracked my friend to Lisbon, three years after he killed my brother. He was living on the estate of the Duke of Trancoso, and I was lodging in rooms on the Rua Augusto Rosa near the cathedral. One day I returned from an errand to find my door handle not at the unusual angle at which it was my habit to leave it. Someone had turned it. Perhaps it was an accident, perhaps not. One does not take chances. I was not sure at the time whether my friend knew I was following him. In any case, I went silently to a window and crawled out onto the roof, which came down low on that side and allowed access to another window in my chambers which was hidden behind a wooden screen. I crept into the room and saw this exceedingly dark stranger sitting at the table upon which I took my morning coffee and upon which I tinkered. He was there, eyeing with interest my latest project.

"I had a pistol in my hand, hidden behind me, Ruttee. The one who introduced himself as Songay Bin never knew. He was one untoward gesture away from a ball to his heart, but something about him made me tuck the pistol back into my belt."

"He never spoke of a weapon," Ruttee said. "And I do not believe he felt in any danger."

"Perhaps," Junipero said, "but he was sitting beside a powerful bomb I had just completed. In any case, as we drank my last bottle of Madeira, he told me of your people."

Ruttee swirled his mug of alleged tea. "Songay Bin had been watching the one called Ordulf for many years. He could not have missed your interest."

"I was not very subtle, I admit. Once I learned who had done those horrible things to my brother, I obtained two muskets and waited on the road outside Santander, hidden in a line of thick shrubs. He drove by in a coach, which I pierced with both balls before his mounted guards could react. Three of them came at me up the slope. I dropped the musket and drew two pistols. I shot one of the guards. Another was thrown violently from his frightened horse after I fired but missed. The third rode around the hedge and charged me at sword point."

Ruttee waited expectantly for the Spaniard to resolve the situation. After a minute, Junipero shrugged as if he had been waiting for his audience to beg for the revelation. "I would have been run through, but the horse stepped in a rabbit hole. Snap. His leg broken, his rider pinned screaming beneath him – and I ran like the Devil was jabbing my ass.

"Some time later I learned this Ordulf had not even been grazed by the two shots I put into his coach. Mind you – it was a small coach, and I am not such a bad shot. That was when I began to suspect this was no ordinary man. When Songay Bin told his tale I was halfway to believing him already."

Junipero looked around the small room. There was no other thing to would serve as a proper chair, so he leaned back against a post. "I learned there were others like my friend Ordulf, others in this evil clan. I was astonished. I asked Bin how many of these sons of bitches they had killed. And you know what he said? Of course you know! None!"

Ruttee nodded and opened his mouth, but the Spaniard cut him off. "I recall his excuses. I admit that these men – if we can even call them men any longer – seek out, befriend and bewitch the powerful and wealthy wherever they go. And it may be true as you believe that if they found it necessary to focus their wrath on the Dibele, they might kill many more of you, and then who would follow them and raise the people against them? Yes, you are a wise and persistent tribe. But you are just a minor splinter to be plucked from the sole of their foot – should they notice you at all.

"I told Songay Bin I was not of your tribe nor bound by its customs. I was going to kill Ordulf, be he man or beast. And we parted amicably.

"Several days later I went to a private club in the Barreiro where I had observed the monster enter on two occasions. He had gone both previous times in by a back entrance, so I set my bomb in the alleyway, inside of a barrel. When I saw his coach at the end of the way, I lit the fuse and ran into a brewery abutting the club. I dove under some pallets and waited for the explosion. You might say now this was not much of a plan, and I will agree with you. Three years had made me no better an assassin than I was the day I was born. There were many flaws in my plan. What if Ordulf did not come close enough to the bomb? What if he had lent his carriage to another man? And so on. But one thing I never expected was what happened. No explosion. The bomb had failed. This I could not comprehend. I make things, Ruttee. I have made things all my life, not just pianos. But unfortunately not a bomb before. So, foolishly, I ran quietly back to the alley to retrieve my device for another day. Providence was watching. Some sense told me to pause – just one heartbeat – and that saved my life." The Spaniard ran one hand over his scarred cheek. "The bomb worked in the end. I woke in the cathedral, in the hospital of the nuns of the Order of St. John of Jerusalem. I was there until the winter came and my broken bones strong enough to leave."

"You did not give up."

Junipero had his hand on an ancient leather yoke hanging forgotten on the wall. He stroked the surface and traced the fine cracks with a forefinger. "My brother was a simple priest. He loved his parishioners, so when some foreign bastards moved into an estate and began plying tricks on the local maidens, he complained to his bishop. Shortly after, he was visited in the night and offered a reward to stay quiet. He could not, so instead his skin was removed in many strips, as one skins a hog, and his body rolled onto the threshold of the same bishop, who would thereafter entertain no more complaints about the foreigners.

"Lying for months in plaster and bandages, I had a long time to think about quitting my new career. I was convinced Songay Bin had sabotaged my bomb. Foolish, I know now, but my mind was clouded by pain and anger. After some meditation, I concluded this Ordulf has some – say, influence – over the essential elements of antiquity: the earth, the wind, the water, and of course the fire. Twice I had used fire; twice I had been lucky to live. I determined the next time we met there would be no fire involved."

"Earth, wind and water," said Ruttee, "do not seem to me the basis for weapons."

Junipero tilted his head. "That is my problem. Or one of my problems. Another is you. The unsigned letter giving me a time and place to acquire a helper in my revenge could only have come from Bin. I do not surely know whether you have come to help me – or to hinder me."

"Why would you have agreed to this if you believed I was

only going to work against you?"

"For one thing," the Spaniard replied, "you cannot really stand across my path. In this country you are my property. I can always sell you to the nearest farmer, and though I suspect you would escape in a trice, you would be hunted and a reward offered for your capture. For another, I have faith you will tell me much about our friend I do not know."

Ruttee considered this for a long minute. "Both are true. I have been given leave to use my judgment. Songay Bin wishes me to teach you. He also hopes I will learn from you."

"Good. Let me remind you of a truth which came to me as I was lying under the care of the blessed nuns. Songay Bin said these men found their power in the Holy Land as Crusaders. In those days, their sway was over men armed with swords and bows. Now they control men with musket and cannon. If we do not kill this evil now, what arms will they possess in one hundred years, eh? Dibele not yet born may curse you for your inaction."

December 10, 1776
Buck's County, Pennsylvania

The Widow Narramore rocked in front of a cold fireplace. She had stripped her bed of its wool blanket and hemp linen sheets and wrapped them around her shriveled body. She would have had a heavy rug as her outer layer, but that old family possession had gone missing from the line out back shortly after the Continental troops chose to bivouac on Narramore Farm. Besides the bedclothes, the widow wore three of her five pairs of socks, two sets of undergarments, her Sunday dress over a garden smock, and had a knit cap jammed down over her ears holding an embroidered tea towel beneath.

Two of her guests sat at a table across the room, their breath misty horizontal gusts over her late husband's chessboard. She regarded them through narrowed eyes. They were officers, leaders of the dirty rabble camped in tiny triangular tents on her finest, flattest field. Their only redeeming qualities, the Widow Narramore determined, were that as officers they were entitled to a somewhat larger than starvation share of salted shad and cornmeal as well as three or four sticks per day of green firewood. All of this bounty they shared with the widow, but she did not consider that just compensation for confiscation of her cows, the contents of her root cellar, her wood piles, her horses, and the hay in the barn by the ravenous maw of the Army as it swarmed over her land. The officers had carefully tallied her losses and paid for it all in crisp Continental dollar certificates, whose only value – the widow was sure – would be in starting the miniscule daily fire.

One of the officers moved at last, picking up a pawn and advancing it. The other looked not at the board but at his opponent, a captain, one of Washington's staff quartered in the mansion two miles up the road, where it was probable the fireplaces were warm and the rations housed fewer weevils.

They were old friends. Captain Bradley Anderson and Lieutenant Chance Dwyer were both natives of Hardwick in the New Hampshire Grants. Dwyer had assumed command of the company camped outside, many of whom were their townsmen, after consumption took his superior during their retreat from the disastrous campaign on Manhattan Island. He had hope of being promoted to captain and permanent control of the company, but Dwyer had no influence other than his old friend, who was himself the most junior officer on the General's staff.

Anderson glanced at his tricorn hat, which beckoned from a nail by the front door. He wished he had the ill manners to go over and cram it upon his numb head. He also wished the same impulse that had urged him to visit Dwyer might at least have reminded him to pack his wool cap, now two useless miles off. It was late afternoon on a clear and sunny but bitterly chill day. He was about to suggest they abandon the game and set out in search of their daily sticks when a private pushed open the door and stomped in. The soldier nodded nonchalantly at the officers.

Anderson and Dwyer both showed mild exasperation. Many men of this and other companies had originally joined local militias that had the tradition of electing their own officers, and these troops maintained an opinion of the officer class as equals who commanded only at the pleasure of the ranks.

"Visitor, Cap'n," the private said, tossing his head to indicate the world beyond. "He'n got a cart."

The two officers sniffed. There was some aromatic scent in the room, something familiar they should have been able to place but could not. They rose stiffly.

Outside the temperature seemed slightly less frigid than inside, perhaps due to the weak sunlight reflecting from the weathered shingles of the house. On the path that led up to the house stood the cart, and leaning against the cart was a thick bearded man at the center of a gaggle of twenty or so soldiers who guiltily turned away as the two officers approached.

Captain Anderson said nothing. It was Dwyer's company. Dwyer pointed to one man. "Sergeant? What is this?"

The sergeant did not reply at once, as he was hurriedly swallowing. After a moment he choked out, "Mister Serra here wants to see you, sir." He motioned to the bearded man, who stepped forward.

"Dismiss the men," Dwyer said to the sergeant, but the men had already walked off a dozen paces – only to slow there to a glacial step, ears cocked back like cats to catch the conversation from which they had been sent packing

The two officers scrutinized the newcomer, who bowed. "My name is Junipero de la Serra," he said. "I am a lover of liberty, and I have come to you with a modest contribution."

He motioned for them to follow him to the back of the cart, where he opened the doors. Anderson leaned into the dark space and saw a heap of irregular cloth-covered objects on one side and a neat stack of large disks on the other. The inside of the cart was intense with the same sweet greasy smell of a moment ago, and this time Anderson was able to place it.

Ham. He hadn't tasted ham in months.

Dwyer peered over his friend's shoulder and made the same recognition, as well as noting there were obviously empty spaces at least three hams had recently occupied. That explained how this stranger had managed to drive through the pickets.

"Mister de la Serra," Anderson said deliberately, fighting back his own wave of saliva. "Do I understand you to say you are making these stores a gift to the Continental Army?"

The bearded Spaniard nodded agreeably. "They are all yours with my compliments, sir."

Anderson swallowed hard, then called, "Sergeant, bring the quartermaster to take possession."

The appearance of ham and cheese had a transformative effect on the Widow Narramore. After a moment of fascinated incredulity at the two miracles the officers deposited on her parlor table, she flung off most of her coverings and ran to the pantry. The three men – the officers had of course invited the donor to be their guest – heard some hammering and sliding, and the Widow reappearing clutching a bottle of homemade blackberry wine, plates, glasses, and cutlery. She made places at the table, filled a glass for each, and the four sat down as happy as any banquet goers had ever been.

As Lieutenant Dwyer sawed at the ham with one of the Widow's dull butcher knives, Captain Anderson politely asked the Spaniard how he had come across such fine provisions in these lean times. Junipero told them he had trained in piano and organ repair in his youth, and his work was known well in the confidential network of the Catholic Church, which still operated with supreme discretion even though the faith had been recently made legal in the colonies.

"There is a monastery in the Lehigh Valley," he said, accepting a thick slice of meat onto his plate. "The brothers purchased a historic organ from France which arrived in such a state that it could not be made to work – so they sent for me. I restored the instrument to its full glory, asking only compensation in consideration of the parts, as is my custom when serving the Church. The brothers said specie was nonexistent in these times and paid me with stuffs from their larder, which you see here before us."

Anderson paused chewing and got out, "For which generosity we thank you again. And offer our blessings to the good brothers."

Dwyer, working now on the cheese, glanced sideways at his friend and grinned thinly. If their hometown pastor could but hear his student praising Papists, he would pass a granite paving stone.

The Spaniard shrugged. "The brothers were too generous – the parts were not dear. Most I fashioned myself. In any case, I did not want this bounty to end up in on the King's plate, which it would have done had I tried to take it back to my workshop in New Jersey."

Both of the officers sat up noticeably. Junipero reached for some cheese. "I have a shop just outside Trenton," he said. "The dios maldito arpilleras – I am sorry, the Hessians – marched in and made themselves at home. I am fortunate to be just far enough away that none are billeted with me."

"You passed through their lines," Anderson said. "Did they interrogate you about your business in Pennsylvania?"

Junipero shook his head. "I mean no disrespect, but these Hessians and their officers have little regard for your Army. They have not made the slightest effort to erect fortifications around Trenton. They do not believe you can touch them – they boast that while you freeze, they will keep warm this winter and sweep up what remains of you in the spring."

Anderson rose, went to his satchel, and returned with a notebook and a thick square pencil. He opened the notebook and wrote one line, then asked, "Would you mind very much describing the state of the Hessians and other forces about Trenton as you have seen them?"

The Spaniard nodded and began to talk.

December 12, 1776
Trenton, New Jersey Colony

The farm Junipero had rented included a barn and a stable, both empty of animals now except for two horses – his cart horse and an old mare purchased for Ruttee to ride to his employment. There was an open shed Junipero paid a neighboring farmer to fill with seasoned wood and an outbuilding for the necessary human reliefs. The farmhouse itself was what had attracted his attention: two stories, clapboarded, with a steep roof. Most important, it had one large room on the second floor with good light. This was where he set up his table and unpacked his tools and where Ruttee now stood outside the open door watching his tinkering owner.

The Spaniard worked with a small plane, shaving minute slices of white pine from the side of what resembled nothing Ruttee had ever seen. Not that the Dibele had much fine furniture in their huts, so it was possible this wooden object, a squat rectangle, was some kind of appointment unknown to Ruttee. It was also possible the dozen or so brass tubes inside had some innocuous function. But Ruttee did not think so.

Junipero finally noticed his audience. "Was he there?"

"No," Ruttee said.

A silent moment passed. Shavings flew steadily from the plane.

"Perhaps tonight."

"Perhaps," Ruttee agreed.

Another silence with only the low scraping of the iron blade.

"Perhaps he has gone," Ruttee suggested.

The Spaniard shrugged.

"In either case, your efforts may be for nothing," Ruttee continued. "Subtle nudges may not be enough."

Junipero set his tool down and contemplated the curly splinters at his feet. He sighed. "Ordulf will sniff out even our most discrete moves – he has done it before. This time we might lose ourselves in the crowd. War is a wonderful and horrible distraction. He may forget about an old Spaniard's hate."

"And if he does not?"

"If you set a trap for a rat," here Junipero nodded to the contraption, "and the rat escapes, do you live with the rat? Or set another trap on another day?"

"Our rat may outlive his trappers," Ruttee said.

The other did not reply, and after some long minutes he took up a chisel and began to round a wooden corner .

December 17, 1776
Trenton, New Jersey Colony

No one, not even the present owner of the Twelve Mile Tavern, knew what the place was exactly twelve miles from. It was only a mile and a half, roughly, from the center of the cluster of buildings called Trenton and less than that from Assunpink Creek. Europeans had been living on the banks of the Delaware hereabouts for over a hundred years, long enough for history to be lost. The building had been a tavern for the last twenty years and before that the home of Twelve Mile Farm. The owners had died of pox and taken the eponym's secret to their graves, which were out back behind the stable.

The main room had once been a large dining room with thick timber bones and high ceilings. Present management had hacked out one wall to install a bar, otherwise the structure was little changed since its construction.

This evening the establishment was a German enclave. Hessian troops quartered in and around Trenton had adopted the Twelve Mile and other taverns and squeezed the local regulars out by force of numbers. Each unit gravitated toward its own, officers of course claiming the best houses for themselves and leaving the coarser commons to enlisted men.

The Twelve Mile Tavern was clean, well-stocked, and separated by a good distance from the other taverns, which were mostly within a short walk of Trenton center. It had been effectively commandeered by the officers of the Grenadier and Fusilier regiments, who considered themselves the cream of the commanding class.

Ruttee entered the back door of the tavern lugging a full cask of beer. His load weighed nearly as much as he did, but he managed it with ease. His employer, Mr. Yates, supervised from his station behind the bar with cool interest and a bit of appreciation. He had been convinced by a Spaniard to hire this black fellow for next to nothing, the Negro's owner himself having no work at the moment, and Mr. Yates determined it had been a very good deal. This Ruttee was doing the same work for far less than Mr. Yates had previously been paying two local layabouts.

Of course this placement had not been chance – Junipero and Ruttee had spent several nights observing local roads until Junipero determined the Twelve Mile Tavern was to be Ruttee's temporary place of labor.

On one of these raw nights, Ruttee ventured they were already in position for an effective ambush.

"I believe I have told you what comes of ambushes," Junipero had replied. "Our friend has an awareness which is supernatural. The time must be when he passes us with his attention fully on some other, more valuable prize."

So they had waited and watched and now Ruttee was in the tavern's employ, doing anything which needed doing. Mr. Yates was happy. He was happy because he was a staunch Tory and because his tavern was now filled most nights with the King's troops instead of local rabble, many of which were too republican and too vocal about it for his liking. True, he would have preferred proper Englishmen instead of Hessians, but the coins of each were the same to him.

Junipero had represented himself to Mr. Yates as a fellow merchant with conservative views - another product of careful surveillance. Ruttee had been given the background of one recently owned by an officer in the Continental Army. Mr. Yates had listened attentively to Ruttee's invented tale of his mistreatment at the hands of the King's enemies, and the act was completed.

This was an evening when the preparations might yield a dividend. The plotters should not have worried. It was inevitable two score of drunken soldiers would talk at length on the business of soldiery, and it was inevitable such talk would dwell on the capabilities or lack thereof of the enemy, and it was inevitable in this particular situation Mr. Yates would, from behind his wooden pulpit, bring the conversation around to include his new hire, a star witness of the situation on the other side of the lines.

That is how Ruttee ended up in the middle of the tavern floor, surrounded by tipsy red-faced Hessian officers as a living font of espionage, slowly turning his head from side to side, taking in all his audience. He did not look directly at the far corner, where an hour before an indistinct figure slipped in among the gaiety and assumed the empty table just out of reach of the candlelight. Ruttee had watched from the back room, and as he went about behind the bar tending his chores, groups of Hessian officers went in turns to the table in the shadows in what he thought much like a state of quiet, uncharacteristic obeisance.

This is the Saxon. He had been taught about the five: the English, the Gauls, and the Saxon. *Junipero was right to follow the Hessians. The Saxon was from a place very near Hessia.* Another inevitability: even immortals seek comfort in the company of the familiar.

"Your old master – why does he defy his King?" The questioner was a consumptive captain of the Fusiliers.

"He was told many lies by bad men." Ruttee had spent some time seeking out local servants and learning to imitate the hesitant patois spoken by the slaves in this area. "They told him God did not crown Kings, but that all men were equals." This drew gasps and murmurs of disapproval.

He answered several more questions about Continental Army officers, forces he might have seen, weapons, etc. Then one officer asked him about Washington – had he ever laid eyes on the chief rebel?

Ruttee shook his head. "No. Maybe we never will. They say the army want to go back to their farms. No pay for a year, no food. If they ever made to attack, Mister Washington going to have to ride his big horse away out in front to shame the cowards – and the sergeants have to come behind them with bayonets. The rebel leaders don't like that. They know one lead ball into Mister Washington and their treason is over."

This pleased the crowd, who cheered and launched into a drinking song more ribald than martial. Ruttee slipped into the back room and immediately turned to peek out through a crack in the door to see how his act had played to the dark corner, but he could detect no change there.

December 21, 1776
Trenton, New Jersey

Ruttee bumped open the back door of the house and entered the kitchen, his arms full of firewood. He laid his load down carefully on the hearth. Junipero knelt in front of a small hot fire frying potatoes and onions in a cast iron kettle. Ruttee sniffed the slick floral scent.

"The oil of olives," Junipero said. Ruttee sat down to observe. The cook removed the browned mixture into a copper bowl, letting excess oil drain. Then he cracked two eggs and stirred it all together. The yellow slurry went sizzling into a skillet preheated over the flame. After a few minutes, he used a wooden paddle to flip the firmed mass and cooked it on the other side for about the same length of time. Finally he upended the steaming golden round onto a tin platter and set it before Ruttee.

The two men carved up the aromatic cake. Ruttee poured

from a bottle of wine, and they ate by the light of the dying fire and one candle in the middle of the table. Outside the wind rose, and they heard the first of the sleet spatter against the door.

They dined in silence, which was Ruttee's normal state but rather an anomaly for the gregarious Spaniard.

Finally Junipero spoke. "I think by summer you will be a free man."

Ruttee did not answer, so the other went on. "You have never asked me where all this finery comes from. It is not easy or cheap to find olive oil worth eating in this place." He sighed. "The truth is, my friend, that our funds are about at an end."

"I assumed," Ruttee said around his mouthful, "you were a rich man."

"Wealth must come from somewhere. This meal comes to us by my father's gift, his estate in Vitoria. My brother and I were the only heirs, so it became mine on their deaths. I sold the land. It was no palace, but could have supported me until the end of my days. It lay on the fertile banks of the Ebro and contained a large vineyard and fine meadows." He picked up his mug and took a sip. "Now I have all this—" He gestured with his drink to the kitchen "and you."

Ruttee grunted.

"In the spring, come what may, I will sell you at auction. I pray – no, I *expect* – you will then escape and make your way back to your people."

Ruttee shrugged. "You plan to carry on alone? Unless, God willing, we are successful."

"Yes," Junipero said slowly, "God willing." Then he looked up. "I am sorry you have to endure this."

"I made my choice," Ruttee said. "When the one you knew as Songay Bin returned to our land and told our Father about you, I was the one who was allowed to come."

"Songay Bin is your brother?"

Ruttee shook his head. "No. Our Father is... the Father. The one who fled the Tower."

Junipero poured himself some more wine. He had never questioned Ruttee about the Dibele. There had been too much to do, too much to worry over. Once he had accepted the existence of one thing that could not possibly be true he had just let the rest go by without what he had considered irrelevant examination.

He motioned to Ruttee. *Continue.*

"Our Father's name is lost to time. He may not even remember it. He was a slave – taken as an actual slave, not like my present imitation – driven far from his home, across the desert in a slaver's caravan. One night under the stars the captives were attacked by wild dogs. The men roped together had no place to hide. Many were shredded, their throats ripped out. The Father was badly wounded, but the beasts had bitten through his bonds. He was able to slip out of them and crawl away from the bloody frenzy. He walked in the sands for days, aimless, lost, and crusted with gore. He fell down dead in a hidden valley – and woke in a cool chamber with water being pressed to his blistered lips.

"He had been taken to the Tower and brought back to life with the water of the other, the healing water in which the celestial being sleeps. Our Father calls it an angel, but Ordulf and his kind wreak their evil with the power of the same water. Perhaps it is a demon – but no Dibele will say that out loud.

"Our Father lived in the Tower for a long time. His saviors were men like him – abandoned or lost in the desert. They were as brothers, guarding the angel and taking his water to sustain themselves.

"Then Ordulf and his friends stumbled upon the Tower and were taken in with kindness. One was saved from death by the water, but they were not grateful – the temptation of power was too strong. The knights killed them all. Well, most of them – our Father was unseen in the chamber of the water when the carnage began. He heard the screams of his brothers being hacked apart, and he heard the intruders searching the Tower.

"Our Father filled a skin with the water and fled. Eventually he came to a settlement, and after some time he was able to make his way back to his birthplace. He had drunk nothing on the wide desert but the water of the angel, which is too powerful for any man to take in such quantity."

"But he lived," Junipero pointed out.

"Yes, and after drinking the water for two days he fell down on the sand and lay as if dead for a very long time," Ruttee said. "There he dreamed – he saw he must be the one to oppose those who had slain his brothers. Who else was there? The secret had almost died with him. From the Dibele tribe he had come, and to the tribe he returned. He began to train the young to go into the world and watch the Giza Mashujaa. I am a Watcher, as is Songay Bin."

Junipero gestured over the remains of their meal. "As I know now, following these bastards grows expensive. Your tribe must be vast to support your agents."

"No. We are a small group. Few of us are Watchers. My mother is a teacher of English and Portuguese. My father travels to the coasts, trading gems from the mines of the mountains near our home. My sisters and brothers are record keepers and librarians of intelligence and the like."

"You may be few, but I have found you widely distributed," Junipero smiled.

His nominal possession shrugged. "The Dibele could not support many more Watchers. You may imagine how the Father has used his powers and what water he is able to gather to preserve our monies. I do not deal with that business. As a Watcher I have lived too much of my life far from Nafase Dibele. I make my contributions from a distance. You see, wherever we are able to raise the people against the Giza, we arrange to be the first into the place from which the knights are driven. We know to search for the water and how to locate secreted wealth. These go into the Dibele treasury."

"Was this man you call Father the one who sold you into slavery?"

Ruttee gave him a strange look. "I was not sold. I traveled to the coast and paid for my passage to Nassau. There I gave Mr. Bullus seventy pounds to transport me in the guise of a slave to your hands."

"You traveled across the ocean as a free man? Why finish the journey in chains?"

"In the British colonies a slave is invisible. If you had been in Bengal–" Ruttee made as if to hold a globe in his hands and tapped with one finger on the invisible side – "I might have made the journey as an Abyssinian merchant. If we were in Egypt I would wear a galabia and be a Nubian. Here in New Jersey, I am an ordinary servant."

Junipero regarded his remarkable purchase. *Anyone who thinks this man ordinary is blind.*

December 26, 1776
Trenton, New Jersey

The attack, when it came, surprised everyone. Junipero, who had petitioned God for it; the Hessians, who had belittled it; even the Continental soldiers were amazed to find themselves on the march. The units had formed up for an afternoon assembly in the bitter cold, but instead of the usual cursory inspection were issued rations enough for three days and led off on a mission whose aim was kept secret even from most of the officers. The troops marched with deadly earnest for once, with little of the quiet jesting and tune humming usual on their trips. For one thing, it was difficult to keep a happy mind while stepping in the bloody imprint of a friend's foot, as a fair number of them had threadbare rags tied about their feet in place of boots. For another, they saw even the bandsmen had abandoned their drums and fifes and were walking beside them with muskets.

Junipero had paid several residents who lived along the Delaware and on the likely routes into Trenton to ride immediately for him if they saw any movement of Continental troops. Hours before dawn, Ruttee threw open the farmhouse door to find the insistent pounding was being applied by a gangly lad, bare-headed and smothered by an outsized greatcoat wrapped over his nightclothes.

"Mr. Serra!" he said rapidly, seeing Junipero behind Ruttee. "The Continentals have come across! They came through the ice!"

Juniper motioned the lad in out of the biting wind and snow where he calmed enough to describe what he had seen from his attic window: troops and horses disembarking from flatboats. And cannons. Junipero pressed him on this detail. Yes, he knew what a cannon was. These were cannons – perhaps a score. Junipero rubbed his chin. The army would not drag its heavy guns on a mere feint.

No, they were not marching on the town yet, but two smaller groups had left as swiftly as the weather permitted, one down each fork of the road to Trenton.

Junipero gave the boy coins and sent him home, then turned to Ruttee. "We must go directly as we have planned. Make yourself ready."

Ordulf approached the bridge carefully, listening for the trump and slaps of massed boots stumbling in the dark, the clanking of kit, the tense breathing of excited soldiers advancing into battle. He pulled his horse to the side of the road to let a squad of Hessians pass, their officer pausing long enough to salute him. Ordulf nodded, then nudged his white stallion forward.

Time enough without careless hurry. Washington might ride at the head of his column or he might lag behind. The Hessians would first deploy skirmishers in front to harass the rebel columns. Ordulf planned to find a spot to observe this operation and determine by the flow of enemy messengers where the orders originated. In the dim light of morning the confusion of battle would blossom, and in that fog he would cloud their minds and creep through the rebel lines to kill their unsuspecting and vulnerable commander.

The stone bridge was short, needing only one arch to span the modest Assunpink Creek. The road leading to it curved left and on the other side bent back to the right and rose several feet before disappearing behind thatch and trees.

Ordulf reigned in his horse as it put its first hoof on the stones of the bridge. The clouds began to show definition, backlit by a sliver of sun rising on the unseen horizon. He scowled across the creek at the high ground on the other side, at the evergreens concealing most of the rise.

He smiled. The knight dismounted and stepped through the snow to the middle of the bridge.

"Show yourself, Spaniard!" Ordulf called – and he pointed to the trees. "I see you skulking in the bushes."

He kept walking until he was on the other end of the bridge and spotted Junipero, frozen in action, one hand on a large wooden box, eyes large as a mouse enthralled by a snake.

"This time is your last, Spaniard. I am tired of playing with you. I must deal with this great Washington."

A stomping rush of boots, muffled by the snow, made him pivot. Behind him another short column of Hessians quick marched to the beat of distant popping muskets. They started to swing around Ordulf, but slowed and then stopped as they recognized him. Ordulf waited for an officer to appear after them, but they were alone.

Ordulf began to address them – and paused when he saw Junipero tremble. The knight refocused his gaze and froze him once more.

"Did you think I would not sense your presence, Spaniard? You have no secrets from me. You cannot hide from me." Ordulf smiled again and turned around. "Nor can your servant."

Ruttee had come up quietly from beneath the bridge, following in the holes the Hessian boots had made through the deep snow, pausing in the shadow of Ordulf's mount. Now he stepped forward until he was mere paces away and sank to his knees, his eyes on the ground.

Ordulf smiled again. This was more appropriate behavior. Perhaps he would let this one live. He could use a servant.

Ordulf barked at the Hessians. "To the town. I will follow

you. Go now!"

He saw more movement. The servant fell prone into the snow, an act of complete supplication.

But the African looked up, no deference in his face. Ordulf hesitated. On the slave's back was a flat box topped with fabric – and the box was pointed right at Ordulf.

Ruttee did not believe the knight controlled fire in all its elemental forms, as Junipero swore, but it did not matter. He pulled a cord attached to the mechanism on his back. There was no fire in the box – only metal. Heavy springs cut from the thickest pipe in an organ, those strong hair-like wires which sounded the purest highest note on a piano, and spheres fashioned from many musket balls melted together.

The springs released their compressed energy with a fierce kick that slammed the box down onto Ruttee's tailbone and drove the lead weights through the sheer cloth. The spheres did not fly directly at Ordulf, though, and the knight felt a flash of triumph – the Spanish bastard's new trick had missed him totally.

But the balls were massive endpoints dragging between them the fine wire at a savage speed – and invisible against the drab trees on this overcast morning.

Instinct made Ordulf throw up his arms. The first wire sliced into his wrists, taking off the right hand and stopping halfway through the left arm. He started to scream, but his howl was ended by another wire cleaving his throat and neck bones as quickly and cleanly as if they had been made from the snow under his feet.

The Hessians pivoted at his shriek, and as the several parts of Ordulf's body dropped gushing red onto the white ground, they spied Junipero running. They leveled and fired a hasty volley, poorly-aimed and uncoordinated. But Junipero staggered.

Ruttee jumped to his feet as he saw the muskets come up, and he dove for the parapet just as Ordulf's horse bolted past. It bumped him, and he rolled awkwardly over the stone wall and spun the several feet to the bed of the shallow creek. He splashed sideways onto the rocks. A bone in his chest snapped. An edge of Junipero's device drove deep into his kidney, and the box cracked with a brittle report he was sure was his spine fracturing.

He lay gasping in pain for several minutes, trying his best to stay quiet. At any moment he expected to see muskets appearing over the side of the bridge. At last he heard shouts and feet pounding on the packed snow. Some of the far frantic calls were in the Hessian tongue, but new ones – the nearer cheers – were English.

Ruttee, soaked with ice water and doubled in agony, shrugged off Junipero's broken machine and hobbled to the road. Both the Hessians and their pursuers had disappeared. Only one figure remained, sitting flat-legged in the middle of red-splattered snow. Junipero was holding up the dripping head of the knight.

They die? thought Ruttee.

Junipero addressed the dead man's slack face. "Remember me, knight? You killed my brother, and now I have killed you."

Ruttee approached cautiously, knife in hand, but the head, eyes vacant and fixed on something in the far distance, did not reply. The body sprawled beside the Spaniard did not so much as twitch.

Junipero looked up. "You see, Dibele? You see, my friend? They are not gods."

But he said this with blood on his lips that could not have been the other's, and more blood seeping from inside his jacket that was certainly not.

January 30, 1777
Harwich Harbor, England

Standing before a bank of bowed windows in the great stern cabin of the Indiaman Agenor, Lord Strain waved a hand at the fishing vessels bobbing at anchor.

"There is your security, gentlemen. There float a fleet of insignificant scows abandoned by their anonymous crews. There will be no eyes upon us today."

Strain was trying to make a grand and comforting motion to his two fellow stockholders, but this became somewhat more comical and thus countered the desired effect when an especially ungainly roll of the ship forced him to grab at a vertical member with the other hand.

His audience was distracted anyway by the effort of keeping their chairs from sliding on the planks. Henry Maddox, normally ruddy and jovial, was pale as his linen cuffs. William Jarvis, who had once captained a ship much like this in the service of the East India Company, gazed upon Maddox with much superiority and considered briefly resurrecting the old mariner's trick of swaying slowly to and fro in the sight of a distressed landlubber. Strain broke in on this imp and chased it off.

"Jarvis? Are you yet satisfied?

It had been Jarvis and his salty instinct that had braked their scheme. His suspicions were infectious and made them all a bit nervous, even Lord Strain, who was otherwise sure the Company in general and he in particular was untouchable.

"I'll be satisfied if this ship goes down with all hands immediately we disembark," Jarvis said. Maddox glanced at him in alarm. Even he knew such a sentiment was a gross violation of maritime philosophy – not to mention superstition. Jarvis shrugged. "I maintain this is treason, dress it as you may."

Strain frowned, exasperated. "And I dress it thusly, Captain: His Majesty and family own a good part of the Company through strawmen. His Majesty's government will expend several millions of pounds dealing with the American issue – none of which *we* will see, mind you. The Royal Army will mount a jolly show while cutting out a healthy portion of the Treasury supplying phantom regiments and purchasing imaginary artillery. They may even contrive to lose the damn conflict. What we are doing here today *is* for King and

98

Country."

All three wanted to believe that, so they did. Their plan was breathtaking in its simplicity. The East India Company would form a subsidiary – or obtain a charter for a coequal entity from the Crown. It would not matter but for the bookkeeping. Strain had even put quill to the top of a blank sheet and roughed out a letterhead: THE AMERICA COLONIAL COMPANY. And underneath, smaller: By Charter of His Royal Majesty. Et cetera, et cetera, as the barristers would insist on saying. He did not yet dare reveal his design to a printer.

What the three did not have to voice was that *their* Army, the efficient corporate military arm of the East India Company, had no phantom regiments. Oh, it had its share of fissures where goods and specie leaked out of the organization, but not to worry – satisfactory portions of that revenue stream also reached the private accounts of upper management. *Their* Army had real regiments and a competent officer corps promoted and recompensed on performance, and performance was more often than not manifested in zealous and ruthless suppression of any native opposition to the Company's ends or threat to the Company's profits.

A fortnight before, Strain and Maddox had dined with two of the Company's generals and queried them how they might conduct the North American campaign if – theoretically, mind you very much – they were in charge of same. Both had been in agreement in their assertions that the past and current commanders had been too sympathetic to the colonists. Both advocated burning Boston, for a start, followed by one coastal city a month until the chief rebels were turned over for hanging. The possibility of introducing a plague was put on the table, along with the potential of paying large bounties to the Indian tribes for traitorous scalps.

The cabin door opened, creaking like the rest of the vessel, and a head poked in. It was their clerk, one of the ever-present note takers the Company demanded record every detail of the enterprise. Strain put up a hand, palm to.

"We are discussing horse breeding, Wadburn. Pocket your pen and go find a mess to join." The head nodded and began to withdraw. "And send in the candidate!" Strain added, rather too loudly.

Just then they heard the footsteps of the Captain above, pacing the quarterdeck in agitation that he had been quit of his comfortable cabin to this brisk exposure. The three conspirators glanced involuntarily up to the swinging cabin lanterns. *Perhaps we are not as at ease as we pretend*, Strain thought. But the hissing of the water against the hull and the rousing chorus of the wind playing the sheets was cover against any eavesdropping. Strain sat back down.

The door opened again, admitting a pale, nervous man in his mid-twenties, dressed in shabby but formal clothes, his brown hair drawn back into a pigtail. He seemed deflated, perhaps undernourished, and overstressed. His eyes bulged more than they ought, and his cheeks sank so his interviewers could trace the outline of his molars in them.

He advanced to the desk and made his leg. Niven Cluny was not of a type the Company would have otherwise selected for its ranks, but Niven did not know that. He was not ambitious or sharp – nor was he charming. He was not even properly connected. He was the fourth son of a minor Scottish noble who had not enough to leave to his oldest son, never mind the rest. His only quality, and the reason he was here this afternoon, was his accidental union to a most lovely young lass named Catriona.

When Lord Strain's intelligence sources passed on the information that catalyzed this meeting, he had merely pursed his lips. When he relayed it to Maddox and Jarvis, the former had protested his disbelief. The latter just smiled knowingly, muttering something about six months at sea being the best tonic.

"But Mr. Franklin must be seventy years of age," Maddox had sputtered, whether in anger or in envy Strain could not tell. "I have met the man."

Strain had also met Benjamin Franklin, that outwardly

guileless homespun colonial. Company sources had observed him attend a meeting of the Royal Society, where the simple rube had been awarded an honorary doctorate by Oxford University, whose deans were not fools.

"Mr. Cluny," Strain began. The young man quivered stiff at attention. "My colleagues: Mr. Henry Maddox and Captain William Jarvis—" Here Cluny nodded to the gentlemen named. "—and I have considered your application for employment with the Company, and we are in hearty agreement you are just the sort of man we seek in our ranks."

Cluny's face crumpled with relief. Strain hoped to God he did not burst into tears.

"But," Strain continued, "there is a little matter of Company honor which must be cleared away before you begin your career."

Cluny showed confusion, then a flash of understanding – followed closely by rage.

Strain nodded. "The seduction of your innocent wife by the notorious traitor Franklin is common knowledge in the Company—"

Cluny put his hand to his hip and drew halfway from its hidden scabbard a thin dirk that promised to be about ten inches of razor-sharp steel. Strain smiled and shook a finger at him, whereupon Cluny just barely managed to stop from plucking his weapon full out and flinging himself across the table at the throats of his new employers.

Strain was encouraged by their candidate's furious energy. "Save that blade for the man who wronged you, Mr. Cluny." And he proceeded to outline for Niven Cluny his first assignment as a Company man. From Harwich he would take a stage to Dover, there to catch a packet ship to Calais, where a private coach would race him into Paris. In that city the Company had informants who would guide the coach to where Mr. Franklin might be lured up some private alley. Cluny would alight from the coach, knock his cuckolder on the head, and make the same journey in reverse.

"Then it is off to India for you and your wife, where you

will live in a mansion with a dozen servants and serve the Company and yourself well and good," Strain finished.

Maddox and Jarvis nodded enthusiastically. It was a lie, of course. All knew but the naïve Cluny. The Company had French authorities on payroll. These would dutifully take the murderer of an eminent American guest into custody. They would publish his confession (already written and lying in some drawer) in the Parisian papers – absent any reference to Strain and present company – and then like obedient magicians, make the insignificant Mr. Niven Cluny disappear.

Cluny clasped his hands together, overcome with gratitude at his good fortune, too choked to even speak to his most generous benefactors.

February 3, 1777
Passy, France

An uninspired snowstorm hovered all day over Passy. By dusk the accumulation was just four inches and only slightly slippery. Pedestrians made their way up and down the narrow Rue des Eaux in a most normal manner. The exception was a rounded figure studiously pacing the street – now deserted but for him – one slow step at a time, backwards.

Benjamin Franklin had spent the day visiting Monsieur Barbaroux, a leading Parisian Freemason with intimate connections in the French government. The visit included each man bringing the other up to date with the events of, respectively, Philadelphia and the American colonies, and Paris and the European hoi polloi. They followed this with discussions of natural science, comparative religion, the wisdom of the ancients, et cetera. Barbaroux kept an extensive wine cellar, and he liked to lubricate each topic with its own bottle from Burgundy or Bordeaux or various regions up and down the Rhone. The two shared a plate of bread and cheese in the early afternoon, but this ballast was not absorbent enough to prevent Franklin from later bidding farewell to his genial host in barely coherent French and stumbling to the street.

He had refused a coach, because the distance was really not far, and he was hoping the walk would burn away surplus wine. Plus, he was always cognizant of the need to conserve every sou while at the same time appearing not to need to. He wished to present to the French government not as the penniless representative of a penniless cause whose lack of pennies made investing hard francs in them an obvious waste, nor as the rich ambassador of a rich continent who desired but did not actually require an infusion of francs. He calculated the content of every one of his days to project the middle possibility. Walking home in a light snow seemed to him the proper combination of frugality and vitality.

Just about the time he turned onto the Rue de Eaux after crossing the bridge over the Seine, he had realized he was lost, but also about this time he became intrigued by the properties of the snow under his feet, so he neglected to ask directions.

The accumulation came to the top of his buckles. Some worked its way into Franklin's left shoe, and the wetness as it melted against his skin made him ponder the equivalency between depth of snow and its water content. He mused rain was rain, and water was unable to be compressed or expanded in its liquid state, but here was solid water in at least two densities – soft where virgin and hard in his footsteps. In the natural world there would be a great variation in the density of a given volume of snow, whether the snow be fluffy and light on the wintery hills of Massachusetts or a dense slush on the fall streets of Philadelphia.

Determining the amount of potential water a snow pack held was an eminently useful exercise. In the mountains, snow accumulated over a winter, away from most observers but for the occasional trapper or Indian. In the spring, snow melted and ran down to civilization. Too much snow and rivers would flood, killing the unaware along the banks. Too little snow and crops that required irrigation would fail, killing in a slower way.

He began to think of ways to assess the amount of snow – it would have to be a measure of mass, not just of depth. Perhaps some kind of platform with a spring beneath, the weight of the snow lowering the platform, which might be connected to a signaling arm arcing along a scale.

But how to transmit the reading from hilltop to distant river valley – and he looked up and had no idea where he was.

He squinted ahead and then behind, which because he was walking backwards was really behind and then ahead, but in any case, he was alone on the rapidly darkening Rue de Eaux.

Except for – and he almost missed her, as she was perfectly camouflaged in her gray dress and under her gray umbrella – one woman slowly catching up to him. He remained facing backwards and watched her approach.

Her skin was pale as the snow, but her hair, gathered up above her head and mostly covered by a gray hat, was red as strawberries in summertime.

She noticed him watching and came up to him bravely.

"Can I help you, monsieur?" She spoke French with a slight accent he could not place. Somewhere along the Swiss border provinces, he would have guessed. Perhaps farther south. Italy? Greece?

Franklin started to reply, but his words coagulated. His eyes had drifted down from her wonderfully beautiful face and full crimson lips to her cleavage. Her dress was cut low, and some stout mechanism beneath squeezed her plump breasts together and lifted them toward Heaven. Franklin saw her take notice of his fixation – he coughed uncomfortably.

Please God let her not be a prostitute. He bowed. "Yes, mademoiselle. I seek the house of Monsieur Jacques-Donatien Le Ray de Chaumont."

"Ah," she said, looking at the backwards footprints. "I concluded you sought for the Hôpital général de Paris."

Franklin laughed. "I assure you I am not mad, just temporarily misplaced."

"Then why are you not watching where you are going?"

104

"Because I desired to see where I had been."

She smiled. "You are either a genius or an idiot."

He had the impulsive desire to sweep off his hat, then realized he was not wearing one – just a greasy old wig, whose sweeping off would not make the desired impression. "I have been both in my time, your grace. At this moment I am a lost idiot."

"My name is Madame Nicole Marcelle du Meudon," she said, taking down her umbrella and shaking off the a dust of snow. "My husband is the Vicomte Jean-Marie du Meudon."

He bowed again. "Benjamin Franklin, of Philadelphia, at your service. I have the honor to be the Commissioner to France of the United States, recently arrived and as you can see not yet oriented to my new home."

She turned so they were both facing the same direction and put out an arm to be taken, so he did. "I know the house of Msr. de Chaumont well. I pass it every day on my way to market."

She is telling me though her husband may be a Vicomte she is not monied. I wonder if she will expect to be compensated for walking me home. He realized with some embarrassment he had not a coin on his person and sighed. *C'est la vie.*

They began to stroll back over their footprints – hers pointing toward them, his away – and he started to explain his idea of how to measure snow in distant mountains, and about the constant density of water and the inconstant density of snow, and how he had devised in his youth an instrument which gathered falling snow into a graduated cylinder of known inside diameter so it could be taken in and heated to reveal the actual water content of the snow and how this could be compared to the depth of the snow. He was impressed she appeared to be interested in natural philosophy and indeed asked several pointed questions about snow and about his instrument. He was more impressed that she appeared lovelier each time he snuck a glance at her.

When they reached the end of the Rue de Eaux, where it curved sharply away to the left, she turned him to the right, down a smaller and darker street. There were no street lamps on this unnamed Ruelle, and the clouds hung down like thick curtains in a dark room.

A coach pulled out from the next cross street and fully blocked their path, the driver backing the reins to freeze his team. They could not see his face or judge his intent. Franklin was about to call out to him to move his vehicle when the coach door burst open and what seemed to Franklin some manner of manic wraith vaulted out and strode at them with a stiff-legged determination.

Franklin was petrified. He had no weapon. Mme. du Meudon pulled abruptly away from him – he had some vague chivalric notion that he should shield her with his body, but she was already gone.

The man stopped within a pace of Franklin and drew a thin knife. It seemed a yard long. Franklin stared at the metallic tip. Was this how it would end, then? In a gloomy French alley, with no credit or advantage to his new nation from his ignoble death?

His attacker started to say something, and Franklin's attention returned to his face, which was oddly familiar. He did not place it, but it was no matter. He could not outrun or outfight or outthink this problem.

Then the man's aspect turned from dark bitterness to wide-eyed surprise. Three inches of a metal blade much like the one in his hand protruded from his chest. He gurgled. A petite geyser of blood erupted from his cloak. He grunted in bewilderment and toppled forward, just missing the amazed Franklin.

In the space where the attacker had stood now appeared Mme. du Meudon, her furled umbrella in hand. Or, Franklin saw, what part remained of her umbrella once its hidden rapier was withdrawn. This weapon, its carved bone handle still vibrating, stuck up straight from the shuddering corpse.

The remnant animal magnetism, Franklin thought dimly.

Madame put one foot on the deceased man's back and plucked out her weapon, then wiped it on the back of his coat and examined it critically in what light there was, as though mere flesh might mark such adamant steel. She turned and fixed her disapproving gaze on the coachman, the tip of her killing metal pointed at him.

That figure did not linger to protest or render aid. He snapped down his leather strips – and horses and carriage bolted off into the night.

Franklin gaped as Mme. du Meudon resheathed her rapier and spread the reassembled umbrella above her as if the murky night above was a harsh midday sun.

"Passy is full of cutpurses and madmen, Monsieur Franklin. I suggest you carry something to keep them at bay."

March 10, 1777
Hungerford, England

King Henry's Copse bore a grand name, yet was but a minor patch of trees long ago stripped of its wildlife by poachers. The only edible creature left in its bounds was the partridge, thriving here to the point of becoming a nuisance due to the killing of all the bears, wolves, foxes, and badgers by the locals in either preemptive self-defense or to forestall the starvation of their emaciated children.

Geoffrey walked softly in the Copse, under the cover of alders and birch. It was too early in the spring for foliage, so he was easily visible among the trunks and bare branches in his emerald coat and white britches. He had optimistically donned a bright ruby hat brimmed large against a putative sun. It was not necessary to hide from the partridge – they would hide from him. It was necessary to frighten them from where they were hunkered down, to get them to flush from cover and fly so he could bring his fowling piece to shoulder.

He had hired a servant in London, a tall narrow-shouldered fellow named Rawls who asked no questions but followed directions in silence. Rawls carried a matching gun and kept five paces behind Geoffrey.

They broke through the trees and entered a meadow sloping away from them. Geoffrey paused and motioned to Rawls, who marched ahead noisily, stomping and kicking at patches of tall grass. Other hunters in this country would use dogs for this task, trained birders who snuffled through the brush and pointed to the prey. They would even retrieve downed birds. Unfortunately for Geoffrey's sport, ever since he had begun to take the water dogs would not come near him. None of the knights had been able to keep one. The animals barked and snarled and frantically clawed at doors to flee the knights. This saddened Geoffrey for a while, who had once owned quite a handsome pack of hounds in Emberton Castle. Now he had Rawls and a resignation to hunting sans canine.

True to reputation, the Copse gave up its bounty as Rawls' driving soon spooked three brace of partridges. Geoffrey swung his weapon up, tracked one bird down the barrel — leading it a bit — and fired. The bird spun in the air, one wing jutting out stiffly, and plummeted to the ground.

Rawls went to the body at a deliberate pace and put it into a canvas sack slung around his neck. He came back to Geoffrey and exchanged guns, then returned to his noisy advance.

Before he had put his boot to the brush, Rawls froze like a pointing dog, but not at a partridge. He tilted his head to train his right ear into the wind. Then Geoffrey heard it too — the pounding of a horse at canter. *Perhaps Rawls was a poacher in his previous employ. He hears the sheriff coming long before I.*

It was not the sheriff, however, only Thomas riding a brown and white mare. He saw the hunters and kneed his mount to them.

Geoffrey studied Thomas. The water had been especially kind to the young lad from his fields. He had not a mark of his true age on him. He had never even needed to shave. *Five centuries on, and he has no beard.*

Thomas nodded gravely.

"I knew," Geoffrey said. He rested his gun butt-first on

the grass. "I felt it in my gut that day. Did you not?"

Thomas said nothing, just looked at Rawls, who stood at a respectful distance with his back to them.

Geoffrey shook his head. "You did. The water connects us all. We have been pissing it out for many years." He tilted his face to the sky and crossed himself. "And many pissed it before. The whole of the world must be connected by the vital energy of it by now."

The silence of the meadow was unbroken. Song birds had been scattered by the gun's report; the partridge squatted quietly, waiting. Minutes passed. Rawls did not move one muscle. Thomas bent forward and rested his forearms on the pommel.

Geoffrey shuddered as if escaping a reverie. "Now our brother Ordulf is gone. You want to know what we shall do about this crime."

"The messenger said he was killed in battle."

"So he would have wanted it. He would also want us to avenge him."

"Would he?" Thomas asked. "I should never speak ill of the dead, but Ordulf wanted nothing more than women and wine. To him the water was only a blessing which allowed him to copulate with the greatgranddaughters of his conquests."

Geoffrey smiled. "True. But do you feel nothing?"

Thomas sat straight in his saddle. "Oh. I feel something – Ordulf was granted by God ten lifetimes and power to make such a time give him his every wish."

"You sound like your wishes have not come true."

"I wish," said Thomas. "I wish to return to the Holy Land. I wish to sit in the sun and eat figs and olives and read of other men's worries."

The old knight extended a hand and swept the meadow. "But Thomas, this is the land of your birth. Wouldn't it please you to buy land in Emberton and build a grand estate?"

"No." Thomas said. "I yearn for blue skies and, above all else, to be warm."

Geoffrey ruminated on this point for a while, then said,

"Now that I put my mind to it, Emberton Castle was a dismal and drafty place. I too loved Jerusalem, but the Holy Land is tiresome. Constant war, strife and complaining, short on water and shade. Let us prepare the ship and go in search of a finer home."

March 23, 1777
New York City

Ruttee pulled his cloak over his head against the sudden rain and continued to trudge down Broadway. He was feeling chilled, damp, and discouraged, due to an unexpected discovery – New York City was chock-full of black faces.

He had arrived last night, deposited quietly on the northern end of the island in a hired rowboat. By sunup he approached the outskirts of the place, which was obviously growing. Carpenters swung mallets on new construction rising amid scattered and shrinking farmland. The road itself was wide and paved with stones, but the stagnant ditch parallel to this engineering work stank. He had passed two bloated, floating cow corpses in the last quarter mile.

Farther into the city, he stopped to talk with any willing citizens. The first few whites he approached hurried past him, but he soon spotted friendlier, darker faces. These told him each a piece of the story until he assembled the essence of the place. He had expected to find slavery here, and sure enough there were well-dressed Africans walking the street with packages and other assorted light burdens, some driving carts, some pushing wheelbarrows. These would speak with him only briefly before returning to their errands. There was another population as well: black men and black women in worn clothing who seemed to have no particular place to be. These were the ones who supplied him the best information.

The island had become a magnet for slaves escaping from their Patriot owners. The British command promised freedom, although Ruttee could not get a consistent answer about just what the conditions to achieve that state were. Some told him they were soon to join the British Army and such service was the key to obtaining their effective manumission. Others had heard the Navy was evacuating them all to an African shore. Or Canada. Or England. Each knew something good lay in their future. That they could not agree on what it was exactly did not bother them much.

Ruttee pondered his gathered intelligence briefly before acting on this new reality. The first thing he did was to rub some mud on himself and rip open a few seams in his outfit, as he did not want to be mistaken for someone's wayward possession. The second thing he did was to turn off the broad street into the section of town that had been devastated by the Great Fire of the year before. Here the background palette of the city changed from spring green and tan stone to various shades of charcoal. All the way down to the harbor he could see the landscape dominated by remnants of burnt timbers jutting up from stacks of ash and blackened remains. Here too was a great concentration of dark faces, peering at him out of flimsy tents, in the darkness of teetering shelters thrown together from charred debris, and from under nothing more than ragged coats and mufflers.

As he walked he passed occasional warm drafts tunneling through the freezing morning air pressed down on the city. Fires crackled everywhere, on what had once been street corners and invisibly behind smoked planes of jagged brick, as if the famous Fire had never been subdued but just deprived by its voracity of most available fuel. These scattered residues of the disaster combined to deposit a grayish-silver smear of smoke over the neighborhood which soon coated Ruttee's nose and mouth with the taste of overcooked grease.

At least the streets had been cleared of rubble. He passed a building remarkably intact for this vicinity. Three of its brick walls stood – one even up to the second story. Some entrepreneur had salvaged burned lumber retaining enough internal soundness to construct a crude roof inside the three walls. Over a doorway was a hand-lettered sign, chalk on a slate fragment: Hell's Cellar. He saw through the large empty window spaces a rude bar and men drinking.

He was about to go into the tavern when a woman stepped out of the shadow of the building. She was older than he, coffee-skinned, with a narrow unfriendly mouth. Pink divots on her cheeks and chin were old souvenirs of smallpox, and matted hair hung to the shoulders of her ratty dress.

"Two shillings," she said.

He did not stop but brushed past her.

She followed him, grabbed his arm and tried to pivot him around. "One and six."

He shook loose. He was about to command her to leave him alone when the scars on her face struck a chime of sympathy in him – and instantly he had a revised plan.

"Two and six," he said, and she showed at first confusion then suspicion. She backed away from him.

"Are you with the provosts?" she asked with venom.

He shook his head. "Meet me at sunset – somewhere we can be alone."

"We can be alone right here," she said with a nod of her head toward the ruins.

"No. I require some space."

Her eyes narrowed, and she stepped up to him, dipping one hand into a pocket sewn into her skirt. "Do you think me a fool?"

Ruttee, wary of a knife, again shook his head – and held up a shilling. She snatched it from his fingers, and as she backed away into the ruins said, "Ask for the Ranelah Gardens."

The Gardens turned out to be an acre or so of mud clinging to the roots of dead weeds. To the east the land climbed suddenly into a bluff. Ruttee waited in the shadow of this feature and watched as the good people of New York lit their streetlamps. He heard the first distant cry of the watchman, and shortly after saw by the occlusion of the town lights a feminine outline coming boldly toward him. She sighted him as he approached from cover. She had her hand in her pocket again and scanned carefully about for an ambush.

"We are alone here," Ruttee reassured her. "I have made a survey. There are two drunken British sailors sleeping under yonder tree—" he pointed to a shrub a hundred yards to the north.

She turned her face up to him but kept her hand in her pocket. "What do you desire for your two and six?"

Ruttee bent to a canvas bag on the ground beside him. From this he drew a whip – an ugly leather scourge sprouting several short, brutal lashes. The woman gasped, and her hand flew from inside her skirt. She brandished a thick knife a butcher would be happy to own.

"You put that devil back into your bag," she cried, a real and raw fear vibrating in her voice.

Ruttee tossed it at her feet. She hopped back as if it were alive. "That is for me," he said reassuringly. "Not for you."

"What do you mean by this?" She eyed the thing – but kept the point of her knife directed at his heart.

He began to remove his coat. "I wish you to whip me."

Her face twisted with revulsion. "I don't—" She swallowed. "I will bind you up, if that is your pleasure. Some men wish to be caned. I will do that. But this, no, not this."

Ruttee folded his coat and laid it carefully on the ground. He wore underneath a white linen shirt he began to unlace. "I want nothing more than for you to apply the scourge to my back. I think ten or so sound strikes will suffice, as long as they draw blood."

She shook her head. "You must find another to do this. I will not."

His torso was bare now. "I need to have the appearance of an escaped slave," he said. "I will pay you well for this service – and I do not want to find another. A man may apply much to his effort and put me in too much pain. A boy would not produce a believable result." He smiled, hoping to convince her he was not mad. One carrying shout and the

113

nearest watchman might just amble over to investigate.

"If this is not for your gratification, then what?"

"I have my reasons, and you shall have your specie. Do you question all of your customers in this manner?"

She did not answer but stooped and picked up the leather by two fingers as if it carried disease. Ruttee could see she struggled with the task and thought it almost amusing this woman, who probably had submitted to the whole range of human deprivation with professional detachment, appeared queasy at this. She would have to remove none of her clothes. Her body would not be indisposed in any way. Yet she fought to bring herself this easy payment.

He turned his back to her. "Would it make it easier if I insulted you or someone you love?"

She hissed at him. "Stop your tongue – and do not cry out. I do not wish to be arrested with this in my hand." She gripped the handle and let out the strands of leather. "Are you ready?"

"Yes."

Her arm went back and then forward. The leather slapped against Ruttee's skin; he started at the sting. Though he had been punished in this manner before, the searing still amazed him.

"Did that draw blood?"

She stepped close and felt his back. "No."

"Try again – harder this time."

She sent the whip ends singing through the darkness. This time he could feel the skin part under the lash. A hot moist trickle began.

"Good. Again."

The slapping again, then again, and he saw actual colors in the dark sky. Each flash of pain threatened to drive him to his knees, and he lost count.

"Enough," he panted. He turned around and saw by the starlight and the distant candles the tears running down her cheeks, shiny and voluminous – as he imagined the blood appeared cascading into the waist of his trousers. She turned away from him, sobbing quietly.

Stiffly and carefully he brought out his purse and removed two guineas. Each movement summoned fresh searing agony as ripped skin parted further. He held the coins out to her back. In her exertions, her cloak had slipped off. Underneath a short dirty blouse – even in this meager light – he could see the crisscross of scars.

March 24, 1777
New York City

The sky brightened before sunrise and revealed Ruttee curled up on the doorstep of an expansive brick house which stood apart from the other buildings on a short street curving from the water. Exhausted, he had been able to sleep only in short stretches before being wrenched awake either by the pain of his back or the cold of his drying blood. Now he feigned slumber, his coat drawn tight about him.

Inside, two men talking, then bootsteps on stairs. The door opened – and the conversation died.

"See here!" A young, outraged voice. Ruttee felt the tip of a boot in his hip. "Move along!"

Ruttee sat up, groaning. He gained his feet ponderously, dropped his cloak, and flexed his back as much as was believable. He glanced up the steps. The man who had kicked him wore the uniform of a junior English officer.

"Away!" The man repeated, drawing his foot back once more, and Ruttee nodded dumbly and began to shuffle off toward the street. He slowed once he was out of kicking range and peeked back. An older officer, preoccupied with reading the top paper of a disorganized stack, filled the doorway.

Ruttee moaned again, more loudly, but the older man still did not note him. The younger officer narrowed his eyes and started down the steps. Ruttee stopped, waited until the young man was within arm's length, then tumbled forward with an emphatic cry of pain – not altogether acted. As he fell, he was already calculating alternate plans. This one was failing, and he felt stupid he had wasted his flesh on it.

"Leftenant!" the older officer cried, horror in his cultured tones. Ruttee hid his face on the ground, scooting a bit to display his bloody shirt to its best effect.

The lieutenant straightened. "Yes, sir."

The older officer came down the steps. "Leftenant, these slaves risk their lives coming through the lines to us. We shall not let word go out we are inhospitable. Please remember – every African who ends up here represents a substantial economic loss to a rebel somewhere over there." He indicated with the stack of documents a direction vaguely to the west.

"Yes, General," the lieutenant said. Ruttee felt this man would continue to kick him once the general was out of sight, but luckily the general did not leave. Instead, he stooped close to Ruttee and examined the bloody cloth and eyed with abhorrence the gory trail Ruttee had left.

"You have been whipped," the general stated. Ruttee hung his head even further. "What is your name, boy?"

Ruttee managed to croak out, "Sam, suh."

"Sam," the general said confidently, his eyes on his subordinate officer, "would you serve His Majesty's Army in exchange for your freedom?"

"Yes, suh!"

The general hmmed, looking him over, then directed, "Go around to the back of the house and have the kitchen give you some hot water to wash your wounds. Leftenant, have the surgeon's mate fetched."

"Yes, sir," the young man said neutrally.

"And direct them to ration you out some soup and bread," the general added to his new charge. "When you are stronger we will find employment for you."

May 8, 1777
New York City

The disembodied words of the butler filtered down to the basement and reverberated in the wine cellar until the original direction of the sound was lost. "Sam – send up three of the very dry Madeira!"

Ruttee, who had gathered the majority of his wine knowledge in the last two months, went to the shelf marked SERCIAL and took down three blue-black bottles, wiped the dust off with a cloth, and set them carefully into a deep square hole in the wall.

This was no mere hole, and nothing like he had ever encountered before his service in this house. Inside the wall was a shaft shooting uninterrupted from the basement up to the second story library. A wooden box, fit inside the shaft, fastened to a rope which ran to the top of the space, around a pulley, and back down to hang inside the hole in the wall, just at hand. The intent of the designer was pulling down on the rope would propel the box and its load up to the desired floor.

This house had been built by a Patriot merchant who considered himself a natural philosopher, an engineer, and an architect. The merchant had incorporated several clever, several unwieldy, and several unworkable design elements in his blueprints. This vertical shuttle was all three: it seemed clever, looked unwieldy, and had proven ultimately unworkable.

There were three more such systems: from kitchen to dining room, from wood bin to fireplaces, and from linen storage to bedrooms. All had been in disuse due to the effort needed to lift more than the lightest load when Ruttee finessed his way inside and began casting about for some way to make himself useful to the inhabitants. He might have known little about wine, but he know a bit about rope and rigging, as he had spent a tedious crossing of the southern Atlantic observing sailors at work and examining sheets, stays, blocks, hanks, winches, and all the other fascinating mechanisms essential to the operation of a sailing ship. The household's system seemed very much more simple than the myriad ropes running hither and yon on that ship.

The surgeon's mate had been kind, and with the ointment supplied by that fellow the lash wounds healed to bearable scab in a week. The keeper of the house assigned him a sleeping spot on the floor in one of the small outbuildings behind the stables, and the cook fed him dutifully if somewhat reluctantly. One day, after he had made a careful examination of the existing technology, Ruttee walked down to the docks and purchased some fine hemp rope, two double blocks, and a cleat. That afternoon he took the old mechanism out of the firewood hoist – which as far as he could tell had never been used – and refit so it was what the tars called doubletackled.

He begged the keeper of the house, a twisted and flinty man who had been cashiered from the 34th Regiment of Foot after taking a ball in the knee ten years before, to come down for a demonstration. Ruttee stuffed the box with a heavy load of hardwood logs and invited the keeper to pull on the rope. The doubletackle configuration caused the lifting force required to be only one-fourth of the load's actual weight. The technical details were wasted on the keeper, but the tactile discrepancy amazed him. He hauled easily on the rope until the appearance of a ribbon tied about the hemp indicated the wood was successfully arrived at the top floor. Ruttee secured the line about a cleat, and the keeper limped up the back stairs as fast as he could to confirm this was not some darkie trick. When he came down convinced, Ruttee had a new permanent job.

He had been issued funds to make the other three hoists functional, and his reputation was secured each time the cook, who was reassuringly obese, sent his employer a full tureen of steaming soup safely up the kitchen hoist rather than wrestling the slopping vessel around two flights of dark winding stairs.

A fortuitous property of the shaft system was that it channeled sounds. Ruttee could hear the butler's demand for wine as clearly as if the two were in the same room. His positions of second assistant butler, apprentice sommelier, woodcutter first class, and lift mechanic, gave him excuses to be in whichever basement listening post provided the best eavesdropping opportunity.

This morning the general was meeting his aides for a late breakfast and intelligence session. It was the kind of session demanding the strictest security, which the participants did acknowledge and impose – in terms of outsiders. But the house staff was invisible to the officers, who routinely discussed matters of troop placement, weaknesses in defenses, and other vitals in front of them. It was as if the staff was part of the structure.

He had just lifted the wine to the library and was easing the hoist back down when he heard the general and two other officers enter the room upstairs.

"...expected to be hosts to bloody pirates, then?" one of the other officers complained.

"Oh, but he has a letter from the King. From the King!" the second officer said, giving the words 'from the King' an exaggerated lilt. Clearly he did not accord a letter from His Majesty the seriousness the bearer expected it should.

The General was silent for a time, then said, "Gentlemen, I caution you not to make public demonstrations against our new guests. I have had word of these men privately. You will not want to make them your enemies."

"Or what?" the second officer demanded.

The General did not answer.

After a moment, the officer continued. "And that monstrosity of a ship. Black! If Satan had a Navy, it would be his flagship..."

Ruttee did not hear the rest of the tirade. He bolted for the servant's stairs and took them two at once. He shot into the pantry on the third floor and glanced out the window there, then flung open the narrow door leading up to the widow's walk. This small cupola gave a view in every direction, but right now he was only interested in one.

Ruttee stood panting, looking out over the harbor. A

tremulous chill seized him, sweating though he was. There at anchor, aloof from all the other mundane vessels of a working port, rocked a ship decidedly not. And just as Bin had described her - glistening black, her furled sails black bulges tight about black yards.

More Giza had arrived.

To Thomas Jefferson
June 5, 1777
Paris, France

Dear Sir,

I offer this brief communication that you may expeditiously be informed of various matters in which we share a common interest. I shall be succinct, as I must copy this out plain three times to be dispatched by three routes, praying God will deliver one into your hands. Perhaps I am overcautious, but on the voyage to Brest our vessel was twice sighted by British men-of-war. Fortunately the Renown is a swift sailor, and, with the blessing of Providence, easily outran her pursuers.

It is clear to me from only a few days intercourse with the French people that there is great enthusiasm for the cause of Liberty among them. The higher up the ladder of authority and power one climbs, however, the cooler that ardor becomes. I do not mean to imply anyone in the Government wishes us ill. On the contrary, I believe them to be in their hearts just as passionate as the populace, the only difference being a practical reserve, as they do not wish at this juncture to overtly side with us against the British. In their view, they have to date been quite generous – and now desire only to see the seeds germinate before spilling any more precious water upon them. I have made arrangements to stay in Paris for several additional months, and I will use that period in an endeavor to point out to the King's ministers all the benefits due them if our harvest is successful.

You asked me to look in upon our friend Franklin. This I did last morning, and the result was not settling to my mind in the least way. He has taken lodging in the house of Msr. Jacques-Donatien Le Ray de Chaumont across the Seine in Passy, where I called upon him. We spoke at some length on my voyage, as he is passionately interested in the flow of the waters in the Atlantic. To my dismay, when the topic turned to my primary mission, and what must be his most pressing business, that of promotion of our infant Union, he all but waved it aside as a transitory fancy, instead calling my attention to a novel apparatus he has fashioned out of glass with the intent to capture and preserve within its walls the fluid of Leyden. He bid me touch a tiny rounded arrowhead fixed to its top, whereupon a goodly amount of the ethereal fluid shot from the apparatus to my fingertip with a white flash and an ear-shattering report. The elementary humour rushed through my whole body like some demonic excitement and left me palsied and infirm in my stance. This greatly amused my host but did nothing to improve my increasing sense of apprehension about Franklin's present state.

I do not know for certain if it has any bearing on his odd disinterest in a cause he was principal in birthing, but during my appointment with him, he maintained the constant and intimate company of a Madame du Meudon, a most handsome woman. The glances and sly nods which passed between them makes me fear our friend's whole energies might, like his jar of Leyden, be concentrated on the generation of vital sparks.

In any case, I shall be in Paris, as I said, for some months. In that time I must endeavor to entice his mind to his office once more.

Yr. Obd. Srvt.
Ethan Woodbury

September 1, 1777
Upper New York State

Thomas had forgotten pain. Several hundred years had fallen away since his last serious wound, so the spasms of shockingly intense agony grinding between his ribs seemed unprecedented and terrifying. Were these the throes of a death long, long overdue? Every slap of his body against whatever was beating it sent another jolt directly up his spine. His head ached. He gritted his teeth until they issued squeaks of protest.

No light. Tightness all about him – bound into something? Coherent thoughts seeped in between the hammers of misery, and he began to reconnect them. Hudson River. He lay in the bottom of a boat, a tiny one, by its quick pitching. Water splashed off oars and against the outer skin, their hidden wakes pulsing a rapid rhythm into the thin membrane of the craft and knifing directly into his heart.

Musky, filthy stench – he was wrapped in a hide. The attackers had dragged him from the river and thrown him onto the bank. Bodies unmoving all about him. The one searching his pockets had seen a twitch, called out. Padding footfalls ran to him. Hands gripped him, rolled him.

The sloop had been sailing upriver. He could not remember the name of the boat nor that of any of the men aboard her: two British officers, four Redcoats, and three sailors. They now floated silent in the water or stiffened on the bank. The excursion was a lark on his part, escaping the boredom of the town, yet deadly business for his travelling companions. He could not even remember their mission, and that made him unreasonably angry.

The river had narrowed, the lookout above shouted with excitement, and one of the officers opened a spyglass to obtain a closer vantage. Two native women splashed in a shallow inlet. The helmsman nudged his tiller, and the sloop edged slowly closer. The sailors and some of the soldiers made rude suggestions to the women, who ignored them but made no move to cover their tawny curvaceous bodies.

The senior British officer had just begun to command them to stop their foolishness when the trees lining the bank erupted with screaming Indians. They sprinted for the water and dove under the surface as the soldiers frantically tried to bring muskets to bear. Officers drew their sabers; sailors scrabbled for axes. Thomas pulled his broadsword, but before he had a chance to get it clear of its scabbard a horizontal hail of arrows zipped across the gap between sloop and land. One hit him in the right breast and spun him around.

He staggered against the rail and saw a thick rope cable pinning the sloop against escape. Natives braced each end up and down stream. He realized the trick: anchored out into the river deep enough to allow small craft to pass over, then hauled to the surface. The sloop was trapped. One sailor leaned far over the side, chopping at the rope with a cutlass. An arrow sprouted from his neck. He screamed and toppled into the water.

Thomas groped at his sword with his left hand, but the blood streaming down his arm lubricated the handle, making it difficult to grip. A pistol blasted near his head and set his ears ringing. He let go of his sword as an Indian dashed at him, wooden spear forward. Thomas managed to deflect the tip with a forearm swipe only to feel the point sink deep into his thigh. The pain reset the glass in his mind so the quick desperate fight on the boat slowed to a blur, then something chopped into the side of his head and blacked out the world.

Thomas felt the texture under the canoe's skin of change from liquid to mushy solid. He heard hands creaking on wet wood and padded feet splashing water and thudding on earth. The canoe dragged over land for some distance, then stopped roughly and tipped. He rolled out, slamming onto hard dirt, each movement accompanied by red-hot embers sizzling in the pulsing flesh of chest and thigh.

Someone removed the hide. It was night, and all he could

see was one open fire and half-lit ghosts of Indians. The same hands that had uncovered him found purchase around his torso and dragged him until his back smashed against a tree. The torment was unbearable, but some sense blocked the scream in his throat. They wrenched his arms behind the tree and bound them with a stiff line which sliced into his wrists. Finally they left him in peace, and by concentrating all his will on shallow careful breathing he was able to sleep.

September 2, 1777
Upper New York State

When he awoke it was just dawn. The remnants of last night's fire smoked feebly as a woman with leaves and dry grasses tucked under one arm poked a stick into the ashes. Wisps of white rose from a hole in the center of a longhouse roof. Men staggered from the longhouse and from the outlying structures and lurched into the woods. Children were already running in threes and twos, whooping and crowing. Women appeared, some carrying bags made of skin and making for where Thomas reckoned the river. Others maneuvered fish and small animals skewered on denuded branches over the resuscitating central fire.

Two gaunt yellow dogs approached him warily. One sniffed a boot, then recoiled. The pair stood close together and barked at him for a while with teeth bared. They lost interest and gave chase when a line of youths ran by.

The smell of cooking meat made Thomas's abdomen cramp with desire. His mouth was leathery. He craved water, any water, but no member of the tribe offered him a drink. None looked at him except for the dogs, who growled on their busy forays through the native activity. The youngest naked child would not attend him. Even through his wracking pain Thomas had to admire the discipline of these people.

All day he watched, sometimes falling into a restless half-

124

sleep. He could not get comfortable for several reasons, not the least of which was the remnant of arrow shaft protruding from his chest. It had broken off sometime during his capture – only about one handwidth remained. This baton vibrated in time with his heartbeat, a telltale metronome, disclosing to all who cared that he lived.

September 7, 1777
Upper New York State

For five days, or at least five days in the alternate calendar of hallucination he plunged into after the first night, the village ignored him. His pain was like surf: a fierce pounding followed by a regrouping lull, then building in a hissing rush to the next crest – on and on through daylight and night.

On the morning of what he estimated to be that fifth day, a delegation emerged from the longhouse. They did not look past him but approached with purpose. Four braves, young and narrow-eyed, trailed one older man, who moved with majestic deliberation, in contrast to the arrogant confidence of his warrior escort.

The Indians stopped two paces from him. The oldest stepped one more.

"You are not dead," the elder said in good English.

It was not a question, so Thomas said nothing. He fought to keep his eyes open wide, though the rising sun was directly behind his interrogator.

"Why?" the elder asked. "Why do you not die?"

Thomas held his eyes but did not make the least movement.

The Indian seemed to sigh. "Some–" here he motioned to the braves to left rear "–think you are a demon. Some–" he motioned to the others "–think you are a spirit."

Thomas kept silent. He was delirious with thirst and hunger, but the elder's words flayed him open more than any physical insult. The clarity of this fantasy was so compelling it seemed to him now the first time the question had come up. Had the water made him spirit or demon? Five hundred years to determine this, and yet he had made not the least progress. His head started to wobble from the effort of keeping it up.

"A man would die of these." The old man held a stout walking stick wrapped with sinew dried to an ebony gloss. He touched this to the end of the broken arrow – and Thomas had to grind his teeth to the edge of breaking the enamel to keep from shrieking.

There was a long pause as the five men eyed their captive. "Many think we should kill you. To be safe." The spokesman started to touch his stick to the arrow again, but Thomas twisted his torso enough to avoid the probe.

"What if I am the kind of demon," he croaked, barely comprehensible, "that cannot be killed? The kind that appears to die, only to rise and take his vengeance on you and your women and children?"

The braves shuffled nervously, elbowing one another, but none came closer. None moved away, either.

Thomas bit down on his tongue. A drop of moisture rose from somewhere in his throat and allowed him to continue. "What if I am the kind of spirit who rewards those who help him with the many things a spirit can do for a man?"

The elder stepped back and studied on that for a time, then said, "The people fight the Redcoats." He made a small tight circle over his head with a pointed finger. "The people fight the bluecoats." He made another, larger circle, out to the side.

Thomas nodded. The Indians up here were loose confederations of tribes and subtribes. The old man was saying this village was on the side of the Americans, but other villages – with whom they probably traded, hunted, and intermarried – would fight for the British.

"If you are a demon, then we are right to fight the Redcoats. If you are a spirit, then we should be their friends."

Thomas had no answer for that, and after an eternity in

which the five men standing and the one man sitting stared hard at each other, the standing men turned and went back into the longhouse.

Several hours later, three braves untied him. They let him flop over onto his side. He had not the strength to sit up on his own. His arms stayed bent backwards at the shoulder, stiff as rusted hinges.

One brave held a piece of hide up to his face and mimed biting it. Thomas, too weak to argue, opened his mouth. The leather tasted of rancid fat and wood smoke and something else his woozy brain was trying to name when the man in front of Thomas took a flat stone and drove it hard against the end of the broken arrow shaft.

The arrow finished its interrupted journey through Thomas' ribcage, erupting from the flesh of his back as Thomas clamped down on his bit and passed out.

He woke up on his left side, naked on a raised bed of soft furry skins. He felt thick layers of grease, clammy on his chest and on his thigh. The air was sharp in his nose as after a lightning strike. He must be in one of the smaller huts, its outer cover layers of hide and pine boughs and long grasses. These were supported by branches bent to meet in an open circle where the tiny central fire vented. But not all the smoke was able to escape, leaving the air inside a translucent gray.

Thomas imagined figures moving in the fog, beams of living light falling down from the vent, dancing in the thick visible atmosphere. He was five hundred years old and felt five thousand. Every joint was swollen and stiff, every muscle was abused and depleted and desiccated, and his wounds burned.

Five hundred years. Not once was I brave enough to reach beneath the water to touch the light, to wake up the being. To ask it if I am a demon or a spirit for drinking its bath.

He slept and woke to more figures in the smoke. These seemed more substantial. They made soft purring noises, and the skins under him resonated. Two smoke wraiths approached and resolved. It was the twins who had lured the sloop to the shore, the squaws whose weapons were their perfect breasts and goddess-like features. He half expected them to draw knives and finish the job.

They moved in unison. It was disorienting, seeing double. Thomas watched as they shed their sheer leather robes. They were naked underneath. They crept carefully onto the bed, one to his front and one to his back, each facing him, each putting her arms around him.

Thomas was too drained to respond as he certainly would otherwise have. He could only close his eyes and breathe.

They don't know either – and he sank back into dreamless sleep.

October 9, 1777
London

The King of England was once more ruling, knickers gathered about his ankles, from a velvet-covered throne. The Royal Physicians had considered the problem for a great time, consulted in a corner with much head bobbing and professional susurrations, and finally presented His Highness with a blue pill and a draught reeking of decayed mutton. George downed both, waved his assassins from the room, and sprinted for the Royal Seat of Ease.

Today His Majesty's shite was the consistency and hue of gruel, heavy on the suet. The only difference being, besides the aroma, was that the royal arse felt to char with each strained contraction.

I will have the cook's head for this, the King raged. *The latest spice from India, my prick. Settles the digestive system. My fiery hole it does. More like raises an army of deviant fanatics to rampage through my gut with torches.*

He groaned once more, the muscles of his traitorous abdomen spasming without his consent, and another trickle of yesterday's dainty dish splashed to the bottom of the putrid, beautiful box.

There had been a window, an all too short window, when the contents of Geoffrey's curious phial had made magic with the regal bowels. For a week and some days more the King's stool had been, well, majestic. Firm but not hard, soft but not liquid, and departing politely from the sovereign rectum with a whispered goodbye. They had even smelled garden fresh, like some kind of flowering plant flourished in his nethers. He had oft on those occasions chanced a glance into the ornate box, as his sessions on the lid were so short he could scarce believe they had been fruitful. But there lay the proof: perfect turds, suitable for casting in bronze and displaying in Westminster Abbey.

That idyllic time had also passed. The King knew Geoffrey had given him just enough of the superb liquid to flaunt its properties, to drive the King to acquiesce. He had done and more. Much more. Now George desired more phials – he lusted after them with a passion such as he had never known.

The King was no genius, but neither was he a fool. After his midnight meeting with Geoffrey and Jean, he had summoned Barrington, and the two put their minds to the task of deducing Geoffrey's home ground. The man had let slip several subtle but telling clues which allowed the two men to narrow the area down somewhat from the whole of the British Isles to one region centered on Bedford. Barrington had sent out three regiments to pitchfork every stack of straw and question every living and sentient being within a five-league radius.

He made out the voice of Barrington, a muffled request to his man Janeway, then a shouted greeting: "Your Highness, you mustle burble mub!"

The King mused on the oak slab door of his royal privy chamber. One of his predecessors had been no fool. The door was designed to thwart axes and rams long enough to allow a beleaguered monarch to slip out the window and make his escape behind the ivy-covered crenellations leading to another flat roof. It also thwarted normal communications, but the King was not about to admit his Secretary for War to see him thus.

The Viscount's mangled entreaties went undeciphered for the most part while the King finished squeezing out as much as he could. He elected to forego the ceremonial bumwiping and did the deed himself, then straightened his coat and britches and wig and made himself into the King of England, Protector of the Realm, et cetera, et cetera, and opened the door.

Janeway stood with averted gaze at the threshold, towel in hand, but George passed this amenity by and went straight to Barrington, who became politely fascinated by some ceiling murals during the time the door to his ruler's intimate room was open.

Barrington pivoted ninety degrees to his left and swept out one arm toward two footmen who formed a human easel supporting a huge wooden panel, rounded at the top and with a gilded border. The edges were raw, splintered in many places. The King suspected his troops had literally ripped this artifact from some uncooperative church. It depicted the figure of a man in ornate robes raising a beneficial hand over a slew of proportionately too-small adorers swarming his ankles.

The Viscount, after practically bellowing against the stubborn door, now was mute. He merely pointed to the large script on the plaque nailed to the bottom edge of the panel.

Lord Geoffrey of Emberton.

The King turned to Barrington. "We have smoked the old prestidigitator out, then, eh?" He was volubly pleased, but for some reason Barrington was pale and quiet. The King followed his gaze back to the plate, to the fine print.

Defender of the Faith. Crusader for Jesus Christ. Lost in the retaking of the Holy Land in the Year of Our Lord 1244.

George froze, the breath stopped in his throat. This could not possibly be – but the face in the portrait, though done in the flat angular style of the period, was without a doubt the man he had met twice.

"Clearly," the Viscount said quietly, "Geoffrey of Emberton has been on a long strange trip."

December 14, 1777
Upper New York State

Another substantial snow had fallen in the night, and the valley below was layered waist-deep. The tribe had wisely situated their buildings in the sheltering lee of a cliff. The village itself had only a few inches of white upon its common.

In the woods just beyond the outer huts the drifts were also passable, and this is where Thomas strung his bow as several braves kept sharp eyes on him while radiating indifference.

Soon after his wounds had healed – and it had been very soon, as his captors had returned his pack unmolested, and in the pack was a supply of the water – he had stood watching a young brave testing the flexibility of a bow. Seeing his interest, the Indian handed it to Thomas. The tribe's attention turned to him, curiosity becoming raucous laughter as he raised the bow and bent it the way he had been taught in Castle Emberton by Geoffrey's archery master: pinning the string against his jaw and pushing his body into the grip – the maneuver necessary to ready a stiff English longbow. The shorter Indian weapon took less strength to draw, arms alone were enough, but the old technique came to him automatically. Laughter quieted a bit when he picked up two arrows, inspected them for straightness and balance, made a minor tweak to the angle of the fletchings on each, and proceeded to send them a hand's breadth apart in the middle of a black smudge of ash wiped on a birch trunk fifty paces away. The braves whooped with delight. Demon or spirit, it could shoot.

They tested him almost every day. It pleased Thomas, who remembered chilly mornings on the damp heaths around the castle bending and loosing, bending and loosing until the

131

bundle of straw roped to roughly resemble a Frenchman instead approximated a hedgehog.

Thomas stepped to the mark and inserted an arrow into the rawhide string. He was certain a proper linen string would produce a swifter shot, but he had none. Three braves looked on from his left. He did not know their names. Members of the tribe had names, he knew, but they shared them only with immediate family. When one was talking about a member of a different family, he just pointed with a toss of his head and said 'that one'.

Ignorant healing Thomas had inadvertently committed a serious faux paux against his captors' mores around personal designations. One day soon after he was able to stand again, he tried to introduce himself properly. But when he pointed to his chest and said, "I am Thomas Banks", the surprisingly considerable portion of the tribe which understood him turned away with disgusted faces, as if he had crapped in their communal stewpot.

So, having no access to their real names, he fixed them with private appellations, based mostly on appearance. His audience this morning was Crooked Nose, Long Ears, and Scar on Left Temple. Not very noble familiars, he supposed, but unless he married one of their sisters he would have no other to call them.

Thomas drew the arrow in the Indian style and exhaled. He centered the tip on the target, then elevated to account for the distance. There was no wind on this still morning, no need for left or right corrections.

He was just about to release when a loud bellowing upset the perfection of the day, and a figure crashed from the bushes in a horizontal flurry of snow and stumbled directly in front of his shot.

As Thomas dropped the tip and released the tension, he thought for an instant a stray shot had found an innocent hidden beyond the target, for the figure was one of the younger braves clamping both hands to a head wound. Blood dribbled at an alarming rate from the tip of his nose and the end of his prominent jaw, but he made no sound after his initial shouts. He stopped, wavering but upright.

He had been slashed open from brow to cheekbone. The three braves who had turned to behold the victim flounder from the woods did so without comment or visible surprise. Long Ears simply took the blood-soaked youth by one shoulder and pulled him toward the village.

The victim was deposited in front of one of the larger huts, one decorated outside with the skins of several colorful birds. A woman stepped out through the flap and spoke just one word to the injured brave. The lad ducked into the hut, and the woman dismissed the others with a wave.

Thomas remained, peering into the dim recesses of the hut where the brave had disappeared. The woman waited. At last she lifted the hide a bit higher and caught Thomas' eyes. He nodded and crept through the small entrance.

It was not totally dark inside. Light came from a constellation of pinholes in the hide covering and from the tiny ventilation hole at the apex of the hut. The woman laid the brave down on a crude cot, then shook a handful of fuzzy emerald plant stuff from a pouch and deposited it into a wooden bowl carved from a burl.

The woman grinned at Thomas, hiked up her robe, and squatted. She pissed a noisy stream into the bowl while Thomas watched, too fascinated to be embarrassed. Robe dropped, she became serious once more and muddled the mixture with a wooden pestle.

When she was satisfied with her potion, she took the bowl closer to the brave, who had been lying silently and still all this time staring at the modest patch of sky observable through the vent. She scooped up some of the greenish mass with one hand and simultaneously pried the brave's fingers from the wound with the other. She parted the edges of the cut with two fingers and squeezed fluid into the pulsing crimson gap. Thomas cringed in sympathetic pain, but the brave showed no reaction.

Thomas watched the woman remove strips of hide from a

clay pot steaming hard by the fire and wrap them around and around the boy's head. After her operation had bound up the loose skin, she applied the rest of the green mush and covered it with what looked like a rabbit pelt with the hair burnt away. She sewed this one piece into place swiftly and expertly.

The young man's eye was probably lost. Briefly he was tempted to fetch some of his water, but he knew revelation of such powers would not be wise. The brave would have to trust in his physician's knowledge and her herbal skills.

Outside was silence, but when Thomas finally emerged, he saw plenty of activity. The men of the village gathered around the eldest, who Thomas had privately christened King Richard. This noble savage had in his hand a bundle of white fur, which Thomas saw on closer approach was an English goatskin knapsack that had no doubt belonged to some deceased Redcoat. King Richard extracted an iridescent black feather and pointed it at a brave. The honored man came forward, accepted this token impassively, and stepped back into rank. The same ceremony was repeated with a broken deer antler, a slightly deformed musket ball, an arrowhead. When he saw Thomas, the King put his hand in and drew out an oval blue stone inlaid with glittering flakes of silver and handed this last to him.

Now every brave — and Thomas — possessed on object. They picked up their bows and began to move quietly in the direction the youth had appeared from just ten minutes before.

Thomas fetched his quiver and bow and followed the pack. The Indians set a fearfully fast pace, yet remained as quiet as the snowfall itself, knocking not a flake from any branch.

After about an hour of this stealth, they were in a section of the forest so dense barely any snow had reached the ground. Overhead was almost solid black only hinting green, a sky woven of pine needles. The braves at the vanguard of the group slowed abruptly.

Thomas stopped altogether, peering into the gloom created by the tightly knit trees and hearing nothing. The men ahead of him moved to the left, and Thomas looked that way – and saw a man fixed violently to a tree.

The young brave was nailed up like a bug pinned to a collector's bench, the nails being sharpened branches as long as a forearm. Blood dripped copiously from his wounds – four, Thomas counted, and all apparently in areas calculated to generate much pain yet small chance of immediate death. Thomas noted grimly that the perpetrators of this ritual had been chased off in the opening act. At the youth's feet lay a casual pile of at least two dozen more thin, needle-sharp skewers.

The men yanked the stakes out of tree and flesh. The wounded man, as Thomas had come to expect, made no sound, but collapsed to his knees on the last removal. Two men picked him up, and the party began to retrace their steps.

Thomas found himself walking next to Scar on Left Temple. Thomas nodded his head back toward the bloody scene. "Who?"

Scar on Left Temple frowned. "Bijinway. Very bad men. Hate Osuanee."

Thomas had learned the proscription on naming individuals did not apply to the tribal groups. His captors were Osuanee, but he had not heard of the other tribe until this moment.

"Where do they live?"

Scar on Left Temple gaped at him like he was being a crazy white man again, and Thomas realized these people lived everywhere and nowhere.

"Where is their longhouse?" he asked instead.

The brave pointed without hesitation over his right shoulder. "One day to walk."

"Then why don't you go and burn their longhouse?"

Scar on Left Temple gave him that look again. "We burn their longhouse. They burn our longhouse. Have to build two longhouses." And he hurried away, shaking his head at the insanity of European logic.

King Richard stepped up to fill the gap.

135

"Are you at war with the Bijinway now?" Thomas asked.

The older man shrugged. "Always war with Bijinway. Sometimes war with Warranawonkongs. Sometimes with Ganienkeh. Never war with Onkwehon."

Thomas considered this Byzantine state of affairs for a time, then said, "Do you do that to Bijinway you capture?"

King Richard laughed. "Of course. If we did not, it would be calling them a woman. Is right to test brave before making them brothers." Thomas thought this was some mistranslation, and perhaps 'killing in a gruesome and painful manner' came out 'making them brothers'. The other saw the confusion on his face and continued, "If we catch Warranawonkongs, Ganienkeh, they become Osuanee. Marry Osuanee woman. Fight with Osuanee."

"You adopt them into the tribe?"

"Yes, adopt. Good word." The old man smiled happily. "But if we catch Bijinway, Bijinway catch Osuanee, no adopt. Maybe eat."

Thomas felt sour bile rising in his throat and turned his head away so King Richard did not see his disgust.

January 24, 1778
Passy, France

Benjamin Franklin is working as hard as he has ever worked. The dedication is on his face: his furrowed brow, his intense frown, his narrowed eyes. Breathing deeply and rapidly, all his great powers of concentration are focused on one goal. He is vigorously rogering the beautiful, naked, and supine Madame Nicole Marcelle du Meudon as, he hopes, she has never been rogered before and may never be so again.

The Madame encourages both this dream and his physical endeavor. Her loud pleas to her Maker, her howls and groans delivered with side-to-side shakes of her head, and her small interspersed sighs, maintain Franklin in a hardened state he trusts would defeat a blacksmith's anvil and hammer. Periodically she grips him with arms and legs like a bear on a tree trunk and trembles in an ungovernable fit.

Or perhaps it is the salve, as she calls it. The salve of essential oils, waxes, and extracts purchased in some apothecary on one of her perambulations on the Mediterranean coasts. Tingling slick grease the color of drying hay the Madame applies to her lover's Johnson as the performance is being cast, the orchestra tuning, the dance steps agreed upon. This ointment is worth whatever she paid for it, he decides in some distant and acutely happy portion of his awareness.

Time rushes past the wrestlers; time freezes the horizontal tableau; time is irrelevant and unknown; time is abolished.

At last Franklin's guts combine their various parts and fluids, a pulsing lock whose teeth finally mesh, opening a door from which a holy torrent is released, invoking a celestial chorus of seraphim and cherubim who combine in a discordant yet triumphant final crescendo.

And he is off. He has rolled from her body – his moving of its own unbidden accord, seeking a lower state in which to recover.

They lie there, barely touching, the only sound their hearts, the fire sparking, the winter wind hooting bass notes as it discovers resonant hollows on the exterior of the cozy house of their host, the happily absent Jacques-Donatien Le Ray de Chaumont.

Franklin looks down. The necessary region is alarmed once more. It has volunteered with no call from its master. The phenomenal pernicious salve again! The good Madame has noticed the hydraulic wonder as well, and she puts out a hand to push against his ribcage.

"Not yet," she says wearily. "I shall burst into flame from the friction."

He thinks to protest this statement. They could not plausibly generate enough heat to produce flame. He knows this. He has seen fire produced by Shawnee ingenuity – a stick rolled between the palms, its bulbous tip inserted into a hole in a timber, that hole stuffed with bristly, wooly....

He feels a throb. She is still observing the region, though, and shoves him again.

"At least grant me a glass of wine first," she sighs. She stands, and a dozen and more ghostly Madams in various aspect ratios stand with her, reflections in the rotund glass bell jars Franklin has been industriously fashioning and wiring in series. The whole crowd of women is disastrously gorgeous. Franklin is transfixed by the lovely choreography. He stands as well, his reflection joining hers, his round pale body made long and lean in the convex surfaces, his protruding member exaggerated in apparent length by the geometry of the optics. He moons hopefully at Nicole, even wagging his eyebrows suggestively, but she ignores him.

He puts one hand over his heart, which is still pounding away. *I am in love*, he realizes. Those hips, that skin and eyes and lips and.... And wit, he admits. And wisdom – often more profound than his own.

The Madame poses in front of her mirror, attempting to rescue some order from the chaos their thrashing created in her tresses. The mirror stands as tall as she and is framed in an iron latticework – thick with cherubs cuddling fleurs-de-lis – mounted by gimbals to a floor stand. She adjusts the angle to let her scrutinize her head and begins to winnow her locks from the shambles left by her lover's eager hands.

Franklin in the meantime has gone to his experiment, his visible enthusiasm for the curvaceous Nicole only slightly flagged. He has improvised a crank affixed to a set of toothed gears on the last jar's base – this he inspects for a minute, touching it to make sure the play is neither too tight nor too loose, then he turns his head to inspect the more important mechanism of the lithe form of Mme, who, with her arms raised over her head accentuating her full breasts and hardened nipples, is the primary experiment on his mind.

She notices him in the mirror and sticks out her tongue. This is so arousing Franklin almost passes out from loss of humourous fluid to his demanding part. He turns away with a superhuman effort, his hand still resting on the crank, and he almost absentmindedly begins to press against it so the shaft it controls rotates.

This action ultimately spins an array of leathery flaps inside the jar. A low hum slowly ascends a mechanical scale from subsonic to notes a harpsichordist would strike by reaching far to the left. A metal spike protruding from the crown of the jar begins to glow, an aura swelling around it, the otherworldly light chaotic like leaves bending in an uncertain breeze. He cranks harder.

The spike transmits a spark, a corkscrewing sustained bolt of lightning in miniature, to an identical spike atop the next jar. Franklin grins insanely. His idea is working. He throws his temporarily dammed romantic energy into the cranking.

In a flash the whole of his interconnected metal and glass fancy is whining, sparking, glowing. Each jar seems to increase the effect of the last until the entire array participates and saturates the room with a web of crackling and fiery beams shaming the actual fire of mere wood. Franklin is still spinning the crank furiously, its several parts a unified blur.

Madame has paused in her coif repair to appreciate this phenomenon, then she shrugs. Life with Franklin is full of such odd noises and lights and smells and sometimes conflagrations which must be quenched with the nearest bucket of water or chamber pot, so she returns her attention to her own needs. She lets go of a handful of hair and reaches out to optimize the tilt of the mirror. She pulls at the top, not noticing the bottom cherub is heading forelock-first for one of the metal supports of the nearest jar – a support coated in the dancing bluish-white light.

The floor in this wing of the grand house of M de Chaumont is stone slab, the color approximating simple gray, but only because the eye integrates all the small inclusions and crystals in the stone into homogenous color. Viewed closely, as Franklin has, it is ripe with metallic flecks that no doubt contribute to the one unfortunate property of the floor detracting from its grandeur. It conducts heat like iron. The floor is always cold. It sucks the warmth from the air, so this wing is preferred in summer and shunned in winter. But for lovers willing forgo the floor and to also stoke a robust fire, it serves.

These fact stumble offstage in his awareness as he watches the horror play out, unable to alter their course. The damned floor is like ice on his bare feet, and the chill coagulates him to the tip of his head as his lover, the exquisite Nicole, pivots her mirror until the cherub's head taps the leg of his machine.

Yet somehow he continues to turn the crank. No matter. There is obviously already more than enough of whatever kind of fluid he has generated. It vaults to her mirror, splits, courses around the angelic ring and meets itself on the other side. The mirror is momentarily rimmed with a dazzling brilliance.

His love moves nothing but her head, toward him slightly, questioning this new development.

Then the light floods across the mirror. It slams against itself at the center with an eerie cricketing chirp and is tossed up and out like waves clashing on a stormy beach. An appendage surges out from the mirror, a bright blue beam outlined with red fading to pink streaks within. It envelopes the naked woman, caresses her for an instant, then seems to find what it was really seeking – the cold stone below. Light, color, movement, sound – all finish their crazed dash from glass and metal to metal and glass and flesh and then to the earth and then, with a thunderous report, are gone.

Franklin is left deaf – and blind in the sudden blackness. His eyes suddenly impotent, his glasses lost hours before in the entwined bedclothes. He gropes his way toward where he thinks his lover must be. He calls her name, quietly, then desperately, for there is no reply.

At last he feels her foot with his hands and begins to recover some sight, though the real fire has almost died. She is lying on her side, facing away. He turns her onto her back and cries aloud. Maybe it is the darkness, but she looks ten years older. Perhaps she is injured. He rises to call for help. A log collapses into itself on the fire, reenergizing the blaze, relighting the room, and he sees more clearly. She is two decades older. He cannot breathe.

She opens her eyes, and he feels a rush of relief. But she does not see him. She stares into the mirror, which has ended up almost parallel to the floor. She is witness to her reflection, and she begins to sob.

Franklin falls to his knees, his ancient and creaking knees, the agony registered but ignored. "What is it, my love? Are you in pain?"

She shakes her head minutely. "My Ben" she says. "My Ben. I am sorry."

He frowns. This is not her voice. This one is feeble and worn. The accent is thicker, unfamiliar.

"I have deceived you, and now I am old and ugly... and horrible."

"No, no, no," he insists. He slides an arm under her neck and pulls her close. "No. You are the most beautiful creature the Creator ever–" But something is wrong – three decades older now, her face all wrinkles, her neck flabby. "Nicole," he whispers.

"My name is not Nicole. I am not Madame Nicole Marcelle du Meudon." She is limp in his arms. He can barely hear her words. He pulls her closer. She feels substantially lighter than just minutes before when they wrestled in passion.

"I do not care what you call yourself," Franklin cries.

"My name is Druda... Gruttadauria. I want you to know this. I did not mean to do anything but love you. He promised me youth and riches. He gave me the water."

"Who?" He fumbles for words. "What water?"

"I do not know who he was. Did I care? My Ben, I was dying. I was worn down to nothing. My family had been taken by plague, down to the last of my precious granddaughters. He came to me then, in the stinking alleyway jammed with the dead and gave me a drink. One long drink and I rose up. Another drink and I was well. Several sips more of his cursed

141

water, and I became the woman who fell in love with you."

"Why?" He hears his voice – the sound empty and stupid.

"To distract you from your duty."

Now she is four decades along, sere and limp, a tattered flag with no wind to fill it.

He starts to speak, but she shakes her head painfully. She mouths, "No more, my love. Just hold me."

And he takes up her wrinkling, stiffening form, now five decades past, six, seven, accelerating until the mass ceases to move and leaves Benjamin Franklin weeping naked and alone on the bitter glacial floor.

Hours later Jacques-Donatien Le Ray de Chaumont, in nightgown and cap and holding a single candle aloft, quietly opens the door to investigate the soft sounds of despair within. The quavering yellow light of the candle discovers his friend clutching to his breast what to de Chaumont's astonishment resembles nothing so much as an unwrapped mummy.

March 25, 1778
Upper New York State

"Smell!" insisted Long Ears.

Thomas obediently bent down and sniffed the brown doughy stuff the brave cupped in his hand.

"How long?"

Thomas wrinkled his nose. "Not too long?"

Long Ears frowned. "Long means deer gone. Not long means deer coming back."

Thomas nodded. Understanding the age of deer shite by its odor was key to the tribe avoiding wasting a day hiding by a deer path, like the one he and Long Ears were watching. They were concealed behind a thick bush downwind of the trail, itself a barely–visible continuous thinning in the spring vegetation sprouting through the forest floor.

Seven other braves hid nearby, though if Thomas had not

seen them melt into the background he would have been certain he and Long Ears were the only men for miles in any direction.

The two sat comfortably with their backs against the base of a straight oak. Each had his bow in hand and one arrow stuck into the ground beside.

They waited with no more conversation. Thomas had never known hunters or soldiers to bide their time without gossip, ribald jokes, teary remembrances of times past, empty boasts, etc. But he had learned to stop himself from speaking in the beginning of such silences, and the longer the vigil the easier he found it to hold his tongue.

Long Ears leaned forward just a hair's breadth, but enough to register in the corner of Thomas's vision. *He must sense the deer*, Thomas thought. Then he heard a clear tone – the high chirp of a bird from one of the hiding places.

He reached for his arrow. That subtle call was not the signal for game.

Six Bijinway braves appeared, walking recklessly and noisily along the path. The first carried a spear, but the next two inexpertly gripped muskets by their barrels.

Thomas had wondered when the local tribes would begin to carry firearms. The Osuanee had shown no interest in using the several they had captured along with Thomas, content instead to display them on the walls of their longhouse, useless trophies of victory. And useless they largely were in the forest, which is why Thomas had made no effort to enlighten his captors. Leave them tied up as decorations, he had decided. They were inaccurate, slow to load, heavy. Their powder, if it could be obtained at all out here, generated blinding, choking billows of smoke, giving away the gunner's position while simultaneously obscuring his sight. Hunters and warriors who relied on stealth and speed were ill served by flintlock weapons.

Now he knew the Osuanee would command him to teach them about muskets – because their bitter enemies carried them.

He searched behind him for Bijinway. If he had been the

one to organize their loud procession, he would have sent flanking troops out quietly to fall on any Osuanee drawn into the open by this ruse. But the parade passed with no sign of support, and Thomas guessed the Bijinway believed a Brown Bess made its bearer impermeable to mortal weapons. How they came to this conclusion Thomas did not know. Obviously they had not learned of the Osuanee taking the river sloop from men wielding multiple guns.

They were about to learn if the magic held, for the Osuanee in hiding began to move. Thomas saw subtle ripples in bushes to either side of him, then Long Ears sprang to his feet and let out a piercing ululating shriek.

He darted through the undergrowth, Thomas behind him several running strides, the other Osuanee ahead and behind. The Bijinway turned, saw they were in a bad defensive position, and ran.

They fled downhill, an instinctive but bad choice, for that way terminated against a sheer rock outcrop. By the time they determined there was no easy way forward over the rock, their escape to either side had been cut off by Osuanee.

The Bijinway turned and flourished their muskets, this captured sorcery their best hope for escape. The two braves who bore the arms aimed them only in a very general sense.

Two reports trembled leaves all about the two parties – at least the Bijinway had learned to prime the pans – and more damaging to the ears and eyes of the musketeers than their target. The Osuanee party laid their bows aside and unlimbered axes and tomahawks. This was to be close work. Thomas threw down his own bow and unsheathed his sword.

Before what promised to be a bloody melee started, Thomas saw Pinpillow break from his fellows and charge the cluster of Bijinway. The young brave had been pierced by this same enemy, and he was still decorated with deep pink dimples angry on his brown skin. The Bijinway recognized evidence of their handiwork and froze as Pinpillow screamed into their ragged line, axe high over his head.

The brave reached within an arm's length of the largest

Bijinway, and Thomas expected to see the plunge of the edge down onto the enemy's skull.

But Pinpillow stopped. Still elevating his weapon, he reached out instead with his other hand and smacked the brave lightly on the cheek, then sprang backwards and scampered to his people.

The Osuanee erupted with shouts and derisive laughter, stepping aside as the silenced Bijinway slinked past, shoulders stooped. Pinpillow danced with wild joy, wheeling his arms and lifting his knees to his chest. After admiring his steps for a minute, the other braves joined in, their raucous celebration echoing in the forest.

Thomas stood still, as stunned as the defeated enemy had been, his heart still racing with the anticipation of combat, not knowing exactly what had just happened.

March 27, 1778
Upper New York State

These deerskin breeches were almost broken in, Thomas felt. He had been wearing them continuously for three days, through prickly undergrowth, through icy rivers, through the thick smoke of the longhouse fire, and now he gripped the waist and peeled them down. They crumpled around his ankles, and his legs were only moderately scratched in the journey.

The twins had spent a day chewing the raw deer hide, sucking in one small mouthful at a time, the greasy stiff skin puckering into wet nipples as they worked their teeth on it. His vest they made out of fox, his moccasins out of doubled moose hide lined with beaver. The day his outfit had been complete, they solemnly undressed him of his tattered English clothes and redressed him in his new regalia.

His old garments were stuffed with dry grass and propped up as a target, reminding Thomas of the faux Frenchmen dummies of his youth. Perhaps the fate of his inert doppelganger should have brought a sympathetic twinge, but in his new vesture, his long hair tied back, his skin darkened by exposure, he looked – and felt – more Osuanee than Englishman. He took part in the ritual execution of the target with great enthusiasm.

He hung his breeches beside his vest on a protruding stub and stood naked in the middle of his home. The hut was mean and tiny, but it was his. The twins, still nameless to him, usually slept in one end of the longhouse with the other single women. They came to his hut often enough that he did not feel neglected.

Thomas could not properly define his relationship with the two beautiful squaws. Like most of the society of the Osuanee, indeed, like most of their whole world, sometimes he thought he understood them – only to lose his grip on it the next moment. They were nonplussed by cannibalism. They were comfortable with torturing captured enemies, then they turned around and embraced those enemies as sons and brothers. They fought with deadly bloodlust, but the highest honor was simply touching an enemy in battle. If they themselves were thus touched, the humiliation clung to them for years, whereas if they were grievously wounded, they bled happy and proud, their passion for the fight returning before the scars were firm.

He was deep in concentration, trying yet again to process these opposing ideas when the twins burst in through the door flap, elbowing each other to be first, laughing and chattering. They dropped to their knees in a limber ease Thomas knew he would never be able to duplicate, supernatural water or no.

They were so alike Thomas often confused them – until they undressed. And even then they were such a matched set his unspoken names for them were better left unsaid.

Slightly Smaller Mole on Inside of Left Breast spoke first. "He," she said breathlessly with a toss of her dark tresses toward the longhouse, "has had a vision." It was clear to Thomas she was talking about King Richard.

Her sister Also Has a Light Streak Perhaps an Old Scar on Inside of Upper Right Thigh followed quickly, "Of you. It came in the smoke."

Thomas regarded them carefully. Perhaps he had gotten them backwards. He shook his head. "What am I to do in this vision?"

They both laughed at this foolishness. "It was not our vision," Also Has a Light Streak Perhaps an Old Scar on Inside of Upper Right Thigh said.

Then they fell silent at the same instant, extreme solemnity freezing their features. It was something they did often, reacting as one, and Thomas had been disconcerted by it for some time. Not anymore. He waited for what they had to say, for this was the attitude they assumed when they had some serious news.

They stood in unison and dropped their robes. They were naked underneath, as was most often the case and so no surprise now to Thomas. But this time they put their palms flat to their abdomens, rubbing lightly in minute circles to draw his attention away from other areas more attractive to the male eye, and Thomas understood instantly the message in their slightly protruding stomachs.

He sank back onto his bed and sat slumped and openmouthed. This provoked the twins to break their solemn air and smile broadly.

"My name is Rain Rushes Down," the one closest to him said softly.

"My name is Leaves Whisper," said the other, just as quietly.

Thomas had mind enough match these names to his old designations.

Leaves Whisper took her hands off of her belly. "She will be called Child of Demon."

Rain Rushes Down made the same movement. "He will be called Child of Spirit."

They paused, expectant, but he was dumb. A roar filled his skull, deafening him. The floor was no longer level. He felt shaky, his guts boiling with the intensity of emotions long dormant.

The twins watched him with concern for a time, then gave each other knowing smiles.

"You are afraid we are too weak now." Rain Rushes Down said.

"But we are not," Leaves Whisper said definitely.

And they dove on top of him to prove their continued ability.

March 27, 1778
London, England

"Well, 'tis about time – look here, Molly – if it in't the Three Graces crossing." Mr. Lambert nodded toward the larger of the two windows at the front of the shop.

Molly, the coffee maid, did not look here. It would of course be the usual trio of Members who came across from the chapel for their afternoon pot. Fyshe, Tomlinson, and Coldbrook, who had fallen into a regular and predictable habit of an afternoon's invigoration from the aromatic bitter specialty of Tacey's House. The routine had been ongoing long enough that Mr. Lambert had plowed through all the low-hanging trio monikers available to his memory – The Three Sillies, The Three Piglets, The Three Blocks, and the like. He had then resorted to strained descriptors, i.e., The Three Horsemen of the Apocalypse, The Three Points of the Compass, etc., which Molly greeted with calculated indifference until eventually her employer stopped his grasping.

The door opened to admit the Graces and an unwelcome volume of chilled spring breeze. The men trooped to their usual table in the corner, which Lambert kept clear of customers for them at this time every day Parliament sat across Margaret's Street. They did not have to beckon – Molly loaded their pot and cups on her tray before they had shed their hats and coats.

They were not the only patrons from government. Tacey's House was a place where Lords and common Members had gathered to continue dry debates with the fuel of coffee these hundred years and more. Tacey was long dead, but the original debate still simmered. It was a two part question: firstly, how much power had God granted the Crown, and secondly, all other details.

The Graces were converts to the Marquess of Rockingham's Whigs, so their answer to the first part was: King George inherited all Heavenly privileges of the throne, but Parliament reserved all earthly decisions. On the second part they much differed as the circumstances evolved. It was the first principle that bound them.

Molly poured as they settled themselves into their seats, and they spent a quiet minute slurping and sighing as addicts long denied their release. At last Coldbrook put his cup down and spoke quietly, "This marsh, at least, has been successfully drained."

His companions smiled. They had spent the whole morning on hard benches listening to a member from up in the northern wastes argue his bill to fund the draining of some marshland which was apparently the only obstruction blocking the Shining Highway upon which this Glorious Nation was bound to some objective or other and so on and et cetera. Refreshment could not have come at a more opportune time.

"God spare us," spoke Fyshe severely, "from debating African slavery, or the conduct of the war, or the servitude of our Irish brethren. No, not so long as there is a single marsh thumbing its metaphorical nose at good John Bull."

This and the kick of the coffee put them onto the subject of marsh drainage in general, and thence they segued into the pros and cons of inclosure, and the effects of same on the traditional classes of farmers, and the observation by a droll Tomlinson that opening the common at Wenlock might enable the preservation of old Shite Brook, thus preventing the erasure of its name from the official maps.

The three had achieved a brisk rhetorical pace when Fyshe, who was facing the door, put his head down and fell silent. The others knew what was portended. Falk approached.

Hye Falk, member from King's Lynn, who sat on one side one day and the other side the next, who was never caught into a corner or in a lie, who had friends in all places, who had one pocketful of favors owed and another of same due. He represented a borough good and foolish enough to grant a vote to any free man living within its boundaries – unlike Fyshe, Tomlinson, and Coldbrook, who represented an owned borough, a rotten borough, and a pocket borough respectively. Owned, rotten, and pocket boroughs sent members ordained by the rich families who controlled the land, but Mr. Falk actually had to go about after an election had been called and convince the men of King's Lynn to return him to his seat on the uncomfortable oak planks. This constant practice whetted in Falk the ability to cajole, coddle, and convince his fellows – talent the Graces did not have and of which they were secretly envious. They shifted nervously, for if Mr. Falk was bearing down on them, he had some scheme brewing.

Falk stood at the head of their table until they could politely ignore him no longer. "Oh, hullo there, Falk," said Coldbrook, acting surprised to see the newcomer. "Come across for a cup, have you?"

"Good of you to offer," Falk said pleasantly to the nonoffer. "But I am in a frightful hurry to get down the Alley."

The three listeners bent their heads imperceptibly and unconsciously toward the end of the table. Falk's business in Sweeting's Alley, where the new stock exchange was located, meant money was going to change hands – and there were six hands here at this table feeling suddenly empty.

Falk smiled as a conspirator and leaned down after searching theatrically to port and starboard. "The thing is," he said softly, "I have just been informed by a most confidential source the King has put up North to install Carlisle as the commander of their new Commission."

His audience carefully made their faces: Yes, we expected

that. Frightfully trivial gossip, you know.

In reality, this kind of hard data could move relevant stocks to increased or decreased value in a twinkling once it was generally known. The Commission in question, a delegation assembled by the government, was charged to sail for the colonies and make such offers there as would convince the so-called Continental Congress to return to the fold, let bygones be bygones, and jigger the fine print so normal trade might be reestablished in the Empire and the damn French kept where they belonged. The Graces were outwardly composed, but each inwardly frothed with possibilities. If an investor could but deduce which stock would move on this announcement, and in which direction, then his fortune would be made.

"So I am off," Falk continued, "with no delay." Emphasis on the word 'no'.

It was Fyshe who at last made the inevitable counter. "I suppose... there is no reason for you to rush straight over. Not so near tea time."

Falk rubbed his beard. "Tea. I do crave a pot about this time. I will probably be delayed about two hours in that endeavor. I do also have some britches at the tailor's which want picking up."

"A minor inconvenience. Is there any service we can do you?"

"One tiny thing," Falk admitted. "I would be ever so grateful for your support in this marsh draining bill. I feel in my heart for those poor folk up there, ankle deep in mud all the live long day."

This, they knew, meant somebody with designs on the new, profitable land which said marsh would become on removal of the overlying glop had as the result of some elaborate maneuvers Falk's note in hand, to be discharged by the stewarding of this minor bill through the House.

"Marshes are dreadful places," sniffed Tomlinson. "I say let them all be drained."

Fyshe nodded, raising his cup to his lips. Coldbrook was

quiet, but at last he also bobbed his noggin in assent. It was as good as a wax-sealed Royal decree. Falk smiled even more widely, wished them the joy of the day, and departed.

The three sat reflecting for the next five minutes, slurping and sipping. Fyshe and Tomlinson were absorbed in fitting this news to their understanding of the present economic system, searching for a crack into which the lever of their capital might be inserted. Coldbrook was not calculating at all.

They have forgotten – perhaps they never knew, he was thinking. *Had I not told them we overlapped two years at King's College? That we often drank together and drifted between taverns with the same carousing herd to mutter clever multiple entendres about the barmaids under our breath?*

No, he had apparently not; otherwise they would have been busy interrogating him. Coldbrook slowly refilled his cup while his two companions ignored theirs. Fyshe and Tomlinson were reckoning with this new data based on their estimation of Frederick Howard's – The Right Honorable Earl of Carlisle's, that was – diplomatic abilities, which estimates were probably low. The Earl was thirty years old and had no significant experience in these matters. But Coldbrook also had personal input to his mental algorithm. Freddie was a rake, a dandy, an ordinary soul whose number had been drawn in the lottery of birth. Coldbrook knew his old chum was not the statesman to set to rights the present schism between the Empire and a whole virgin continent full of rebellious malcontents. Therefore, no matter how poor the chances for success his companions might project, the odds Coldbrook set on the ripening of that enterprise were exactly and decidedly zero.

And it smacked him like Divine Revelation: *The King did not want peace.* He did not want this senseless war to end. For whatever reason, the naming of Carlisle was George's message that the Crown would endeavor to win this conflict at any price.

Coldbrook could not help but smile. It was the smile of a gentleman in his club playing for serious money with marked cards – and only he could interpret the markings. In a moment the three men would make wholly trivial excuses for leaving, apologies all around, then each would dart out to find their man of business. They were sure Falk was at this instant using his information to influence other Members. He had promised them two hours – they would be lucky to get thirty minutes.

March 28, 1778
Hudson River Valley, New York

He had in the course of his life often woken suddenly in the night. It was the ingrained awareness of the serf – and later of the soldier – that alarms in the dark brooked no delay. Not this time. This night he swam comfortably to the surface of sleep and bobbed there relaxed and undisturbed. Slowly his body became aware of the physical. He had an arm around a warm pliable body, his hand cupping a breast. Behind him another body molded to his, knees behind his, chest to his back. All three breathed as one.

Thomas opened his eyes to the dark. Nothing was visible in the hut, not even in in the apex hole. The moon was absent; the stars vanished.

I am twenty years old. I have been alive for hundreds of years, but I am still twenty. Now I have two – are they wives? – perhaps sixteen years from their own birth. And two babies whose years have not begun to accumulate.

He decided suddenly. He was tired of being forever twenty. He would never go back to that world of stasis. He would stay with the Osuanee. He would stop taking what water he had left. He would save it for emergencies, for his women and his babies, until it ran out. From that moment he and they would live as people were meant to live.

I may not be a spirit, he resolved, *but I will show them I am no demon.* He closed his eyes and fell back asleep.

Sunlight through the hut door warmed his face, waking him. He sat up, groggy and for some nameless reason quite happy. Then he recalled his nocturnal resolution, his two pregnant women, and he smiled.

He put on his breeches. The girls had gone while he slept, as they often did. They were young and full of energy. He listened for the song they sang while preparing the morning meal.

There was no song. No sound of men shuffling about, no women gossiping, no dogs growling. Only blanketing silence and enveloping trees.

Thomas stopped his breath. Still there was nothing. He stooped, picked up an axe propped beside the door, and slipped outside.

The village was lifeless. No smoke billowed from the central fire pit or from the longhouse roof. He ran quietly to the longhouse and poked his head into the main opening. The structure was stripped. No weapons, no pots, no blankets – empty.

He retreated to the center of the clearing, rotating to brandish his axe at the four points of the compass, anticipating whatever evil had taken his people, fear rising as scalding bile in his throat. He wanted to call out the dear names he had just learned – but could not make a sound.

Crashing in the trees behind him made him whip about, axe drawn back. Whoever approached was not wise in the ways of the forest. They were clumsy, cracking twigs underfoot, kicking leaves.

Men broke through into the clearing, and Thomas had not seen such in so long that at first he did not recognize the red uniforms. He took range on the leading figure, calculating whether he had time to rush or should first hurl the axe. The soldier aimed his musket at Thomas's breast, and three behind and flanking him did the same.

"Hold your fire!" a man roared, and Thomas turned to face this new threat. The English captain held a saber, but as the men lowered their barrels, he ostentatiously sheathed his weapon and made a small bow.

The native the officer saw before him was as dark as any Indian, long-haired and half-naked, but he was thickly bearded and clearly had the features beneath of a white man.

The captain stepped forward and extended his hand. "Thomas Banks?"

April 21, 1778
Atlantic Ocean, Off the coast of France

The Atlantic Ocean in spring was never still. It was often violent – stiff winds shearing white tops off mountainous, racing waves. Sometimes it was merely uneasy with long rolling swells bobbing a ship like a fisherman's cork. But it was never as flat and the air as hushed as this morning.

Captain Friday might have been woken by this unnatural lack of motion. Or perhaps it had been the barometer, whose mercury plunged precipitously at a rate he had never seen. Though the quicksilver itself was silent, his four decades spent on wooden planks had brought his bodily humours into resonance with the salt water. He could feel in his throat and stomach when the meniscus of the instrument swinging over his bunk changed.

Whatever had roused him from a sound sleep and kindled his apprehension sufficiently that he had flung just a slicker over his nightshirt for a quick turn, it was not apparent on the quarterdeck. The lieutenant of the watch was sighting his glass across the deep purple of the northern horizon. The helmsman glanced back at as the Captain appeared, and Friday thought this ancient mariner himself had an uncharacteristic foreboding in his weathered face.

The lieutenant lowered his glass slowly and wheeled to face his commander. He felt a vague sense of guilt he had not called Friday out before, but what was he to report as the cause? A lack of wind? A glassy surface? No ships, clouds, nor land?

"Good morning, Mr. Proctor," the captain said. "And a fine morning."

Proctor saluted. "Nothing untoward, sir. Clear sky and no sails in sight."

Friday nodded. He bent back and considered calling up to the maintop nest, the very highest manned point in the ship. He could see the lookout there, eyes diligently on the distance. No. The Captain knew his ship and his crew. If there were anything to see, it would be spotted and called down instantly.

The men knew where they were and who they were up against. The mighty British Navy sailed hundreds of ships; the nascent America only a dozen or so. Many of the British ships carried more cannon and threw more hot iron than did the Dauntless. If any of those got close enough, the Americans would be in peril.

The Dauntless' defense was speed. One of the newly constructed heavy frigates, she could outrun any ship larger and outfight any ship smaller. Still, those larger opponents were best identified while far off.

To utilize her best qualities required a captain who was not bound by ego but would raise all sail and make haste to avoid an engagement if he entertained any doubt. Shadrach Friday was the man for this ship. As a young boy he had followed his father and his father to sea, and at twenty years of age had become the captain of a cutter hauling dried cod to Jamaica, Maine timber to London, and rum to every city with an Atlantic port. Over the years, his ships had increased in size and tonnage so by the time of the Declaration he owned a fleet and a large mansion on Milton Hill from which he could inspect his properties as they negotiated the Harbor. He had become affluent by hard work, diligent planning, and an abundance of caution.

But a merchant ship was not a warship, though Friday's commercial commands had always carried several cannon to repel pirates and the French. Now he commanded a floating fortress whose hold was filled with powder and shot instead of lumber or potatoes. The Dauntless carried twenty-four twelve-pound cannon and several six-pound chasers. This did not compare to the massive thirty-two and eighteen pounders his opponents might carry. Friday knew many of the English hands were pressed men, unhappy and poorly fed, yet not to be therefore underestimated. He also knew even on short rotten rations they were excellent gunners, rapid and accurate from daily practice. He prided himself, however, that his cannon were served by volunteers desiring to retain their sudden liberty – free men who would fight just that much harder. Plus, he worked his great guns twice a day – once in the morning running them in and out to harden the muscles of their crews and once in the evening firing for speed and effect at empty casks put out on rafts.

Friday had his eyes on the perfect line of the horizon. His only fear was the sudden appearance of a British squadron which would try to use its small fast ships to harry him toward the slower dreadnoughts. But no ship could catch him unawares on a morning like this. The crow's nest far above provided the watch a view ten miles off, and unless the wind picked up, it was impossible any vessel might approach the Dauntless this day. They would still keep vigilant, however.

"Please join me for breakfast," Friday said to Proctor.

"Yes, sir," Proctor replied. "Thank you, sir."

The Captain returned to his cabin, sat down at his desk, and opened his logbook. There was just enough illumination from the predawn sky in the great cabin windows that he did not need to light a lamp to read his bold entry from the previous day. As he was reviewing the account, someone pounded urgently on his door.

"Enter!" he called.

An ashen ensign practically fell over his feet as he pushed the door in. He caught himself and lurched upright. "Mr. Proctor's compliments, Captain. He requires your presence on the quarterdeck."

Moses Proctor did not turn as his captain appeared beside

him at the port rail. It was impolite and against naval tradition, but Proctor did not apologize and his superior did not upbraid. They were both fascinated by a thick cloud clinging to the sea, a bank black as peat smoke lying a half-mile off. It lay heavy upon the water, rising to what Friday judged a hundred feet or more, its slab sides sharp and smooth as a human construction. He could not see any waves in front or to the sides of it. How had it gotten so close without being noticed?

He glanced up at the topmost lookout, who was not asleep. The man was staring at the phenomenon himself, open-mouthed. *He probably had not known what to call out*, Friday realized. *Neither would I.*

"Captain..." Proctor whispered, but the sea and the ship were so deadly silent it seemed as if he had screamed. "I don't know what that is. It just appeared."

Friday held out his hand for the glass and scanned the formation for several minutes. Every man on the ship was doing the same with naked eyes and various instruments of magnification and ignoring the rest of the wide empty sea. Friday lowered his instrument angrily.

"Belay that skylarking!" he bellowed. "Keep a close eye all about!" Then he muttered to himself and perhaps to Proctor, "Could be a trick."

He regarded the peculiar bank for some time, scratching the stubble of his beard. The Dauntless was pointed east, though in this stillness it could not be described as cruising. The sun began to rise a point off their port bow. The strange black cloud was just to their northwest. The morning light should have lit the side of the cloud which they could see, but it remained as black as the rest.

Friday drummed his fingers on the rail. "I have heard of such things in the southern seas," he said. "Whalers tell of undersea volcanoes which spew gasses and rock right up to the surface."

Proctor was not convinced, but he did not voice his opinion. He had seen drawings of volcanic plumes in history books. Assuming the artists were not bald-faced liars, this sharp-edged anomaly resembled those vast billows of ash not at all. It looked to him more like the Parthenon rendered in quiescent brimstone smoke. He did not offer this impression to the Captain or the several other officers who had slowly accumulated beside them.

"It is moving toward us," Proctor said.

The Captain nodded. No feature on the water provided them reference against the cloud, but still it evidently grew larger and more distinct. They could make out curls and bulges, as if the material comprising it was boiling.

A collective disbelieving moan escaped the company. A ship edged out of the inky cover. They saw its bowsprit first, then the figurehead hanging below, a mermaid with a twisted smirk on her black wooden countenance.

Black not because she was a Negro mermaid, but because the ship itself was painted entirely in black, a gleaming burnished ebony. More of the vessel emerged, confounding those experienced seamen whose jaws went slack at the sight of a ship moving faster than the air and the fog around it. Her sails were black as her hull, leaving the sailmakers on the Dauntless stunned as they contemplated the enormity of dyeing such expanses of canvas.

Friday felt oddly relieved. Here was something of substance, something he could understand. "She's got Spanish lines," he said to the officers assembled about him.

"She flies no flag," the sailing master pointed out. The other ship's mainmast had just cleared the fog or smoke or whatever it was, and indeed their tops were unfettered by banners of any kind. Nor did a flag appear as the rest of the black vessel emerged from cover.

That did not worry Friday. The flying of false flags up until the point of actual cannon fire was a common and accepted ruse de guerre. The Dauntless herself was at the moment flying a Dutch flag. It was somewhat odd to show no flag at all nor any colors in the rigging. No signal flags or pennants denoting ranks of officers on board could be seen.

Friday picked up a speaking trumpet. "Ahoy the ship!" he

159

bellowed. "This is the USS Dauntless! Identify yourself!"

There was no response. The black ship somehow slowly came about to match their heading, leaving the black cloud to their sterns. The officers shuffled nervously – not a puff of wind moved the black sails. Perhaps they had sweeps out on the far side the Dauntless could not see.

Friday knew all the legends of ghost ships – unmanned apparitions that appeared and disappeared in mist and night – but this one was here, in the waxing daylight. She did appear to be unmanned – but for one lone unmoving figure standing on the topmost aft deck which in the ancient design corresponded to a quarterdeck. No crew was visible or audible, even as the two ships closed.

Friday had also heard of mirage ships, real ships whose images were bent by tricks of the atmosphere so they appeared miles from their real positions. There was one dependable method of sorting phantasm from material.

He turned to the bunched officers on the quarterdeck and found the ensign of the watch. "Mr. Highbridge, would you be so good as to put one shot across her bow?"

The ensign tore his eyes away from the black hulk and, gulping loudly, saluted and ran below.

The mystery ship was now well clear of the black fogbank. Proctor half-expected that smoke to disappear, as if it had spawned and should die in the birthing. It persisted.

The officers heard muttering on the gun deck below, then rasping and squeaking as the great gun was wedged to the proper elevation and levered to orient the muzzle. With a sharp grunt the gunnery captain pulled on the lanyard. The firing pin dropped.

The Dauntless had been quiet as a ship is at night in enemy waters and had managed become even more silent at the awful sight of the dark ship, so the boom of the powder and the crash of the recoiling cannon carriage made not a few of her crew literally jump from the deck. Friday followed the flight of the ball as it howled across the black ship's bow and skipped three times on the perfect ocean surface before slowing into its final splash.

For a minute there was no sound but the gun crew tugging upon the ropes to return the carriage into firing position. The dark figure on the other ship's deck did not shift. The two vessels and the sea returned to an unreal silence.

The spell was broken by a broadside – a dozen or more cannons thundered in unison. The side of the black ship erupted in flame and smoke, and the Dauntless shuddered as heavy iron struck home.

Friday staggered, and some instinct in his mind cried danger even over and above the obvious attack. *This is not right!* He grabbed the rail to steady himself.

"Fire!" – even as he screamed the order he realized what was wrong. The enemy fire had raked his ship – balls disintegrating the thin planks of the stern to careen through the unprotected crew. He heard screams, the surprised howls of men impaled by splinters and battered by hot iron. On the main deck men were down and writhing. In places he saw only bloody rags mixed with the remnants of their owners.

How had the shot come through his ship at such an impossible angle? It was as if the cannon had been fired from the fogbank aft instead of from–

Friday ran to the helm, yelling at the man there to turn the ship hard to port, but his voice was obliterated by the broadside from the Dauntless's own cannons. Part of his mind noted several absences from his answering barrage, guns no doubt torn from their carriages by the raking fire. He whirled back to see what damage those surviving guns would inflict on the enemy – and his heart sank. No black splinters flew, no sheets parted, no opponent shrieked in pain. It was as if the Dauntless's iron had passed through the idea of a ship. The Captain turned slowly to face the stern and the black bank still floating just two ship's lengths away.

Proctor was helping the sailing master to the gangway which would take him below to the surgeon's cockpit. The master had been pierced through the thigh by a wooden splinter two feet long, and blood spurted in pulses through his breeches. Something familiar in the rounded and weathered side of the spear made Proctor quickly inspect the masts as the master half-fell down the stairs. The mainmast had been shattered at its base by a cannonball. He looked up and could see yardarms swaying out of level as the weakened timber bent under its now unbearable load of sail, rigging, and men – marines and seamen who had swarmed up to their fighting positions just moments before.

"Abandon the mast!" he screamed. The marines knelt on a firing platform sighting their muskets at the enemy ship, searching for targets. Stark, the Captain of the Marines, peered down at Proctor and shouted something swallowed by the din and chaos.

Proctor began to repeat the order when the enemy released another broadside. This time grape mixed with the round shot. The impact of the broadside shook the Dauntless and knocked Proctor to the planks. As he lay on his back, he heard the crackling of multiple small projectiles buzzing over, a flock of metal hummingbirds scouring the Dauntless's deck from stern to bow, and he followed one cannonball as it rebounded off of the scuppers and arced high into the air.

When he rose he saw Captain Friday was down and motionless, one arm taken off just below the shoulder.

"Get the Captain below!" he bellowed, but nobody came running to help. All about the main deck and up from the open hatches came the screams of the wounded, the moans of the dying. And too much silence – the dead chiming in.

The main mast had fallen while he was down, its loud splintering adding to the cacophony of battle. Stark, trapped underneath a tangle of stays and spars, made frantic gestures to attract Proctor's attention. Proctor leapt down to the main deck and reached for Stark's hand, but the injured man avoided his grip.

"Get one of the six-pounder shells," Stark gasped. Proctor saw the Marine's lower half had been crushed cruelly by the weight of the collapsing mast, and he started to protest. Stark cut him off. "Fetch one and draw out some of the charge! Quickly – we haven't much time!"

Proctor stood up. The Captain sprawled motionless on the quarterdeck at the center of a spreading red puddle. The First Officer was nowhere to be seen. Moses was the senior officer and must stay on the deck and fight the ship, but there was precious little left to fight with or to defend. Smoke billowed from the aft hatches, uncomfortably near where the powder magazine lay twenty feet below. He counted five men working to aid the fallen. Not enough to suppress a blaze and man the cannon.

"Please," Stark moaned.

Proctor raced to a locker and rolled out a six-pound shell. He used his knife to pry up the brass fuse plug and then shook some of the powder onto the deck. He ran this to Stark and knelt down.

Stark grabbed the shell, removed something from about his neck, and pushed it into the hole. That done, he seemed to lose most of his vitality and laid his work at Proctor's feet.

"Plug it," he said weakly. "Load it into the stern chaser and fire it into the cloud."

Proctor did not know why, but he jammed the plug back into the shell and ran, hurdling debris and the dead and dying, ignoring pitiful pleas from the wounded. He found one of the chasers amazingly still on its mount and spun it around to shove in one of its small bagged charges. Decking was on fire a few paces away. He reached over and lit the shell's fuse on one edge of the flames, the whole time expecting another killing broadside – to which he was wholly exposed. The charge and shell rammed home, he picked up the firing line. He performed this drill with no expectation it was anything other than a delirious man's dying fantasy, and as he aimed the piece and pulled the lanyard, he bid goodbye to his life.

The small gun coughed, just a footnote to the deafening tumult of the enemy's cannons, and delivered its tiny ball into the roiling black cloud.

Nothing happened, and Proctor's senses began to return to his duty. He filled his lungs to order the survivors off the ship, but his eyes were still fixated on the strange fog bank. His command froze in his throat – a fiery point had appeared inside the mass, visible somehow through the opaque matter. This incandescent speck extended tentacles – spinning arms of red and yellow flares that began to revolve and race through the interior of the mass. To Proctor's awe, the bank swirled and shrank. It circled upon itself as if some drain had been opened. It thinned, evaporating to mere gray vapor, then white mist, then nothing. Inside was the enemy ship.

Proctor glanced at where the black ship had just been, but she was no longer off their portside. It was suddenly clear from where the deadly raking fire had truly come. The smoke from the fire below decks was thicker now, and he limped through it to the nearest hatch. "Fire as they bear!" he roared down, wondering if there were surviving men and mounted guns. The smoke was too dense for him to see.

He climbed onto the rail to get a clear view of his position. The combined momentum of the enemy shot had turned the Dauntless a few points to starboard, so the aft guns there might be just be brought to bear on the enemy.

Now the deception is exposed, Proctor prayed. *Let us have a shot at her.*

One of the Dauntless's guns fired, and a shockingly few voices remained to cheer as the shot struck home. Ebony fragments flew from their opponent, then another gun discharged, and the black ship vibrated visibly from the point-blank strike.

Proctor braced for a return broadside. Minutes passed, time without sound. Proctor had been struck deaf by the cannon fire. He could see men on his deck with open mouths. They must have been crying out, but he could not hear anything. No more shots came from the Dauntless. *Two cannons only. The next broadside from that black bastard will be the end of us.*

But it never came. Before the two guns below could be reloaded, the black ship heeled over as if there were a stiff wind she alone could feel and began to put distance between herself and the listing, smoldering Dauntless.

Proctor let out his breath, suddenly as tired as he had ever been. He realized he had never had his promised breakfast. His stomach rumbled. Somehow, that sound he could hear clearly.

He walked the deck, seeking out those still able, directing them to launch the boats. Two ensigns picked their way below to gather survivors and put them over the side. Moses stopped next to Stark and knelt. Stark opened his eyes and smiled grimly.

"Do not bother yourself with me," Stark said with a painful effort. "See to my men."

One of the ensigns reappeared, his face and uniform black with soot, and reported the fire approached the magazine. Proctor indicated the young man should help him free Stark from the tangled mass.

Stark began to resist the rescue but soon fell silent. His eyes closed. Proctor touched his neck. It still pulsed, so the two officers attacked the mound of debris pinning Stark down.

April 25, 1778
Atlantic Ocean, Off the coast of France

Isaac Stark, Captain of Marines aboard the USS Dauntless, died before dawn this day of injuries sustained in action against the enemy.

That was the beginning of the entry Proctor was making in his mental log. When he obtained a proper logbook – not if, he had to remind himself – he would bring it up to date with the events which had transpired in the three days since the sinking of the Dauntless.

It would be a proper read, too, he imagined. It would open with Lieutenant Moses Proctor (acting Captain) and Ensign Cornelius Ward extracting the unconscious Marine from under the crushing timbers and leaping with him into the sea as billowing flames piped them off. They splashed together near Captain Friday's overturned gig, onto which they scrambled and dragged the inert Stark up out of immediate peril. They and two charred and bleeding shipmates kicked and paddled with hands to urge the gig away from the blazing frigate. They were not much above a hundred yards off when the fires reached the powder magazine. The good Dauntless detonated in a fireball. The shocked air hit them hard, blowing one of the sailors clean into the water and concussing the rest into near-insensibility. Smoldering pieces of wood and hot chunks of metal hailed down upon them as they shielded their heads as best they could and entreated God to grant nothing of any great size be propelled toward them.

After some time they were able to look back into the soaring pillar of smoke and ash, but nothing remained of their former home. Not a scrap floated above the level of the water. Off to the south, the black ship showed them its stern as it merged with an indistinct haze.

Proctor, when he was fully satisfied the enemy had done with them, dove beneath the gig, and after several attempts managed to extend the daggarboard. This long stout board rose slowly up in the midst of the exhausted survivors, who summoned the last of their energy to lay hold of it and slowly lever the gig over onto its side. From that position it should have been normally a minute's work for such experienced seamen to recover the boat, but it took this battered compliment a whole torturous hour.

Finally the gig was righted, and Stark was placed gently onto the bottom planks. Proctor told the men to lie down and rest while he took inventory, a task too quickly completed. The gig had gone into the water without its mast, without tackle or oars, without sails, without rations or water. It had retained its tiller and an abbreviated length of light line tied to a cleat amidships.

They drifted for several hours, listening sharply for any cries from their lost shipmates, but the ocean was bare and silent. In the afternoon a front raced over and refreshed them with a deluge of sweet rainwater – then tormented them with a fierce wind driving the sea into ten-foot waves. Working furiously as the front approached, Proctor and Ward stripped their uniform coats and used the line to fashion from them a very unseamanlike sea anchor, which they tossed out to stern. When the swells began and the ocean ran, the drag allowed the gig to just barely keep its bow into the wind. Proctor leant his whole weight on the tiller arm as the gig rose up and up the steep face of the first large wave, then came slicing down the far side into the calm of the valley for the briefest respite before the next ascension.

They continued on in this precarious manner for a day and a night, taking turns at the tiller, calling on their Maker to protect the two blue wool coats below, for if their rig split, or the line parted, or their hasty knots came undone, the small gig and her miserable crew would be turned sideways in an instant and driven under the surface of the icy Atlantic.

Sometime after the rain, Stark had regained his senses. He called Proctor to him and told him what he knew of the necklace – of Caroline, of Warren's death, of the Dibele and of the cabal of knights. Proctor would have believed none of it four days ago, and even now it sounded like the ravings of a delusional madman. Except he had seen the black ship disappear and reappear and its massive black cloak dispersed by a mere drop of this water.

Proctor accepted these impossibilities now with equanimity. He understood the water might have saved Stark's life if he had chosen instead to put the amulet to his lips as he lay stove by the mast, but Stark had given it up to save his shipmates. *He would have been disappointed*, Proctor thought. None of his marines had made the gig. Stark had forfeited his restoration that four sailors might drift on the uncaring ocean until thirst and exposure granted the mercy of death.

At dusk they had put the marine gently over the side without a salute of musketry. They had no shroud to sew him into, no cannon ball to sink him with dignity. They could perform none of the traditions, but there was never a dead man laid beneath the waves with as much appreciation – though it was only Proctor who knew the full measure owed.

As the light grew on the fourth day, Proctor sat in the

stern, upright only by virtue of one numb arm crooked over the tiller. The others sprawled listless in the bottom of the gig, washed raw by the ceaseless sloshing of the undrinkable salt water they were too weak to bail. The sun blazed down upon them. They had removed their blouses to wrap their heads and left unprotected torsos now horribly crimson and blistered.

It should be cool and cloudy. We should have a mast and a sail. There should also have been a hogshead of water lashed to the gig. There was so much gone wrong he could not even manage a hopeful grunt for his fellow castaways when the sail rose up over his horizon. It must be close by, he reckoned, to be visible from his slowly declining altitude. He slumped farther down into the gig. The dazzling sun lay behind the ship, and Proctor could not make out the flag. Not that it mattered. It was no doubt false.

April 27, 1778
Hudson River Valley, New York

It was his story, Thomas decided. Like his name, it was private, shared with no one but family. And the British force which discovered him in the middle of the deserted Osuanee camp was most certainly not his family. When they treated him as a recovered captive he did not correct their presumptions. He guarded his tongue, played the part of a traumatized Englishman held against his will by savages, and meekly followed the troops back to their sloop, accepting their sympathies and a ration of their rum.

He found himself watching the banks during the run downriver, searching among the trees for glimpses of his wives. He knew it was hopeless, but he could not look away from the forest. The men in the boat seemed crude and dirty. They scratched at lice and stank of moldy boots. Thomas forced down a piece of hardtack handed him. It sat adamant in his stomach, unfamiliar to his digestive process.

When they reached the fort on the outermost edge of the British occupation, the colonel in command took him to a cabin where a servant drew him a bath, shaved him, and presented him with a set of mismatched but reasonably fitting clothes suitable for a civilized man. Thomas pulled on the britches and blouse and sat staring at the stiff black boots for a long time. His comfortable moccasins had been taken away, presumable tossed in a trash pit or even burned. He longed for them, but knew he could not wear them now while keeping his family secret.

The boots turned out to be a size too large, which was a blessing. The colonel loaned him a horse from the fort's string, a filly whose legs seemed to be of all different lengths so even at a walk Thomas thumped down on the hard leather at every step. After a short while he had to stand in the stirrups to rest his chafing ass.

He left the fort at dawn, stopping only to let his sorry mount graze and drink. In late afternoon he emerged from a thick stand of budding trees and confronted the house which was the endpoint of the colonel's detailed directions: a monstrous stone mansion, three stories high. Wide steps led up to an ornately carved entrance of red stone arching around a doubled timber door. As Thomas drew closer, he saw the land behind the place appeared to end abruptly. He walked his horse to the side, his curiosity bristling at the illusion – but it was no trick of the eye. This imposing building had been built precisely on a precipice overlooking the Hudson River.

Hated his own castle, thought Thomas, *and always seeking to replicate it.*

He heard Geoffrey calling his name, so he dismounted and led the filly to the front of the house. His Lord stood in the doorway, dressed in an emerald green suit over a ruffled white blouse.

"You are just in time for tea," Geoffrey said.

Thomas had been dreading questions about his long absence. On the ride south, mostly paralleling the wide slow river, he mentally edited several versions of his recent history which might be submitted to his old patron. None included the whole truth, and he worried he was not in Geoffrey's class as a liar. There was a fair chance any invention would be obvious.

His concern was for naught in the end; Geoffrey seemingly had no interest in the details of Thomas's disappearance. The earl had certainly used his influence with certain persons in the Army to initiate the search for Thomas. But now found, the past was seemingly irrelevant. Thomas had ventured out to see how the land lay and had seen it and was back.

It had not been that simple. Thomas had been bored in New York. The town was hip to shoulder with Loyalist refugees, speculators, and soldiers. Resident rebels kept sullen silence by day but jeered the Englishmen in the night, pelting victims with stones and balls of horse shite, then scattering without leaving a witness brave or foolish enough to name them. When he learned of the small confidential expedition sailing upriver to communicate with friendly tribes, he inserted himself in its company. It was only to relieve his tedium. In the end, he hadn't learned anything about the Indians of use to any other white man but himself.

They had tea and scones with cold beef and sliced turnips in a huge dining room, at a table built to seat forty or more. As they ate, seated together at one of the ends, Geoffrey described the property.

"The man who built this fortress did not love his King as much as he did the rabble," Geoffrey smiled. "And so he is in flight and we are in possession. You complained about the awful stench of New York, and you were right. If we have business there, we can take a staircase down to a landing on the river and be in the city in half an hour."

"Is Guy to join us?" Thomas said.

Geoffrey cut a turnip slice in half. "Guy is taking care of matters in France. The French desire to put their greedy fingers into this pie. Guy contrives to crack their knuckles."

Thomas did not ask of news from the Tower. Jean was

serving his time there, and Thomas knew Jean was as likely to be found in a brothel in Cairo as at his station.

After the meal, Geoffrey showed Thomas the rest of the interior. It was an empty, depressing place in Thomas' eyes, decorated throughout by someone who overly revered the past. The cavernous library, its high windows giving a spectacular view of the river far below, boasted two suits of armor flanking a huge fireplace. The walls groaned under a scattered collection of broadaxes, pikes, and swords such as he had not seen since picking his way through the dead after the battle to retake Ascalon.

Thomas wondered the Earl was here at all. Geoffrey had not disliked New York. He reveled in the adoration he received from the Army and the politicians who were attached to the Royal teat. He totally ignored any disapprobation from the surly rebel faction. His tastes were in line with the excessive drinking and carousing of the officers, so why decamp to this remote and apparently deserted billet? No, this was part of another of Geoffrey's schemes, he was certain. And he would be informed of it in good time, as always.

At the same moment, a wagon approached from the south. It was a small wagon, drawn by two unremarkable horses and guided by two bored men. The team stepped along at a comfortable but unhurried pace; the men watched with seeming disinterest the scenery pass in the rapidly fading dusk of early spring. In the wagon bed, a soiled tarpaulin covered what might have been five stout timbers. The deliverymen left the reins slack. Whatever this harvest was, they thought it in no danger of soon spoiling.

The wagon made the same revealing turn to approach the house Thomas had taken just hours before, but unlike him, the two teamsters showed no appreciation or surprise at the precipitous placement of the estate. It was as if they had been here enough times to be thoroughly used to the looming stone monster. The driver guided the wagon around to the side of the house, a stone's throw to the riverside cliff. Neither man showed any apprehension at the nearby danger.

Geoffrey stood in a cramped hallway expounding about the thickness of the walls and the soundness of the construction techniques. A torch sputtered in its sconce, filling the space with trembling yellow and making the place much like the uncomfortable medieval castle the builder had intended. Thomas ached from the ride and wanted to retire to his quarters. His belongings had been fetched from New York and stacked by unseen hands in the middle of a large suite next to a bed which looked most comfortable. He longed to stretch out upon it.

A knock. Geoffrey turned without surprise and opened a stout wooden door to the outside. On the step waited two men, hats in hand, eyes submissively downcast.

"Our delivery," Geoffrey pronounced, and the two men put their hats back on and went to the wagon.

Geoffrey took Thomas by the arm and led him farther along the hall to a large high-ceilinged kitchen. A soot-crusted fireplace took up one whole wall. In the middle stood a wide table made of wood yellowed by age, stained by decades of various juices, and crisscrossed with knife marks.

The two deliverymen reappeared, each carrying one end of a plank upon which was balanced a naked man, quite dead. They slid the cadaver onto the table and hurried out. Four repetitions and the table was lined with five corpses.

Thomas noted the bodies were all in relatively good shape – for being dead. *They should all be alive, holding their wives and children. But for this useless war.*

The shipment complete and the outside door rebolted, Geoffrey stood by the table evaluating the dead as if they were turkeys being considered by a cook. He contorted their arms and legs, checking for rigor mortis. He worked his fingers into their mouths to see how far the jaw would open.

Thomas turned away, sickened. In his centuries he had seen piles of dead exuding tumbling rivers of gore, but something about the tranquil row of innocents moved him.

One had died eyes wide, and the empty unfocussed orbs seemed to follow him accusingly.

"These come from the prison ships in the Harbor," Geoffrey said. "They would have gone into the water otherwise. Fed to the sharks. A waste, don't you think?"

Thomas did not think and did not reply.

"My men there bring them straightaway. Only the pick of the crop. Fresh as can be. No consumption, cancers, abscesses. No missing limbs." Geoffrey smiled at Thomas.

Thomas had heard of the prison ships run by the British authority. They were hives of disease and starvation in which captured colonials were stuffed to repent of their rebellious nature – and rot doing so. He had a strong suspicion obtaining such plump, muscular corpses might have taken some active intervention by the two deliverymen, who he had to admit were not technically grave robbers. These dead had never had a proper grave. They showed no obvious marks to suggest cause of death, but given the proper financial incentive, Thomas was sure there were ways to hasten fresh inmates to their sad but inevitable end without damaging the product.

Geoffrey, meantime, had gone to a cupboard and taken down several colorful ceramic urns and a mortar and pestle. From an inside pocket he produced a slim leather-bound notebook, which he lay open on the counter top to consult. Guided by its contents, he pinched, spooned, and poured ingredients from urns into the mortar. He ground the mixture vigorously with the pestle. Then he reached back into the cupboard and took out a black carafe.

Thomas was expecting this. A score of similar black carafes had been fashioned in India specifically for the knights. They were cut from pure obsidian, hollowed out by some method unknown to the Western world, fitted with ground black stoppers which made the interior tight and leak proof but which were removed with a simple push and twist. Geoffrey thus opened the carafe and inserted a long piece of straw. He covered the end of the straw with a fingertip and withdrew it. He held this over the mortar, and a trembling drop shining from within formed and then fell, a tiny shooting star. Three more sought the mortar, and he carefully returned the rest to the carafe.

Geoffrey picked up the pestle and began to gently mix. "I commissioned an Arab alchemist some years ago," he said. "A man called Bakr ibn Mayyam, probably the most accomplished practitioner of the art there has ever been. I gave him some of the water and let him see what it might do to enhance his potions."

Thomas was shocked. "We swore never to share the secret of the water."

Geoffrey shrugged. "It was a unique opportunity. Have no fear – ibn Mayyam will not be revealing any of our affairs. He wrote this– " he tapped the open notebook "–as his final testament, though he did not know it at the time. Do not look at me with such reproach. I left a satisfactory quantity of gold on his widow's doorstep."

He located underneath the working surface a silver spatula and a wooden tube perhaps a foot long and as thick as a thumb. The tube closely surrounded a solid cylinder within. Geoffrey picked up some of the mortar's contents with the spatula. The blob of dark green sparkled with shining points pulsating within the gummy mass. He shoved this into the end of the wooden tube, displacing the cylinder a bit. He took the charged implement to one of the bodies and inserted the tube into the gullet, then shoved on the projecting cylinder, impelling his compounded potion deep into the corpse's throat. He repeated the procedure on a second guest.

"These two seemed the most suitable," Geoffrey said, watching them closely.

Thomas's apprehension and sickness were overwhelmed by a terror the likes of which he could not remember when one of the infused dead began to kick its heels.

The corpse writhed, its hands tightening into fists. Then the other body began to spasm – almost gently at first, then intensifying rapidly until it was bouncing on the table.

Geoffrey smiled broadly. "Two successes. A good day!"

He threaded leather straps through slits in the table and looped them around the animated remains. The two seizing dead men danced horizontally in their flexible cages. They began to moan, mindless awful sounds of something lost and damned.

Thomas's eyes brimmed with tears of rage and fear. Nonetheless he had a burst of clarity: these were monsters, the dead snatched from the abyss against God's clear plan. *What then does that make me?*

He backed unconsciously away from the awful sight, then spun around at a noise behind him. A slight, dull-eyed man moved without inspiration toward the table.

Geoffrey, noticing his presence, slapped the three corpses not treated, and the man nodded slowly and left as dispassionately as he had come.

"Yes," Geoffrey said, seeing Thomas' question on his face. "One of the first useable ones. There were many failures in the beginning, but each batch becomes more capable. I will replace him shortly with one a bit sharper."

The impassive servant reentered the kitchen, empty now but for two drooling, thrashing bodies and three inert lumps of flesh. He showed no sense of kinship with either group but wheeled a low cart to the table and rolled the first limp body onto it.

He pushed the cart slowly out of the kitchen and down a long shallow ramp to a square hole set midway up an outside wall. The opening was covered by a metal grate pivoting on complaining hinges. He tipped the corpse from the cart into the hole, the top of a descending chute, stared blankly at the empty space for a time, then turned to fetch another discard.

The last body fell tumbling and slammed face first into the unyielding icy water. It slowed abruptly on impact, then sank immediately down six feet before reaching a temporary equilibrium of buoyancy. The corpse drifted slowly and rotated a half-turn, its arms floating up as if reaching for the disappeared sky.

Then the head jerked, snapping back and forth.

He knew what was happening, if not exactly where he was. He could remember everything – every sound, and many sights. His eyes had been open the whole time, and the visual memories were clear – until the surface of his orbs had begun to lose their humour and die. The pictures after that were fogged. He knew he had fallen into the sharp frigid water and if he breathed in now he would quickly be truly dead.

In front of him shone a wavering half circle of mottled alabaster. He reached out for it, kicked for it until his head broke the surface. Even with his ruined eyes he discerned the shapes of banks, trees, and the reflections of the moon broken into many pieces on the water.

It was a granite upthrust, bare as a pensioner's head, and inhospitable in the January gusts. But it would have a damn good sight line, so he sharpened his axe and trimmed down the intervening pines and oaks and used them to build a small camouflaged shelter at the top of the formation. He worked at night, and quietly as an axe allowed, often in the snow and always in whistling winter blasts which discovered the most minute passages through his several layers of clothing. When he was done he had an acceptable place to retire from the elements. It would not stand out – he had used a drawknife to remove the bark from the outer side of the logs, and in a few days the color of the wood was approximately the same as the rock. He daubed the seams with mud and moss from the riverbank, wove dense evergreen branches into covers fitting into the door and window, and made his hut almost air tight.

A fire here put up a plume visible for miles, so he denied himself. When the cold became intolerable, he slid down below the crest of the hill where two boulders had edged apart ages before leaving a crevice wide and deep enough for him to stand up and lie down and cache a supply of food in the back, safe from wildlife under a cairn of rocks. Emissions from small fires here diffused through the trees and blended into the frequent fog.

176

By early spring conditions improved. He was able to relax in his blind and watch the mansion through his glass in comfort. On this pleasant April day he had been outside most of the afternoon, soaking up the sun like a lizard, his attention mostly on his business with his mind wandering only occasionally.

Those times when his focus did slip, Ruttee went back to the same topic that had come to the fore of late. He was absorbed in the mental exercise of rethinking his entire life and reason for being on this hard lonely ground.

He had trained from his youth to become one of the Watchers, to go into the world and observe the Giza Mashujaa. He would post reports back to the Father. He would stir the populace against the knights until the people were ripe for tipping into action. When the cabal's debauchery and intrigue became intolerable the Dibele Watchers would transform into catalysts of action and urge the locals to turn against the Giza.

They simply move on, Ruttee thought. We do nothing but annoy them. We lie on the beach and watch the storm clouds gather. We never prevent the deluge or save those drowning in the flood.

He stretched his hands out in front of him. *I have touched a dead Giza. I took great care moving the pieces of his body, but I know his blood touched my skin. I breathed his ash. How has it changed me?*

He was long done ruminating when he saw the wagon. The light was fading, but he was sure this was the one that had visited about every three days for the past fortnight. It approached the house in the same manner and went to the same door. The two men unloaded their cargo and departed as they had. Ruttee knew what came next.

The half-moon was bright enough to show the river and its banks when the bodies began to fall. They went down flopping and lifeless like dolls and splashed into the water to founder slowly and sink out of sight.

What was Geoffrey doing? He was going to some trouble to bring in corpses, hold them for an hour or so, then toss most of them into the Hudson. He kept one or two from each batch. Ruttee could think of no sensible reason, but a few which were dreadful. One of these moonless nights he would have to go down to the mansion and find a way inside. He became permeated by dread at the prospect, but it might be the only way to discover what game the Giza played here. He could waylay the deliverymen on their next trip and try to trick information from them, but they would know only the history of the bodies – Geoffrey was too cautious to reveal his schemes to the help.

He sat up abruptly and scanned the surface of the water. He imagined one of the corpses had moved, deep beneath the surface where it was almost invisible, just a pink smudge under the white lunar paint strokes.

There it was again. It *was* moving – struggling laboriously for the surface. Then the head broke through, arms flailing, and Ruttee was up and tearing down the hill.

April 28, 1778
Yonkers, New York

Major Jeptha Newman of the 1st North Carolina Regiment had endured many olfactory insults in his military career: close-packed unwashed troops, spoiled tins of beef, small pyramids of gangrenous limbs rotting outside the surgeon's tent. The nose, he knew, could grow accustomed to the vilest vapors. But this one – this one drove spikes through his entire being, seized him with two bony clawed fingers thrust into his nostrils and wrenched him up from the blackness.

He saw diffuse light as he struggled to rise up and escape the acrid demon, and as he slowly reclaimed partial sensibility he also became aware every last part of his body was in some degree of agony. He tried to complain but could only summon a weak childlike whine.

"He's back," a wavering voice said in a triumphant cackle.

"I've never known this concoction to fail."

A shadow moved, and the unholy stench attacked his nose again. Jeptha sputtered, then held his breath.

"My master is in your debt, doctor," he heard another voice say – this one deeper, younger. He heard the muted metallic plink of coins dropped onto an open palm.

"Well, boy, you give him this draft three times a day with some rum and hot water, and drop this oil into his eyes–" the older voice hesitated as if he had been reminded of something deeply upsetting. "Though I doubt...."

"Yes, sir, doctor. I will make sure my master follows your directions."

Footsteps went away from the bed, and the older voice said, "You tell your master to start carrying a pistol with him when he is on the road from now on. This fighting has spawned all sorts of Godless behavior."

Newman struggled. He tried to form words, to say there was some mistake. He owned no slave, certainly not this one who claimed to be his, and he did not recall being attacked on the road. A hand clamped around his lower arm and squeezed hard. The pain made him sigh.

"Yes, sir. Thank you, sir."

A door opened and closed. Someone descended stairs. Another door opened and closed below. Silence, a long silence.

Hollow scraping on the floor. A chair probably, yes, because he could feel someone sitting down by the bed. The man leaned down very close to Newman's face.

"Don't move," the stranger said softly, and Newman felt oil dripping. It was wet and soft but hit his eyes like hot skewers. He shut the lids and choked back a scream. He wanted to raise up his aching arms and rub his fists into his eyes. It took all of his will to resist the urge.

"You were dead – or what passed for dead, anyway. Do you remember what happened?"

Newman shook his head as much as he could within the bounds of the pain. A fraction of an inch.

"You were in a wagon with other men. They were actually

179

dead. You were all taken into a house for a while, then you were dropped into the river."

Newman remembered. He could feel his flesh breaking the surface. It had been memorable because he was surprised how hard water became when you fell into it from a distance. He tried to nod, and the nerves screamed at him again.

"Do you remember your name?"

He nodded.

"Good. I will give you the doctor's potion and fetch you some broth when you feel like you can take it. You must lie here quietly and recover your strength – then you can tell me what you know of this."

He knew he had crawled to the surface, desperate to fill his lungs. When the image of the ivory half-moon steadied, no liquid between him and it, he had sucked in sweet air until it felt to burst him from within. Then he blacked out. That was the last of the images he could muster. This voice must belong to the man who pulled him from the water and saved his life. He lifted one hand an inch above the sheet, not knowing what motion he could make to convey his thanks.

The man rose and walked away in the direction of the door. There he stood silent. Newman got the impression he was listening to the stillness of whatever building this was, monitoring to see if there were any strange ears about. He moved quietly again, to where Newman had been aware of a patch of light. The window. Again the man stood for a long time making no sound, then he came back to the bedside.

"I am going to tell you a story. A normal man would reject it as the most outlandish fantasy, but as you now have an intimate acquaintance with it you may be more receptive."

July 18, 1778
Baltimore

Mrs. Fuchs lined the eligible boys up on the shady side of

the rickety brick building, where it was incrementally less inhumanly hot. As she had explained to the man in the humid oppression that was her office this torrid day, the Baltimore Children's Home and Foundling Hospital currently housed, among its other guests, thirteen young men who more-or-less met his parameters. These being a stout constitution, a cheerful disposition, the ability to drive a small wagon, and perfect eyesight.

The man approached the line, shuffling as if he could move only with great concentration and effort, his solicitous Negro close behind. Mrs. Fuchs had not been so impolite as to ask the man about the quality of his vision. She could not see his eyes behind the large tinted lenses of his spectacles but suspected by the way he moved he had only partial vision. This deduction was reinforced by the way the darky moved with his master, muttering observations into his ear.

The man with the dark glasses wanted a youth to travel with him and be his eyes. Perhaps he was going to sell his slave – again Mrs. Fuchs had not asked. She protested such employment would not be as beneficial to the chosen boy in the long term as would his other destiny of entering into an apprenticeship for carpentry or printing or the like when he turned fourteen. The man had put pay to that objection by constructing a stack of gold coins on her desktop.

The man was examining the fifth in the line, a skinny lad of thirteen. They were all skinny, reflected Mrs. Fuchs. The orphanage could not afford to feed children of this age the volume of food it would take to fatten them. At least they were all – so far – standing up straight with some semblance of respect on their damp faces. Maybe she would not have to apply her switch when this exercise was complete. She wished so, as she had overdressed for the afternoon. Her paper fan was abandoned upstairs, it being unprofessional to wave it about during a business transaction. Sweat pooled under her hair and ran down her neck.

The two moved on and stopped in front of a lad even shorter than the rest. He had jet-black hair and skin as pale as flour, and he looked back at them as coolly as the day was not, meeting their eyes without flinching. The slave muttered something to his master.

"What is your name?" the man asked.

The boy fidgeted for an instant, then caught himself. "Nat." He thought about this, then added, "Sir."

Mrs. Fuchs nodded to herself. The switch dodged for now. "Nathanial Quentin Robards," she said. "He is twelve years old, as far as we know. He came into our care two years ago, after his father killed his mother and then himself."

This revelation did not draw any overt emotional response from the boy, something the man and his servant seemed to note. The man took a book from his pocket and held it open in front of him. "Read the first line," he demanded.

Nathanial Quentin Robards' eyes moved on the page, then he said in a rhythm as if it were poetry, "But there is another and greater distinction for which no truly natural or religious reason can be assigned, and that is, the distinction of men into Kings and subjects."

The man closed the book and said, "Can you drive a wagon, Nathanial?"

The boy's shoulders slumped just a bit. "Maybe."

"Come here and put your hands in mine."

The boy took a step forward and put out his arms. The man captured his small fists in his much larger ones.

"Now – try to escape," the man ordered.

Nat hesitated, glancing over at Mrs. Fuchs as if to confirm this was not a beatable offense. When she did not object, he began to twist and turn violently, his torso writhing. He kicked his legs up in as if in some fast dance and gained leverage. The man winced in pain and turned his captive loose. Nat flew out of the restraint, lost his balance, and fell to earth. But he somersaulted backwards and bounced in the same motion to his feet.

Several of the other boys could restrain themselves no longer and began to cheer and hoot. Mrs. Fuchs made a mental list, sighing. Switching on a day like this — she would have to remove her hat and coat.

"He will do," said the man with the dark spectacles.

August 3, 1778
Monticello, Virginia

Jeptha Newman was getting better at surveying his surroundings by supplementing the degraded images available through his damaged eyes with audible clues. Quick echoes of his boot scuffs told him the space he was in this morning was small — much smaller than what he had imagined his host would inhabit. The room, illuminated by two high windows, was jammed with furniture. He detected white rectangles on the dark floor — books left open to a page the reader was interested in revisiting. The windows were without drapery, and the furniture padded in leather rather than cloth, and there did not appear to be any large paintings on the walls. These all contributed to the harsh acoustics. An upright clock ticked and tocked with a ringing, echoing clack and click.

Finally the rustling of a paper as his host lowered the letter of introduction. "Major Newman, I do not have the honor of being personally acquainted with Doctor Trumbull," Thomas Jefferson said. He had a soft high-pitched voice. Newman reflected that before the unfortunate insult to his vision, he might have had trouble making out the man's words, but his ears had sharpened themselves through exercise. "He has been selected as an aide de camp by General Washington, so he must be a worthy military — as well as medical — mind."

"He is," agreed Newman. "And it is in both of those capacities he has sent me here to petition you for help."

He could hear the leather squeaking as Jefferson moved on it. "The Doctor supplies no specifics."

"He desired those details not fall into unfriendly hands. I carry them secure." Newman gestured to his head. "General

Washington – let us be blunt – suffers from certain gastric and digestive problems which often oblige him to be long... ahh... indisposed."

Jefferson made a sympathetic noise. Anyone who traveled much was unhappily accustomed to the convulsive result of tavern fare.

Newman continued, "Doctor Trumbull was referred to one of your servants, a Miss Caroline, who allegedly is skilled in the art of preparing dishes which ameliorate the specific complaint the General is prone to present." He could see the dim shade of Jefferson nodding.

"I do not buy and sell my slaves, as a rule, Major Newman. Miss Caroline was given to me by my friend Pierre Beaumarchais, the esteemed playwright. You have heard of his works, perhaps?"

And Beaumarchais no doubt got her at a fabulous bargain from a slick operator who put the gift into his head by magical suggestion or by hard coin, thought Newman. *The string of ownership surely might be followed all the way back to the band of tricksters from which my new companion hails.*

"Doctor Trumbull knows of your practical management, sir. He suggests you consider this a loan. He has entrusted me with funds sufficient for you to secure a proper replacement." He then named a sum and brought out a leather purse, which he dropped onto the desk.

The hook was set. Of course, the good Doctor had no idea his name was being employed in this ruse, but by the time if ever the two ends of this thread met, the gold would have irreversibly bound this deal by sinking into the plantation's books. Newman guessed Jefferson would expend this sum in a month. It was common knowledge and public record Monticello was perpetually in arrears.

Jefferson made a pleased sound deep in his throat. The great man was assaying the purse with ill-concealed anticipation.

"I have always tried to obey the Commandment which

forbids theft," Newman said. The four were on the road to Richmond and well out of Jefferson-owned land and the hearing of any Jefferson-owned people. "And apart from a few watermelons taken pretty much before I could read Scripture, and leaving out some necessary provisions requisitioned from the populace to supply the 1st North Carolina Regiment, I have done what any reasonable person would have to admit is a passable job of it." Ruttee smiled at Caroline. Something about the recent transaction had ignited the Major's loquacity. "But that bit of bamboozle I just participated in has surely set my accounts before the Lord with a balance due."

"I thought you paid for her," Nat observed. He sat in the driver's seat, reins thick in his tiny hands. The Major perched next to him, and Ruttee and Caroline reclined in the back of the wagon trying to take what comfort might be found on the top of Caroline's two canvas bags of personal effects.

Newman gave the lad a sharp look and tried to remember if the rule about a child being seen and not heard was contained in the Bible. "Indeed I did – with gold of a questionable provenance," he added to the side for the benefit of those behind him. Ruttee shrugged.

The first thing Ruttee had done once the wagon was off of Monticello proper was to tell Caroline why she had been brought bewildered from the main house and told to pack. Submissive and cooperative – yet Ruttee had observed from where he and Nat lay sprawled in the shade under the wagon that she still made note of all, keen to intercept whatever danger this new development represented. When she spotted Ruttee, she made no sign of recognition.

He told Caroline about Junipero and the death of Ordulf. She had him recount the events on the bridge several times, each time concentrating intently on the details of the dismemberment.

"I can scarcely believe it," she said at last. She wondered where Lieutenant Stark was. He would be happy to know the death of Doctor Warren had been avenged.

"Nor could I," agreed Ruttee. "That a knight of the dark

force might be killed – it was unimaginable. But it is so. I gathered the pieces and saw them returned to ash."

He continued, recounting the Major's astonishing escape from the Reaper and laying out what they knew about Geoffrey's plan to create reanimated dead with the power of the water and some Arabian alchemy.

"Ah," she said. "He is raising golems."

Caroline saw every eye upon her. Even the reliable Nat put his faith in the horse and scooted sideways to listen. "There is an ancient text of Hebrew magic," she said, "called the Sefer Yetzifah – which means the Book of Creation. It contains a method of animating clay which has been molded in the shape of a man by writing one of the true and mystical names of God – a manifestation of the essence of God – on a scrap of paper and putting the paper into its throat. The clay rises and becomes a servant to the magician."

Seeing Nat's gobsmacked expression, she added, "The dead Giza was a Saxon, so the Dibele study legends of that land and others nearby." *Watchers may need no more classes in Hebrew*, she decided.

She sat quiet for several miles, digesting this new reality. At last, Newman broke the silence to recount his recollection of the exchanges between the Giza.

"He said, specifically," Newman said, "that the head of the serpent must be removed."

Caroline nodded grimly. Washington was more precious to the American efforts than Jefferson. "How I am to be inserted into the General's household?"

"You are a gift from Jefferson," Ruttee said.

Newman glanced back. "Officers are always short of cooks, especially good cooks. Your kinsman here tells me you are resourceful. You will no doubt make yourself indispensable."

December 11, 1778
Kiev, Russian Empire

Three castaways stared into an inferno. One was melancholy and meditated on lost friends taken by the ocean and the unjust chances of war. The second was inquisitive and contemplated the huge logs combusting in the cavernous fireplace. So much usable board feet within those heavy timbers – under the deep snow this land must be awash in valuable wood. The last one was envious and glanced from the roaring blaze to the white blanket outside and wished he were out there and chilled to the bone in a certain sled rather than comfortably hot in here.

The melancholy one shook himself, shedding sadness like a retriever sheds pond water, and looked up, suddenly animated with anger. "This is imprisonment, not quarantine. I will wager you doubloons to dolphin turds the Koron is back in the Baltic by now, not laid up in Yevpatoria or Bahkshivishi or whatever damned name they are calling that festering shithole this week."

Enoch McCue, ship's carpenter – though at the moment without a ship to carpent – rotated and took one small step backwards toward the fine hardwood being wasted now on warming his bum. "If this is an act put on for our amusement, the sisters are playing their parts convincingly. I have to agree with you – the most leprous prison and your best hospital are not distinguishable. So which are we now occupying?"

"Oh, we are in custody," Joseph Scudman stated. "The threat of plague was a crude ruse. Do you see any of the Koron crew here with us?"

McCue's head wobbled as he tried to nod and shake it at the same time. The four Americans alone had been invited off of their rescuer, bundled into the hold of a small sloop and dispatched to this nunnery outside Kiev.

Ensign Ward was still searching for something out the window. "The British sail in the Black Sea," he said without turning, "and the Mediterranean is thick with them. We were lucky to make it to Yevpatoria without being detected."

Scudman was perturbed. "The British Navy has no right to stop and board a ship of the Empress Catharine."

McCue nodded. Scudman, able seaman on the ship's list, had read the law with an uncle for a year before following the American banner onto the Dauntless. He therefore became the self-appointed spokesman and decider of any and all belowdecks discussions of legality – domestic, foreign, or maritime.

"And yet they do," said Ward. He was the youngest in the room, but the only officer by commission. McCue, a carpenter, was by naval tradition an officer, but his office came via warrant and had no command responsibility. Ward took his charge seriously, though he was only 20, half of the carpenter's age and a decade younger than Scudman. "They might apologize later. That would do us no good should we rot in an actual prison rather than this pretend one."

McCue nodded. Scudman noticed he was cheering for both sides and scowled at him. McCue grinned and said, "Joe, we draw pay for every one of these days under the sisters' dominion. Isn't it right, Mr. Ward?"

"True," Ward said.

"So what is the hurry?" McCue continued. "Are we not treated like honored guests? The Countess provisions her nunnery with food and drink far better than the quartermaster ever allowed the poor doomed Dauntless, or any other ship in his parsimonious grasp. We are warm and dry. There is no plague, or at the least no plague has manifested itself. I see no reason to lament this comfortable fate."

Ward turned to face them at last. "'Tis our duty to make our way back as soon as we are able."

"I would like to do just that," Scudman said. "And I would like to hear your proposal for accomplishing the feat, because I do not think our Lieutenant is out fashioning our escape plan."

Ward reddened but said nothing. It was too true to rebut.

Proctor was with the Countess at this minute, somewhere out there in the perfect ivory countryside, bundled with that beautiful creature.... He sighed.

"Five months we have been idling about here," Scudman pressed on. "I think we should slip away by enlisting in the Russian navy. We drink vodka every day, and we have come to love our borscht. We will easily pass for Russians." He scratched his thick auburn beard for emphasis. "The British will never pick us out." He turned to McCue and said, "Kak pozhivaete?"

The other threw up his hands. "Ive bylo khuzhe" he replied.

"You see?" Scudman said triumphantly.

Moses Proctor, their immediate commander, was indeed not thinking about the fate of his small crew at the moment. He was instead admiring once more the angelic profile of their hostess, the Countess Ekaterina Mergasova, who was tucked in beside him under mounded furs. He had plenty of opportunity to contemplate her handsome face on these rides. The Countess was insatiable in her longing for his descriptive and detailed account of life in the American colonies, as she insisted on calling them. Any other person in the world a prideful Proctor would have corrected, but the Countess could take such liberty with him and he would just beam like a lovestruck fool.

She was especially fascinated by the indigenous peoples of his homeland, so he had wrung his memory to recall the various names of the Indian tribes in and around Cape Ann: the Agawam, the Moswetuset, the Pennacook, and several others. He told her what he knew of their tribal structure, religion, social life, diet, clothing, and relations with the white man. All this history she took in with a delighted smile, which disappeared only during one of her frequent coughing episodes. These were the reason for the excursions – her physician had counseled her that exposure of her lungs to chill dessicated air would harden them against the damp miasmatic air of the city. Taking his advice now that the Russian winter was upon the region, she loaded herself daily into this sled drawn by two black geldings and driven by two burly, hard-faced bodyguards. For several weeks Proctor had been her companion and entertainment, but several weeks had not been enough time for her two servants to cease regarding him with suspicion, a potential threat to be kept constantly under surveillance by one of them as the other held the reins.

Proctor stopped talking, and the Countess turned to look at him.

"I fear I have run dry of facts," he said weakly.

She laughed. "Then you have my permission to invent some – as long as they amuse me."

"I admit I have acquainted you with the more pleasing aspects of the Indians. I have omitted certain of their customs which would offend you."

"Offend me?" She said, taking mock offense. "The late Count loved to regale me with the most gruesome details of his battles with the unholy Turks. The bon sauvage of your colonies cannot have vices more unsettling than those. Are you hiding cannibalism? The sacrifice of virgins? Torture, mutilation?"

The guard not holding the reins narrowed his eyes, bushy black eyebrows almost touching his red cheeks, and glared at Proctor. The gaiety of the Countess' voice as she catalogued potential horrors was lost on the huge bodyguard.

Moses cleared his throat. "Yes, Ma'am. All those may be true... at least, I have heard...."

She laughed and clapped her mittened hands below the furs. "Then why do you want to ever return to such a place? Wouldn't you like to stay here, in a peaceful and civilized land?"

The guard continued to strangle Proctor with a glower, daring him to refuse the Countess' hypothetical.

"Yes... er. No. Please, Countess, I am an officer of the Continental Navy. When we are released, I must return to my duties."

The Countess stopped laughing and inspected him with wonder. "Why do you say *when you are released*, Lieutenant? You are not a prisoner."

Proctor stared at her, his mouth rudely open to the freezing air. He could feel his tongue drying before he recalled his manners and closed his lips. He frantically interrogated his memories. Captain Senyuvin had said there was plague in Spain near where they had loaded the cannon and all aboard the Koron were under quarantine. The four Americans had been dispatched upriver, unloaded on a quay and driven directly to the nunnery on the vast expanse of the Countess's estate. No one had said a word about confinement – or mentioned quarantine again.

"I....," he said. "The plague...?"

The Countess shook her head. "There is rarely a plague. It is just an excuse to make people obey. Admiral Ushakov sent a note asking me if I would be so good as to provide a home for a few displaced Americans, and I agreed. You are free to leave. You have always been free to leave. I believed you were enjoying my hospitality." She seemed hurt by his revelation.

Proctor's head pounded from the daggers of icy air infiltrating under his fur cap and especially from the abrupt realization that he had been shockingly derelict in his duties. He had not demanded of the Countess on the first day she justify their imprisonment. He had been too overwhelmed by her grace and loveliness. And here she had thought them shipwrecked foreign friends enjoying her charitable gifts of soft beds and fattening foods.

He could not even face her now. He was convinced his cheeks burned with shame. *She must think me a thorough dolt – which I am.*

The Countess sighed, and this triggered another round of deep and helpless hacking. Her bodyguards politely turned their heads away. Proctor gazed out over the rolling snow.

"I am being unkind and selfish," she said at last. Proctor turned, a protest on his lips, but she spoke before he could. "I see now I have shackled you with too much kindness, but only because I wanted to know more about your country. I would love to travel there."

"I would be honored to show it to you," Proctor said.

She felt under the furs for his hand and gripped it tightly as another cough seized her.

December 30, 1778
London, England

By the Grace of God, King of Great Britain, France and Ireland, Defender of the Faith, Archtreasurer and Prince-Elector of the Holy Roman Empire, The Duke of Brunswick-Luneburg George William Frederick surveyed his capitol from a hilltop north of the city. The rising sun was just reaching the tips of the sails on the Thames traffic, tinting them marigold and rust as they began to tremble with the waking of their crews. The King heard the clang of cooking pots being dragged into breakfast service. He smelled the greasy smoke thick with ham and bacon. His mouth watered.

This hill, what was its name? Ah. Primrose, he remembered. *I have been here before, but never on such a superb day as this.* He had a walking stick in his hand. He struck it on the grass and began to stride toward London. The path was a road, dirt then stone, and the buildings he passed were sturdy and in good repair.

All he beheld was his. A kingdom of artists and craftsmen, of learned old souls and dashing young adventurers. He was their King, and it was wonderfully fulfilling.

Into the town proper he walked. He thought it noteworthy that he had covered the distance in so little time, but such was the illusory nature of happiness. A woman carrying two buckets of milk spied him and made an ornate curtsey. He nodded regally. On the other side of the street two little boys ran past, hallooing and laughing.

He turned to watch them. He and Edward had run

together just so, once. His little brother had been happy and bright.

The King returned to his journey, but the elation of perfection and fitness had evaporated. *Edward should have been heir to the throne.* George knew they whispered it – all their tutors, coaches, servants. It was Edward, chattering bubbly Edward who seemed born to rule, not his reticent elder.

The breeze turned frosty, and the light lost its hues. Gray clouds rolled over the city. He shivered and hurried on. Head down, navigating by memory, the map unrolling in his mind.

A corner. Familiar and yet curiously not. Alarmed? Should he be alarmed? Where were his guards? Ahead was a palace. He knew it, yet it was unfamiliar. Who had commanded this new palace be erected without his consent? The floor dark and hard, echoing his footsteps and the feeble tapping of his walking stick, now an old man's cane in his shaking hand.

A hallway. Narrow, crushing. The claustrophobia began, his chest throbbing, and he ran, stumbling, fighting heavy boots that would not be directed. Into a huge open space, washed by flat color and hard noise. Servants and courtiers milling about. Diplomats and representatives, all waiting – but not for him. Not a face turned, not a bow made. The fear of the tunnel still choking, he could muster no cry to attract their attention.

A throne. The back to him, the center of all their worship, and he tumbled forward, his legs unable to move. Just one arm left to his will, he reached out and touched the hot golden chair with his fingertips, the pressure enough to turn it as if it were balanced delicately on some clever gimbals, and it rotated to him.

The King!... but this was Geoffrey in the seat of power! Crown and scepter and ermine robe, lording over him with the benign smile of absolute, unquestioned command.

George bolted his eyes open with conscious force, destroying the dream. His bedchamber was beginning to brighten where the rising sun found opportunity between the lush drapes. Knotted sheets wound about him, drawn tight like bonds of punishment and soaked with sweat.

He lay there for an age as the room slowly grew more distinct and regained its daytime colors, his heart by turns skipping and pounding until his imagination believed in the reality of this and not the other and he was able to feel his muscles slowly unclench.

September 10, 1778
Tarrytown NY

"This is where we part," Ruttee said. The fire was not dying, but he rose to put another of their scavenged logs onto it.

Newman nodded. Nat lay on his stomach, chewing on a piece of jerky, toasting the end in the flames every once in a while.

"You return to the watch?"

"Yes," Ruttee agreed.

"I will go home for a time," Newman said.

The new log, a prime piece of old maple, ignited. The reinvigorated blaze reflected hot off their faces; the evening was cold on their backs. Newman sat relaxed against a wagon wheel. "I mean to kill him," he said indifferently.

Both Ruttee and Nat turned to look at him. Ruttee saw a weakened man able to detect only shadows. Nat saw the Major, the hero who had rescued him from Mrs. Fuchs' monotony. Neither doubted he would keep his word.

Newman felt Ruttee's eyes on him. "With your help. Or without. I understand your craft – your calling – is the sentinel. Perhaps you could remember me in a correspondence and let me know where that son of a bitch goes."

"I saw one die. They can be killed, but it will be very dangerous."

Newman, taking this as good as a handshake, rose silently

and took his blanket from the wagon. He wrapped it about himself, stretched out in the fringe of the firelight, and went straight to sleep.

October 2, 1778
Tryon County, North Carolina

He heard them in the pine trees and in the thickets of rhododendron. He would not be able to seen them, of course, even if his eyes were whole, but he might have been able to note stirring branches contradicting the wind or shadows flitting under shining green leaves – as he had once done and would never do again. Now what remained of his eyes registered only the broadest strokes of color, and he protected their tender state behind the dark glass.

"Three men," whispered the youth next to him on the seat. "One behind and two ahead to the right." The quiet words were almost drowned in the intermittent squeal of the springs and the pounding of the wheels against the rocks salting the slimy shallow ditch the locals called a road.

The man nodded, though it could have been just the rough motion of the wagon – the men hiding along their path would be chagrined if they knew a city boy had smoked them. The boy gave the reins a flick as the their horse slowed to eye a particularly menacing hole.

"Steady as she goes," the man said normally, seemingly amused.

As if it were their cue, two men stepped out into the lane, and the youth drew back the reins to check the horse. "Two men in front of us," he said to his passenger. "One is pointing a long musket. The other has a gun with a shorter barrel."

The man with the dark glasses smiled grimly.

"State your business," one of the men growled. To the youth, it sounded something like *Steet yer bidniss* and took him several seconds to decipher. The man with the dark glasses had been born and raised not far from the spot, though, and understood the dialect perfectly even though he now spoke with neutral unaccented authority.

"I am carrying no valuables," he said.

"'At's's not what I–".

A louder voice from the trees cut him off. "Are you a King's man?"

The man with the dark glasses sat very still, seeming to contemplate something in the trees. "What has become of the famous hospitality of the Blue Ridge?"

Silence for a moment, then the voice from the trees again. "We took in too many scorpions lately. Now we like to know who's coming into our parlor. Are you a King's man or are you not?"

"Depends on which one you dislike the most today."

The voice almost laughed. "They take their turns."

"Have the Loyalists been recruiting hereabouts?"

"You don't answer questions very well," the voice said. Then after a pause, "We had some Redcoats come with promises. The others come now and again with their own propositions. Both of them have been told to go to Hell, so I ask you again. King's Man or not?"

"Not," he said, then aside to his driver, "Please describe our two interrogators."

"The one with the long gun has red hair. Curly hair. Freckles all over his face. Short nose, close eyes. I can't make out the color."

The man with the dark glasses nodded. "That will be Beene Wilcox."

"The fellow with the short gun is taller. Thin. Wide nose, bushy eyebrows. Black hair. Got a scar on his chin."

"Joshua Teague, most likely."

These observations did not make the two men any happier. They brought their weapons up suspiciously. "How do you know our names?" demanded Wilcox.

The man in the wagon slowly – as if it were part of a ceremony – doffed his tattered felt hat and held it up at arm's length. "Boys," he said, "I am amazed you fail to recognize your old comrade Jeptha Newman."

The gunmen squinted against the high sun, then lowered their weapons.

"I'll be damned!" cried Wilcox with a wide smile. "It *is* you!"

The other man, Teague, maintained his sour expression. "What t'hell happened to you, Jeptha?"

Newman replaced his hat. "It is a long and unpleasant story. I will tell it to you anon. Perhaps Mr. Rutherford will show himself now I am welcomed home?"

"Been some time," said Rutherford, materialized from the greenery. "Who's the little feller?"

"Nathaniel Quentin Robards is his name," Newman replied. "A natural hand with the horses and a pair of keen eyes for a battered old soldier. Now, if you gentlemen will be so good as to step out of Mr. Robards' way?"

They moved on, past splintering barns and indifferent cows, unpainted shacks, fields carefully tended and fields gone feral, stone fences and rail fences, until they reached the center of the town Newman called Kittlekern. The community consisted of a two-story unpainted store and smithy on one side of the muddy road and a long low wood slat structure bearing no signage on the other. That, Newman told Nat, was the inn and tavern. He did not tell him it was also the whorehouse and the hospital as required, both those uses being disreputable and unfit to mention to a child.

Three miles on, Newman bade Nat to nudge the team off the main road onto an almost invisible track which led over a hill and down into a broad hollow through which flowed a stream too small to be named river and too big to be named creek. They crossed over on a log bridge. On the other side horses grazing in meadows, and they began to pass small outbuildings and free-standing roofs sheltering stacks of hay.

"This is where I grew up," Newman said.

Nat imagined himself here as a child, riding one of those

friendly horses and fishing in the stream instead of spending twelve hours a day separating rags into piles of wool and cotton. "Why did you leave?"

"You recall your Virgil?" Silence told Newman the orphanage had not been strong on classical instruction. "In ancient Rome, the oldest son inherited the estate. The second son went into the Legion, the third into the law. Any more issue had to pick up sticks, I guess. My older brother Danil and his family work this land."

They soon came to the main house and environs – a large barn, a rambling stable with many windows, a chicken coop, several paddocks with whitewashed fences, and a two-story house with an porch on three sides. From all these places streamed the curious of several sizes, and by the time the wagon stopped under a huge chestnut in front of the house the crowd numbered ten. Eight were children aged from about five to fifteen. Two were adult. One man looked to Nat like a rounder, taller version of the Major. This man came up and embraced Newman as he stepped down.

Danil – Nat assumed this was he – greeted them profusely and ushered all into the house, to a table set for dinner. Nat noted there were places already for him and the Major. Somehow the information of their arrival had traveled faster than their wagon.

Nat was placed down the long table approximately according to his height, which had been retarded by nature and an orphanage diet, so he was shoehorned in between two girls younger than he who were quiet through the opening prayer but then began to pepper him with questions, sideways and sotto voce so nobody but the gawking boy on the other side of the table could hear.

Nat was handicapped by his gluttony. The fare under Mrs. Fuchs' husbandry had been spare, mostly potatoes and other root vegetables boiled with chunks of pork fat in which showed the occasional meat fiber like a vein of gold in quartz. Food the Major had purchased on the road had not been much better. The Newmans, on the other hand, served up to their growing flock the bounty of this land. They had potatoes, sure, but also a pitcher of fresh milk, warm bread, biscuits from which a plume of steam rose when halved, tubs of butter, smoked turkey, fried fish, plump sausages, boiled cabbage, and some kind of porridge which tasted like sweet corn. Nat was unable to empty his mouth long enough to answer interrogators coherently. He figured this no loss, as he could barely understand these people, so perhaps they would have the same problem with his accent.

While the girls on Nat's left and right satisfied themselves giggling and kicking his shins under the table, Danil systematically recounted family news and the progress of the farm over the past few years, the time, Nat surmised, which the Major had been absent. The elder brother never once asked about the dark spectacles, which his brother did not remove at the table, nor the several scars. Nat did not know if those marks had been there the last time the two had seen each other or not. The eyes, though – he had overheard the slave Ruttee and the Major talking about the treatment of them as if the injury was recent.

Mrs. Newman sat less than she hovered, refreshing plates. She had an oval face and prominent nose – features reflected in the older children. Nat thought her the most beautiful woman he had seen since his own mother. She patted him maternally on the head as she passed, probably out of habit. Nat stopped chewing, as he suddenly had to set his face sternly to suppress tears. The girl on his left jabbed her toe into his calf and tittered, which helped restore his equilibrium.

After the dessert, a baked dish of apple slices with a sweet crunchy top that Nat's eyes followed from kitchen door to table like it was the Ark of the Covenant borne by rural cherubim, the company dispersed. Danil called for a pitcher of persimmon beer, and he and his brother went out to the porch. Nat wondered if he was to follow or if his fate was to be cast into this pool of energized children. He slipped outside.

Danil and Jeptha rocked in twisty-willow chairs, a table between them holding a stoneware pitcher and two pewter mugs. Nat hugged the wall and skittered invisibly sideways so he not be ordered away. He stopped a little ways off and dropped to the floor, then noticed pairs of eyes peeking up at him from between gaps in the boards and heard suppressed laughter. There were no secrets in this place.

"...near a place they called Whitemarsh, in Pennsylvania colony," the Major said, "although it was no marsh that day – all solid, frozen as hard as stone, and us nearly. The Regiment had moved north the previous winter, a mild one here, as you will recall. Few of us had brought necessaries for the brutal cold Nature delivers there."

His brother did not interject but reached over and topped up both mugs.

"I marched my company to the far right flank before the Colonel who sent us received a dispatch noting the flank itself had wheeled about. We snuck through the trees and emerged right into the middle of the British line. Fifty men faced two thousand." He took a drink and held it for a long time on his tongue before allowing it down. "We fired one volley for our honor, and of course the enemy fired one for theirs. Theirs did more damage."

He stopped, facing into the distance, brow furrowed.

"What was left of us was taken aboard a prison ship in New York harbor. I was ill with some fever rendering me so much like a corpse that one morning they tossed me overboard. The cold water revived me – and here I am."

Danil raised his mug. "Praise God for His merciful hand."

The Major nodded and returned the toast. The story was ended.

"Brother," Danil began in a hesitant tone. "As I said, I lately purchased some acres bordering our western fields and planted them in tobacco, which is in great demand. Our beef and pork fetches the highest price I have ever seen. We have enough and more. There is room now that you might build yourself a house and take a wife."

Jeptha seemed to deliberate the hypothetical arrangement. Nat was stung with fear. A wife would certainly send him packing back to the orphanage – far from the hot bread and cool butter he had on his plate only several minutes ago.

Finally the Major said, "I hear in your voice you have already identified the possibilities."

Danil chuckled. "I have. The Widow Legett asks after you almost every Sunday. She owns five hundred well-drained acres."

Jeptha whistled – the first frivolous sound Nat had ever heard issue from the man. "The late Mr. Legett was industrious. He had only one hundred last I knew him. How many children would I inherit?"

"Three. Two strong boys and an clever girl."

Nat could feel the icy drafts of the Baltimore institution on his skin – sure as sunrise. He was doomed.

"I appreciate your intelligence, brother," the Major said. "And I may yet take advantage of the opportunity – after I have concluded one last campaign."

Danil looked incredulous. "Forgive my presumption, but are your eyes fit for such an enterprise?"

"They are not, but what I mean to do is of a personal nature."

"Thank God for that. Can I assist you in any way?"

Jeptha shook his head. "No, but if you would be so good as to let Nat and I inhabit one of the cabins, I should like to let my body rest from its recent depredations."

"Join us in the house, Jeptha."

"You are too kind. One of the outer cabins would be ideal. You remember my nocturnal habits. Nowadays I find myself up late into the night studying on coming events, and I do not wish to disturb the order here."

Danil shrugged his assent. "Shall I alert the Widow Legett?"

Nat saw a rare smile on the Major's face. "Five hundred acres, you say? I don't see why we cannot indulge an old friend."

February 11, 1779
Passy, France

The citizens of Passy knew they were superior in all ways to their Parisian neighbors. The streets of Passy, they declaimed, were wider, in better repair, and covered with far less shite than those in Paris. The buildings of Passy were painted from a more discerning palette. The sun shone more brightly in Passy. The air did not always reek of piss. Every detail of city life was preferable in Passy. Of course, the people of Passy were paramount as well. It stood to reason. They were smarter and more attractive. The inhabitants of Passy constantly wondered aloud how much improved life was compared to the unfortunates of Paris, though the two communities were separated only by the one or two hundred meter width – depending on where one chose to measure – of the Seine, which snaked between them.

These conceits all occurred to the scholar as he leaned on the balustrade, gazing out over the river and sucking on a red clay pipe. Under his arm was tucked a copy of Voltaire's Dictionnaire philosophique disguised in an old cover sliced off an Te Deum nicked from the Temple du Marais. Hiding the banned work in the skin of a sacred musical seemed to the scholar a proper nose-thumbing to the decadent clerical pigs all right-minded thinkers detested.

Across the river and upstream milled a small crowd of boys. They were not dressed in rags but in respectable short coats against the raw afternoon. The scholar guessed they were on recess from one of the minor Parisian academes, which were not to the standards of the learned institutions of Passy. The boys stared down at a barge making its way slowly down the Seine. The vessel undulated awkwardly under its load of barrels and livestock – normal trade stuff seen every day on the river. What attracted the attention of the boys was four figures standing in the bows forward of the sheep and goats. Four bearded men dressed in long coats and strange, tall hats of dark glistening fur.

The scholar smiled. Russians. He heard the boys call out at the men as the barge passed beneath. The youths waved and hollered and made rude noises. The four Russians glanced up at the high bank and ignored all entreaties to respond.

Cossacks, no doubt, the scholar thought excitedly, and once the barge had come close enough, he called out "Dobroye utro!" The men turned their bearded, fierce faces up to him, unsmiling. Finally one raised his hand and replied "Davay pazshe nimsya!" The scholar nodded and waved his pipe, pleased with his worldly knowledge.

The vessel steered close to the Passy side, toward a narrow wharf. The boatmen hurled rope lassos around stanchions fastened to the structure and heaved hard to drain their craft's momentum. The barge crabbed sideways, struck the wharf hard, then stilled. She rocked hard as her own wake caught up, yet the four Russians jumped nimbly off.

They trooped in formation up some stone stairs to the street, where the scholar watched them from a distance. Suddenly, he hoped they would not come his way and expose his lack of any more of their language, but one Cossack produced a piece of paper from his pocket, consulted it, and waved a hand in the opposite direction.

The hirsute band arrived eventually at a blocky white house enclosed by a stone fence. They marched through an unlocked gate and knocked on the blue door, which was opened after a time by a cadaverous man who peered at them down the impressive length of his nose.

"I am Lieutenant Moses Proctor of the Continental Navy," the Cossack in front said. "We wish to see Mr. Franklin."

The servant reviewed each of the supplicants in turn, then said in a thick French accent, "Which Mr. Franklin shall I notify?"

Proctor fantasized briefly about knocking the old fellow right on his obstructionist ass but held his temper. "Benjamin Franklin, if you please. I did not know there was more than one about."

"So it appears," the other said carefully. He began to close the door. "Please wait here."

The sky blue portal slammed in their faces. The four looked at each other. "I propose we kick it right in," said Scudman, "and set to teaching them their manners."

A lesson was not necessary. They heard excited voices beyond the door, then it swung in, showing them a scrawny young man in a violet suit and powdered wig who waved them to enter.

"I am William Temple Franklin," he said, "my grandfather's secretary. Please come in – you are all Americans?" He scrutinized them doubtfully, but Proctor set him to ease by introducing his shipmates.

"I need to speak with Mr. Franklin," Proctor said when he had finished.

The other Mr. Franklin nodded. "Certainly. He is always happy to receive our countrymen, but at the moment he is conferring with a most prestigious delegation from the Royal Army." He led them down an ample corridor, past a room filled by men of varied station, judging from their dress, who eyed them – some anxiously, some jealously.

"It may be some time," young Franklin continued. "You see we are besieged with callers, as seems to happen most days. Every person in France who has an idea about a novel weapon to use against the British or an obscure strategy to secure victories over the Redcoats comes to petition my grandfather for funds to develop their ideas. Some come to offer their services as Governor of a State, based on experience in the French colonies. Some want to sell us blankets, or shoes, or dice. Others want a piece of the free land rumored to be available in America upon application." He dropped his voice. "And a few are probably spies."

They arrived at a smaller room, this one deserted. Franklin herded them in and closed the door behind him. "I shall go and whisper into my grandfather's ear when it is appropriate, but I do not expect the meeting to be concluded until late this afternoon. I shall have refreshments brought."

"You are very kind," Proctor said. "Just please relate to Mr. Franklin that I and my shipmates were saved by Isaac Stark's use of Caroline's water."

William's eyes narrowed just perceptibly. Proctor could tell he wanted a less obtuse message to pass along, but the young man just made a terse bow and went out of the room.

"Why didn't you tell him how far we have come to see him?" Ward asked after trying to control his exasperation.

Scudman reached out and caressed the embossed cerulean and cream paper on the wall. "Because the High Mr. Franklin is de facto Ambassador to the French Court, is why. Because he ain't got to care much about some castaways which washes up on his doorstep, is why."

This opinion quickly proved in error. Only a short time after they had entered the room, they heard doors creaking open and banging shut and many men speaking French all at once. Above them all was the voice of a different man whose French, Proctor judged even with his limited grasp of the language, was spoken with confidence but wandered off the mark from sentence to sentence. This lone voice made apologies; the many other voices protested their business was not concluded. Arguing and confused footsteps faded into the distance, then one set pounded back.

Ben Franklin tore the door open and stepped breathlessly into the room. "Tell me!" he demanded.

Proctor made the introductions again. The four needed no naming of their host – his identity was unmistakable. He had barely patience enough to tolerate Proctor's good manners and flapped his hands during the niceties.

"Tell me about Stark," Franklin said abruptly.

So Proctor told the story. He began with what Stark had said as he lay dying in that blowing desolate night on the Atlantic, of Caroline and her tribe and the gift of an amulet filled with some manner of occult fluid. He described the battle with the dark ship, the sinking of the Dauntless, their rescue by the Russian Navy and how the four Americans had helped the

Russians put ashore their load of furs in Valencia and muscle aboard six cannons.

"The Koron's mission was to hide these cannon in a cache under an inaccessible cliff along the Black Sea coast for use if the expected difficulties with the Turks should arise. After we had worked our damndest for them, they sent us up the Dnieper stowed away in the hold of a riverboat, under the pretense there had been a plague in Spain and so we must be quarantined. We suspect the hypothetical plague was an invention to remove us diplomatically from the scene. The Russians did not want us about, spilling their secret."

He related how they had been taken in by the kindly Countess Mergasova, who, when the weather had improved, outfitted them and funded their overland journey back to Paris. He did not volunteer the information that, due to his shameful dereliction of duty in not immediately establishing their exact status, they had lingered in Kiev eating sautéed wild boar and drinking French wines while their fellow countrymen suffered on land and sea.

Franklin did not seem to care much about the comfort of their absence. He asked Proctor, and then each of the other three, to retell their memories of the appearance and subsequent battle with the dark ship. He interrupted them with many questions, most of which they could not answer. It took almost two hours to finish this interrogation, during which time the same servant who had been unimpressed with their appearance at the front door delivered brandy and some petit fours.

Finally Franklin had no more to ask. The five sat around a polished, japanned table; four clogged with sweats and saturated with drink. Franklin the younger was presumably busy assuaging the needs of the petitioners in the rest of the house. Ben was suddenly less the energetic diplomat and more an exhausted septuagenarian. "Gentlemen," he said, rising laboriously, "I appreciate the effort you have made to bring me this news, and I congratulate you again on your survival of that most horrible encounter." He paused. "I have much to think about, and much to arrange if you want to be returned to America. In the meantime, I invite you to stay at a chateau a member of the Royal court has made available to me. William will fetch the carriage. Please rest there for a few days until I send for you." He made a small bow and went out of the room.

"Well, well, well," Scudman muttered. "A royal chateau. Every country we visit, they at least manage to stuff us into the most interesting brigs."

June 29, 1779
New York State

The mountain had been carved neatly in two, the other portion taken away to wherever God takes half mountains. Thomas stood at what remained of its peak. He leaned forward and gazed straight down, a thousand feet of nothing between him and the sharp rubble the Almighty forgot. Yet strangely he was not afraid.

I have worn out every emotion. Put on too often until threadbare. I barely recall having true fear. Or anger. Or love.

Blue sky above behind schools of flat clouds. The air moved inconstantly. On this day he was not trying to hide. He expanded his lungs once more and roared, almost a scream – calling for his wives and for his children. This open use of their real names was Osuanee blasphemy, but too much of him knew no one would hear.

He cupped his hands to bellow again and saw on the back of his right hand a spot, the size of a fingernail and darker than the surrounding skin. He had stopped taking the water – was this the beginning of his true age emerging from an unholy preserved skin? He did not shout after all, but looked again at the great drop and the huge serrated rocks directly below. He could step off. This minute, and be done with it all. He would vanish from history, as he should have five centuries past.

His eyes roamed the tops of the trees below, his mind trapped in a maelstrom of doubt and sadness, and he saw lower leaves moving in contradictory patterns. He focused on the disturbance. Perhaps the wind swirled down there. He studied the sway of the branches until he was sure.

With a hunter's instinct, he dropped to one knee, reasoning it must be a bear or deer, but a human figure broke from the brush. Thomas threw himself flat against the rock, leaving only his eyes and brow exposed over the ridge.

He could not see faces from this distance – only form and gait. The man bent, scouring the ground. A tracker? This place was remote, but trappers ventured far in search of the dwindling beaver. Perhaps the stranger had heard his incautious screams – no, Thomas decided. The man came from upwind.

Another appeared some way behind the first, and Thomas' pulse raced. He filled with a white-hot anger, which in a strange way reassured him. His humours might be decrepit, but there was passionate fury in his breast.

The second man – or being – lurching awkwardly down there could be nothing other than one of Geoffrey's revivals. Thomas was certain even from this distance, and thinking about being followed by one of those unholy creations intensified his rage until he had to roll onto his back and take deep breaths to calm himself.

They were climbing up the way he had come. He visualized the path, then jumped up and began to run sliding down the tree-jammed slope.

There was one feature he was racing for – a place where a rock ledge jutted up higher than his head. A path led through a broken gap as wide as stretched arms could reach. He had seen tracks of several animals converging on this natural chokepoint.

Thomas lay down behind a stunted pine about twenty paces off and scooted forward under the camouflaging foliage. He checked the pan of his musket and tried by will to moderate his galloping heart.

Birds whistled staccato arias to mark their territory. Somewhere far away an animal wailed in pain. Nothing sounded from over the rock.

Then the man padded through the gap. Silently as an Indian but not an Indian, he unwisely read the traces instead of checking for muskets protruding from branches.

Thomas laid the line of his barrel on the man's chest. He could hear Geoffrey in his head. *Chivalry*, the old knight was fond of saying, *is praise they carve on the loser's headstone.*

He pulled the trigger.

The report boomed out across the quiet hillside, and the air filled with gray-black smoke. Thomas saw in the corner of his eye a flock of small golden birds bolt from a tree, but he could not hear them for the ringing in his ears. He scrambled to his feet, drawing out his pistol as he ran to the downed man.

The unlucky stranger lay writhing on his back, clutching at his neck. Blood spurted from the wound and gushed in thick crimson flows from his mouth. He tried to speak but produced only a grisly froth.

Thomas pointed the pistol at the dying man's head but could not bring himself to interrogate him. It did not matter, really – the man would not answer, could not answer. He began to convulse, a ghastly volume of blood pumping rapidly out into the growing pool underneath him.

A garbled shriek snapped Thomas' head up. *I am distracted and stupid and it will kill me yet.*

The creature had come at last through the gap. It charged, gripping a knife-pointed pike, and as it lurched toward him Thomas had time to wonder if Geoffrey was afraid to give his creations firearms or if they were yet too clumsy to load and aim. He raised his pistol and fired, but he had hurried. The ball went wide. The thing did not slow.

Thomas's sword was in his hand and instincts took over. He feinted to the right and stepped to the left, deflecting the point of the pike safely past. Then he drove his sword into the creature's abdomen.

The being staggered, and Thomas kicked its near leg out

from under it. It tumbled backwards, but Thomas did not wait to see if the thing would rise. He snapped up the pike and drove it down through the ribcage, throwing all his weight into the thrust.

He held the pike in place and looked back at the human, who lay unmoving, eyes open and unfocussed. The stuck creature continued to spasm. Thomas wondered how long the power of the water would animate the once-dead flesh.

He wished his first shot had not been so mortally accurate. He had questions and now no one to ask. Would Geoffrey wonder where his searcher and his creation had gone? It did not matter – they would be just two more swallowed by the wilderness.

Thomas gathered his guns and stripped the corpse of useful items. Geoffrey's creation still seized from time to time. He briefly considered reloading his pistol. If it had been a dog or a horse he would have ended its misery. Ultimately, he turned to the gap and walked away.

October 20, 1779
Kittlekern, North Carolina

The little enclave – it was too tiny to deserve the appellation hamlet or village, much less town – of Kittlekern had been named after the two otherwise long-forgotten pioneers Kittle and Kern. Or else it was a corruption of a word local savages had used to describe the region. The second hypothesis was as unprovable as the first, the tribe in question having been wiped thoroughly out by the founders of Kittlekern. Now there were no Indians to corroborate or rebut either legend.

The crossroads it barely straddled had for one brief glorious moment some decades before been notorious following the discovery of gold in a small Appalachian valley nearby. Impatient hordes rushed through Kittlekern on their way to fortune, stopping only long enough to snap up the available picks, shovels, flour, and pork belly and pay outrageous prices to the local profiteers.

That had also been the pinnacle of the whorehouse business. The structure pointed out to Nat as the inn and tavern once was the heart of the community – and as a proper heart, palpitated round the clock. When the sun shone, thirsty travelers crowded the tavern, and the rooms out back were in full passionate occupation. At night, poker games ground on to piano music, and the rooms out back rumbled with the snores of opportunists dreaming of tomorrow's nuggets.

Presently there were no ladies for hire in residence, and if the odd rambler wanted a pint or, God forbid, a bed they were to apply at the smithy across the road. The proprietor of that concern would send his son on horseback to fetch the man who possessed the key to the front door.

Major Newman did not need a key. He had come in through the kitchen, which was never locked, and hung his dripping overcoat and hat by the cold fireplace. It was raining like the twentieth day of Moses' cruise, so instead of conducting business in some private hollow he had put out the word to meet at the tavern.

"Build us a fire, Nat," he requested. He went behind the bar and lifted a pony keg onto the counter. There were mugs shelved on the wall, probably clean enough. His eyes had not healed over the last year, but he could discern mugs from pitchers – if he was close enough. He had resigned himself to never again telling pewter from clay. Luckily, that talent wasn't of interest to Penelope Legett.

Nat stripped his sopping gear and set about fetching wood from the attached shed. He had grown six inches in the past year and was the same height as the Major, but he was still a stick. What muscle he had, however, was hard as any adult's from working both the Newman land and occasionally the Legett. He easily carried in an armload of oak logs his orphanage body would not have been able to lift off the ground.

The fire was just catching when two men burst in cursing and stomping. Beene Wilcox went directly to the fire; Joshua Teague put his elbows on the bar and watched Newman pry the bung from the cask. Four mugs were filled from the tap and arranged in a row.

Nat silently counted the mugs and the men. Newman said, "This ain't Sunday school. Drink up, son." Nat hopped onto one of the stools and took a sip. He had drunk beer before, despite the Major's dry jest. This brew was dark and bittersweet. Teague liked it – he had finished his already.

Wilcox ambled over and hoisted his portion. "You want to start your spiel, Major?"

"We are waiting for one more," Newman said and took a drink.

"Rutherford?" Wilcox asked.

Newman shook his head. "Alexander has a young family. You two do not."

Teague's head came up. "You got something dangerous in mind?"

"Would it deter you?"

"Never has before," Teague said. "Depending on the pay, of course."

"Of course," Newman agreed.

"Who's missing, then?"

Nat cocked his head. Another set of squishing footfalls. The door from the kitchen filled with a huge figure, and all eyes turned to it.

"Filly?" Teague strangled disbelief. Nat saw Teague and Wilcox exchange a concerned glance. The Major motioned the newcomer to join them. The big man sat down next to Nat and accepted a mug. Nat looked him over closely, but he could see nothing to cause the men's reaction – other than sheer size. The new fellow's bulk eclipsed Nat, but his face was pleasant and unmarked.

"Nat," Major Newman said, "this is Filly Buckminster."

Filly squinted down at Nat but did not extend a hand or even nod. Nat smiled and got nothing in return, so he returned his attention to the waning foam on his beer.

"Not that I want to go back out in this," Teague said nodding toward the deluge, "but I am itching to hear your proposition."

Newman nodded. He sat his mug down carefully. "I mean to kill a man."

Teague shrugged. Wilcox reached over and refilled his mug.

"And you need us because of your eyes?"

"No," Newman said. "I need you because he may not be a man."

This got even Filly's attention.

"He may be some kind of warlock. I don't know. I do know he will not be easy to kill."

Teague pointed at the Major's face. "Is it the fellow who did that to you?"

Newman nodded curtly. "But it is not – altogether – my motive. I wish to kill him because he is a supporter of King George and has powers which ought not be used against us."

Teague and Wilcox shared another look. "This sounds like a recruiter's pitch," Teague said. "We've already heard enough of those." He made a motion as if to rise.

Newman put out a hand. "Stay. I am not under commission. I propose to hire you as private citizens."

"That so?" Wilcox said. "It's a good thing, then. I hear colonial salaries are a few months tardy."

"I do not pay in paper." Newman said. "This job will be too dangerous. I will provide for your food, lodging, equipment and transportation – and give each of you three hundred Spanish silver dollars upon completion of the task."

Again Teague and Wilcox consulted wordlessly. Nat tried to decipher their faces but could not.

"Major, if near any other man was making that promise, I would call him a liar.... You ain't never been known to lie." Teague relaxed and lifted his beer.

"I am a God-fearing man," Wilcox said. "And I know my Scripture, having had it beaten into me pretty regular. I recall

213

the Lord being down on witches. Seems to me such would cover warlocks."

Teague nodded. "When do we start?"

November 28, 1779
Paris

The massive roots of the Louvre Palace ran deep. One part of Benjamin Franklin's mind pondered the fact. He had explored every room, chamber, cellar, and crevice in the sprawling structure, and though the simple majesty of the newer wings and pavilions put up by several recent monarchs made the central plaza the natural focus, he was more impressed by the substance of the ancient foundation. The huge volume of rock holding up the modern Palace had seemed ice cold on the blistering summer day he first descended into the bowels of the building. On a bitter winter's day like today he knew the atmosphere down next to the ancient walls remained comfortable. His old friend Professor Black of Glasgow lectured on the ability of elements to take up and dispense heat each according to its own nature. Black would say the foundation was a mass with a gigantic heat capacity. Its nature was slow to warm and slow to let go of its warmness, like Spanish houses constructed of thick adobe bricks which held the heat of day into cold night and held the cool of night into torrid afternoon.

His thoughts ran to heat and the theory of heat because it was damned frigid in this tiny workspace in the Louvre Palace. He labored too far from the moderating rock below and too close to the many large, drafty windows favored by French architects. This had been a storage pigeonhole off of the main rooms occupied by the Académie des Sciences. Lavoisier suggested Franklin clear it out and use it as a shop, and the two of them had removed their coats and personally made it habitable, Lavoisier even lending his friend a compact but efficient forge. That forge was at the moment filled with coke glowing a dull red, not because he needed to work any great quantity of metal, but to keep the space habitable. Franklin wished at least one of the Kings who had applied their layman's conceit to the design of the several parts of the Palace had consulted with a living natural philospher or a dead Roman engineer. The place needed central heating, a hypocaust at the minimum. The French system of huge fireplaces was, in Franklin's opinion, hugely wasteful of wood and labor and only served to cool the parts of the interior not immediately in front of a blaze. *If God grants me years, and the King forgoes his iron grasp on tradition, I should like to install my stoves throughout this Palace. And perhaps then a system of privy pits so my learned colleagues do not have to squat in the corridors.*

He had on the table in front of him several tiles of mirror, cut by his own hand from the looking glass that had focused and passed the electrical fluid that horrible night. The ponderous sheet would be there still, safe in its beautiful old frame, tucked into a corner and on its long journey to antiquity, had he not tripped.

Chaumont had found him cradling what remained of his beloved Nicole. Jacques gently removed the dried and twisted thing from his lap and helped Ben to his feet, where he tottered for a second. He lost his balance, slipped from his friend's grasp, and stumbled into the mirror. Franklin gripped it to regain his equilibrium and in the process glanced through the aged glass.

What he saw made vitality surge through him. All grief fled into dark corners. He moved his head away to confirm what was visible by the Chaumont's single candle, then swung back to peer again at the horrible shimmering image filtered through the imperfect metal layer. The silvering, tarnished and thinned by the years, had been transmuted in some manner by the bolt of energy passed to and through his lover's body. Naked and shivering, he yet concentrated only on his hypothesis: some sympathetic harmony had established between the power of whatever Nicole had been given to regenerate her body and the electrical fluid from his cranked generator – and the glass was now imbued with a sort of memory of the water which had sustained Nicole's perfection.

Tapping one of the squares, he forced the image of her perfect nudity from his mind. He had mounted one of his lens cutters, a simple tool of his own design, on the table. A wooden arm floated above the surface. At the end of the horizontal arm was fixed a vertical rod. A screw handle was bolted to the top of the rod, and at the bottom of the rod another, smaller arm secured a piece of hardened clay set with a tiny diamond. Franklin took the handle and pushed down so the diamond tip touched the glass, then rotated the mechanism once. The glass received a perfect scored circle, which he liberated by the application of tangential lines via a hand-held scratching tool, followed by careful pressure to snap the glass at the scores.

He pinched the resulting circle and polished the edges on a hard leather square dusted with corundum to remove any sharpness. Scooting his stool closer to the comfortable glow of the furnace, he wrapped two finished circles with a circumference of black metal ribbon and plucked a glowing brazing iron from the coals.

Three miles away, Moses Proctor and William Franklin approached the city in a shaking coach. Proctor was well bundled against the biting wind whistling unchecked through the ill-fitted windows. He wore wool stockings rolled on the outside of his boots, his long beaver coat which the Countess had presented him, thick felt mittens, and a dingy woven hat pulled down over his head and eyes. He had on five distinct layers of clothing, but he still froze. It certainly did not help that he was groggy. Not from actual grog, however, but from the innumerable bottles of wine uncorked last night for him and his mates by a hospitable group of boisterous Frenchmen at a musty hole in the wall called le Grande Taverne de Nanteuil-le-Haudouin. Such excess had been their habit in the last several weeks, from vodka and sweet Saparavi in Russia to

Burgundy and brandy in France. The wine flowed here in a copious volume. Any venue where the four Americans appeared turned swiftly into a raucous celebration of French-American solidarity as locals packed into the establishment. Proctor had not had to put his hand into his purse at any time during his stay at the Chateau de Flaux outside the village of Mauregard, nor had he to suffer many lonely nights under his plush down comforter. It turned out French spoken haltingly in a New England accent was a powerful aphrodisiac to the lasses of this parish.

The coach hit a rut remarkably deeper than the normal and levitated Proctor off the seat an inch or so. He suppressed a groan of pain and peered out from under his cap at his companion.

Franklin had picked him up with a terse command summoning him to an audience with his grandfather, then spent the ride in silence. Which was acceptable to the fuzzy-headed Moses, who would gladly have napped the whole way, ruts or no ruts. He didn't particularly care for the younger Franklin. The callow young man was a fop with an annoying habit of tilting his head back just enough so he actually looked down his nose at you. Moses guessed he had never suffered an honest day of labor in his life, born as he had been to an elevated station. William Franklin wanted a week or two crewing a fishing schooner, Moses decided, and he burrowed down into his coat and tried to drift off. Franklin turned his head away from his contemplation of the desiccated landscape.

"I beg you," William said, "whatever my grandfather wants of you – please placate him. Agree to do whatever he asks."

Proctor opened his eyes reluctantly. "Why would I not?"

Franklin shrugged.

"He has been arranging our return to America." Moses yawned politely behind one hand. "I expect he has details of the journey to discuss."

Franklin became suddenly occupied in the minute inspection of his right shoe. Moses, a faint alarm attempting to

217

gain the surface of his thickened mind, sat up straighter on the uncomfortable boards.

"He has not," Franklin said almost with shame, "been arranging your return."

"I don't understand. He–"

"I am his secretary," William interrupted. "I make all arrangements and handle all business so he is free to talk and think. I have no ship for you, nor have I heard of any being readied. Yes, he had been busy, true, but he is busy with some kind of craft. Making mechanical devices for his natural philosophy." Franklin spoke the words 'natural philosophy' as though they were blasphemous.

Moses glared at the young man. "But your grandfather is well-known for his interest in the subject. He is famous in many quarters for his discoveries. Honored for them, I judge, and part of the reason why this country loves him."

Franklin breathed out a plume of steam. "He had a mistress. Such is not unusual in these quarters, and not unusual for my grandfather, as you must know. But this one seemed different. She was captivating, intelligent, charming – in her company he seemed more at ease than I had ever known. She disappeared some time ago, perhaps returned to her husband's bed, and since then he has been in a state I find, frankly, disturbing. You have just made his acquaintance, so of course you have no reference, but I do. Others among his friends have made discrete allusions to see if I would volunteer some reason, but I have no explanation to offer them."

Proctor had no opinion on the matter and was in too much discomfort to care. Franklin took his silence as interest.

"He thinks I do not notice, or perhaps he is beyond caring of it. He purchased a musket and keeps it loaded by his bedside. Sometimes I surprise him in the act of scowling at nothing. Lieutenant, believe me – my grandfather has many faults, but blood lust had never to my knowledge been among them. So I beg you again to humor him."

The very idea of this callow popinjay plotting to neuter the great man's interactions gave Proctor the inspiration to seize the lad by the shiny seat of his silk britches and fling him out the window, but the conversation was making his head throb again. So instead Proctor pretended to be asleep. Franklin fell silent, his attention again on the winter landscape of the Parisian suburbs.

Proctor was nudged awake and deposited on the Quai du Louvre, facing the river and with Franklin the Younger's directions to Franklin the Elder rammed painfully into his sensitive ears. He was to go through the Gate of Something and look for the Tabernacle of Someone. Commerce on the river was brisk. Small rowed boats, heeling scows, and enormous barges passed up and down, their masters calling and swearing. Crewmen of craft still at anchor leaned over the sides with poles, thrusting to break up the night's encircling ice.

He turned around. The gigantic structure on the other side of the quai was busy with Parisians. A score lined up awaiting entrance into a central doorway while others came out in spurts of twos and threes. He crossed the stone-paved way, starting and stopping to avoid carts and horses, to join the line. More quickly than expected he was granted entry to an expansive enclosed square, its walls tawny three-story wings bordering four-story pavilions, all decorated with elaborate carvings. The wind outside had been biting. Inside this topless huge box the moving air split into small vortexes pummeling Moses in turn as he crossed. He heard scattered bits of conversation carried past him on the gusts. The high walls blocked the low sun, and it felt colder here than along the river.

He asked a man where the wing named Lemercier might be found and followed the indicating finger past a drained fountain.

As he transited the icy square, he saw peppered in among chattering Frenchmen plenty of citizens of other and distant lands – Scandanavians of several flavors, true Russians, some Ottomans, turbaned Indians.

Moses entered the Lemercier and discovered what had

drawn such travelers. The walls of the great gallery were shingled with paintings, splashes of intense colors cradled in spectacular gilded frames. He halted in the middle and pivoted about. There were voluptuous nudes, battle scenes, hunts, saints, depictions of Jesus and his torments, Jesus and his Mother, Jesus generally being Jesus. In front of these works clusters of visitors paused in awed reverence. Below some squatted students with folios open, copying in charcoal or watercolor. Hushed discussions came to him from each wall – explanations and observations, many in French and many more in languages unknown to him.

He was embarrassed he could not definitely assign a single work to a specific master, though he could recognize the signs of the Dutch school, the Italian Renaissance gang, and some he thought Spanish. Others he had no idea, and he felt like a simple bumpkin who had just ridden a dairy cow into town.

He exited that place into its antithesis, a confined dim hallway reeking of urine and shit. He waited a minute to let his eyes and nose adjust, then walked on, stepping carefully over dark pools and lumps. The next door opened onto another impressive space, this one jammed full of marble, bronze, and stone statues. They seemed to him in no particular order and arranged with no noticable care as to their preservation. Greek gods leaned up against Egyptian pharoahs, and at the base of one huge alabaster nude a drunken Frenchman sprawled. He was of high birth, according to the quality of his silk stockings and satin-lined jacket. Proctor mused the coating of vomit on his chin and pumps contained the remnants of a meal such as the common folk would not see even on high holy days. He moved on, not disturbing the snoring noble.

He smelled the next room before he came to it and was yanked back to sea by the odors. He peeked into the space and saw a class of youths daubing on canvases while a wild-haired older man strode silently about frowning his eternal disapproval. Moses breathed in happily vapors from substances common to a ship and to artists – varnish, glue, tar, paint.

The interior of the huge interconnected buildings went on

in such schizophrenic manner for a time. Stench followed by perfume; airy lightness followed by claustrophobic gloom. Finally he came to a high arch adorned by a sign: ACADEMIE des SCIENCES. He went through the portal and wandered slowly amid a collection of bronze and glass retorts, ceramic crucibles, stuffed mammals, stacks of rocks remarkable and mundane, beakers holding brushes, tiny hills of unknown powders on charred tabletops, branches of flowering trees and fruited vines drying on threads attached to the ceiling, tumble-down rows of books bound in leather, a large magnifying lens set up in front of a globe. He heard tapping from somewhere, and after tiptoeing through the Academy's collections located a petite door hidden by a stack of papier-mâché geometric shapes each the size of a wine barrel.

Franklin glared as Proctor entered his workspace. That was a surprise to Moses, who was still walking as quietly as he could manage. He had imagined he would have to politely cough to get the old man's attention, but Franklin detected his entrance like a predator lying by the burrow of his prey.

Mary and Joseph. He does appear dangerously angry – and I don't think it is just because he has been interrupted.

Franklin stood and motioned Proctor to come closer. Moses crossed the room and looked down at three pairs of spectacles – large round lenses set in black wire frames – on the workbench. There was something unusual about these. The glass was translucent and did not appear to bend the image passing through as a ground lens would.

"Do you like plays?" Franklin asked.

Moses paused before nodding. "I do." He refrained from asking if that was all the great man wanted to know. *I could have stayed under my warm mound of covers with Mademoiselle Whateverhernamehadbeen and sent him a card with 'I do' written on the back.*

"I prefer the comedies, myself," Franklin said. "Molière or Dryden – things in that vein." He smiled happily, the deadly serious mood pushed aside. "Put away the cares of the world for a time. But on occasion I find myself obliged to attend the performance of a mystery, for which I can find no patience. The natural world contains within itself mysteries abundant. All one needs do is observe and reflect. Conundrums begging clarification will present themselves." He picked up a pair of the eyeglasses and spun it idly between forefinger and thumb by the temple piece; two faint pinkish orbs of reflected candle and forge light raced about the opposite wall. "My dear friend Warren. Your Dauntless. The clues are presented in Act One. Forms decay without reason."

Franklin turned away. Proctor thought there was a glint of welling moisture in the man's eye, but it was not clear through the bilayered lenses of his own glasses. When Franklin looked back his face was again hard. "The first act concludes. Curtain down. Refreshments and discussion. Now we find ourselves somewhere in Act Two."

Proctor had no inkling where this line of metaphorical reasoning was bound. His head, which had been clearing, began to throb once more. He removed his cap, hoping the cool air would sooth his aching brain.

"The clues need to be bundled and tied into a coherent form, but the audience is weary and stupid from wine and fois gras. They do not wish to exert themselves. The author brings onstage a narrative device in the form of a stranger who knows much, to reveal—" He put the glasses down. "Lieutenant Proctor, do you trust me?

Proctor had been fixed on the flickering form of the nearest candle flame, mesmerized, his attention in divers places and only partially in this room. "I– suppose I do."

Franklin nodded. "Do you trust your eyes?"

What secret society is he tapping me for? Proctor considered the question soberly, as it had been proposed without the faintest glint of levity. "Before the Dauntless was lost, I did, absolutely. And since, mostly. But that day... perhaps not."

Franklin nodded again, a tutor hearing the correct response from a pupil. "The wise stranger in our production comes in the form of my friends in the French intelligence services. What a collection of observations those fellows possess! One has only to approach them with an organized hypothetical, no more than mist and whispers, and those fellows will ruminate upon the problem. They set to work plastering flesh onto the skeleton using bits gathered from all corners of the earth, until the audience can almost make out the true form of the villain."

Proctor was fully attentive. "What do they know of the ship which attacked us?"

"Widely spread crumbs. Separately without merit, but given a focal point—"

"Do they know where she is?" Proctor interrupted.

"No," Franklin said coolly. There was a long silence punctuated by the hissing of the coke combusting in the forge bowl. "But I know where her power lies. And I think I know how to destroy it."

Captain Moses Proctor stood once more on the riverside, on the curb of the Quai du Louvre's cobble stoned width. *Yes, yes. Captain Moses Proctor.* He liked the sound of it. He liked even the thinking of it.

For Franklin had, with whatever power was vested in him by his young nation – and Moses hoped it was as considerable a power as he suspected – declared Moses Proctor was now and immediately promoted to the rank of Captain in the Continental Navy with all the privileges and responsibilities such rank entailed.

Responsibilities. The newly minted Captain shivered, and this time it could not be blamed on the weather. Benjamin Franklin, his unexpected new superior and friend and conspirator, had charged him with his first mission. It had the potential, Proctor had to admit, to be his last.

February 17, 1780
Morristown, New Jersey

"'Tis all I could find." The young servant spread her apron, showing Caroline a dozen of the most hideous and unappetizing excuses for potatoes seen in this kitchen since the day before. "I dug to the bottom. Rooted in the dirt. All gone now."

Caroline sighed. It was probably true, though she would go and rake out all the straw from the bin later just to make sure. Even tiny ones would be welcomed.

"They froze," Caroline said, pointing to several which were almost wholly black. The land outside lay far below freezing and was scoured by gusting wind and driving snow seemingly every other day. She overheard locals in the parlor complaining this was the coldest season hereabouts in recorded history – even the stoic Indians of the region grumbled. The relentless frost overwhelmed the ability of the root cellar to protect their storage vegetables.

The girl's name was Lucy Ann, one of the General's house servants fetched up from Virginia, and Caroline could not now tell her age. Lucy Ann had arrived in Morristown with some of the other gaggle of servants in December, plump and cheerful and probably fifteen. Now her cheeks were sunken, and her arms were sticks. She might have been sixty years old. Caroline refrained from looking at herself in the mirror shard hanging in the servants' sleeping room. They were all, servants and officers alike, gaunt and ill-tempered as wild dogs.

"These will never do to serve the General," Caroline said. "Though the taste may be little altered, the insides will boil up as black as we." She contemplated the puny tubers. "We shall resort to trickery."

Her sorcery turned out to be a sack of rye flour secreted in the pantry. She set Lucy Anne to boiling the potatoes, then they removed the horrid skins and mashed the dark remainder, folded it into some rye flour, and blended into the mass by vigorous handwork molasses and some starter.

Caroline wiped both palms on her apron. "Knead this for a time, then let it rise in a warm place."

Lucy Ann's eyes widened in desperation. The kitchen by this time of the day was crowded with most of those in the General's service as well as the three Irish women who remained in the mansion to wait on Mrs. Ford, whose late husband had built the place. All jockeyed for a spot near the large fireplace or the baking oven. Lucy Ann did not know where an acceptable dough-nurturing location might be found. Plus it was not unknown for edibles – including unbaked dough – to be nibbled to extinction by the ravenous. Caroline instructed the girl to make loaves and then beg the old man who was the resident baker to include them with his own, as he always watched his handiwork increase with a massive cleaver nearby.

The snow had drifted up over the window again, leaving only a slit through which she saw only relentless clouds. It was her habit to work near this spot and keep watch for the arrival of visitors. Before the first snow, this had been an effective surveillance method, as horse hoofs on the coarse graveled path produced a satisfying tell. But now the only manner of transport was by sleigh, and these glided silently up to the house masked by the incessant howl of wind. Unless the horses or humans made a racket, Caroline was not certain to be aware of newcomers.

Neither, she mused sourly, was she certain to recognize the threat even if she gazed out the iced window directly at it. All of Newman's memories and Ruttee's additions had given her no clear picture of how to distinguish Geoffrey's creations from the mass of dull-eyed shuffling hulks normal soldiers became in such a punishing winter. Especially as Ruttee predicted the quality of the golems would improve. Suppose they became indistinguishable from a man?

She would have to be lucky to intercept one, and this assignment might have consumed its ration of luck already. By rights, she should have been sent packing to some other owner shortly after she had arrived, as there were sufficient cooks already. The General kept her for a time out of politeness for the false gift, but then one cook fell down with dropsy and died and another ran off with an assistant butler. Suddenly there was a shortage.

And blessed was the household, because Caroline had learned at her mother's hearth many ways to make plain foods palatable. Even though the General was rich, the available supplies were mean. Caroline found no cassava, plantains, or ndoleh – just potatoes, parsnips, and carrots. These along with rice and maize served her purpose. It was odd that for all of the Father's tricks she had mastered, this knowledge that served her just as often and often as well she had absorbed before she had been sent for training as a Watcher.

Training had prepared her to work alone, but she preferred to be part of a team. In this place, however, the color of Dibele skin was a bound on cooperation, so she had to be content with building a network of unknowing confederates who fed her by their gossip and were directed by her most subtle suggestions. From time to time she wished she were a free operative in Italy, or India, or China, but she was not – she was in New Jersey and a slave. The training had also prepared her to accept circumstances and adapt to them.

A movement on the far side of the doorway caught her eye. She blinked and shook away dullness. One of the servants had stacked a wasteful number of logs on the fire, making the kitchen temporarily and unnaturally warm, and her lethargic. It had been a man. She closed her eyes for a moment, forcing the memory up. Dark. Serious. Nervous. Face and uniform unknown to her. The damning detail was that he looked well fed.

She snatched up a boning knife – eight inches of steel honed over the decades to little more than a pick – and folded it into a napkin. She put this into a wooden bowl and walked quickly out the door.

The man crept toward the front parlor, where the General conducted his business of war, and paused short of the entrance. Caroline approached. Was he composing himself? He seemed to be breathing more rapidly than was necessary, and his hand opened and closed on the ornate sword hanging from his belt. He carried no visible firearms.

She came up close behind him, but he did not attend. Her hand was in the napkin, fingers on the knife handle. She focused on the nape of his neck, where the small knob of bone jutted from the skull.

If he draws his sword or goes into the breast of his coat, the knife goes just below — up, hard, then twist. He will be dead in a heartbeat. Unless these monsters had no heartbeat.

Her breathing was rapid, matching his, and a voice called out from the study. An unfamiliar voice, loud, and speaking Spanish of all things. The man grabbed for his hat. Caroline's arm quivered, and the blade showed before she was able to stop herself.

He tucked his hat under one arm and marched into the room, where Caroline heard him being introduced to the General in heavily accented English. She sank against the wall, suddenly nauseous and at the same time hysterically hungry.

May 9, 1780
Charles Town, South Carolina

Uncontrollable waves of contractions streamed down from his head, down to his ankles, then rebounding and ascending. Behind the spasms his insides blazed. Before them he was ice. He shivered, his jaw a musical instrument, teeth tapping out an inhuman rhythm. How long it went on his brain could not judge. One second was lived as a lifetime. The colors below deck here were black and less black, then everything red in spirals as his eyes inflated to bursting. In his ears a barrage of drums, though the deck must be silent but for coughs and moans. He could not hear the men in extremis all about, even the quivering forms abutting him, and was thankful for that during his fleeting dips into coherence. Then the shakes took his whole body, his back arched, he breathed out a long, long breath. He did not breathe in. He relaxed, neither hot nor cold. Numb, paralyzed – he was dead. But there was no ascension, just a continued view of the rotting boards above. He glided on a downy cloud magically infiltrated between his throbbing back and the hard deck. Someone came out of the dark and kicked him. And again. 'He's gone,' a voice stated. Conclusive and bored at the same time. Bony hands lifted him off his beloved cloud, and he tried to protest but the mechanism of his mouth had sprung and they carried him to the port and began to pass him out over the hissing foam of the bay–

He groaned and sat up, fumbling for the amber bottle of oily elixir prescribed by his latest physician. He shook the container vigorously, then threw his head back and let several slippery drops fall into each eye. Instantly the laudanum began to dull the ache.

Jeptha Newman no longer remembered his dreams. Be they nightmare or erotic pleasure – all the tender emotions of his sleeping fancy were these days rudely torn away by the agony of waking. Exiting sleep triggered his eyelids, and the movement of those over his withered eyes was like the dragging of sharp salted stones over raw flesh.

The sun threatened to rise. He could make out violet sky in a rectangle of window, and some fuzziness that might be treetops. He turned away and detected a figure sitting on the other side of the lightening room.

It was Nat, woken and worried by Newman's murmurings. So it must have been a nightmare. Certainly he did not detect the happy residual blush from a romantic saga. He wondered if the Widow Legett would want to test him on her feather mattress before committing to a marriage. Would his unconscious but vocal protests during such a foul dream make her hesitate to the contract? He stretched. There was little he could do to control it, so he put it aside.

"Good morning, Nat," he said. "Fetch us some coffee, will you?"

He dressed as Nat ignited the wood stacked carefully in

the fireplace and made coffee and toasted bread, the water drawn and the bread to hand on a board under a cloth weighted against breezes by a knife. Nat paid close attention when the Major laid out the plan for attacking breakfast.

Newman received his meal at a table in the large upstairs room where they slept and demanded Nat again go through the steps of deciphering the message. The syllabus of Nat's exercise was a copy of Baskerville's Cambridge Bible, three sheets of handwritten communication, and a large piece of ebony slate broken ragged along one edge. Nat read the letter slowly, marking certain numbers on the slate. He then flipped through the thick Bible, consulting often with his figures, and laboriously copied words onto the black surface.

After a time, he looked up. Newman had long since finished eating and was honing his knife. "Ready," Nat said.

On a nod from his guardian, he began. "The dark one flies to the king's town south. Sorcery intentioned on the living flesh." The first time he had deciphered this, he had been mystified. The Major explained Ruttee was still watching Geoffrey and had discovered by means not transmitted that the disagreeable fellow himself was coming to Charles Town. Newman had paused to compose himself before he could comment on the second line. After a while he managed to say, "And he is no longer content with the dead." He did not explain more.

Nat was still in the dark about what the second line meant, but he knew it greatly disturbed his friend.

Newman's team waited covertly in a two-story wooden structure previously occupied by an exporter of rosin and beeswax, a Patriot who had fled before the fall of the city to the British. His two main products not being of immediate utility to the occupiers, this building had been left untouched except as temporary quarters for a unit since marched into the countryside to unearth things more edible.

To the rear on the main floor sat the wagon they had driven into the city. Newman, Nat, and Filly entered as representatives of Harnett's, a North Carolina brewery. It was a real brewery, and the stacks of casks were authentic product, though the wagon was only freshly painted with the firm's name. Newman bore a bill of sale stating The Loyalist Association of Wilmington had purchased beer and cider by subscription for the pleasure of His Majesty's forces in Charles Town. They had not been closely questioned, free drink being a self-evident certification of merit, and had delivered their load to the senior quartermaster. That whiskered person scribbled them a pass permitting them to find a place to rest before going back for additional barrels, his eyes fixed with piratical anticipation on the unexpected refreshments.

Teague and Wilcox joined them later by sneaking past the inattentive sentries. They bore forged certificates of parole such as were distributed to the defeated local militiamen who had piled their muskets and sworn off the conflict. These papers did not immunize them from John Bull's naval press gangs, however, so they had to lie low in the garret of the building.

All in all, Newman judged it not a seamlessly tidy scheme, born as it was in a scramble. It held together so far, but time was running out on their plausible presence in the occupied town. The quarry had still not emerged.

He went to the window and out of probably needless habit stayed carefully behind the thin ripped curtain. From up here an observer could see the front quarter of Geoffrey's lair – a mansion faced in gray stone, its windows blocked by dark curtains certainly in far better shape. This was the third day of their vigil, and between this view of the front and the view of the rear alleyway obtained by Teague and Wilcox from their garret, there had been no visitors. At night no lights shone in the place. The coachman informed them he had delivered to that address an odd fellow who could only be their prey. If he had departed sometime between that coach ride and their arrival then they had wasted time and effort. They would soon have to load up and try their escape.

He felt Nat behind him. The boy walked lightly. This

pleased Newman.

"Have you checked the pans?"

"Yes, sir," Nat said. "All loaded and dry."

Two of the casks on their wagon had been empties not delivered to the British. Inside these, their weapons were fastened to the inner wall with twine and tacks so the contraband would not rattle. Each cask held pistols, ball, and powder. Newman's men had stove in the barrelheads and loaded the moment the door of their hideaway closed. It fell on Nat to slide into their hiding place under some loose floorboards and inspect their cache twice a day.

May 11, 1780
Charles Town, South Carolina

They almost missed it. The sun was low, the street dark in shadow, and a lone rider walked his horse slowly past, leading two mules with long canvas-bound loads slung over their broad backs. Nat sat on the floor, his chin on the windowsill, his eyes barely opened. The Major had told him to watch for a wagon, so Nat noted the horseman through his lashes and did nothing. He turned his attention to the two mules, wondering idly what they were carrying – carpets? – when one bundle trembled with a frequency the plodding mule could not have caused. Nat sprang in the air and ran for the door, hissing "Major! Major!"

By the time they had gotten up the boards and laid hands on their pistols, Geoffrey was in the street talking with the rider. Teague and Wilcox burst out, Filly and Jeptha close behind. Nat trailed all, the remainder of their weapons cradled in his arms.

The attack was to have been executed with stealth – as the imagined wagon drew to the house Newman's men would filter out quietly and form up invisibly to flank Geoffrey as he emerged. If he did not emerge they would rush any door opened for the delivery and cut him down with superior fire.

No contingency had been made for the target seeing them as far away as this, and Newman cursed himself for a greenhorn.

Yet Geoffrey was not alarmed. He pivoted to face them and raised his arms as if supporting a giant globe. Nat had seen the pose in a picture book of myths but could not dredge up a name to it. He slowed, fixed by the unfolding disaster.

Teague ran wide, into the street, and approached Geoffrey from the far side as the man on the horse, recognizing an attack, yanked aside his reins and kicked. Wilcox aimed his flintlock at Geoffrey, but suddenly Major Newman shrieked some obscenity Nat could not make out, ran forward, bumped against Wilcox, and fired two pistols at once.

Nat threw up his arms against a sudden blast of wind saturated with needles of grit. A violent dust devil formed in the street, obscuring all vision, and when it died Geoffrey was gone. The horse and rider were far down the street, galloping as fast as bellowing mules could be pulled. The stunned attackers were left alone – except for Teague, who lay unmoving in the dirt.

December 2, 1780
Ossining, New York

The structure was built a barn, but in its present incarnation all the internal stalls had been demolished to leave one continuous space filled on the one side with shelves holding dried, salted, and pickled foods, rope coils of various thicknesses and lengths, oars, rolls of canvas, small hardwares, snowshoes, clothing on a crude rack, and tellingly, an assortment of traps arranged on pegs driven into the wall. On the other side of the space leaned stacks of furs large and small, brown and black, glossy and dull, smooth and rough.

In one corner the stall lumber had been reused to fashion a room several paces on a side. In the middle of this cozy chamber a potbelly stove vented through a freestanding brick chimney, which at the moment shimmered with radiated heat. The occupants were combusting logs at a furious rate to hold the weather at bay.

Outside was the dead, or perhaps the height, of winter. The storm shot ice against the boards; the wind huffed eerie musical notes over the top of the chimney, which backed from this fury every so often and filled the room with aromatic sooty smoke. The four men inside endured the flaw, as the alternative of opening a door was unthinkable, and besides, smoke killed lice.

Three of the men were trappers, driven by nature to this vacation. One of the three also owned the store. The other man was just a traveler who had apparently mistimed his journey.

"The game is Klaverjas," said the oldest trapper, who introduced himself as Huub Broos. The owner of the store, a Mr. Tonjes, sat to Broos' left at the wee table, and to his right a small man who mumbled into his shaggy red beard some introduction the newcomer could not make out.

"I am not familiar with it," said the traveler, a pale, dark-haired man. Englisher by his manners, they had decided, and dangerous by his carriage. He had made amiable small talk with them over beer for an hour before Broos judged he was no threat.

"I will be your partner," Broos said, indicating their opponents, Mr. Tonjes and Red Beard. He laid down a deck of cards and summarized the game rules. Broos then dealt several hands, which they played slowly as Broos and sometimes Mr. Tonjes described the unfolding strategies of Klaverjas.

When the Englisher's understanding at last seemed adequate, Red Beard mumbled something. "He says this is how children play," Broos interpreted.

The Englisher grunted. "And how do men play?"

"Ah — half a stuivers each hand... that is, perhaps a pence."

The Englisher grunted again, and the cards were distributed. Broos caught the eyes of both of his nominal opponents and with a subtle nod make a pact to share in the fleece.

The Englisher and Broos managed to take the occasional hand due to the Dutchman's steady and conservative bidding, but they were soon far outpointed by their competitors. The Englisher accepted his growing debt with tranquility, even becoming more talkative as he sank into poverty. This enlivened the table greatly, and soon Broos and Mr. Tonjes and even the mostly-unintelligible Red Beard were relating details of the trapping season along and near the Hudson River. It was not good news.

"Twenty-three years ago when I first paddled up the river, I had to club beavers out of my way to make the shore." Broos slapped down a seven of clubs, nodding significantly at his partner to indicate they should bid in that suit. "Last year I returned with enough pelts to pay for my flour and bacon and nothing left over."

"Someone remind me what was trump – oh yes," Mr. Tonjes glanced at his hand. "You see the furs in there? When the river thaws the company boat will make its monthly visit. In the old times the stacks went high over my head, and the boat came twice weekly."

They both blamed the Indians, who had become infatuated with the stuffs beaver pelts could be traded for and so who now took many more than they needed for their own purposes.

"You know the tribes upriver, then?" asked the Englisher.

Broos nodded. "I spent last winter – it was almost as mean as this one is turning – buried under the snow as a guest of the Warranawonkong. One of the most tedious stretches of time I ever suffered. They were at war with the Bijinway and did not dare to venture far from their village – not that any could when the snow was hard packed and rose up to the neck. Now remember, a white man would not be able to distinguish a Warranawonkong from a Bijinway. They are alike in every respect – except fancy takes them on occasion, when then they caper in a war dance and commence trying to kill each other.

234

The next season they are just as likely to mix together into one big happy tribe."

"I was told in the town," the Englisher said, carefully calling it neither New York nor New Amsterdam to avoid those old grievances, "about a tribe called the Osuanee, who some claim to have discovered a rich source of gold."

Red Beard, who was in the middle of taking snuff, snorted it back out in a laugh.

Broos brushed some flakes of tobacco off his sleeve and tossed down two cards. "Seventy point roem," he said in triumph. "Do not worry yourself. The Osuanee have removed themselves some ways into the wilderness, toward Shining Water Lake. If they had a flake of gold, they would be here, trading it for beer and bacon."

The Englisher reached into his coat and took out a leather purse. He burrowed two fingers inside and flicked a gold guinea onto the table. It rang a clear note, spun and wobbled and eventually came to a full stop with the haughty profile of George the Second glaring at Broos. The three Dutchmen ogled the coin.

"It is my pleasure to pay the debt of our team," the Englisher said. "I consider it fair recompense for the lesson."

His hosts dropped their cards, game forgotten. His purse was not small, and if it contained the volume of Englisher coinage it promised, well then this stranger was toting a sum worth as much as all the goods and furs in the store. The three men were Calvinists, as each proper Dutchmen should be, with partial but not exact grasps of those details in their theology which dealt with robbing your guests. Each rapidly came to the same conclusion: this Englisher could kill each of them and all of them without much trouble or regret – which settled the religious argument in his favor.

"I wish to find the Osuanee," the Englisher said, looking only at Broos. "I will pay you to take me up the river."

Huub Broos glanced from the coin to his partner's face, then back. Several times he repeated this, thinking hard. Finally, he took and let out a deep breath as though letting go of his most fervent dream. "I can not."

The Englisher scooted close to the table and leaned toward Broos. "I have many more of those," he said quietly, nodding to George's metallic portrait. "When the snow is gone, we go up the river, just you and me. You will still be able to trap your season."

Broos shook his head slowly. "It is true I passed the winter with the Warranawonkong. We were in perfect harmony, brothers and friends. The day came when I made it clear to them I must return to my traps and go back down the river. This agitated them for some reason I still do not perceive. They chased me to my canoe, knives bared. I made it into the stream seconds before they laid hands on me, then they raced on the bank for several miles, screaming and calling promises to remove my watkchimka and feed it to the dogs." He paused. "Do you know what watkchimka means?"

Thomas shook his head.

"Good," Broos said. "No, I will not go upriver this year. And... maybe not the next. I am going to try the western rivers."

January 26, 1781
Nafase Dibele, Central Africa

Travel back to Nafasi Dibele was a journey down a long wooden staircase. On the deck of a merchantman ploughing across the equatorial Atlantic, averaging three meters above the water. Then at Lagos, transfer to a packet boat, two meters dry, say. At Boma, make arrangements on one of the lateen-rigged dhow that sail up and down the lower part of the Congo. Those passengers now a meter over the river, whether they lie about at leisure in a favorable wind or are pressed into working the sweeps when the breeze fails. At Mangai, beyond which only vessels with little draft can go because of the shifting shallows, pay some fisherman and stand in his dugout for the final leg. In one of those craft, carved from the trunk of a Tola tree, the feet are finally about level with the water. At the bottom of that staircase, Ruttee stepped onto the riverbank.

Three times he had gone into the world and returned home. The first came after he had finished his training. The reward for completing those years of mental and physical sharpening was a trip to see the actual Tower. His mentor and he went the now familiar outbound route: canoe to dhow to sloop to frigate. They landed on a sandy shore and rode rocking atop camels in a caravan across a hard land that had shocked him with its sere lifelessness. Ruttee was used to the noisy creatures and dense greenery of the jungle. This quiet landscape where you could see for miles was disorienting. Days and days they slogged across the hot ground, until one night his mentor shook him awake. The caravan slept outside a small village, and in the dark his companion led him quietly on a wide path around the settlement and into a narrow gorge where they flitting from shadow to shadow with the stealth of Watchers. They emerged from the passage into a long broad valley where Ruttee saw in the distance a perfect alabaster column in the bleaching moonlight – the legendary Tower from which the Father had fled. The Tower where the Giza Mashujaa obtained their powers from the bath of a sleeping angel.

Ruttee had been seized with the sudden mischief of desire: to run across the valley floor, to bang his fists on the front door of the Tower and demand the slumbering being wake. Wake and assure all the world it was indeed an angel. But the Watchers that night just watched.

His second journey had been to Palermo, where he was absorbed into the household of a Moorish trader named Tariq. By day Ruttee, whose name there was Philadelphio, opened casks of spices and repackaged them into small clay pots, but at night he slipped out of the town. About a mile into the country was an estate guarded by men with long guns. Ruttee lay on a low rise and watched to see who came and who went. In the morning he reported this to the man who oversaw the spice warehouse, who heard him out silently, never giving Ruttee any clue where his information went.

After six months of exhausting service, he was recalled to make his report, which he thought unnecessary, and to sharpen his skills in English conversation. Then he had ascended the wooden stairs to Brazil and slavery and a new name.

The bank felt familiar under his bare feet. Loamy and soft. His weight squeezed out a faint sweet scent of decaying leaves. Nafasi Dibele was the same as ever – an array of forty or so wattle and daub huts with thatched roofs, those belonging to single men and women mostly smaller and round, the ones built for families larger and elliptical. A greenish-blue wall of vines and trees encircled the community. Even without counting, he could sense the living fence had been hacked back and several new homes built since he had last stood in this spot. The Father's home in the middle, the largest structure, was flanked by two of almost equal size. One was a storehouse, the other classrooms where Ruttee had been taken daily as soon as his tongue learned its purpose. There he had been taught Portuguese, Spanish, Italian, and English. He and his fellow students of various ages played what were presented as just games: hiding, seeking, finding, remembering. Watching.

Everything here was the same, but the young man who had submitted to the slaver's chains was no more. He left this place with certainty in his mission but returned with a different name and an altered perspective on what was possible – and on the limits of immortality.

He had decided to keep the name Ruttee. It was good luck. More importantly, it was a tribute to his dead friend Junipero. He would go first to see his mother and father, who would call him by his old name and hug and inspect him and make happy sounds over his gifts and beg to hear all of his stories. His brothers and sisters and cousins and extended family would come around to pinch his belly and demand a retelling. His friends would later herd him into the middle of their gaggle and ask their own impertinent and ribald questions and make him drink from a calabash of pito until he was laughing too hard to continue.

He turned to the thin canoe and hefted out his two sacks, then pressed a silver piece into the palm of the expressionless owner. This was the second half of the fare, as no experienced man paid full in advance on this part of the river. It was not unknown for a gullible passenger to end up swimming among the crocodiles and hippos, although no operator would dare let a fare bound for Nafasi Dibele come to harm. Such was the respect for and fear of the Father up and down the river, a most useful apprehension that had left the Dibele untroubled for hundreds of years even through periodic outbreaks of tribal unrest and outright war.

Ruttee watched the man pole his craft back out into the main current, then picked up his baggage and walked into the village.

One of the Children came for him after he dropped his bags at the doorstep of his natural father, before he had the chance to embrace anyone. The Children cared for the Father. They fed, bathed, clothed him. They surrounded him day and night. Certainly not to protect him, for it was inconceivable the Father would need protection from any mere man. The Child who came for Ruttee was one who had been two years ahead of him in the school, a slab of a youth selected out into the ranks of the Children primarily due to his strength and fighting skills. He came up behind Ruttee and touched him on the shoulder. The pito would have to wait.

The Father sat on the floor of his home atop a plump zebra skin pillow. He had not changed, of course, since Ruttee had last seen him. He had not changed since the first time Ruttee had been admitted to his presence at age five. *He will be sitting here just like this the day my ancient bones are laid in a grave.* He knelt waiting for the Father to finish his meditation.

Ruttee sweated, though he wore only a simple skirt. Another gradual transformation as one came home from the outside world – layers of clothing shed. When he left Trenton he had on a greatcoat, blouse, trousers, long boots, and wool undergarments. One by one these were stripped off and stuffed into his sacks as latitude and temperature increased. The Father did not appear hot, even though he had dressed in a ceremonial top of carmine and indigo beads and an ivory-barred headdress for this debriefing. One of the Children moved the air with a long-handled rattan fan, but it didn't feel to Ruttee to be doing much good. Sweat beaded in his hair and dripped impolitely onto the woven reed ground cover.

At last the Father opened his eyes. "Tell me of your journey, my son," he said. His voice was soft, almost a whisper.

Ruttee inclined his head and began his report. He started with the day he had left the village and floated the several legs downriver and to Lagos, where his contact had put him aboard an English merchant ship bound for Recife. He closed his eyes and summoned the memories. Not just where he had gone and when but also the minutiae he had been trained to gather – the intense rainbow of the fruit in Brazilian markets, the bitter stench of the lower decks, the slick strangle of the iron restraints. In Recife, how he had contacted an American trader, a Mr. Bullus, who took him aboard a frigate, outfitted him most amicably with chains, and delivered him to the slave agent Teeler in Georgia. How Bullus had ripped his blouse and then applied several lashes with a whip to make the costume authentic, shouting almost in joy, "Nobody's going to buy a buck with no scars on his back, brother!"

The Father watched with sleepy eyes, as though he really had no interest in the perfunctory performance, but when Ruttee began to describe the mechanism Junipero had built and what the internal components were, the Father straightened noticeably.

"...and while the Giza was focused upon Junipero and his decoy, I fell to the ground, pulling the cord to release the springs." Ruttee saw it all again, the visual of his imagination synchronizing to the words as he spoke them – the invisible wire hacking Ordulf, pieces of the knight flying off in bloody spurting arcs as if enchanted, the Hessians' musket balls staggering Junipero, his own dive off the bridge. He still felt an

240

occasional dull pain in his healed ribs.

The Father leaned forward, unreadable emotion flickering in his hooded eyes. "The Giza – what became of him?"

I wondered that too. I squatted for hours near the dismembered knight and waited for him to reassemble.

"I burned his remains...," he said slowly.

He had stood unmoving on the snowy bridge, his mind churning. He was paralyzed with grief; he was enervated with triumph. The body of his friend lay to his right, the head of Ordulf grimacing in his lap. In the distance musket fire, screams, shouts, cheers, and the occasional boom of a cannon, all muffled by the dense falling snow. After a long time with not a shiver from any pieces, Ruttee had gathered up the knight, careful not to touch his blood. He carried them deep into the woods, where he built a pyre out of fallen timber and brought it to life with Junipero's flint box.

The knight for all his magic burned in the end like a mere man, emitting plumes of greasy smoke and the stench of burning hair, until at long last Ruttee stood over a warm pile of ash in the twilight wondering where the power of the water in Ordulf's body had fled.

No demons came. No spirits emerged from the darkness of the trees. The knight had become one with the forest at last, joined together in this heap of black against the carpet of pristine white. Ruttee had unfastened his britches and pissed on the embers.

"...and scattered the ashes," he continued.

The Father stared at him dumbly. He was not sure the Father would even hear any more, but he had to go on. The Child stopped waving his fan and stepped uneasily toward the Father. This Child was Ruttee's second cousin on his mother's side, but nonetheless he shot a malevolent glance at Ruttee as the probable cause of this upset.

"I searched his quarters."

The Father's attention refocused, and his eyes pierced Ruttee. He did not have to ask. Ruttee had earlier settled a slim leather bag on the mat in front of him. Now he opened it and removed a gleaming black object, long and narrow at the top, like a stone gourd. The Father leaned forward eagerly and extended a bony arm.

Ruttee found this water in a locked strongbox in Ordulf's room, along with other items he chose not to mention to the Father. There had been pistols, knives, notebooks, a considerable weight of gold ingots and coin, jewelry and gems, and metallic boxes and ceramic orbs and other objects of mysterious and unknown provenance and utility. The Father did not think to ask if there had been more than water, which was his miscalculation.

The interrupted homecoming resumed. The traveler was overwhelmed with family and friends. He dispensed gifts; he retold the adventure again and again. He ate some of every dish carried to his father's house; he drank some of every draft offered him. When the sun sank into the western jungle, he was escorted to the schoolhouse, where his contemporaries brought out the more powerful drink and begged him to give them the real story. The one where the violence and the women – especially the women – had not been expurgated so as not to offend his aunties. None of his aunties were in audience here, so he crafted a tale of his voyage embellished for his peers. It was his special gift to them, and he narrated loudly and colorfully, for he knew the girls of the village sat outside the windows listening and giggling and blushing.

He left out only the death of the knight. The Father had commanded him to tell no one a Giza had been killed. Part of Ruttee rebelled. Were they not the enemy of all men? It was the central tenant of the Dibele culture, and it seemed to him a reason to celebrate. He ached to share this great feat with his people, but Ruttee recognized that the news had made a powerful impression on the Father. Perhaps the actions in America were part of a larger purpose, one to which Ruttee was not privy – so he talked all the way around the slaying of a Giza, leaving a hole in his tale none in the assembly even dreamed of noticing.

January 27, 1781
Nafase Dibele, Central Africa

Ruttee woke before sunrise. His head throbbed from the pito, but he could not rest. He dressed quietly, snuck through the partitioned interior of the hut, and walked into the jungle. Birds cawed and trilled. Insects hummed and cracked and popped. Some unknown beast in the distance growled, and he felt at home.

He stayed a few miles on a trail that led to the top of a hill giving a view of the village and a long stretch of the river. Some miles beyond this rise he saw faint through the accumulation of sultry mist the higher tops of the uneven range defining the eastern reach of this long valley.

Halfway to the crest, something struck him on the chest. He swiped at it with one hand thinking a large beetle had blundered into him. Then another strike like the first, and this time he saw the pebble rebound off his skin. He looked around and grinned broadly when he recognized the impish face of Songay Bin high up in the branched nest of an umbrella tree.

Bin swung down the trunk like an eager child. Ruttee expected he would have slowed by now. Bin was years older, one of Ruttee's father's cousins, but he slid from limb to trunk and back as limber as ever. He leapt the last six feet, landed next to Ruttee with a thump, and wrapped his kinsman in a constricting hug.

Of course Songay Bin was not his original name, as Ruttee was not. They called each other by their old family familiars in the traditional way of greeting, then Bin stepped back.

"Junipero—" Ruttee began.

"I know," Bin said gently. He saw Ruttee did not understand. "The Children speak to me when the village is quiet. I know your story. Now you must tell me the parts you kept back."

"Why do you think I would hide anything from the Father?"

Bin smiled. "You have always had a face under your face. That is why you were sent into the world. It is why Junipero trusted you."

"I failed him. I let him be killed."

Bin waved, maybe at a mosquito, maybe at the guilt. "You were not there to protect him. I could tell from my first meeting with him he would never be prodded from his course. Did you bury our friend in his holy ground?"

Ruttee made a slight nod. "He was of the Roman church, which is not favored in that region. I took him to the Presbyterians and gave the minister a sum of gold to agree he deserved to lie in their yard."

"It is almost the same god," Bin said. "Junipero will charm him. Now tell me – what of the death of Ordulf?"

They went cautiously up the hill, brushing aside vines, watching sharply for snakes, until they arrived at the summit, such as it was. The Dibele kept the top shorn of all vegetation, and the view was spectacular. At the apex stood remnants of a foundation, some ruined structure predating their tribe. The stone was of a kind not found within a hard day's walk of this location, so the hill had at one time some import to whoever bothered to haul here such a great quantity of rock. The meaning was lost now, the blocks of gray speckled with pink and silver just part of the landscape. They sat on two, facing each other, and Ruttee told the whole story once again, but this time with all the specifics reincorporated for his kinsman's consideration.

When the tale was finished, Bin asked, "Did you note the day this happened?"

"It was the day after the great Christian holiday."

Bin crossed his arms over his chest and contemplated the distant mountains. "On that day – I know the European days by my calendar – a part of my habit now – many in the village were woken by cries from the Father's house. People went running to see what had happened, but the Children came out and reassured them all was well."

"What did the Children tell you?" Ruttee asked.

"The Father was sleeping," Bin said. "And woke up in great agitation."

"A nightmare?"

"The Children say he has never had one – before, anyway. No, he felt the death of Ordulf."

Ruttee's eyes widened. "From here?"

Bin nodded. "The water unites all who have drunk it."

"When I told him the story of Ordulf's death, he seemed... fascinated. But he did not seem surprised."

"Ah." Bin paused. "Did you ever contemplate the details of the Father's flight from the Tower? The story goes he filled some skins with the water and ran into the desert."

Ruttee waited. This was history all the Dibele knew well.

"You and I have seen this desert. It is a wide dry place. If the Father was in a hurry and took with him the water of the angel and no other, he would have only that to drink. Day after day. How much liquid does a man need to survive?"

The implication slowly came to Ruttee. The tale had been told him and them all that the water was mighty. The guardians took it with every new moon, and a mouthful was enough to give them powers and protect them from the erosion of normal time.

"His humours must have been disturbed by so much water," Bin said. "I think he needs it yet. Oh, he accepts all we capture and deliver him with sufficient gratitude. But I have seen subtle signs that he craves it like some men crave the poppy."

Ruttee shook his head. "Even if it is true, what of it? He has water enough to suit him."

"Perhaps. And what if the great Dibele tribe is not protecting the world from the evil of the old knights? What if we are just stalking them to steal what dregs of the water we can for the Father's need? What if this recent commitment to aiding the revolution in the American colonies is only to block the Giza from the New World – so they and their water are kept near?"

Ruttee was stunned. He opened his mouth but had nothing to say.

"I tell you this, nephew," Bin continued, "you and Junipero have shown us the Giza can be killed. When this news spreads to our brothers out in the world, they will try to kill another. Eventually we will succeed, or perhaps the Giza will first come down the river to wipe out our tribe with hellfire as the Father has always warned. I do not relish either of those futures, though you should think destroying the knights a good thing. Consider – if the water is no longer being brought out so we may easily obtain it, Dibele may be ordered across the desert to capture the Tower. You have seen the village of the guardians. They are ruthless warriors. We are not."

The sun was fully above the eastern mountains, and already the air was wringing wet and as hot as a bath. The busy symphony of the jungle ascended as with the raising of a conducting baton. The flying insects contended in volume with the beetles, which strained to outdo the birds in crackling beats. In the bass line beasts invisible in the thick greenery growled deep in their huge chests. Ruttee sat still as a statue, not even trying to flick away the several flies maneuvering to land on his face.

"The Father did not send me to Junipero." It was not a question.

Bin merely raised one eyebrow.

"He would never have given support to the Spaniard if he suspected his ability." Ruttee moved at last to face his elder.

Bin concentrated on a hawk circling high above. "When I was young, I would sit with older Watchers and listen to them talk. Sometimes the pito would shake old memories from their shackles." He paused. "One, who was my uncle's wife's brother, told me of two Watchers who had grown tired of being eyes and had decided to become instead fists." He waved at the bird, which ignored him. "It did not go well for them.

But the story was a glance into a past the Father would never have us taught. There have always been Dibele trained as Watchers who went into the world only to discover their blood ran too hot to hold back. Working alone and without proper training or preparation or support they were easily crushed by the Giza."

"All this history from one drunken evening?"

"I knew it was true in my bones, but I did attempt to find out more. My travel as a Turk was blessed by the Father, who desired I maintain a network within the Ottomans. To track movements of the Giza living in the Tower whenever they popped out to gorge on the pleasures available in the cities under the control of the Sultan. I did, of course, and in addition I engaged a number of scholars to compile intelligence from many places the Giza had plied their wickedness over the years."

"And you found evidence of Dibele violence and Dibele deaths."

"Enough to know I was not the only Watcher to feel impotent in the face of Giza evil."

"And then I came along."

"Yes, cousin," Bin spoke softly. Ruttee could barely hear him over the buzz of the jungle. "I convinced the Father that Junipero was not a threat but a great asset. He would follow the Giza with only a little encouragement and training, which you would provide. I knew our friend was bound to try his will against the knights, and I had great hopes he would put a dent in their armor. I did not know you would be in any danger."

Ruttee stood up abruptly and paced a few steps away, then turned. "There *is* news I have not shared with anyone. Junipero left a father and two sisters. After I arranged for Geoffrey's moves to be noted and forwarded to me, I traveled to Spain to find these heirs. Eventually I located them in Madrid, where I went to tell them of his death and deliver to them his possessions. In the course of the search I heard some interesting gossip from a Jesuit in Catalonia, which led me to Paris. In that place one of our friends informed me that a force of Americans and French had been dispatched to find the Tower and destroy it."

It was Bin's turn for disbelief. After a time he said, "I suspected someone would eventually assemble all the rumors. But why destroy it? If they even suspect it contains great power, why not capture it?"

Ruttee shrugged. "Your concern for the Giza and their property is touching, cousin, given your recent machinations." Bin smiled guiltily, and Ruttee went on, "It does not matter. They do not know where it is. As you say, you and I have been there. They will not find the Burj al Janna unless they have a great many men or a great deal of time."

"What is their strength?" Bin asked.

When he heard the answer, Bin stood and sighed. He did not even have to speak it. Ruttee looked across the horizon of bulbous emerald treetops, over the clearing of the village. The sun shone down through a veil of steam, and they both sweated profusely. It was their home, and they loved it. But instead of the calming greenery of their birthplace, each was seeing good men wandering dangerously close to destruction in a hostile desert.

May 10, 1781
The Holy Land

Ward's camel was, he concluded, the worst camel in their small fleet. It might be the most useless camel in the entire Holy Land; its feckless incompetence was possibly of Biblical proportions. The animal's name was Mahmud, which Scudman said meant 'praiseworthy'. No creature in these parts could have born a more inappropriate moniker. Mahmud managed to slip his saddle so that Ward fell off the other side when the camel rose from the ground. Mahmud pretended to be deaf when Ward called the kneeling command 'Baruk! Baruk!', leaving Ward up in the air hungry and thirsty as everyone else sat down to refreshments. Mahmud went lame, or affected lameness, several times on every outing. But all these offenses were followed by the beast turning his monstrous shaggy head to let Ward see the hurt in Mahmud's large brown eyes and know none of these troubles were the camel's fault, for Mahmud loved his rider and would do anything for him.

Mahmud was limping at the moment, of course. The party was almost back to Amman, and all members were exhausted. Ward thought about waving the others to go on ahead, but the threat of bandits even this close to what represented civilization hereabouts meant all four had to slow to Mahmud's halting pace.

Ward sighed. He had tried to choose a different mount after his very first ride on Mahmud. The camel would have none of it. He had adopted Ward and would rush up trumpeting outrage if the man approached any other of his herd. Mahmud would butt the competition aside, then give Ward an assured look to tell him they were an inseparable team.

The other camels slowed knowingly. Behind Ward came Private David and Lieutenant Lefevre, two French infantrymen who rode stoically. The combined forces had been camped in the desert outside Amman for eight months now, but it had only taken a week for the unhappy Frenchmen to let it be known that if they had wanted their asses to become permanently calloused, they would have joined the cavalry in the first place. And if they had been so rash, they would have opted for horse cavalry, not camel. But there was no time to walk these desert distances, so the blue coats stuffed padding in the seat of their pants and suffered their orders.

Bringing up the rear as usual was Scudman. Today he had spent most of the return trip singing a Bedouin song. Wade knew some of the words to the chorus, but Scudman knew eight verses in addition. Scudman – scuttlebutt lawyer, chronic complainer, a common seaman who grumbled and sighed at every command no matter how minor. Yet it was Scudman who seemed happy and at home. He wore the robe and headdress of a native tribesman, which – with his burnt face and dense black beard – he resembled more than an American sailor. When they went as they had on this trip to ask questions and listen to gossip and legends, it had become obligatory to include Scudman. The sailor could usually be found at the center of a throng, conversing with its members, receiving an impromptu lesson in the regional dialect. Fifteen minutes after the first sharp-eyed child spied the stranger, the whole population of the place would be crowded about him, howling and shrieking with laughter. He plucked copper coins from dirty ears and removed vast lengths of tied cloth from his fist. He let the village elders cut a piece of rope which he magically made whole; he made small balls of clay disappear, then reappear, then redisappear. After such an introduction, whatever the rest of the party wanted was theirs for the asking.

What they wanted was the location of the Tower. Ward and Lefevre posted in the main square of whatever hamlet they were calling upon a bill bearing Arabic, French, Turkish, and Aramaic texts, each identically desiring information regarding this formation and promising gold in exchange. Most of the people being unschooled and thus ill equipped to read their very pretty announcement – which was printed on heavy stock and bore an artist's imagining of the Tower – the two lieutenants also stalked the markets and alleyways. Lefevre bellowed out their offer in French and Arabic. Ward's invitations were in English as well as Aramaic and Turkish – which he had haltingly read from a paper at first before memorizing his lines.

This trip, to a tiny town outside of Madaba, turned unfortunately typical. Yes, yes, oh yes, indeed the famous Tower was well known to all inhabitants, and where was this golden reward? Pressed for details, the secret would be shared in whispers: the Tower was in the north – or the east, perhaps the south, but probably not the west. The Tower was the last pillar of the ruined Garden of Eden. The Tower was at the bottom of the Sea of Galilee. The Tower was inside the Great Pyramid. All these true facts they heard ad infinitum and ad nauseam, and they ushered those offering up such flawed intelligence rapidly and politely from the queue.

In this village, though, there had been one man whose accounting of a journey struck them as not impossible. Previously a caravan guide, too old now for that strenuous job, he told them of a valley far to the east, along one of the minor paths by which some in the past carried cedar oil from Beirut to Baghdad and dried dates from Baghdad to Beirut. He marked the location on Lieutenant Lefevre's map and described the Tower in great detail. Ward's hope had risen and risen with every believable twist of the old man's story, but when the ancient traveler told them he had actually seen inside the Tower after a jinn snatched him up and flew him through a hole in the top, the two officers looked wearily at one another. The rest of the tale was left behind in their dusty wake.

Wade cursed. He used words and phrases which should never contaminate the mouth of a gentleman officer. He cursed his camel, he cursed the desert, he cursed Proctor, he cursed himself. Most of all, he cursed Franklin. Why had that madman sent them into this hell? What evil powers gave him control over a sensible man such as Moses Proctor? Wade swore if he ever made it back to Christendom he would throttle Benjamin Franklin, no matter how old or venerable he might be.

It's my own damnable fault. Greed and ambition. Pride led to this downfall. It is God's punishment on me.

Proctor had gathered his small peripatetic squadron that blessedly cold day back in Mauregard and informed them he was traveling to the Holy Land on a mission of which he could tell them little because he knew little. He had made for the rest of them preliminary arrangements for their return to the United States, but the three mutinied. Ward would not leave due to Proctor's sudden ascendance to the hallowed rank of Captain – albeit without accompanying ship to command. The ensign was gripped by the desperate instinct of a junior officer jammed on the promotion list among his equally competent and equally determined peers. He smelled an advantage over his brother ensigns, who were occupied with traditional floating duties. If Proctor had hopped a rank, then Ward would stick onto Proctor's coattails and pray Franklin might work his wonder one more time.

It came to pass as he had dreamed. Good old Benjamin declared practically as he ushered them out of France's door – Ward was henceforth a Lieutenant, and Ward was on the path to command – of a camel, though that small addendum was months in the future. McCue would not be left, as he desired adventure. Ward had listened to enough wardroom tales of Mrs. McCue to suspect that returning to his Massachusetts hearth was not the kind of dangerous adventure the carpenter had in mind. That left Scudman, who moaned and sighed and finally consented with great reluctance to attach himself to the endeavor so they might benefit from his wisdom and mastery of international and maritime law. Now, more than a year from their initial flush of audacity, they were all ready to be quit of this misguided chase. All except Scudman, who declared his new ambition was to become a desert chieftain, or perhaps a sheik or sultan – whichever rank came with a harem.

Down the hard final slope they rode at last, into the natural bowl where they had established their camp. The site had once been the home of a Roman temple, but to which god was lost among the broken arches and toppled columns. Off to the left their string of camels shuffled and snorted. The hired Bedouin who cared for them was busy hobbling one for a medical procedure; his two sons saw their returning stock and sprinted toward them. In front lay the temporary home of four American sailors and fifteen French infantry – a cluster of tents surrounded by stacked supplies. To the right was the newest addition to their ranks. One week ago a procession of twenty pack mules had appeared, filing slowly between the stubs of two fluted Roman columns. The beasts were led and tended by a dozen Mughals under the charge of a blocky energetic man who introduced himself as Zafar Mizra and begged the three bewildered French privates guarding the camp that day to accept this gift, forty maunds of the finest gunpowder, sent by the Great Peshwa.

"Franklin," Proctor had shrugged upon returning. It was just another act of wizardry. Franklin had waved a diplomatic wand and caused to appear what Ward estimated to be two tons of powder.

One of the French corporals, a former artilleryman, touched a burning splinter to a petite cone of the dark stuff. It popped into a roiling cloud of grayish-white smoke, and he smiled broadly behind his bushy mustache. "Tres bien," he gloated. It was damn good powder.

But, Proctor pointed out, they had no cannon and no target at which to point them even if they did. At least they could use some of this gift in their muskets and reserve the remainder to blow into infinitesimal shards any obstacle that dared block their path.

The next day two parties rode to different compass points, seeking once more any clue to the location of the Tower.

June 6, 1781
Cape Fear, North Carolina

If there had been a window, Major Jeptha Newman could have gazed out over the sheltered inlet and wondered if it were filled with fresh water from the river or salt from the Atlantic. If in addition his eyes were sound, he might have swept them up and down the shoreline and appreciated some of the quite ingenious if unorthodox engineering the neighborhood builders had employed to cant the butt ends of nearby buildings out over the anchorage.

But there was no window and so the state of his eyes was irrelevant. The room was black as pitch. This did not put him at any kind of disadvantage, all things considered. Newman could hear the sucking, rasping breath of the man sitting across the unseen table. He caught the moist hiss of waves splashing on the building's pilings, the whistling pipes of sea birds fighting over a piece of food, the grunts of a distant crewman hauling a line.

"I fish," the voice in the darkness pronounced. "No more."

"It is what I was told," Newman agreed. "I was also told you are often at sea for weeks."

Shifting in his chair. "What is your business?"

"Four men, put ashore south of New York."

"Horses?"

"No."

A long pause. "If we are boarded, you may be pressed."

"You have never been boarded."

"The rabble should keep their own counsel."

"I heard only admiration," Newman said.

"The offshore fleet comes and goes. If we are intercepted, are there any among your party who would be hanged?"

"None. Two farmers who have never been in service, a boy too young to march, and myself."

"It is you who concerns me."

"My name is Jeptha Newman, lately a Major in the First North Carolina Regiment, separated as unfit."

A grunt from the other side of the table. "I would be more at ease if you had a letter of introduction."

"Alas," said Newman. "All I have is gold."

Wilcox and Filly, left to their own supervision, sought the nearest – and in the case of this tiny port, only – establishment which dispensed drink. It was a leaning stack of sticks two buildings farther from the water than the one the Major had entered, and as such defined the other side of town. A weathered board painted with a yellow anchor twined in black chain decorated the splintered steps. The men determined this advertised a tavern. In Nat's opinion it could as well be a supplier of marine hardware, but he followed them obediently into the quiet interior.

Inside were three round tables, several mismatched stools

and chairs, and one door set flat on sawhorses. There were no anchors or chains for sale. Wilcox eased down onto a stool at the horizontal door, ignoring the baleful eye of the lone patron sprawled with his head atop one of the tables. An apish man in a grimy apron hammered a cork into a jug with the side of his fist. Filly stood nervously as the man slammed the jug down and turned to ogle the three intruders with his unnatural bulging eyes, which looked off in separate directions.

There was an uncomfortable silence, which lasted until Wilcox tossed a slim silver triangle onto the tabletop. It rang for a second, its pure tone testifying to its authenticity. Their host smiled. It was a terrifying expression, and Nat almost bolted.

He stayed just long enough to drink a mug of beer, then he slipped out the door. He stood on the sorry and probably unsafe excuse of a porch for a while, taking in the quiet of the day. The harbor was empty of boats and the streets of men. He decided the whole town was off fishing, leaving only the sounds of women. He could see none, but he could hear the small notes of domestic industry through open windows.

He snapped about at a movement – a figure darted back from the porch rail. Nat jumped into the street and walked to peek around the corner of the tavern. The space was empty. He heard a giggle behind and spun toward it, again seeing no source. He stopped in the middle of the rocky street, tipped his head so his hat brim shaded his eyes, and searched carefully. The shack next to the tavern building had many large cracks running vertically between sun-shrunken exterior boards. An eye inspected him through one particularly wide gap. A blue eye, sparkling in the dark. Feeling impudent and brave, he stepped up to the door and pushed it open.

"Your horses are sound. Why do you wish to risk the sea?

He has been watching us – or someone with an eye for detail has kept him informed.

"We rode as far south as Little River to get here. The Tories are still active in the north. I do not mean to fight them

255

or to have my men volunteered for a militia."

Another interminable spell of silence. Newman feared the man might have fallen asleep, so he said, "We can leave as soon as you are ready."

"I have not agreed."

"Do you fear we are Loyalists as well?"

"I fear only God," the voice came. "I will ask him to judge you."

"How long will that take?"

A sputtering laugh. "The Lord sets his own watch."

"Where is your ship? I did not see one which looked able to make the necessary trip."

"You did not *see* her—" the man said, emphasizing his lack of trust in his visitor's visual abilities, "—as she is safely in her own private berth."

Newman nodded to himself. If the British sent a patrol up the river, this captain's ship might stand out as useful and be taken into service. Or it might mark the owner as a blockade runner, or even just as one capable of running through the offshore squadron. It would be torched with no apology or compensation. This man's vessel was not out casting net, nor was it on public display. Newman felt somewhat better about his plan. He did not long to venture into the teeth of the British Navy in a fishing boat.

The girl was about his own age, Nat judged, but she bore herself like an old woman, apart from the occasional giggle. She had invited him in – once he was already fully into the crowded shadowy room – and directed him to a rickety chair. She dragged a crude table from a corner and set it in front of him, then obtained a crate to seat herself.

"I am a witch," she said earnestly. She seemed to want the fact out of the way as early on in their relationship as possible. Nat looked around him for the first time. The walls were papered with bills and flyers: theatre acts, revolutionary calls to arms, covers of almanacks, and municipal proclamations of all stripes. On the floor planks, boxes piled haphazardly on crates, open ends filled with brown glass bottles and buff clay pots, tiny cloth bundles, and bunches of withered vegetation tied with twine. He could think of no polite response.

"My mother is a witch, and her mother was a witch."

Nat started to mention the only witches he had knowledge of were those condemned to death in Scripture and those actually put to death in Salem, but held his tongue.

"Do you doubt me?" Her voice rose.

"No," Nat said.

"I know why you have come here."

Again he said nothing. She brushed the hair back from her eyes, perhaps in frustration. Her audience was not participating properly.

"Attend me, oh spirits!" she said dramatically. A manipulation Nat could not follow in the gloom, and her two hands were cupped together. She shook them vigorously, blew onto them three times, and parted them over the table. The payload clanked and clattered on the surface, bounced and skidded and came to rest. Nat saw three stubby bones, very white, a copper coin worn smooth of its device by countless fingers, two buttons – one as blue as her eyes and one as red as his face, and the miniature and perfect skull of some rodent.

She studied the final arrangement of these items. Nat studied her. She had black hair and pale perfect skin which Nat was unable to reconcile with her existence in this sunburned region. She was not the most beautiful girl he had ever seen, but she was very far from the ugliest. He determined her straight overlong nose was the defining feature of her face. Her plain olive dress was unadorned but also unripped, though it showed signs of wear at the elbows and along the hem. She did not meet his expectations of a witch. But he had never actually met one to compare.

Finally her head came up and she pronounced, "You are on a great quest."

"That's right," Nat said with real surprise. "We are going north to kill a demon."

She stared at him, her eyes gradually narrowing until they

were accusing slits.

"The demon took the Major's eyes and is set on killing General Washington. So we have to go and kill it first."

She swept her soothsaying utensils from the table and into her lap with one angry motion. "You may not play me the fool in my own house," she hissed.

Nat put up both hands. "I swear on..." He glanced around. There was no Bible in sight. "Well, it's true."

She put her bones and beads into a leather purse as she considered this. At last she demanded, "Put out your hand."

Nat obeyed. She unstopped a miniscule glass jar and poured a charge of reddish-gray powder into his palm. "This is mummy powder," she pronounced. "Cursed by an ancient Pharaoh. If you lie while holding mummy powder, you will certainly fall ill and die a horrible death. Have you ever held mummy powder before?"

Nat shook his head, staring warily at the ominous stuff. It contained flecks of black, which for some reason made him uneasy.

"Very well. Tell your story. And mind any deception. I cannot be responsible, as the recipe for the antidote has been lost to human wisdom."

He kept very still and told her everything he knew about what had happened to the Major's eyes and how they had fired pistols at the demon in the streets of Charles Town with no effect but the death of Teague. How they had barely escaped disaster without their enemy being scratched. How the bearded man who was a demon had lifted his arms to summon the confusing, obscuring wind and disappeared into dust.

A popeyed tavern keeper has an advantage in that he always looks intrigued by his customers' tales, which keeps the trade talking themselves dry. Such was the case with Wilcox and Filly, though it was Wilcox who was doing all the talking. Filly's role was to nod confirmation at appropriate intervals.

"There we was," Wilcox was saying, one finger pointed into the air. "In broad daylight, surrounded by ten thousand

Redcoats with muskets and bayonets and us with naught but empty pistols which we had just cleverly popped off so as to alert the whole of the King's bastard children to our crime."

The keeper smiled eagerly, one eye on Wilcox and the other wandering as if on its own accord over Filly...and the other patron...and the door.

"Our commander blind. Our most sound man lying dead in the dust. And the beating boots of two regiments and more thundering ever closer to investigate."

Wilcox paused to drink. Filly nodded. The keeper tapped his fingers on a half-full jug. He was sure the tale was a fancy, but still he was curious to hear how it ended in anything other than the death of the narrator.

The girl was up, searching through the items on display in the several crates. She selected something and came back to the table. "Have you any money?"

Nat reached down, untied a knot in the corner of his shirt, and put three halfpence on the table. She did not have to know another knot held silver specie.

She studied the three coins for a moment, then separated one and replaced it with a square of dark brown leather. She turned the coin in her fingers.

"That is a grigri." She nodded at the table. "I will bless it."

Nat put out a hand and touched it with reverence. The object looked as old as antiquity, older even than mummy powder. It was tooled with flowing characters, none he had learned from Mrs. Fuchs' teachers. "How?"

She combed her fingers through her thick black hair and held the hand up for his inspection. Several dark strands corkscrewed from her fist. She rolled these into balls, then picked up the grigri. It was a small pouch, Nat saw, with a flap over a top opening. She lifted the flap and extracted a long length of leather string. Into the opening she stuffed the unruly cluster of hair.

"Now we are bound. As long as you wear the grigri, my powers will protect you."

259

Nat slipped it around his neck, letting the leather pouch down into his blouse.

"If you are ever in peril, obtain a hair or fingernail from your enemy. Put it in the grigri – and I will defeat him."

She watched him fiercely with her beautiful blue eyes. He wanted to lean over and kiss her.

"Give me something of yours," she said. Nat did not question her. He glanced down, as did she. He had no rings or belt. His shirt was a jersey – no buttons.

"The buckle," she suggested. He leaned over and unfastened one boot, removing the plain hammered iron buckle from its fastenings. He laid it on the table.

She took it up and sheltered it in one hand. To it she added the contents of her leather purse, blew on them three times, and again shook her hands over the table.

"Attend me, oh spirits! Search the heart of this one!" She tossed the objects onto the wood. They clacked and came to rest. Nat was fascinated by her face and was studying on it when the noise stopped. She looked puzzled for a second, then concerned, then horrified. She drew a deep ragged breath.

Nat gaped at the table. Two of the bones had come to rest across one another. Above them was the rodent skull, its fragile needle-sharp teeth parted and clamped onto the copper coin. And on its head an improbable crown – his boot buckle.

The girl shot to her feet and began to shriek.

July 17, 1781
Istanbul

Songay Bin's voice was muffled, his words garbled and unclear. Ruttee cocked his head, but that did no good. So he shook it to indicate he did not comprehend.

Bin stopped speaking. It was surprisingly difficult to make oneself understood while hanging upside down. He had never considered the problem before this moment. The tongue muscles needed to be commanded altogether differently, and the lips did not seem to want to cooperate.

He tried again, more slowly. "You are not in their book. I do not think they will be too hard on you."

Ruttee laughed, not very convincingly. "That depends on what you consider too hard. Hanging is a kind of hardness I had wanted to avoid. The Sultan must have you on his list as a minor spy to deserve a mere noose. If you were a threat to the Ottoman Empire I am sure they would draw, quarter and burn you in a public square. Yet if you are even a minor agent, what am I? A fellow traveler with a spy, comforter to a spy, kin to a spy? No, I am tarnished by your company – an enemy of the Empire as well, by their standard."

Bin frowned, but he was upside-down, so maybe it was a smile. "Do not assume the worst. You are too valuable to hang. The Empire has many galleys which need rowers, and you will easily escape."

"You have had better plans."

The dungeon was cramped. The mossy walls and sooty arched ceiling were stone slabs held tenuously by crumbling mortar. A gate of iron barred a narrow staircase leading up, and down the staircase came the faintest reflection of a quivering yellow flame. Water dripped, a plinking metronome, into an unseen pool.

They had taken passage on a Berber coastal trader as citizens of the Russian Empire. Upon ascending to the Istanbul docks they were arrested by the Janissary unit with the port concession. Their names checked against a thick volume in a tiny hut, in a breathtakingly short time and with an unexpected efficiency they been sentenced to death and forcibly removed to their present accommodations.

"Junipero said you did not make a believable Turk," Ruttee observed. "And the Janissaries obviously thought you a poor Russian."

"I could be in the pay of the Tsar."

"Agreed. Still, you may be wise to travel under your real name instead of the one which draws the Empire's curiosity."

Bin sighed – the same in any orientation. "In this case the truth is a bizarre concoction – and the most likely path to our goal."

They had not once voiced that goal to their Turkish hosts. The simplicity of their intent would have annoyed the Ottoman mechanism, which was used to dealing with elaborate plots – usually by generous grants of overtime pay to the executioners' guild. The two Dibele were drawn to the Tower by their common bond with the dead Spaniard who had been friend to both. They acknowledged it silently by voyaging with the names he had called them. Bin and Ruttee sought only to contact the expedition sent by Franklin and reveal the location of the Tower. They were not so simple as to keep the only copy of the location inside a head that might be parted from its body at the whim of any local potentate. The two had shipped gold and a marked map to trusted contacts in Istanbul, so if they were to be knocked on the head in some alleyway – or hanged as spies – the information would still eventually reach the expedition. But the possibility was deeply unsatisfying. Songay Bin craved to witness the death of at least one knight as had his cousin, and Ruttee, having touched the blood of one Giza Mashujaa without suffering for it, desired to plunge his hands into a puddle.

Scuffling footsteps echoed down the stairs. Ruttee, chained only at one ankle as befitted the spy of lower rank, crabbed closer to the gate to try and see who or what was coming. Songay Bin, firmly fixed to the wall, could only move his head a little. Even small motion caused him much pain. His brain seemed to be swollen and tender from prolonged inversion.

Feet appeared, then legs, followed by the torso, arms, and head of a guard. The man yawned as he unlocked the gate. In one hand he held a wooden stave wrapped thickly at the end with leather. He took a working stance and began to beat Ruttee. His blows were not particularly violent. He seemed distracted and did not put his whole heart into the job.

Ruttee took the first few impacts in silence, then began to

moan and gasp helpfully, but the punisher was not inspired by his encouragement. He turned away and gave Bin about the same number of lackluster strikes to the ribs. The guard went back out of the gate, locking it carefully, and ascended the stairs. His tapir's light diminished, the growing shadows it cast ran to and fro, and then the prisoners were again alone in the near total darkness.

Ruttee eased back onto the floor. He was not injured; indeed, he had caused himself more pain in his life by tripping over tree roots. Perhaps the trifling torture meant their jailers hoped the two would be ransomed, and the warden wished to preserve the goods. Or else they were soon to be killed and were just not worth the effort of a good and proper beating.

They waited, which is a thing the Dibele do very well. Some time later four guards came suddenly into the dungeon, blinding Ruttee and Songay Bin with flaring torches. The men unchained their prisoners and dragged them up into a large courtyard, tiled underfoot with red squares and decorated by blue mosaic fantasies running up the walls and around the deep windows and galleries overlooking the space. Ruttee noticed immediately the wooden gallows – two nooses hanging from the cross member.

Opposite from the gallows a man stood in an archway holding a scroll. He wore a golden robe under a flowing crimson coat unfastened at the front. His careful white beard was like frosting on skin creased and darkened by age and sun. On top of his head balanced a stiff silver turban rising straight up and expanding at the top like an enormous mushroom. Ruttee concluded that this utterly impractical garb meant the wearer must be a representative of the Sultan.

The party stopped, and the man began to read from his script. It was Turkish, or so Ruttee assumed, and delivered rapidly as though the speaker did not expect his new audience members to understand the proclamation – just a pro forma exercise obligatory before the Empire carried out its sentence.

But Songay Bin had done more that just masquerade as a resident of the Turkish territories. When the turbaned man took a pause to breathe, Ruttee was amazed as his cousin responded in the same tongue.

"I do claim the right to speak," Bin said loudly. "I claim the right to beg the indulgence of the Empire and of the great Agha."

The Agha dropped his paper a bit and fixed the prisoner with an evil glare. He had just finished promising that the Great and Benevolent Empire of the Ottomans granted all men the privilege of addressing charges brought against them, but he had not dreamt it possible in this case the pledge might have to be kept.

"Speak," the Agha said warily.

Bin, as he later told Ruttee, gave the man the whole story. Who they were, where they came from, what they were about. Not long into the narrative the man in the high turban rolled up his scroll and pushed it into his sleeve. His face was set in a studied indifference tinged, as Songay Bin's tale unwound, with a bit of resigned annoyance.

Bin concluded his statement with a bow as low as he could accomplish in the grasp of his two guards. The Agha eyeballed the two prisoners for a moment, then motioned one of the guards to approach and whispered a few words close to his ear. The guards turned Bin and Ruttee around and marched them back down the stairs and rechained them just as they had been before. One of the guards stayed behind and administered the obligatory beating without causing either much discomfort.

The light was taken away again. Ruttee found himself breathing deeply, his heart racing. That had been very close.

"The fellow in the impractical hat was the Agha Okuz," Bin said. "He is the Janissary in charge of this place. I told him why we are here."

Ruttee exhaled slowly. "I was never so happy to hear words I could not understand."

"I may not appear a believable Turk, but I studied the part."

"What happens now?"

Bin rattled his chains squirming, trying to get less uncomfortable. "Nothing happens in the region leading to the Tower without eventually coming to the attention of the Empire. I am sure the expedition we seek is there with the full knowledge and blessing of the Sultan Abd Al-Hamid. Remember the saying, 'If you cannot find your bull then slap the nearest cow'."

"I never understood it until this very moment, thank you."

The first guard later returned and beat them with apathy, but this time he left a pan of water and a small loaf of bread which was still warm inside and smelled of cardamom.

July 20, 1781
New Jersey

At first light, the captain put them into a shallow skiff and landed them on a gravel bar two hundred yards from the coast. They hoisted their packs and waded ashore in the icy tide. Just past the beach stood a freshly whitewashed barn commanding a meadow full of brown goats. The barn proved to be deserted, so they gave themselves permission to toss down their burdens within and relax on a pile of straw, flexing and rubbing their numb feet while their boots dried.

Nat soon rose and walked out into the field. Several curious nanny goats approached to nibble at his loose threads. A skeptical billy tilted its head as it contemplated him with its strange Satanic eyes, perhaps judging whether to put its horns forward and charge the intruder.

Major Newman came after him and stood massaging the soles of his feet on the thick close-shorn grass. "Something troubles you, son," he declared. Nat had been obviously uneasy the whole of their voyage up the coast, but there had never been an instant of privacy in the boat to question him.

Nat hung his head.

Newman waited patiently, patting goats as they came amiably up to thrust their noses into his pockets.

Finally Nat straightened his back, as if facing a firing squad and resolved to die bravely. "You will want to return me."

"Return you to what? The orphanage?"

Nat nodded.

"You are fifteen years old, Nat. You're a man – too old for an orphanage."

Nat looked suddenly panicked. "Then... what will I do?"

The Major sighed. "Begin by telling me what eats you so."

"I lied." He paused and closed his eyes. "I know Mrs. Fuchs told you my father killed my mother and then himself and left me an orphan. That was a lie."

There was nothing to say to it, so Newman just stood and rubbed a very happy goat under her ears.

Shaking his head, the boy said in a rush, "I told her a story. I... couldn't tell her...."

Newman's eyes began to ache, so he rummaged in his pockets searching for his ointment. The goats bleated and milled around the two.

"He was not my father. He and my mother never married. I don't remember my real father. He died in a fire at a brick factory. This man was a drunk and a bastard. He beat me. He beat my mother. One night he hit her with her own iron pan. She was down... and he kept hitting her. I was ten years old. I wasn't big. But I could pull a trigger–" He choked on the words. Newman heard the wetness of Nat's tears as he tried to blink them back. "The only truth is that I am an orphan. I am sorry I lied to you...." His voice faded out, the energy of courage consumed.

Newman used his hip to nudge two goats from his path and stepped over to the young man. He put one hand on Nat's shoulder. "I stand by my judgment," he said. "Now let us go and see if this country offers any horses for sale."

August 5, 1781
The Holy Land

The young recruit they picked up in Haifa talked nonstop. Birol Erdem did not try to check him but just interjected a grunt from time to time. It wasn't a burden as long as the convoy was in motion, for the young man was mostly drowned out by the grinding of the wheels on the road, rattling of chains, huffing of the horses, and so on. It was only when they were halted by a rockslide before a steep pass on the Nazareth road that the chatter began to erode Birol's calm. As the civilian laborers passed in single file on either side of the wagon on their way to clear the rubble, he briefly considered backhanding the lad off the seat. He checked the impulse, for he remembered being himself once a freshly minted graduate from the Cebeci School of Artillery. Plus, the wagon was full of explosive shells. They were probably stable enough, but he had not personally packed them or fitted their fuses. It was better not to tempt fate, not to become a bad example for future Cebeci. *Remember Erdem who blew himself up on the Nazareth Road?*

Instead he waited for the young man to pause for breath and asked, "Is Tatim the Snake still teaching metal craft?"

"He is," the lad said. "Was he your instructor as well?"

Birol nodded. "I am not that old – and Tatim the Snake is not that young. Tell me what he teaches you these days about bore corrosion."

They began a conversation on the topic, which the young man knew only in hypotheticals, but Birol made solid from experience in actual war. The cannon ahead of them in line was aimed more or less right at them; sunlight illuminated the first few inches inside the muzzle. Birol pointed.

"See how the bore looks like a pebbled stone? Pitting is the beginning of corrosion, a mark the piece has not been properly cared for. At the end of every day where a cannon of the Cebeci has been fired – and often when it has not – we swab out the bore with a pounded mixture of limes and oyster shell to prevent such dangerous nonsense."

The lad showed confusion as he scratched his scraggly struggle of a beard. "Are these not Cebeci cannons?"

"No," Birol said. "These are Spanish made. We captured them from the Russians."

The laborers ahead were making slow progress with the unstable obstacle, so Birol reached back for a canteen and began the story. His unit of Janissary Cebeci had been training at their barracks in Trabzon for the war which all knew must be coming: the battle to retake the Crimea and other lands of the Empire stolen by the Russians. One day they had been gathered, issued ordinary clothes to wear, and queued for loading onto a ship with some Janissary infantry.

"We naturally began to prepare the great guns for the journey, but our Corbaci told us to leave them. We were taken aback by this deviation and even more confused when we began to embark – and none of the gunners were there. This we had never experienced."

In mufti they had sailed up the coast of the Black Sea. They landed, drew muskets, and were told to wander up the beach pretending to be local militia patrolling for smugglers. Any persons they found in or about a certain concealed inlet they were to kill.

"We came upon a group of hunters on the shore there. Well, they claimed to be hunters, though they had set out pickets like military men and spoke with Russian accents. We professed to believe them until enough of us gathered – then we stopped smiling and opened fire."

The eyes of the young man were wide. Education at the Cebeci Janissary School of Practical Artillery had prepared him for the transportation and care of cannon. Close combat with small arms had not been in the curriculum.

"We killed them all, but they managed to defend themselves for a time." Birol took a drink. "Three Janissary infantry and one Cebeci dead." He pointed at his companion. "Which is why you are here today."

The rookie was suddenly uncomfortable. The dead man was no doubt a friend of all these hardened Cebeci. Would they somehow blame him for the loss?

Birol slapped the canteen against the youngster. "Don't worry. Ten years I have been a Cebeci, and that was the only time we had to get our hands dirty. We leave violence to the infantry. They are too simple to do anything else. And never listen to the gunners. They will brag about themselves as if they are the Sultan's golden shite, but any idiot can point a gun and hold a match. If it weren't for the Cebeci the cannons would not be there to fire. If it were not for us, the cannons would fall apart in a month. And the Empire is built on cannons." Birol looked up to see how the removal was coming along, then remembered his place in the story.

"After the slaughter," he resumed, "we found, as had been promised, a cave at the base of a nearby cliff, within arrow shot of the water. It had been blocked with rubble and covered with earth. We would never have found it by chance. Inside were these six cannon with their carriages and many shells, solid shot, and canister."

"But why were they in a cave?"

Birol shrugged. "Russians. Who can know their minds? They were to be turned on us in the next war, you can be sure."

The lad was puzzled. "Are we going into battle?"

Biral shrugged again. "I have not been told so, but why else would we be taking the gunners?" He moved his head backwards to indicate the tail of the column.

Six wagons led the convoy, of which they were the third. The wagons were stout, their beds heaped with rounded shapes under tarpaulins, and each wagon also pulled one cannon carriage. This was a combined load of some weight, so the wagon had been fitted with a long tongue to accommodate four horses. Even with this rig the trip had been a ponderous haul up from the Mediterranean shore.

Behind the last cannon came three supply wagons handled by six more Cebeci, followed by eighteen mounted

Janissary gunners, who were trailed by three score of assorted women and small ambulatory children. Next in the cavalcade milled a pack of lean hounds of various breeds, sniffing and growling. Last, far back and down the hill, bounced two men on donkeys. They were hooded and robed and some way off, but the lad could see their faces were very dark.

"Who are the Africans trailing us?" the youth asked.

Biral squinted. "Probably some traders trying to pass. They should have gone down the coast."

August 9, 1781
Paris

The God of summer had determined France needed tenderizing and so brought the whole region to a simmer. The day began clear and hot, and as the sun ascended, the heat rose and the humidity increased to create such an environment that sane Parisians descended to their cellars to wring out their undergarments and wait out the onslaught.

On the top of the Louvre Palace, however, members of the Académie des Sciences whose interests included meteorology assembled in the early afternoon to catch the peak of the phenomenon and document it for their records. When Franklin finally stepped out from the staircase onto the flat roof, he was puffing like a hound and sweating streams under his clothes. Leclerc was already there, and de Caritat, and several other members he had not seen in some time. The junior associates had been prevailed upon to haul up the crates of equipment now being put to their use, and for the next hour or so the temperature was measured in Fahrenheit and in Celsius, the relative humidity was monitored with the hygrometer of Lambert, and sightings of the sun taken with a sextant to set the time accurately. Three different anemometers waited in vain to spin with any flow of the static atmosphere. A barometer tube leaned uneasily against the parapet, upended in a beaker of quicksilver – someone had forgotten to bring up the stand for the glass, and Franklin eyed the arrangement with apprehension. That mass of quicksilver was worth a good part of the total yearly assessment upon the members of the Académie. The barometer had been knocked over just two years ago, and most of its mercury had run down between the floorboards and disappeared forever. One careless nudge of the apparatus and the fluid metal would flow into the drains and cascade down into the courtyard. He edged past the barometer carefully – but did bend down to note the reading.

The learned men labored for the better part of an hour before de Caritat paled, teetered on the edge of falling, and had to sit down. None had brought hats; no one had remembered a carafe of water. The Compte had to be helped to the stairs by the party and aided down them until they had reached their laboratory, where drinks were fetched and the day's observations discussed. The distinguished philosophers mopped their soaked heads with kerchiefs, and when those were thoroughly soaked, with a pile of greying linen squares an absent member had gathered to use in construction of a box kite.

The academicians subsequently retired to their respective homes to recuperate, but Franklin had no rest. He had been invited to a salon at the home of the Madame de Montesson, and he could not send his regrets. This learned Madame happened to be the public mistress and secret wife of Duke Louis Philippe d'Orléans, who had the ear of the King.

Franklin turned the problem over as de Chaumont's coach bounced him on the cobbles and lack of cobbles along the rue Saint-Séverin, the day being too damnably hot and his body too sapped to even consider hiking from Passy just to maintain appearances. The Duke had the ear of the King; the Madame had the testicles of the Duke. To what part of the Madame should Franklin attach himself so a chain of communication be established?

The answer to that question, realized upon his introduction to Charlotte-Jeanne Béraud de La Haye de Riou, the aforementioned Madame de Montesson, was: *Any available part*. The hostess of the salon was most exquisitely beautiful.

But the invigoration of perfumed curves and cerebral discourse had not lasted. Franklin reclined on a divan, his tired legs elevated, a glass in hand. He was the last of the guests but for the Madame de Gouges, who stood trying for fresh air at the nearest open window and waving away the moths which fluttered in upon the barest of breezes.

Madame de Montesson perched on a simple wooden dining chair, sipping port and surveying the debris of her salon with an air of accomplishment. "My dear," she said to the Madame de Gouges, "next time you must read us your essay."

Madame de Gouges' hips moved a bit, hinting at a curtsey. "I would be honored, Marquise, but—" she looked pointedly at Franklin "—it is impolite, perhaps, in its passion."

Ben sighed quietly. *It will be Le Question Grand again and again. I will have to calculate an excuse to miss such a tedious salon.*

Franklin loved salons dedicated to the discussion of natural philosophy – although no one calls such meetings salons, for some reason, but rather just plain meetings. Or as he had styled his own Philadelphia group gathered to discuss topics of mutual improvement, a Junto. He had always come away from those assemblies animated. The ideas whizzing about set his brain spinning like a flywheel and sparked his old limbs.

Sparking limbs brought to his mind the dish of frog legs he had left out a bench at the Académie des Sciences. Had he covered it? He could not recall – the heat had burnt away memories of simple tasks. A member had come to the last meeting and delivered a note on his travel to the Papal States, where he had interviewed a Professor Galvani at the Accademia delle Scienze dell'Istituto di Bologna. This Bolognese gentleman had observed that a frog leg, freshly separated from the remainder of the frog, might still be induced to move upon the application of an ethereal fluid he was calling the animal electricity. Franklin had immediately ceased all other activities, scoured the nearby taverns, inns, and monasteries for any legs they were willing to part with, and proceeded to subject them to all sort of electrical, chemical, and mechanical investigations. His last experiment was no doubt covered at the moment with a layer of flies and would be thick with maggots by the time he could return to it. He shrugged. The stray dogs of the Louvre courtyard were in for a treat.

His attention returned to the night. He was sluggish, yes, precisely because of it. These salons, of ordinary philosophy, or play reading, or literary criticism, left him depleted. Tonight the attendees had been writers, and they had descended on the topic of human slavery like the flies would have on his poor tray of frog legs. Suffused with indignation, they had gathered momentum en masse as birds do, coordinating their collective energies to fly in the same direction. And though Benjamin Franklin might be to much of France the rustic genius, the self-effacing homilist, to this gang he was a man who had been so indiscrete as to actually sign his right name to a document blatant in its hypocrisy. They were insulted by the very boldness of the thing, the sheer audacity to declare all men equal and then bear sober witness to such a statement as the owners of subjugated men.

Madame de Gouges herself, who still stood absorbing the evening air, and was as lovely as any fresh flower, had opened the barrage upon him by turning the attention of the company to a recent report from the new state of Georgia about a slave rebellion which, real or imagined, had been ruthlessly suppressed by mass hangings. This brought the company around to several questions, to wit: Were all men (here an animated and flushed Madame de Gouges piped in her correction, "–and women!") created equal? (Answer: Yes.) Were all men men? (Here the only hint of natural philosophy in hours staggered out to buttress the argument. Answer: Yes.) What gave men the right to own other men? (Answer: No such right existed or should be allowed to exist.) What was to be done by right-thinking citizens about this vile injustice? (Answer: Many possibilities, no consensus. Franklin at this point recalled the parable of the mice proposing to bell the cat but had the good manners not to voice same.)

Now, the amusement over, Franklin was tired. Tired of the tedious Parisian summer; tired of standing up physically; tired of standing up morally. He was consumed by defending the indefensible. Not that he tried so very hard. He stayed acutely aware any one of the salon participants could be close to someone in government. Indeed, one or more *might* be tapped tomorrow to occupy some office themselves, in which they *might* then do Franklin and his nascent nation a favor. Not to mention their hostess and her intimate contact with the Court. No, he was not able to unleash his full oratorical powers upon them, which in a normal venue he might, and remind them of the French sugar plantations on Saint-Domingue which existed only by the delivery of an endless stream of Africans fetched in bondage by ships with cruelly ironic names such as Amitié and Liberté. Instead he nodded and drank endlessly to their health.

Madame de Gouges sat on the divan, forcing him to scoot his legs to the side. Her gown flowed over his lower body, and she patted the general area of his knees. "My dear friend," she purred, "you must be spent with parrying the lunges of this legion. Really though, you should be here when they confine their critique to literature. Oh, how the blood flows then!"

Franklin peered over his port. She had turned her head to address him, giving him a clear line of sight across the uplifted tops of what promised to be a set of firm and symmetrical breasts. A younger Ben would have proposed they continue their fruitful discussion in his coach, and eventually over a late wine, and inevitably in the bedroom. Tonight's Ben just shook his head. Was this what an old man felt, or rather did not feel? Had the unparalleled ministrations of his late beloved Nicole – for such was the name he chose to remember her by – removed from his type case the letters necessary to spell passion?

"I do not fault them," he said. "There is a dichotomy at the heart of our union, and some day it will surely split our heart in two." He tipped his glass. "May our children be wiser than we."

Jefferson's letter lay open on his desk in Passy. It contained no confidences worthy of locking it away; it was a simple reply to Franklin's polite note dispatched in April. In a mundane communication, Ben had done his rhetorical best to nudge his friend by implication. He had resisted the urge to scrawl ASK YOUR GIRL CAROLINE ABOUT THE GIZA MASHUJAA on the sheet, seal it, and send it away. He did not know the extent of the knights' influence or how vast their network of agents might be, so instead he had tried to induce Jefferson to interview the girl in private – she might realize her master knew enough to warrant receipt of the remainder of her intelligence. Perhaps he should have encoded his true desires under the writing, or within the text, but again he was ignorant of his opponent's capabilities.

It had not worked. Jefferson's reply was obtuse and off-target in a manner that left Franklin shocked and saddened in equal parts, but now he realized the attempt had been buggered from birth. His colleague possessed a brilliant mind cursed with the ability to hold within its vastness two opposite and wholly incompatible concepts: Equality and Ownership. He had his world divided into separate countries whose citizens did not mingle. Jefferson would give as much credence to Caroline's narrative as he would to a talking horse. The girl might be a brilliant agent operating under the most trying circumstances – and according to Captain Proctor's information she was – but to Thomas Jefferson she was in the end no more than his property.

My mind is too simple for such contortions, I admit. I must choose between the two abstractions. One must be paramount; the other must sink into oblivion. And I must now find an alternative plan.

As it happened, even inspired persuasion would have been for naught. Jefferson had sent the girl to General Washington at the behest of a medico for some reason or other. Franklin's brain had stopped absorbing the words at about this point in the missive. He had no doubt the movement had been a ruse orchestrated by Caroline's organization, and the realization made him sit in uneasy silence for most of an hour. The evil bastards were stalking the Commander-in-chief. The obviousness of it smacked him like a rebuking palm. How had he not seen this? The nation had no one else with the singular characteristics of Washington. Without that rock of a man to guide and shelter them, the states would surely founder and sink. The Crown would be ascendant once more.

The hateful possibility disturbed Franklin. He tried to swallow, but there was no moisture in his throat. He gulped his port as the two women politely tried not to stare.

I might have to live out my years in Paris.

September 18, 1781
The Holy Land

Moses had gotten into the habit of hauling his full bladder up the modest hill dividing the village of Amman from the Roman ruins. As he pissed, he imagined his stream running down into the present on one side and into antiquity on the other. He wondered how many thousands of men and women long dead had shamelessly stood on this vantage point to relieve themselves. No one from the village complained, anyway. The ragged place where the stone and dried mud dwellings became thick enough to mark the probable edge of town was a half-mile off. A priest of whatever god or goddess this temple had been erected to honor might have once chased away the defiler, as there was a line of toppled columns at the crest, perhaps marking some kind of ceremonial function – probably not the practical one he was using it for today.

He fastened his trousers back up and turned toward the camp. It had been almost a year since the four Americans and sixteen Frenchmen arrived here to pitch their tents on the bare expanse. Now it resembled a bustling country fair. Their camels had been joined by a score of mules, forty or so horses, and two donkeys. The rather plain military canvas tents of the original settlers were flanked by the multihued fringed cloth dwellings of the Indians and the boxy red-and-white quarters assembled by the various flavors of Janissary who had lately joined the mission. Six such bright shelters surrounded six wagons parked in a circle guarding six cannon on carriages. Moses shook his head. The practice of having one group who fired the guns and a wholly separate group who transported and cared for them was an insult to both his efficient New England upbringing and naval tradition from time immemorial, but such was the way the Sultanate organized artillery. He could not quibble with their success. They had after all built an empire in this manner.

Separated from the military quarters by just a short distance was a patchwork of enclosures stitched together by the women who had arrived with the Turks. He could hear them singing, laughing, and arguing. There was the dull bell ringing of cooking pots roughly handled, and the shrill cries of children wanting. Dogs barked, camels bellowed and groaned, horses whinnied, and the donkeys conversed pleasantly in a nonstop trading of brays.

Moses took out his watch. It was near four o'clock. Time for the elements to come together.

The French had brought the largest tent in the camp, a rectangular pavilion. This served primarily as their dining room and reinforced the awe of their American allies in the gustatory precautions taken by the French military. This afternoon it was clear of furniture to make room for the assembly. Proctor had gone around and asked every group send two representatives, but his request had been treated only as a lower bound. The Mughal contingent, for example, was Zafar and his second, a thin man named Kashi. But they also brought an interpreter for Kashi and Zafar, who spoke no and little English respectively. And Zafar had to have his assistant or butler or manservant or whatever he was – Moses was never quite sure.

So there were four Indians in the tent. The prideful Turks could not be outshone, and there were two distinct sets of Turk – Janissary gunners and Janissary Cebeci – who had each to be separately represented and supported, et cetera. This escalation meant that Proctor and Ward found upwards of twenty rubbing elbows instead of the six expected. Even their Bedouin camel wrangler had seen fit to slip in, not wanting to admit an Arab deserved less standing than a lousy Turk.

Moses realized he should have scheduled this conclave outside around a nice fire. For some reason it had seemed more formal and binding to be inside, even if inside meant canvas walls about a packed sand floor. The crowded, boisterous atmosphere almost made him move immediately for adjournment.

Instead he went to the middle of the tent and put two fingers into his mouth and whistled the way his father had taught him, a piercing shriek sufficient to get the quick attention of a dory invisible in the fog or a milling batch of polyglot adventurers. The tent fell silent; some of the nearest occupants put hands to their ears, grimacing.

"My name is Captain Moses Proctor of the Continental Navy of the United States of America," he said rather more loudly than was necessary. Part of him took a quick aside to appreciate Franklin's foresight in advancing his rank. "I have come here on orders of the Continental Congress."

He had the attention of all now. He looked at the variety within the allied forces – the faces pale and dark and in between, the tight precision of the French uniforms, the flowing lines of the Turkish. This was all Ben Franklin. That pudgy pale lecherous old man had pulled levers and strings and damned if he hadn't caused the strangest fighting force in the history of the world to show up in the middle of a wasteland.

He had thought long about how to tell them why they were here. They had some inkling – there was so much gossip and conjecture that even the Turks, who had been here only a few days, had heard ten different versions of what was afoot. Proctor knew the scuttlebutt. It was the Holy Grail, buried in the sands. They had found the Arc of the Covenant or stumbled upon the True Cross. A second Mecca was rising from the desert floor. They were to beware of Cossacks, of pirates, of the ghosts of Roman legions, of English Redcoats. Best to tell them the unvarnished truth.

"Somewhere in this area there is a fountain, and from this fountain certain men are drawing power. Mr. Franklin calls it a life force, a vital energy. Whatever it is, it is being used for evil. I have seen this with my own eyes. The ship I was serving on was sunk by this power. Two hundred and more of my countrymen were drowned by these men, and I have come here to find the source of their strength and destroy it."

The tent filled with muttered asides as this development was translated and discussed – neither with much happiness. Moses inspected the turnout apprehensively. One of his first ideas had been to present the Tower as a place where a fantastic treasure waited, but there were too many chinks in that fiction to employ it with any confidence. He took a deep breath. The next step was critical.

"You have all reported to me that your superiors have charged you with cooperating in our mission. I am therefore taking command of this operation and full responsibility for its ultimate outcome."

He held his breath, expecting if any of the several factions were to dissent and advance a claim for its own primacy, this would be the time. He had no way to force any of these men to obey him. It was not clear if he had legal command even of the three Americans who had volunteered to follow him, as this was not a maritime concern.

But all he saw was shrugging of shoulders and slow smiles. The senior officer of the Jannissary gunners, a man named Yildirim, who held the rank of Chorbaji, came up to Moses and hugged him effusively, jabbering in Turkish.

"Chorbaji say," said his interpreter, close behind the entwined pair, "we are here for you."

The equivalent officer of the Cebeci embraced Moses and said much the same thing, as related by his own interpreter.

279

Zafar Mizra waited for the voluble Turks to be done with him and then stepped forward.

"Our Peshwa has delivered us into your hands, Captain Proctor." He bowed. "We will follow you. We have great admiration for the wisdom of the Franklin."

He turned, but Moses put out a hand to stop him. "Zafar – tell me. Why did your Peshwa agree to this?"

Zafar spread his two hands as though what was to follow was nothing but the obvious. "He reads the almanacs of Poor Richard. They are a source of great truth."

Proctor suddenly felt pity for the enemies of Benjamin Franklin, wherever they might be.

Their alliance codified, they sat on the floor and began to hammer out the practicalities of the thing. The Turks sent for tea, the French brought in wine, Mizra unleashed an imposing silver hookah with a myriad of hoses snaking from it. Soon the air was filled with aromatic smoke and several different conversations on strategy.

The common sticking point in any and all of their imaginings was – they simply did not know the location of the Tower or even what it looked like, other than observers had in the past characterized it as a Tower.

Proctor fetched the large map they had been using to track their searches and pinned it to one wall of the tent.

"The red lines show where we have traveled." He pointed to the nexus of the crimson explosion, which skewed away from Jerusalem, then to the end of one long trace to the west. "This is the farthest trip we have made, some one hundred nautical miles." There was muttering as this was converted into whatever units of travel each group was more familiar with. "We chose Amman because what we do know about the Tower tells us it should be within the boundaries of where we have already searched."

Lieutenant Lefevre spoke up, "We have also conducted extensive questioning of local peoples, but they have not been fruitful."

Proctor did not append that the original questioning methods of his French allies were going to include hot irons and pliers before he forbade them. Instead, he said, "We still have many places within this area to survey. Now we have additional men and will be able to extend our reach."

More muttering, this time in a mutinous tone. The Turks had come ready to fight, not to sift the sand for targets. Wandering aimlessly through the desert was for the untrained Arab, not the Janissary. Potential for discord was curtailed by the appearance of the women followers, who bore in platters of rice and lamb and passed them around to the whole company. This distracted the hungry men for some time and gave Proctor a chance to consider his next remarks.

"My friends," he said at last, chewing impolitely, "Almighty God has brought us together with a purpose. He has supplied powder and cannon and men to care for and fire them." He nodded respectfully toward each group as he mentioned it. "He would not have done so if he did not intend for us to discover our enemies very soon."

There was general agreement at this and much head bobbing, even among the Marathas, who Proctor knew were Hindus. Which was about all he knew, not even whether their theism was mono or poly. He would not have been able to pick which pagan god to cite for their pleasure and so was relieved to see his invocation of the Abrahamic deity had seemingly not offended them.

Songay Bin and Ruttee had been lurking outside since the beginning of the meeting, listening to the proceedings. A grim-faced Janissary with three pistols crammed in his wide belt refused them entry. They could not agree if he harbored any special animosity for Africans or if he was just keeping them out because they were – as the whole camp knew – common traders, skulking the fringes of the camp waiting for a chance to sell whatever wares they had to offer.

The guard abandoned his post and followed his growling stomach inside to the lamb, so the two parted the folds of the entrance and walked in. Some of the occupants in the back turned their heads, and the guard growled, but most of the party was facing the map on the far wall.

"Pardon me," Songay Bin said in perfect English, "might I have a minute of your time?"

Moses was about to order them out, thinking a sales pitch was imminent – when Bin repeated his question in fluent French, then in what Moses knew was Turkish but could not understand, then in some tongue full of swishing vowels which surprised the Indians and made them sit up to attend.

Ruttee had a map of his own under one arm. He bowed and passed it to Proctor.

"We have some information which might be of use to you," Songay Bin said four times in four different languages.

October 11, 1781
The Holy Land

They had been almost one hundred miles too far north. While Proctor examined the new map, Songay Bin told an attentive tent the legend of the Giza Mashujaa. Proctor saw he would have been able to make a much better guess at the location of the Tower if he had known about the knights' flight from Jerusalem into the east.

"It is better you had not," Bin reassured him when Moses pointed this out. "You would surely be dead now." For, he went on, the Giza had built and populated a village near the entrance to safeguard their secret. If any of Proctor's force had traveled by this place, which was called Daskara Hafiz, asking about a Tower, they would have been set upon and murdered.

But it looks so peaceful, Proctor thought.

He lay in the shade of a bank of boulders, examining Daskara Hafiz, half a league away and a little below, through his glass. He scanned an unremarkable collection of mud block houses clustered around a patch of palm trees and vegetable gardens. It did not seem a den of murderers.

"I count perhaps sixty houses," he whispered to Songay Bin.

"Meaning we have sixty men to fight."

Proctor focused on the corrals. These were filled with horses, not camels. Women filled pots from a central well, men walked about in pairs and singly, dogs and children ran about playing. "At least," he replied. He was curious how such an isolated group supplied themselves. Were there ever new recruits? Brides from other regions or outsider grooms initiated into the communal business? He had many questions, but the time to ask them would probably never come. The men in his objective glass would not stand aside or invite Moses and his party into the valley, so today the proposition was how to kill them.

"Sixty men trained in fighting, on familiar land, with fast horses," Songay Bin said.

Proctor nodded. The allied forces were no match for the guardians. Another half mile behind, paused behind some rock outcrops and high dunes, were the rest – three Americans, sixteen French, eighteen Janissary Cebeci and their wagons and cannons, the same number of Janissary gunners, a dozen Indian drovers, and one more Dibele. Mounted on a mixture of camels, horses, and donkeys, and bearing a hodgepodge of small arms.

"We have the cannon," Proctor pointed out, not very enthusiastically. The artillery could barrage the village for a time, probably killing mostly women and children, whereupon the guardian menfolk would charge on horseback and overwhelm the allies. He put down his glass and turned to Bin. "Any wisdom?

"Ask the Sultan to send Janissary soldiers," Bin said.

On the other side of the village, the land rose up to form a glacis on enormous stone upthrustings, rock molars set in the gums of the desert, continuous but for several narrow breaks – one of which must be the entrance to the valley. Now that he was here, Proctor's predatory instincts seized him. His heart beat faster at the prospect of gaining access to the land beyond – the valley where something mysterious and evil lurked, waiting. It was the same dizzying elation he had felt when a great shark circled his dory one morning long ago. Crouched with a pike in hand, he had silently invited his competitor to rise once more alongside the boat.

"You are sure there is one in the Tower?" Proctor asked. The tale of the Giza Mashujaa told by the two Dibele included the knights' arrangement for safeguarding their treasure. In addition to the village of the guardians, they always left at least one member of the cabal resident in the Tower while the other three traveled.

Bin nodded. "In it or close by. A lone knight is known to remove as far as Crete, but that is rare. More often the one responsible for the Tower will venture to Jerusalem or Damascus for short entertainments."

"If we wait for reinforcements, do you think we will be discovered?"

The Dibele considered this, looking into Proctor's face with respect – and concern. "Almost certainly."

Lifting the glass back to his eye, Proctor felt the thrill once more.

The strategy was far from perfect, and none of the parties was happy with it in its whole. The Janissaries of course wanted to bombard the village back to sand with cannon shell. It was pointed out to them this would kill many innocents, warn the occupant in the Tower, and leave them open to counterattack. The French wanted to march a column proudly into the town with the invincible eagle standard of Le Roi before them. This possibility was not given much consideration. The Indians, who counted a couple of ex-sappers among them, sketched on the ground a system of tunnels to be run under the buildings so they might be blown to infinity with some of the most excellent powder they had brought. Proctor promised, quite insincerely, their proposal would be tried if the primary scheme did not succeed.

It was Ruttee's idea. "I shall walk to the east for a time," he said. "Until I am quite burnt and thirsty. I will keep to hard ground and rock to leave no track, then turn back, seeking soft soil so my steps are clear. I carry gold – I have brought a bit with me – which I will represent as having come from a caravan." This imaginary caravan, carrying gold from the mines outside of Tabuk, was betrayed and ambushed by bandits. In the subsequent battle, most of the bandits and members of the caravan would have been killed, but not before they secreted the gold – buried unmarked – in the featureless expanse of that arid inhospitable region. "I will keep the secret just long enough to be convincing, then agree to lead them to the gold."

Songay Bin had argued he should be the deceiver, but Ruttee insisted it was his design, and he must bear the responsibility.

"What if they just kill you and take the gold?" asked Mizra.

Ruttee shook his head. "Would you risk losing a fortune to gain only what I will be carrying? I do not think so. They will ride out – I will agree to guide them if they are serious about defeating any remaining bandits we might encounter. This will encourage them to send out as many men as possible, leaving fewer for you to fight."

"But they will surely kill you when you cannot lead them to gold or even to the remains of a battle," Mizra pressed.

Ruttee shrugged. He would slip away, the way Dibele were trained to do.

October 13, 1781
Hudson River valley

A skunk had nested here. Luckily, it had departed, leaving only its aromatic memory. Countless mice, of course, and probably possums, raccoons and squirrels. There were signs the natives had poked about but probably did not like the atmosphere enough to stay. Only one human artifact remained – the name 'Evian duChambre' carved into the log sill of the north-facing window.

Filly and Wilcox toyed with the name for some hours. It was Wilcox who posed most of the possibilities. Was Evian a trapper? A Roman priest fishing for souls to entice with his Papist lies? A disgraced French nobleman in silks and lace freezing to death far from a doomed love? The least this Evian could have done was to leave a body, or at least his bones, so they might have some tangible clues.

After this lively conversation, carried mostly by Wilcox, they settled down to the ways each preferred to pass the time. Wilcox scoured the area around the hut for a thick piece of oak to carve into a walking stick. Filly opened his worn copy of Tacitus' histories, and they took turns keeping an eye on the movements around the mansion below.

Major Newman had guided his band of four to Ruttee's hut based on memorized directions, then took Nat and departed with no discussion. This rankled Wilcox, who sat taking his doubts out on the wood.

"I dunno, Filly, can you make any sense out of this plan? Us with no equipment of destruction besides the guns we carry, and we already mourn the capability of those to do the job. I will let you recall the last time we set against that thing down there – which is at this very moment likely looking up at us and laughing – we came up one good man short."

Filly grunted and turned a page.

Wilcox attacked the stick with new vigor. "I am as good as my word, and I still anticipate earning my pay here, but ain't you with me in wondering if there *are* tools on this earth that can give us the drop on the old wizard?"

Filly shrugged.

Wilcox opened his mouth to continue – but instead made a shushing sound and grabbed for his musket. Filly, more nimble than his size suggested, was on his feet with a pistol in each hand and peering out the door as Wilcox was just bringing his weapon up.

Nat broke out of the trees, Newman close behind.

The night fell chill, and the Major had them retire down the hill to Ruttee's cave where they huddled around a humble fire, brewed coffee, and roasted a rabbit Filly had caught in a snare.

"Fellows," the Major said staring into the flames, "tomorrow this matter will come to a head. I have made arrangements, and now it is time for you to learn your roles." He swirled his mug and took a sip. "It is a simple thing. The local concern that brings the house—" he nodded in the general direction of his nemesis' mansion below on the bluff "—its lamp oil will deliver in the morning a supply indistinguishable from their usual product, except that this oil will not support a flame. Tomorrow at dark Nat will shinny up to the roof and blanket the chimneys with wet canvas."

Wilcox swallowed a mouthful of rabbit leg. "When the old sorcerer is stumbling around blind with a lung full of smoke – we advance with our muskets?"

Newman shook his head. "You and Filly will go up the road to the house where his guards are stationed and prevent them from answering any alarm."

"Major," said Wilcox, "we gave it our best in broad daylight, and the feller wasn't scratched. If I understand the disposition of forces you propose, you will be alone. I don't see any cannon lying about. What kind of ordnance are you going to be carrying?"

Newman drew his knife – a wicked piece of steel with a marbled blade and a bone handle. "Beene, you have the essence of it. We need to get close enough to our enemy to lay hands on him and not be deceived by trickery." He rotated his wrist so the weapon caught the yellow flames on its blade. It seemed to glow like a living opal. "In the dark – I will have the advantage."

October 13, 1781
The Holy Land

Two days after Ruttee's departure, a small group closely observed Daskara Hafiz. Proctor was still wrapped in a scratchy wool blanket. He had spent the night flattened against observation on the top of the largest boulder, which gave him a clear view into the village. The monotonous raw night had brightened into a cloudy chilly morning. He had always imagined the desert to be constantly hot, and when reading his Bible as a youth visualized Moses and the Children of Israel trudging slowly about for forty years on burning sands. Now he realized they had spent half that time freezing, for the desert here got very, very cold in the winter months.

The others slipped up at dawn to join his vigil. They crept about to stay out of sight of the villagers, but it had not been so necessary as Proctor had imagined. The guardians were remarkably unconcerned, it seemed, with possible intruders. They did not set out guards at dusk and had no one up in any of the high points of the town watching out for approaching visitors. Proctor decided they had realized long ago their remote location was security enough. Apart from the rare caravan passing benignly, probably for centuries the only uninvited had been half-dead unfortunates like the one laboring now toward the town.

"There he is," Tayar Dogantez called down softly. The tall Turk, the Chorbaji of the Janissary Cebeci, had slithered like a lizard up the smooth boulder the rest were using as shelter. The Americans found both he and Yildirim had been taught very usable English in the Janissary training schools, which might have had a bearing on the choosing of their respective squads for this endeavor. Their employ from time to time of an interpreter was pure diplomatic show. "Just there, beyond the stand of saltbush."

All eyes turned to the east, to an indistinct shape emerging from some head-high scrub. Proctor focused it in his glass – it was Ruttee, looking now rather three-quarters-dead. His skin was peeling, his clothes were torn and dirty, and his face strained with the effort of keeping his feet. Proctor was duly impressed – the Dibele were actors of the first rank. Or else Ruttee really was about to fall down desiccated and expire while Moses watched.

Ruttee stumbled into sight of the village. A child called out, then two women took notice, and finally a man with a great sword strapped to his hip strode out to intercept the stranger. As the man approached, Ruttee sank to his knees, wavered, and collapsed sideways. The villager turned and shouted something which caused several more men to hurry out, hoist Ruttee up, and bear him to the village and into one of the larger houses.

The life of the community seemed to regain normal fairly quickly. A cluster of women gathered around the watering place to gossip, probably about the derelict, but the group lasted only minutes before dispersing. Proctor could see nothing moving through the one window visible of the house they had carried Ruttee into.

"They will strip him," said Mizra. "They are desert people. I think their first instinct will be kindness. They will bathe him."

"And find his gold." Yildirim's eyes had not left the village. "That is when they will decide what to do with him."

"I would ask such a man, 'Where did you get this gold?'," said Mizra.

Yildirim nodded. "And is there any more?"

Songay Bin watched tensely, praying they were right. They heard no sound from the house in the village, no screams of a tortured man being compelled to yield up a secret. But Dibele trained to take such treatment. Death could come in silence. He clasped his hands together tightly. *To be a Dibele is to wait and watch. Ruttee, my cousin, make them believe.*

Nothing happened the rest of the day. The spies heard no cries of torment. They saw no fevered preparations for travel.

As much as the men observing could tell, it was a routine day. Men and women went in and out of the house – where Ruttee was being either tortured or nursed – without visible excitement other than the buzz a stranger would induce in such an isolated community. The sun went down, but none of the party up on the hill went back to the wagons.

October 13, 1781
York County, Virginia

The boil looked like a musket ball had lodged in his leg and stretched the dark skin into an angry crimson dome with an ivory apex.

"The bilious humour is intact below," Caroline said. She pressed against the roundness with her index finger, and the patient drew in a sharp breath.

"God save–" he groaned. "Can't you drain it?"

She swung the lantern away and set it on the planks serving as an operating table. "Yes, but that will leave the flesh bleeding and swollen. Better to draw the bile and let the insult be given up gently."

Down the gentle slope the cannons continued their unending chorus. The American pieces, nearer but firing away, sounded the bass chords, while the British cannon, two miles farther on but pointed toward them, chimed in with counterpointing treble notes.

Billy exhaled hard and sank back on the boards to watch her prepare the poultice. A pot simmered on a makeshift oven made of salvaged bricks. Into the water she stirred crushed oats, a lump of clay the color of a bloodstain, and a handful of peppercorns. After mixing this thick concoction, she spooned out most of the steaming mush into a square of flour sack lying at her feet and tied the corners up with a bit of twine.

Billy eyed her approach with apprehension and groaned again as she eased her poultice onto the swelling. "It is going to burn my leg clean off," he hissed.

"You may present to the surgeon if you would rather," she said without any sympathy. "He would have it clean off in his own cheerful manner." With her free hand she made a sawing motion.

Billy stifled another protest. Actually, it was beginning to feel less painful. He had ridden beside the General all day as the lump increased steadily in size and sensitivity. He could not even contemplate another day in the saddle with this throbbing bulge on the inside of his left thigh.

"If it does not resolve, tomorrow I will give you a dry poultice as a cushion," Caroline said. "You can bear it."

It was not much of a hospital, just a foundation sprouting splinters suggesting where walls once existed, remnants of a large barn which had been pulled down for use in some military project. The house the barn had once served stood nearby, a burnt out husk. The owner of this modest plantation had been a Patriot, and the bearers of the torch the local Loyalist militia. Both sides agreed on the utility of a chicken coop, and so that expansive structure survived the conflict. The tasty contents had not. Today the lost poultry's home was servant quarters. Divided in the middle by a hanging sheet cobbled from muslin and burlap, it housed males on one side, females on the other.

Billy had requested treatment here in the ruins of the barn, as he did not want to risk his complaint returning to his master. He had been Washington's groom and riding valet for many years. Now they hunted Englishmen instead of foxes – but foxes had never shot back. He could not leave the fortune of the General to a substitute who would not know the length Washington liked his stirrups or anticipate the instant a hand would be put out for its field glass.

The patient turned his face to the stars. "I must bear it. Tomorrow comes the crisis."

Caroline, cleaning up her operation, did not speak. She had been too occupied with the logistics of feeding the headquarters staff and transient officers and the steady flow of

French dignitaries minor and major and sizing up each new face for its potential to be a puppet of the Giza to absorb details of the siege.

"The moon is new," Billy said. "In the dark we will take the two redoubts protecting the city. Without them Yorktown will surely fall. Without Yorktown – and the army within – the British must leave the south."

October 14, 1781
The Holy Land

They dozed, chewed on dried apricots and flatbread, shivered, and were woken in the violet predawn by a cacophony. Loud talking, urgent. Horses whinnying and clopping about in agitation. The light gradually increased until it was clear a group on horseback was forming near the edge of town.

"He has persuaded them," Lieutenant Lefevre said, and they all hoped he was correct. It seemed so, as there was no other reason they could think of which would fluster the villagers like this.

The men below whistled and shouted, then turned their horses to the east and kicked their sides. The excitement of the group on the hill increased to a giddy happiness as they counted the number of mounted riders trotting away from the settlement.

"Forty-six," whispered Mizra, "so far, and–"

He fell silent, as did those around him, all suddenly sober. The second to last horse came into view – it did not have a gold-frenzied rider tall and eager. Over its back was slung a man, chained firmly to the mount by wrist and ankle.

Songay Bin stood and turned away. He began to walk back toward the allied forces.

Ahmad ibn Abbas sat restless and angry beside the fire in

his house. He ran his stone with uncalled for violence up and down the cutting edge of his shamshir. This ancient weapon, his father's and his father's, was already worn thin. Ahmad's stone technique threatened today to make it vanish before his son could inherit.

He had yelled at his beloved wife and cursed at his adored children, all of whom repaired hastily to far corners of the village, leaving him alone with his rage.

He was furious that he had been forbidden to ride out in search of the African's caravan. His older brother Ghazi had volunteered Ahmad to stay behind, and as the eldest in the family his rule was not to be denied. All had burned to rush out. Soon after the derelict's tale had made it to the well, each man imagined himself rich. They had only the inconsequential task of finding and killing the bandits and following the African to the buried gold. A couple of cautious old men had wondered if the newcomer was telling the truth, but most thought if anything, there was more treasure out there than the dessicated dark fellow let on. Why would he exaggerate? Besides, his tale had leaked out in fevered visions while the women sponged water onto his shivering frame. The poor wretch did not even know where he was. No, it was certain he spoke from his true heart.

Once firmly excluded from the enterprise, Ahmad was seized with righteousness, upset with the lack of obedience his fellows were displaying. *The Giza Mashujaa provide.* Meteoric sparks flying from his blade. *They will be angry with us for our rashness and our greed.* It was his patrol duty tomorrow, one reason he had been left behind. Three men would ride the traditional path as prescribed long ago by the Giza – into the valley, twice around the Tower and to the base of the three seemingly impassible alternate routes into the valley, closely inspecting for traces of intrusion. What if the anger of the Giza Mashujaa were unleashed on him as the representative of the unfaithful village? It was not fair. Not fair he was not at the moment riding for gold, not fair he might suffer punishment for the sins of those who were.

Two hours later he squatted outside, still seething, this time taking his frustration out on his saddle, rubbing it furiously with date nut oil until he could see the reflection of his dour face in the leather. The sun was bright but the ground frosty, the streets quieter than normal with so many gone. The children played somewhere in the distance, not making enough noise to fill in for the missing.

A man shouted, and Ahmad stood on his toes to search what horizon he could see. A small mounted group approached, riding as fast as it appeared they could. He counted six. Three on horses; three riding camels. Ahmad did not pause to inspect them – this was clearly not friends visiting. He sprinted for his horse, which was tethered in his stable, and jumped onto its bare back. There was no time for the saddle.

He urged his horse through the nearest alleyway and out of the town. Two others were beside him when he emerged – three others hard behind. When the bandits saw them, they wheeled their own mounts abruptly and began to flee.

Their leader seemed to be a bearded hook-nosed man on a camel. *An Israelite*, Ahmad thought. *Not your usual bandit.*

He glanced over his shoulder. The men not out lusting for gold were racing after. He reined his horse in and waited for them to form up. There was no glory in foolish attacks when you were outnumbered. But there was also little glory in defeating a wandering band of inept thieves, which this group appeared to be. It sometimes happened, out here far from any other community, that desperate men appeared. If they were judged to be truly lost, or on some earnest journey, they were treated with hospitality and sent on their way. If they tried to enter the valley of the Giza Mashujaa, however, or made indiscreet inquiries regarding a tower, they would be slain summarily and their bodies left for the buzzards.

These attackers were little more than pests. Probably a random accumulation of desert outcasts who could do no harm to the guardians except disturb their sleep or perhaps snatch up one of the young or a woman wandering too far.

They were a nuisance to be swept from the land.

Ahmad and his fellows watched the band retreat in panic down one of the tall narrow canyons in the rock wall forming the near side of the valley of the Giza. The newcomers did not know it was a dead end. Ahmad looked to his right and to his left, and the conclusion was on every man's face. The bandits would come to a sudden whirling halt against the sheer rock. They would turn in horror to see the guardians advancing with steel in hand. The men of the village would take out their goldless frustration on this rabble – it would be a slaughter. Ahmad raised his shamshir and let out a shriek, then kicked his horse and charged toward the mouth of the canyon.

The men knew this gouge in the earth well. It was about a half a mile deep and constricted on the middle – from above an hourglass shape. As they entered they could see the would-be bandits jostling to pass through the narrowing. The vermin would know shortly they were trapped.

The men of Daskara Hafiz trotted forward, forming up two abreast so as not to bunch at the restriction. Each had his weapon drawn and leaned forward with an air of determined murder. Ahmad found himself in the next to last row going through and came out expecting to see the villagers forming for a galloping attack. Instead he saw his men ahead slowing, their horses dim shadows in the thickened air. The pounding hooves of so many animals raised a powdery, choking haze in the windless canyon, reducing the visibility to near zero. This did not concern the advancing men, who anticipated a fight at close quarters.

But the incompetent bandits were not milling in panic. Gaps in the dust showed them kneeling calmly on the ground, muskets trained on their pursuers. Ahmad jerked the reins of his horse to the side. It was an ambush! Turning brought the end of the enemy line into his view – and he shouted a warning as he stared directly down the throats of two cannon.

The cannon and their crews disappeared in a cloud of smoke, and instantly a powerful shock wave of scalding heat bowled into him. Even as his horse staggered, his heart lifted –

it was hot air and little else. Two cannon balls had faint chance of doing any damage to the dispersed targets his fellows presented in this veil of risen earth. Then he saw to his right – where an instant before had stood three men and their horses – only red glistening clouds. Small shot buzzed past him like furious steel bees. He had never seen canister before, but he instantly comprehended its implication.

Another cannon materialized in the swirling turmoil. Ahmad slewed his horse to escape its path just as it boomed out a shot that obliterated two more villagers. He slid down low on his horse and smacked it with the flat of his sword to urge it back toward the entrance.

This is treachery, he was screaming in his head. *I have to catch the others – and that African liar. It is–*

He never finished the thought, for on the other side of the restriction, positioned up behind camouflaging rock, another great gun was aimed squarely at the only exit from this trap. Ahmad ibn Abbas's last sight this side of paradise was of a turbaned man lowering a smoking torch.

The Turks wandered among the dead, overly eager to dispatch any wounded with their scimitars, but none on the ground drew breath. The combination of twenty-four pound canister shot and musket balls had made the confined space into a killing field. The lack of living enemy proved unsatisfactory. Possessed by inflamed bloodlust, the Janissaries desired to storm Daskara Hafiz and deal it the treatment any defeated city might expect after a siege; namely, carnage, rape, and plunder of all valuables.

Proctor managed to disabuse them of this craving. "The rest of the village may return at any time. We do not know how long Ruttee's deception will hold, and we do not have the cavalry necessary to meet them," he pointed out. "And whoever is in the Tower must know we are here by now. Cannons are not a common sound in these parts."

His arguments were reluctantly taken by the Turks, who contented themselves with stripping what scraps remained from the pieces of dead and vigorously cleaning their cannon.

Proctor and Ward were organizing the reformation of the allied convoy when McCue sought them out. He was agitated, twisting his hat in his strong, scarred hands. "Captain," he said in a rasping voice, "you and Mister Ward need to come with me."

It was Scudman. Scudman, who had lead the feint on his faithful camel wrapped in tribal scarf, yelling wildly, yelling believably. He lay on a blanket, the blood soaking cardinal the whole side of his white robe. His face was as pale as it must have been the day he reported dockside at fourteen years of age. Someone had untwisted his headscarf and folded into a pillow. He smiled weakly when Proctor and Ward squatted down beside him.

"What happened, Joseph?" Moses asked quietly.

Scudman coughed. Blood showed in the saliva trickling from the corner of his mouth. "Just a splinter of rock, Captain. One of them Turkish shots went a bit long, it seems. Probably got excited and used a touch too much powder. They ain't sailors, you know." This long declaration seemed to empty him, and his head sank back.

Proctor looked across to McCue, who had once been a surgeon's mate. McCue gave a slight shake of his head.

"Well, then –" Proctor began to rise, but Scudman, in a sudden burst of vitality, grabbed his wrist and held him.

"I know what you're about – them Africans has the magic with them. The Devil's water– " he coughed again and let go of Proctor. "I don't want any. I have enough sins to count against me–"

"John–" McCue began, but the dying man cut him short.

"No!" And he grabbed at Proctor's sleeve. "Promise me, Captain Proctor. Promise me on your honor you won't put the spirit of Satan into me."

Moses nodded, which Scudman took as affirmation. He closed his eyes.

October 14, 1781
York County, Virginia

In the morning, her patient's predictions were supported by an increase in the barely organized chaos that was headquarters. Colonel Tilghman, one of the General's aides, appeared in the kitchen before the sun rose with a list for the cooks: the number of officers who would be breakfasting with Washington, the number who would come at midmorning to take coffee, the number who would be lunching, etc. As he read these off and consulted with the quartermaster, Caroline and the other servants trooped to the back of the tent to inventory the supplies brought by the sutler in the night: beef, bacon, onions, barley, peas, flour, rice, salt, various cheeses, and sundry necessities.

Past the tent tramped units of Americans and French, each bunch with its own particular uniform and convention of dress. Some sported dark blue coats with red facings over white britches. Others wore coats of black with beige over tan. Some coats were long, some short, some cut to the belt in front and let hang to the knee behind. Britches were of linen, bleached or dyed, or of leather, shiny or rough. They moved each in the style of their unit's temper. Marching, trotting, walking, running – and every one toward the unceasing, booming cannons. They sang, they chanted, they were silent. Caroline glanced up from her chore every so often, knowing whatever they were, they were all hungry.

When the eastern sky showed a stripe somewhat less than black, she shouldered her two-bucket yoke and negotiated a grassy incline to where the headquarters' cows were penned in an rude enclosure whose bounds were braided branches left over from felling trees for firewood. The young servant who fed and guarded the dozen head helped her milk them. It took six trips to transport the morning's yield and pour it carefully into kegs.

On her last trip down she passed a redheaded woman,

taller than her by several inches and hollow-cheeked, who carried a baby strapped to her back. A camp follower, one Caroline did not know, but with so many new troops it was not a surprise. The woman was still there when Caroline struggled up the incline with her heavy slopping burden. Something in the woman's face and pose made Caroline pause.

"Do you have any for sale?" the woman asked hesitantly. Her baby began to cry, so she reached around and pulled the cloth sling until the child was in her arms. As she bounced it to hush, she continued, apologetically gesturing to one breast, "I lost my milk on the march."

Caroline nodded to the canteen hanging from the woman's belt. "We shall fill that, if you tell no one."

The woman unscrewed its lid and tipped a bucket to pour in a stream of milk on which cream crusts floated like ice on a winter river. She held out a worn cloth purse inclined to let Caroline see the contents – a few shillings, mostly pence. Caroline shook her head.

The woman's pure green eyes suddenly brimmed. "Dear Lord, thank you," she said, and she grabbed her benefactor's hand and squeezed it hard.

Washington was up, dressed, and holding court as the sun peeked through the pine trunks. The cooks moved in their efficiently choreographed process – mixing and rolling in the tent, carrying iron pots out, fetching back black containers seeping steam from under their lids, passing in frying pans filled with bacon and flat corn cakes and brown-topped biscuits.

Caroline tended one of the fires, adding chunks of wood to keep the flames constant, stirring the beans and the porridge so the bottom did not burn. They were some distance away from the two large tents and on the opposite side of the main entrances so the smoke would not annoy the officers and their mounts. She heard but could not see the constant commotion of martial business in front. Out here in the back were only scurrying cooks, servants bringing supplies, and two members of the Guard.

These two soldiers were distinctive, at least in their uniform. The members of the General's Life Guard had the awesome responsibility of defending Washington against sneak attacks, kidnapping attempts, assassination plots, and any other kind of menace to his person. They dressed in blue coats with buff facings and britches and wore stiff black leather helmets with white plumes fixed to the sides. The buttons on their coats were not the ordinary state regimental devices worn by other men. The Guard's pewter buttons read simply USA, the bold letters entwined in relief.

These two, Caroline noted, did not have the lean menacing visage shared by many other Life Guardsmen. The private looked oddly out of shape and portly, though his simple dim face was thin. The mercurial sergeant next to him, ruddy and with the broken veins on his puffy cheeks revealing his love of drink, affected to be put out one minute and bored the next. She supposed they had been appointed as a political favor to some functionary, as the General's aides took care to distribute memberships in the Guard more or less equally among the states.

The fire constant, she stirred the four pots in her care, then went over and removed two large pieces of bread and two thick slices of bacon from a frying pan at the next fire, ignoring the objections of the young girl protecting them. She carried these to the two Guards.

"Thankee," the sergeant said, licking his lips. The private grunted, his eyes rather distant. Caroline nodded and backed away. The two were no more impressive close than from a distance. Posting these two at the rear of the headquarters' tents to guard the fires and the officer's latrines was the decision of a wise officer.

Sometime before noon, an exhausted Caroline was helping to inventory fresh stores brought in as gifts by the French. Two wagons had been accompanied by two dozen infantry, dazzling in their natty robin's egg blue coats with yellow facings, white breeches, and high black boots stropped to a glossy shine. As she reached up for a box, several of the troops came marching past so closely they brushed her. Calling "Pardon! Pardon!" and laughing gaily, they continued on without pause. When her arms came down, she felt a lump in her dress pocket.

It wasn't until well after the midday supper she was able to excuse herself and dash off for a private moment. Something told her not to trust even the barn for this errand, so she continued on a hundred yards past until she came to a thicket of small pines and brush. She forced her way into this concealment and found a small volume within, probably a deer hideaway.

She removed the lump – a thin pasteboard box sealed with wax and secured with ribbon. On the top was carefully written the word CAROLINE.

She took a deep breath. A reading slave played a dangerous game. Inside the box was a pair of plain spectacles wrapped in a flyer for musical entertainment: CONCERT SPIRITUEL AU CHATEAU DES THUILLERIES, etc. Her French was passable enough she could tell this was nothing more than an ordinary handbill, but one faint pencil mark over the A in AU told her what she needed.

Returning the parcel to her pocket, she left the thicket. Some minutes later she was back. She built a tiny fire and set over it a tin cup to which she added a teaspoon of vinegar. Once this liquid had commenced to steam, she unfolded the handbill and carefully held it so every part of its area was eventually exposed to the acidic vapor.

This treatment developed the secret writing on the blank side of the paper. It was in a scrawl, somewhat less legible due to the author not being able to follow his product by eye, and read:

Sister Caroline,
Word has reached me of your watch over our farmer friend. Accept the enclosed, which will sharpen your fluid

vision.

Franklin

I wonder it took so long, she thought in amusement. *He has joined every other secret society – why not ours?*

Caroline put the handbill and the pasteboard on the fire. They flared up and filled her cramped blind with an acrid smoke that took several minutes to seep out. She put her hand to her throat and pulled on the chain about her neck.

Most Dibele did not like to be near the water. It was the embodiment of the evil they dedicated their lives to fighting; many could not even fall asleep in the same room with it. Ruttee was typical. He had a quantity inherited from the dead Giza but stored rather than carry it. Caroline, however, had never shown fear of it. The Father recognized this and sent her out from Nafasi Dibele with an amulet containing a drop. Some urge had compelled her to spontaneously gift hers to Lieutenant Stark, and she had felt unarmed and oddly naked without it. When Ruttee arrived with the blind man to purchase her from Monticello, he had confided his possession of a quantity, so she obtained a tiny glass vessel into which he obediently placed a drop of his stash.

This hung from her chain, sealed with wax. Sometimes when the world was hushed all round and conditions – what exact conditions she was not sure – harmonized, she could feel her necklace pulse with energy. But she had never removed it.

She looped it now over a branch stub, unfolded Franklin's spectacles, and put them on. The glass was clear and apparently unground; the image coming to her eyes uncorrected, as if she were gazing through a well-made window. Then she noticed colors reflecting inside the lenses and turned her head. A rainbow surrounded her necklace. Like the halo of clouds about the moon on an icy winter night – but shimmering – yellow and purple spikes stabbed out and retreated. Bands of hideous orange and garish crimson chased to and fro with such intensity she had to snatch the glasses from her face. Her vision of the fluid was sharpened indeed.

Billy came into the tent in midafternoon and begged her services. She followed him to the ravaged barn, watching his stiff-legged gait with trepidation. Once in partial cover, he sank to the ground with a deep groan. Caroline uncovered his thigh and prodded the skin surrounding the infection, which now looked like a freshly cut slab of beef from which a round plug had been removed.

"The salt has drawn the yellow bile," she said. She slung the sweaty linen holding the used poultice into a corner. "Please hold your tongue." She took out a flask of rum and poured a stream straight into the volcanic wound. Billy jerked violently for a moment – but did not cry out. Caroline nodded and began to apply a new bandage. "Do we still attack tonight?"

"Yes."

"Do not let a ball ruin my good work."

He smiled weakly. "I will do my best. Now I must be quick." He stood up and fastened his buttons, thanked her, and was gone.

On her way back to the cook tent she took a wide detour toward the river. This brought her in behind some rocks and dense rhododendron bushes and let her peep out at the milling crowd in front of the General's tent. She slipped on the spectacles and spent a time studying each individual, but none had an aura or an accompanying rainbow or displayed any other supernatural manifestation. Nor did she know exactly what that might be, or how like the lights that played about the pure water. She trusted in Franklin's art. If there were one of Geoffrey's creations about, the glasses would betray him, but time was running out. Surely the Giza must try to prevent this victory by destroying the army's inspiration. She made one more sweep, then reluctantly removed the glasses and went back to work.

October 14, 1781
The Holy Land

Three hours later, the crisis came. Joseph Scudman, American able-bodied seaman who had discovered his talent for adventure a little too late in life, shuddered and convulsed and finally relaxed into silence. Proctor had left just minutes before, searching for Songay Bin, willing to dishonor his sacred vow if it would save this man who had proved more valuable than any of his officers had imagined. But Bin was nowhere to be found. One of the Indians said he had ridden out on a borrowed horse in the direction of the fictitious plundered caravan.

Moses cursed. Songay Bin was a volunteer and not subject to Proctor's tenuous authority, and by the time Moses returned to Scudman's desert bed it was over.

The allies were ready and anxious then to move, so they wrapped the man in his bloody garment and buried him quickly in these sands so far from his home.

The allied forces snaked past the village in the fading daylight. The houses were dark; nothing moved. Some of the French and Janissaries hedged their orders and swung out of line to get closer, but they heard no sound. Many burned to sprint into the defenseless town, but none were brave enough to further defy their officers, so they turned away and rejoined the long procession.

The moon rose as the allies entered the hidden valley, but it was a meager crescent. Their vision was limited to what the stars illuminated. They picked their way carefully for several hours until a pale vertical presence in the east grew distinct.

They paused as one, as if waiting for this beacon to recognize their trespass. But no light appeared, nor any other sign.

When they were somewhat less than a mile from the target, the Janissary gunners passed the word to the Cebeci wagons. They slowed and spread out with practiced skill evident even in this darkness until the cannon were arranged in an arc and all were pointed at the Tower.

October 14, 1781
York County, Virginia

As the sun was just gathering for its descent behind the western hills, Caroline visited the servant's privy beyond the cow pens. On her way back, a troop of frontiersmen came hiking from the woods. They dressed in buckskins and moccasins and carried their long rifles nonchalantly on their shoulders. She shrank into the shadow of a stunted birch and surveyed them with Franklin's gift. None of the serious-faced men had any hint of extraneous light about them not due to the low slanting rays of the setting sun.

She glanced up at the headquarters tents, wondering if anyone had noted her long break. Standing at his usual place was the Life Guard sergeant, officious and glancing suspiciously about. Several paces away stood the private, seemingly bored with the whole affair, slightly slumped and inattentive – and surrounded by a beating glow.

With a gasp, she scuttled behind the tree and waited there for her racing heart to slow. Then she peeked around and confirmed what she had seen. The private was haloed in alabaster streaked with rainbows of light achingly sharp, and his skin seen through her spectacles had an unnatural translucence so profound she was sure she might be able to see his bones if she were closer.

What was he waiting for? She looked at the General's tent. The rear entrance was undone; the flap of canvas waved slowly in the capricious breeze. Just beyond, Washington sat with his aides and many of the commanders of the units surrounding Yorktown. The private could step inside without being challenged. He was Life Guard. No one would stop him. They would be frozen with surprise as he raised his musket or ran at the table with his bayonet. Why did he just stand there pretending to be a man?

She leaned against the birch, her mind working at a rolling boil. She did not know what to do. She had formulated a dozen plans for dealing with this threat, but now each clever scheme seemed naïve. The only thing certain was that doing nothing was impossible.

After a while she ran to the chicken coop, then turned her back on the headquarters and walked briskly down the long line of tents and camp fires where many of the Colonial army units slept and ate. The men were gone, called to formation, leaving only a sparse population of women, children, and packs of dogs. She was in luck today. The tall woman's head of shining red hair was like a beacon.

"I need your help," Caroline said quietly when she was close.

The woman examined her visitor carefully. Caroline knew if this were the wife of a soldier from Virginia, or the Carolinas – much less Georgia – this plan would never work. But Caroline had noted insignias on worn uniform parts simmering in the laundry pots as she had approached. This unit was from Pennsylvania, so it was possible the fair woman would not automatically shun a request from an African.

The redhead nodded, rocking the sleeping baby slung in front of her.

Caroline extended a folded slip of paper. "Give this to the private in back of the headquarters tent. That is all."

The woman took the paper and unfolded it. Caroline noted she could read, and quickly. The redhead had dark, almost black eyebrows, which elevated as she considered the words.

She hesitated and met Caroline's eyes with a profound scrutiny. *She is going to refuse me, and perhaps expose me.*

But the patriot's wife did not even ask why this improbable and improper act was being proposed, nor why she had to be the vehicle of such a shameful and potentially disastrous assignation. Instead, the woman asked, "Don't you think I should give him cause to obey me?" She fluttered her eyelids and tilted her head and forced a wide toothy smile. Caroline laughed.

October 15, 1781
The Holy Land

Proctor, Bin, and Yildirim mounted in front of the battery and rode closer to the target. Yildirim wanted to inspect the structure for signs of weakness, areas where his projectiles might inflict the greatest damage. Bin came along because he was the only one among them who had seen the Tower before, and even though he had never been inside might have some salient suggestions for Yildirim.

Proctor felt naked. He was sure there was an intelligence inside watching the three enemies – for the Tower had no friends – come closer in the predawn glow. The hairs on his neck stood up. *I am a cat, trying to make my attacker think I am something larger and more dangerous than I actually am.*

He had seen spires similar to this, but those rose from the sea in shallows or near islands – remnants of rocks worn into cylinders by the relentless action of the sea. Those had not been hollow, as this one was alleged to be. Some large part of him did not believe it. It was a fantasy, a legend imagined real. They would waste powder and shot on this pillar, knock a few chunks off, and be none the closer to accomplishing the mission.

Proctor made a note to have Ward calculate the height of this strange peak – he would estimate the distance back to use as a baseline. Proctor guessed it would come out to be five or six hundred feet. They rode twice around the base – Proctor made the diameter about one hundred and fifty feet – but could not see a door or window or any other possible entrance. It was irrelevant, really. They were not here to enter politely.

By the time they returned to their line the desert was purplish-pink with enough predawn light to commence. Yildirim gathered his gunners and pointed out an interesting bulge in the rock one-third of the way up and some kind of hidden fissure right up at the top. He assigned four guns to attack the bulge. The other two would elevate and probe the feature at the top with twenty-four pound iron fingers.

Proctor, Ward, and Bin withdrew behind the cannon to observe the firing preparations. McCue worked with the Indians shuttling bags of powder to the six emplacements. Back at Amman, once the Turks had shown up and the caliber of the cannon was known, he had volunteered his sailmaking skills, cutting up tents into rectangles of several sizes and sewing them shut around carefully dispensed weights of powder. The Janissary gunners watched carefully, nodding reluctant approval at his technique. In the end, he and his Maratha recruits produced hundreds of loads in different sizes so the gunners might combine them into a charge sufficient for the desired shot.

Next to Proctor's group the Cebeci swarmed nervously in an irregular formation. Apparently once the cannon were placed, these troops took no further interest in serving them or supplying them. Proctor still thought it an odd arrangement, made even more counter to his admittedly limited infantry experience by the revelation that the Cebeci were normally just audience to the fighting. On this day, Tayar had acquiesced to Moses' suggestion that his men be ready with muskets and scimitars, which they stood holding with a disquieting unfamiliarity. To the left of the Turks the French stood in a professionally dressed line, fixing bayonets.

Yildirim stood at the end of the arc, watching his crews yaw and elevate their muzzles in a percussive ballet of shoving and squinting and tapping with mallets. Satisfied with their aim and loaded, they stood at attention beside their cannon. Once all were posed stiffly and formally, the Chorbaji spoke one quiet word Proctor could not hear. Six men brought six wooden staffs holding slow match down to six touchholes, and the celestial stillness of the desert morning was blasted away by the hellish stuttering roar of six cannon firing nearly in unison.

Two of the shot went home, and the French cheered. None of the Turks, gunners or Cebeci, made a sound – for one of three was far below their standards. The gun crews again fussed over their alignments, loaded, and fired the next rounds. Four of these struck, and the crews proceeded to carefully reload and resight before touching match again.

Proctor, watching the Tower through his glass, saw shot hammer against rock, birthing gravel blooms that arced out and fell in graceful parabolas. The thing still looked solid to him. He brought his glass higher up. The gunners targeting the odd feature at the top were having a harder time hitting it, perhaps due to the extreme angle their barrels were forced to assume.

A jagged sheet of bluish light filled his lens, and Moses gave a startled cry. Bin and Ward snapped their heads to the top of the Tower.

Lightning struck. It erupted as if from a great churning storm cloud though the morning skies were clear. Bolts flashed from the top of the Tower out toward the allies like white probing fingers. But they seemed to run out of power – they curved down and cracked into the ground much nearer the Tower than the cannon. More crackled out yet went no farther than the first.

"What is that?" Ward shouted above the booming thunder echoing against the valley walls.

"Their magics are powerful, but they are old knights. They did not count on cannon which can reach a mile." Bin pointed to the top of the Tower. "A Giza is up there now."

Moses stared up with his naked eyes, thinking for the first time that the massive pillar might indeed be hollow. But it was still too possible they were surrounding some reclusive and innocent natives and the lightning was just a coincidence. He had once watched entranced as St. Elmo's fire engulfed the whole of his schooner's rigging off of a stormy Cape Cod. He had witnessed a waterspout rise from the North Atlantic on a clear day, lightning bolts playing from its top down to the flat water with the reports of thirty-pounders.

The Janissary gunners, who had paused to marvel at the display, shrugged and went back to work. They were used to operating under counterattack. Yildirim barked out an order, and the captains of two more cannons drew out their wedges to aim at the top of the Tower.

October 14, 1781
York County, Virginia

"It is time," she whispered to herself. Her battered canvas and leather traveling bag sat on the dirt in front of her. Inside the fragmentary barn the light faded. The wind shifted to the west, blowing away battle sounds, making the constant pounding of the big guns seem farther than it was. Caroline pulled out the thick wooden plank that shaped and strengthened the bottom of her bag and balanced it on edge. She raised a brick and began to pound on it, but very precisely, just at the point where one who examined it would have seen a faint joint line hidden in the wood grain. After several hard whacks, the line grew wider and finally separated until she was able to work a flat rock into it and twist the two glued halves apart. These had been hollowed to leave a secret compartment concealing a petite double-barreled flintlock pistol, several paper twists full of powder, and six lead balls.

The wind began to stir loose straws, so she shielded the weapon with her body, protecting the powder as she poured in two charges and rammed home two balls. She glanced about sharply to make sure there were no observers to this – she did not want to find out what the attitude of the General's staff would be upon finding an armed slave in its midst. She secreted the gun in an inner pocket and crept out to find a spot where she might observe the rear of the headquarters tents.

Lying under a prickly shrub, she watched the private.

Without the assistance of Franklin's glass, he was unremarkable. His sergeant was not in sight, probably called away for some duty in the excited crowd preparing in the twilight for battle. Her fellow cooks and servants sweated, hard-pressed as they hurried about, which was good for Caroline. Her absence would not much matter to anyone as long as all were preoccupied with urgent tasks. At the most they would assume she was fetching something. Half of them were at any one time fetching something.

Her accomplice had also been watching. Now with the sergeant absent, the redhead approached the private, slipped him the note, and walked off without looking back.

Servants drove torches into the turf to illuminate paths to the cooking fires. The private just stood slack-jawed, the note hanging ignored from his fingers. Caroline cursed him. He was too hollow to be tricked. He had forgotten how to read. He had never known how to read. His lust had been extinguished by the water. He was a neuter, and a siren would have no effect on him.

But eventually he opened the note and stared at it for a time. He refolded it without expression and tucked it into a pocket, then deserted his post. He wrenched a torch out of the ground and started into the fading light.

Caroline pushed up and ran for the barn. She had to skid to a stop once to avoid another cook lugging a crate – and sprinted on as the other called her name. She hurdled a low gap in the barn wall and scrambled behind a pile of rotting straw.

The private shuffled in. He inspected the area by the light of his torch, then stuck it into the ground and took the note out and opened it to read again.

She rose and tiptoed toward him, silent on the soft dirt. He finally sensed movement and raised his eyes to find the small barrels of her pistol two paces away and trained on his head.

Caroline had only one hard plan – kill this threat. After that was improvisation, which she might possibly survive. Her fate was secondary to the elimination of this Giza creation. Still, she did not fire. There was much she wanted to know. *You do not need to know. Just fire!* Yet she hesitated.

The private started to laugh, and Caroline's aim waivered. Her finger tightened on the triggers – then she heard a harsh familiar voice behind her.

"Lower your weapon," the sergeant said.

October 15, 1781
The Holy Land

Proctor was impressed by these gunners. His experience aiming heavy artillery at sea had invariably involved nerve-twisting periods of waiting for the roll of the ship to bring the guns into proper firing elevation, a process which could take an alarmingly long time in a battle on a slow swelling sea. Here on solid ground, the Turks got off shots at a rapid clip.

He saw Tayar and one of his men sitting on the seat of a wagon, Tayar shading his eyes with one hand and speaking continuously to his assistant, who scribbled furiously in a little book. Moses went to the wagon, jumping to avoid the determined gunners dashing to fetch ball and powder. He did not interrupt Tayar but listened attentively for a minute. The Cebeci was keeping a running tally of how many rounds had been expended. Proctor began to worry. A frigate like the Dauntless, with ample room in her hold and magazine, could carry shot and powder aplenty. Her ability to fire had only been limited by the quixotic generosity of the quartermaster of naval stores. The Cebeci did not have such luxury. They had to haul the heavy iron shot hundreds of miles, over rocky roads and clutching sand. He looked into the back of the wagon. The stack of round iron was not as high as it had just a few hours ago.

Then the gunners cheered. Huzzahs roared from the rest of the force, and Proctor's mind was eased.

An immense slab of rock cracked visibly at the top of the Tower. Two more balls slammed into it, and the thick strip loosened and fell, tumbling and scraping and bouncing off of the Tower's side until it smacked into the valley floor with a volcanic plume of dust and a deep and sustained rumble.

Behind the hole it left they could see empty space – the top of the knights' hideaway. Moses found himself making fists so fiercely his fingernails dug into his palms – and he had to restrain himself from shouting.

Yildirim switched four of his pieces to shell, which slowed down the pace of fire, as the gunners had to carefully calculate the time of flight and trim the fuse accordingly on each round before stuffing them down the muzzles. The shells exited trailing a plume of dirty white from the burning fuse, smoke which formed a tight spiral tail behind the spinning round. The first few firings were not inspired. Some shells exploded before hitting the target, some glanced off and detonated either as they fell or as they bounced on the hard valley floor. The rest flew past the rock needle and blew up far on the other side.

"They are missing badly," Bin said worriedly to Ward as Moses climbed back up to their observation point.

Ward nodded. "They are unfamiliar with these rounds. The shells and fuse were made in Spain. The cannon as well." He noticed Proctor. "Isn't that right, Captain?"

"I pray it is," said Moses.

They didn't have to wait long for the skill of the Janissary gunners and the combination of theory learned in their academy and lessons gathered the harder way on the battlefield to make itself evident. The gunners studiously cut the fuses against graduated wooden marking sticks and bled measured volumes of powder from McCues' canvas sausages until they had shortly achieved the ideal combination of time, energy, and direction.

"Look!" Ward hollered in awe. One of the guns had dropped its projectile directly into the roughly rectangular opening at the top of the Tower, delivering it there as softly as ever a twenty-four pound sphere of iron and powder propelled at near a thousand feet per second could be humanly placed. Moses imagined he could hear the rattling of the deadly marble as it fell down the hollow, and he stopped breathing anticipating the explosion.

Which he could not possibly hear, of course, it being too far away, attenuated by rock and his ears ringing and calloused by the continuous report of the guns. But he saw its effect. Just about at the place near the bottom they guessed might be vulnerable, he saw the dust jump off the wall as if the inside had been rapped with a giant hammer. Another cheer, this time without a pause. The cannon continued to pummel the Tower from within and without.

The guns fired continually, each to its own careful yet deadly pace, as the sun climbed from the eastern horizon. More shells dropped into the Tower as others lashed the structure from inside. Others, either due to minor defects on the shell surface ruining spherical perfection or just the natural distribution of shots from a smooth bore barrel, missed the small opening and exploded harmlessly outside.

Moses was amazed at the accuracy the Turks were able to achieve, and as he watched the Tower he imagined he could see it vibrating like a reed. He had fancied it upon first viewing as stout and solid – now he was convinced the walls were as thin as new ice. When the shearing began, therefore, he was perhaps the only one watching who was not dumbfounded.

A jagged vertical line developed suddenly, starting at the very base and extending fifty or sixty feet up, then the rock layer pulled away from the cylinder, opening up a gap which allowed the allies their first vision directly into the enemy's stronghold.

It was so much like the deliberate opening of a door that all activity ceased. The cannon fell silent. No one tried to speak. Ears rang in the eerie and sudden cessation of concussive reports. They waited and watched the dark interior.

Lieutenant Ward leaned close to whisper, "The Maratha are terrified. They are sure whatever serves as their Satan lies inside that place."

"Count me also," Bin admitted, "but the being which sleeps here cannot be your Devil. Think of all the evil and sin which has afflicted men while this one slumbered here, harmless."

"I used to have a dog," Ward said, still quietly, still eyeing the broken Tower. "He often slipped the back door in the night and killed rabbits while I was unawares in my bed."

"Still...." Bin gritted his teeth. "I would rather face a devil than an angry angel."

Proctor had run down to confer with Yildirim and Lefevre. Four French soldiers marched past the cannon and started for the Tower, bayonets presented. The allies watched intensely as the small group edged forward, employing boulders and high points in the land as temporary shields. At one point some loose rock detached and fell from the ruined apex of the Tower. The four men dove to earth, and all the observers drew a quick breath.

But there was no other movement, and after a slow approach and a few signs of the cross, the men stepped into the blackness.

Proctor had his glass trained on the opening, and for many unendurable minutes he detected nothing. No one along the allied line spoke. Proctor heard only the soft whistle of the wind, the shuffling and spitting of the men, and the muted sounds of the animals behind them.

He stiffened and said, "There!"

Indistinct movement in the darkness came forward and resolved into four sound Frenchmen. Proctor could see their wide grins in his glass. One hoisted a chunky red mass impaled on his bayonet. Proctor refocused.

"God save us," he breathed.

Ward was trying to identify the object through his own glass. "What is that?"

Proctor dropped his telescope and turned away. "They have a leg." He handed his glass to Bin, who eagerly put it to his eye. The Turks began to cheer.

315

After a council of war among the leaders, the Cebeci hitched the cannons to their wagons, and the force advanced slowly toward the Tower. Proctor ran forward and back prodding them to move with more urgency. The sun was climbing to its apex, and he did not want to get caught out on a moonless night with an enemy of unknown abilities nearby. Most in his little army were noticeably hesitant. The Maratha drovers produced amulets of various sizes and kissed them fervently in one hand while leading their beasts with the other. The French stopped to add their amens to a prayer offered by a private who had been within one month and one comely maid of the priesthood. The knight was most and truly dead, but his master might yet dwell inside that dark gap.

The French troops graciously shared their prize. They positioned the bloody leg so the allied train had to part to pass around it. The Turkish gunners cheered anew – this was their work, after all. The Cebeci spat on the ground; the Marathas shuddered and looked away. The French laughed and poked the meat with their bayonets.

"In some ways it seems a shame," observed McCue as the three Americans walked by the horrible pile. "If the bugger was a hundred years old and more. Like an ancient fish in a pond your grandfather tells tales of finally getting caught."

Ward was fascinated by the gory sight and almost bumped into Proctor. Moses put out one hand to steady his friend. "That may not be the biggest fish," he said.

McCue scratched under his cap and began to philosophize on the point, but he was not heard. The Arab youth, the son of their camel tender, scampered to them, his heels turning up sprays of sand. His agitated Arabic overwhelmed Moses's limited facility in that language.

"English, Hafiz," Moses urged, but the boy was too excited to do anything but point back the way the allies had come.

Proctor froze. The appearance of the other men from Daskara Hafiz at this point would be a disaster. The allies were strung out, easy targets for cavalry swords. "Mister Ward," he said as calmly as he could force his voice, "give my compliments to Lieutenant Lefevre and ask him to make a square with his infantry. McCue, run to Yildirim and Tayar Dogantez and tell them we may be soon attacked from the rear – beg them to be so good as to make their cannon ready with canister."

Then he sprinted for the nearest high ground. He could hear Bin hard behind him. Once there he could see the approaching form – it was not a mounted troop of agitated villagers but a covered wagon accompanied by three horsemen. He brought them into view in his glass, but they were not familiar. He handed the telescope to Bin. "I do not know them," he said pointedly, for the men were as black as last night.

Bin held them in the lens, frowning, and did not reply.

As the newcomers drew close, Proctor sent word to the French and the Turks to resume their advance and waited with Bin. The new party halted, and the riders greeted Songay knowingly in some language Moses did not recognize – his guess had been correct.

"Friends?" Proctor asked quietly. The French, just falling out of their small phalanx, eyed the riders with suspicion.

Bin nodded. "These men are from my village. They are the guards of–"

The driver of the wagon reached back and opened the cloth cover, revealing a much smaller, older man, black as the others. Two of the riders slid from their saddles and helped him gently to the ground, where he faced the Tower with what Proctor thought a distinct appearance of loss.

"What is this?" the old man cried. His voice was dry and creaked like new boots. "Songay Bin – what have you done?"

Bin bowed low. "Father, allow me to present Captain Moses Proctor–" here he pointed at Proctor with an open hand "–of the American Navy. Captain, this is the Father of the Dibele tribe."

Proctor made a leg. "Honored, sir."

The old man Bin had called his Father ignored the social

niceties. "You must stop this at once," he said to Proctor as forcefully as he probably could. "I demand you leave this place."

"Is this man really your Father?" Moses whispered to Bin.

Bin shook his head ever so slightly and said more loudly, "Our Father once lived in the Tower."

Proctor pondered the shriveled old man and did not ask the obvious question: *How long ago?* Instead he said, "Sir, I have been sent by the government of the United States of America with the support of His Highness the King of France and the Most Righteous Sultan of the Empire to destroy yonder structure and any inhabitants which resist us. I am afraid I must respectfully decline your demand."

The old man seemed dumbfounded. Proctor decided he had not ever had many people say no to him. The four powerful men this Father had brought along were armed with pistols and swords, but the French troops had their muskets barely lowered and still had not turned their backs on this meeting.

The Father turned from Bin to Proctor and back but said nothing. He turned to the wagon, and the two men lifted him back inside.

Proctor faced Bin, who shrugged sheepishly. "Lieutenant," Proctor called to the French officer, "let us continue."

Moses walked quickly through the Cebeci wagons, which were being reversed after the false alarm. He wanted to see inside the Tower for himself. Ward was by his side, and Lieutenant Lefevre and Songay Bin caught up to them as their intent became clear.

The four reached the opening. Proctor looked warily up at the ominous rocks overhead. The layer peeled away was about two feet thick. Chunks had already broken from the bottom edge and fallen, partially blocking entrance. He expected the rest to slide at any minute and had a strong inclination to just back away and let Nature take her course.

They were in the shade here, and as his eyes adjusted to the shadowy light he could see over the obstructions and into the chamber. He took off his cocked hat and held it above his brow to try and block out the ambient glow of the outside.

"Cornelius?" he whispered.

Ward crept a bit closer. "It looks like a candle inside a hurricane lamp."

It bore some resemblance, Proctor agreed silently, except this light was an odd violet and flickered wildly as if several candles were striving for supremacy. He took a deep breath and began to climb over the rocks.

The others followed him into a vaulted cave littered with giant blocks and shards shaken from the broken walls and ceiling. The air was syrupy with some essence, bringing to Proctor's mind flowers crushed and left to rot.

All eyes were drawn to the center of the room, to a rectangular stone just above the height of a tall man and twice as wide and long. The unnerving light came from inside this imposing rectangle. Indigo patterns splashed on the ceiling and reflected upon their faces a sickening blue.

Proctor touched Bin in the gloom. "Is that the being?"

"It is as described in the Father's tales," Bin whispered. "But look there."

He pointed at the far corner of the block. The rock or whatever material the structure was crafted from had been cracked. There were scorch marks on the side. One of the Turk's shells had careened down from the top of the Tower and detonated beside it.

Ward crept to the damaged face. He took out a tinderbox and struck a spark onto the linen before Proctor could call out a warning, but the small flame flared up – and nothing more happened. Proctor let out a long breath.

"It's leaking," Ward said.

The other three approached, almost blinded by the small point of light. The bottom of the crack was wet. A trickle of moisture seeped out as they watched.

"Is it... l'eau?" Lieutenant Lefevre asked anxiously.

"Yes," said Bin. "The healing bath of the being who lies within." He glanced warily up.

Ward slowly extended a trembling hand toward the moisture, but his fingertips stopped a whisker away from touching it. "Who fills the bath?" he said. His voice cracked like a youth.

Bin glanced at Proctor and jumped onto one of the ceiling pieces that had come to rest nearby. From this advantage, he grabbed onto the lip of the rectangle and pulled himself up to peer over the edge. A purer, more intense blue played on his face for an instant, then he let go and tumbled to the ground.

"The water decreases," he said. "There are marks above its level."

"What does it mean?" Proctor demanded.

Bin shrugged. "I do not know. But I think we should leave."

They climbed over rubble back out into the midmorning sun and began to walk back to their line. Proctor saw McCue among the powder stores and waved him over.

"Lieutenant Ward," Proctor said, "would you and Mister McCue be so good as to come with me to my wagon? And Lieutenant Lefevre?" The Frenchman stiffened, and Proctor continued. "Please deliver my best wishes to both Yildirim and Tayar Dogantez and beg their forgiveness of my ignorance of the necessary precedent which I should follow, but I desire the loan of one of their cannon."

Lefevre saluted and dashed off. Ward and McCue followed Proctor to his private wagon, from which he hauled a large wooden box. McCue, who was never without a hammer, opened it expertly. Proctor removed the lid to show a cylindrical object packed tightly in excelsior. He lifted it out, and they saw the thing consisted of several long wooden pieces carved to fit together like a small keg and fastened by bands of heavy white fabric.

"Gentlemen," he said, handing his wooden treasure to the carpenter first as a professional courtesy, "this was crafted by Mr. Franklin. The oak forms a sabot which contains a special shell."

"A sabot?" asked Ward. "But how did he know—" Then he remembered, as did they all, that Franklin had seemed particularly interested in the caliber of the Spanish guns hidden away by their Russian saviors. *How had he known what diameter to make the sabot? Because they had told him. Franklin had been planning this whole enterprise even before the vagabond sailors had appeared in Passy. They had just brought him the final details.*

Proctor proceeded to relate to them the instructions regarding the arming and firing of the weapon. "In case anything happens to me, one of you must use this." The two stared gravely at the cylinder.

Ward began to ask something, but Proctor turned away. Yildirim was shouting and waving toward the Tower.

The newly-arrived Africans were making their way quickly toward the opening, skirting the allied positions. Two of the men shouldered a small sedan chair bearing their – and Bin's – Father. Moses swore and began to run to intercept them. The group reached the opening before him and hoisted the old man over the rubble wall – and the remaining three of them turned to face the allies, a pistol in each hand.

Proctor skidded to a stop. He turned to call the French infantry forward. The smaller group would have to yield in the face of muskets, and if they did not, well, he had a job to do, and they were in his way.

But the French were dropping their muskets and swords in the dust. Proctor was stunned, his cry stillborn, and he watched open-mouthed as the two groups of Turks trained their own weapons on their one-time allies. Ward flicked his sword impotently. McCue tossed his hammer onto the ground with a sour display, muttering something blasphemous.

Tayar Dogantez came to him, holding a pistol carelessly, as though it had materialized unbidden in his hand. "I am truly sorry, Captain Proctor." He actually did look sad, though the situation was his creation. "The Great Sultan has commanded us to bring him whatever we find in the Tower."

Proctor was apoplectic. He could not make his mouth

form words, so he just unbuckled his sword belt and handed over his two pistols and powder horn to the Turk. Finally he was able to spit out, "Why don't you take him the water—" he jerked his head in the general direction of the Tower "—and let us destroy the rest?"

"A most excellent compromise, Captain," Tayar agreed. "If I were in command I would readily agree to it. But the Sultan has ordered, and no man wants to be the one to disobey the Sultan."

"Are you going to kill us and leave us here to rot?"

Tayar laughed. "What an imagination you have. We only wish to keep our Sultan happy. No – we will all leave this place together and depart – perhaps not as friends, understandably, but maybe as comrades in a great adventure, eh?"

Proctor turned his back on the man in a moment of pique and gazed absently into the dark gap, past the Africans, who had lowered but not discarded their arms. The sun, in its winter inclination, was lower in the sky. He could just make out movement inside the chamber. He began to walk toward it, and Tayar followed him, still gripping his pistol but unsure whether to attempt to restrain his new prisoner.

"What is he doing?" Tayar asked, standing beside Moses. The Father stood high up on the lip of the huge sarcophagus. The reflected colors, now dancing more angrily than ever, made his body seem to quiver.

They were several paces from the three guards. Tayar lowered his pistol's muzzle; he was also fixated on the old man inside. One of the guards finally gave in to the temptation and glanced over his shoulder, then said something excitedly in their strange staccato tongue. The other two whirled around so all five now peered over the boulders.

The Father's perch seemed precarious. He waved his arms in what could have been some religious benediction – or just a frantic windmilling pursuit of balance.

Proctor felt it first. The air rushed away, hesitated, and slammed back. The pressure change pushed on his gut the way mercury is squeezed in a barometer. Then he heard the pulse.

It was deep, almost so low as to be beyond his ear's abilities. He imagined they were standing on a colossal drumhead – and some giant had struck it once.

The men swayed and grabbed for boulders and each other to stay upright. The drum beat again. One of the Africans fell over and took Tayar down with him. Proctor lost his equilibrium and toppled sideways, striking his shoulder on a sharp rock. The drum beat again, then again.

Proctor managed to get to his knees and scrabbled to stand. He looked up between a gap in the rock and saw the old man teetering. With a sharp cry he fell backwards off of the altar – or sepulcher or whatever the hell that damned structure was. The walls boiled with rainbow flashes. More bands joined in the chromatic display. Red and yellow waltzed with blue and violet, and the whole inside of the chamber was lit more brightly than the desert. Proctor no longer had to strain to see the action inside, indeed, he now had to shield his eyes against the dazzling power emanating from the pool.

The ground shook again, this time with a sustained energy, but Proctor's attention was riveted on the top of the altar. One huge black hand reached dripping up from inside and clamped its claws down wetly on the rim.

October 14, 1781
York County, Virginia

She did not obey at once, so the sergeant stepped closer and pushed something into her back. It felt like the end of a musket. She could at least be sure of the one in her sights – but that would leave her dead and the sergeant alive. Franklin's spectacles had showed he was not a golem, but he was clearly here to support the assassination of the General. Her gaze wandered from her target, and she saw a green eye and strands of red hair through a gap in two upright board remnants.

Caroline lowered her arm and dropped the pistol onto some straw, still eyeing the hidden woman, trying to mentally convey a signal. If legitimate soldiers appeared, a slave's account of the evening would weigh little against that of a sergeant from Washington's own Life Guard, but it would buy her time to think of an alternate ending to this performance. The red hair did not budge. It was not certain shouts – or shots – from this barn would even be noted amidst the ceaseless pounding of the cannons. The wind suddenly increased, swirling up old hay and dry manure .

"Lord Geoffrey said there would be one of your kind about," the sergeant said. "We just had to draw you out."

"There are more of us on the way," Caroline said. "Drop your gun and surrender now."

The sergeant laughed. "I don't see anyone coming to your aid. I think you are as good a liar as His Lordship warned."

"There is still time for you. We will go to the General and tell him what has happened. Geoffrey needn't harm you."

"Harm me?" The sergeant was incredulous. "You do not understand the situation. Very soon our dear General, old Stone Face himself, will be dead – and in a most spectacular manner guaranteed to quail the heart of the army. The rebels will piss into their boots and slink back home. Geoffrey, Lord of Emberton, will become the Emperor of America, and his friends who have rendered him services most valuable will be dukes and earls."

"Not all of Washington's guards are as wicked as you," Caroline said. "They will strike you down before you can touch him."

The sergeant laughed again. "For some reason known only to him, Lord Geoffrey desired you see how it will end. Show her!" The last was louder, directed to the private.

The private unshouldered his musket and leaned it against a pile of stones, then unbuttoned his coat and vest. Caroline saw what she had thought his fat was in fact an inner garment circling his torso. It was made of canvas sewn in vertical strips and reinforced with leather. She had never seen such a thing and had no idea what it was. The private reached down and fingered a small tin box attached to his vest by a rope-like tether. The wind suddenly became even more fierce, and high overhead, curved lines of silver clouds like individual sword blades raced over the sliver of moon.

"When our friend here opens the box, a clever mechanism strikes flint and lights the quick fuse. Then we count one two three, and the powder charge in his corset does its duty. There is a layer of razor-sharp iron pieces atop the powder, just in case the blast is not enough. Before they even know what is happening, your treasonous leader and his aides will be cut to ribbons and on their way to Hell."

Something about this repulsed Caroline beyond the obvious. "But he would be–" She addressed the private. "You will kill yourself. This is madness."

"Do not waste any more of your remaining breath on him," the sergeant said. He pressed the muzzle harder into her. "He came from the dead and desires nothing more than to return to that peaceful rest. Once I kill the rebellious slave who was found in possession of a firearm, our friend will run to Washington's position carrying a dispatch satchel. All the soldiers and officers around the General will part for him – then gather close to see what new intelligence has come in the heat of the battle. The men in the trenches and the men gathering for the assault will look up to their dear leader while the private fumbles clumsily for the message. And as easy as can be, the spirit of this rebellion will disappear in a brilliant flash and a cloud of smoke. It will be like a magician's spectacle. Many men tonight will come into abrupt possession of bits and pieces of the famous General Washington. They might pass them down to their grandchildren as reminders of his folly in denying God and his King."

October 14, 1781
Hudson River Valley, New York

TO ALL BRA
DISPO
IN THIS NE
THE TR
FOR T

Thomas cupped the rectangle of folded paper in both hands, like a congregant might cradle a relic of a saint, and reread the bold print. It was a cipher. An unintended message from an unknown printer, data added to an incomplete puzzle, and he did not possess the key to bring meaning from it.

He opened the page and read the whole announcement:

TO ALL BRAVE, HEALTHY, ABLE BODIED, AND WELL

DISPOSED YOUNG MEN,

IN THIS NEIGHBOURHOOD, WHO HAVE ANY INCLINATION TO JOIN

THE TROOPS, NOW RAISING UNDER GENERAL WASHINGTON

FOR THE DEFENCE OF THE

LIBERTIES AND INDEPENDENCE

OF THE UNITED STATES

AGAINST THE HOSTILE DESIGNS OF FOREIGN ENEMIES

TAKE NOTICE,

The broadsheet continued with illustrations of stern, capable, well-equipped troops loading, shouldering, and pointing muskets. Fine print below informed the reader how he might throw in with the sober fellows pictured above and receive ample provisions plus SIXTY dollars a year by producing himself at such and such a time in such and such a place.

Thomas considered he was most probably one of the foreign enemies, though he had no hostile designs these days.

He just wanted to find his wives and his children.

He turned the page over. On the back Huub Broos had traced his recollection of where he had been encamped with the Warranawonkong and the lay of Bijinway hunting grounds the fall before. Toward the edge of the page snaked the path a tribe might take if it were bound for the lake of shining water. A pretty picture, but it was mostly conjecture, Thomas admitted bitterly. How many of Broos' triangle mountains, broken trees, and stream fork landmarks would appear the same in life as on the reverse of this recruiting appeal? Distances and compass bearings were very roughly approximate, the scattered recollections of the old Dutchman.

At least Broos claimed to know the half mountain where Thomas had killed the golem and his handler, and he had set that feature as the starting point of the inked route. All Thomas had to do was return to the spot and strike out as directed.

Except now there were several thousand Colonial troops in the way by land, and rumors the rebels had forged a huge iron chain and deployed it across the whole of the river some ways upstream to block surreptitious voyages.

Nevertheless, he was prepared. He had bought two sound horses and stabled them a few miles away at a farm where he had also stockpiled provisions. The ride inland would be harder than sailing, but he could swing wide of the American troops and return to the river valley once he was north of their camps. He would find the half mountain as he had done before and see where Huub Broos' memory took him.

Thomas did not know if Geoffrey would send another golem and keeper to follow him. He had never discussed the fate of that first pair with his lord – and did not care if Geoffrey sent a dozen of the monsters after him. Thomas would destroy them as he had destroyed the last.

October 15, 1781
The Holy Land

Proctor went limp with fear. His lungs were sheathed in copper plate and would no longer expand. His heart hammered erratically as the unbelievable played out not a yardarm's length away. Another horrible set of fingers appeared beside the first. A head rose above the rim – a huge human-shaped head with liquid eyes. It scanned the room and finally fixed its gaze on Proctor.

Moses felt his body stop living. All his humours and energies froze solid as the being regarded him. The eyes were not the deep red he had imagined of a demon. They were turquoise. The color of the deep sea at noon, the color of the eyes of a girl he had once loved.

Then Moses was looking at the wall. The being seemed to flicker out of existence. It was some kind of projection, a trick shone out of a magic lantern, he thought wildly. Someone is blocking the lens.

The image reappeared. The being heaved itself out of the bath. It was the height of two men – Proctor's brain worked automatically, taking a mariner's necessary observations. It took the shape of a man. It had ears, nose, mouth, arms, legs, hands, feet. But it was not a man. Water streamed from its skin, which was not pink or black. It possessed no color and every color and seemed to shift through the spectrum as it moved, like the iridescence of hummingbird feathers. It dematerialized, and Proctor's throat loosened enough to let wind into his chest. He surveyed the damage. Tayar was gone. The three Africans were rooted to their spots, hypnotized by the piercing gaze of the being.

Movement brought his attention back to the sarcophagus. The being was again visible. Moses wondered if its inconstant existence was a symptom of its injuries. It had not rested in the healing water long enough – they had woken it up, and it was not pleased. He began to breath rapidly. His mind had accepted the thing. He was still in awe but no longer paralyzed.

He heard the Father calling, weak and plaintive, hidden behind rubble near the tomb. The being did not even notice. It jumped down and landed with a sickening crunch and a grunt from its victim. Moses gasped – it was no shadow. The Father did not make another sound.

This shook the guards into action. One discharged both of his pistols at the thing while his fellows climbed over and between the blocking boulders to try and reach their Father.

Proctor turned and ran. After several strides he heard shrill screams behind. He rushed by Turks nervously aiming their muskets at the opening. They gesticulated plaintively at him, but he did not stop until he came to the French troops. They had regained their guns and were frantically checking priming pans and adding powder to the ones emptied by the shock of being tossed down.

Lieutenant Lefevre grabbed his arm. "What is going on?" he demanded.

Moses saw the gunners swarming their cannon, depressing the muzzles to bear on the commotion. He tore loose of the Frenchman's grip. "Tell your men not to fire unless they can see it!" he yelled, and he ran on.

He spun one of the Turkish gunners around. "Leave me one!" he cried, but the man did not speak English. Proctor repeated his plea to the left and right but none of the men showed any recognition nor paused in their tasks.

The desert winds had mounted to squalls, filling the air with gritty sand. Proctor heard Ward calling his name from somewhere in the dust and ran to the sound. The Lieutenant was cradling the wooden sabot containing the shell; Proctor pointed at the wagon. "We need the box as well," he said, and Ward passed him the sabot as if it were a fragile baby and sprinted back to the wagon.

Proctor pivoted at a ragged volley of muskets. The creature had emerged from the chamber. It advanced upon the line of Turks with a limping gait made more uneven to the eye by the occasional sudden transparency. The Cebeci were not holding their weapons like strangers now, but firing them in good form – yet musket balls did not deter the thing. It raised one thick arm and brought a monstrous fist down on the nearest terrified Turk. The man collapsed, his skull cracked and deformed like an egg squeezed too tightly. The Janissaries panicked and scattered in all directions. The giant chased slower ones, catching one by the neck and twisting off the screaming unfortunate's head with a nauseating moist cracking sound. It disappeared – and reformed directly in the path of a fleeing man. The thing raked its fingers across the Turk's chest and the saber-like nails sliced the flesh and ribs and guts into gory spurts.

The French stood firm in the face of this horror. Lieutenant Lefevre gave the order to aim and to fire, but their volley bothered the being no more than a soft breath. Before they could reload, the colossus flashed closer, right in their rank, and began to tear into the nearest soldiers.

Proctor saw from the corner of his eye the captain of the nearest cannon touching slow match to its hole. The shock of the muzzle blast caught Proctor full on the side, and he fumbled with his grip on Franklin's weapon. They had loaded canister. The deadly cluster of ball raged out and tore through the French troops, dropping three or four into red piles. But the being was not moved. It turned its piercing eyes upon the cannon and began to stalk toward them.

The next gun fired, with the same lack of effect except to kill two more Frenchmen. The Turks ran screaming as the being loped from cannon to cannon, tossing them off of their carriages as if they were dry sticks instead of three thousand odd pounds of bronze. Then it looked at Proctor.

Its eyes narrowed as it regarded the wooden object in Proctor's arms, as though it could tell this was something more threatening than mere shot. The thing started for him, ignoring several surviving French troops who reloaded and peppered it with ineffective musket balls.

Proctor backed up slowly as the being approached. He could not run. He could not drop Franklin's trust and run, and even if he had the ability he had seen how the creature could move faster than should be possible. He searched his mind for a prayer but could remember none.

The creature was three human paces from him when it stopped. Its face registered – pain? And it glared past him.

Proctor turned his head and saw Songay Bin walking quickly toward the being. He discarded two smoking pistols and drew out two more from a wide belt holding several others. He aimed at the creature and fired.

The being swiped at the air and shook like a wet dog. Canister shot had not affected it, but these small balls were somehow causing damage. Proctor remembered Stark's improvised shell containing the water and realized Bin must have fashioned ammunition with some of his own hoard of the liquid. The creature actually faltered and almost fell back before catching itself.

Ward appeared, dragging the wooden box with one hand. In the other he gripped a pistol. He had several more tucked into a bandolier. He dropped the case at Proctor's feet and, with a maniacal grin as though this was the most fun he had ever had, turned to the creature and put a ball into it. The monster actually opened its mouth in a grimace, and Proctor heard a bass note of pain under the screaming of the wounded and the crackle of small arms.

Behind them the Maratha drovers stood in a tight cluster, loading muskets. One raised his gun, shaking with obvious terror, and fired. This ball had the blind luck to find its target. The being flickered and vanished.

Bin and Ward, fresh pistols in hand, crouched warily back to back, sweeping their gaze to and fro trying to not be surprised by the reappearance of the supernatural enemy.

October 14, 1781
Hudson River Valley, New York

Night fell deeply black after thick clouds rolled in from the west and curtained the thin crescent moon and the stars. Newman crouched behind a thicket two hundred yards from the mansion listening for any sound from Nat's advance. The young man had put on his moccasins, and the Major heard no hint of his motion or any whisper of movement from the dwelling.

Newman wore his moccasins as well, and his dark spectacles were stowed in a pocket. He padded softly as a kitten to his left, toward an overgrown garden of ornamental bushes leading to the side of the mansion. The designer of the grounds had imagined them a small tribute to Versailles, but Geoffrey had not retained staff necessary to groom the place. Newman's intelligence – confirmed by Ruttee's observations – was the old warlock let no servant stay past sunset. A cook, a maid, and two butlers packed up and departed each evening, returning at first light. There were events in the night, Newman guessed, no human was to see.

He felt his way along between the shaggy high shrubs, sometimes having to thrust his body between branches interlocked over the path. The closer he got the more convinced he was that his oil ruse had worked. The only rectangle of light he could make out, high up in the building ahead of him, seemed to be wavering on the edge of extinction.

The door was solid and latched firmly. Newman slipped his knife into the gap below the handle and lifted the tongue. He pushed gently. The hinges chattered, which froze him for several anxious minutes. As he listened to the distant unformed noises of the building, his excitement at the operation cooled, and to his dismay was replaced by a tangible dread he could not throttle – his body's recognition of these surroundings as it connected with his mind's horrible memories of lying naked among corpses. His pulse came up into his ears; his guts filled with uncontrollable liquids. He had to lean against the wall and will his lungs to work deeply and slowly before he was confident he could move without shaking.

He tiptoed to his left, keeping one hand moving, fingers skimming paintings and furniture, lifting one foot at a time, gliding each slowly forward to feel for trip hazards. In this fashion he proceeded until the wall turned him to the right, then right again. Eventually he felt an open passage and went forward, still in contact with the wall. The floor underneath changed from stone to wood, and he began to hear muffled pulses of sound but could not determine their bearing.

The room was heavy with wood smoke, indicating Nat had negotiated the climb to the roof and delivered his stopper. The acrid air rushed past his ears in volumes greater than should be sucked into fireplaces, especially ones damped by canvas. It contained clean, humid pockets – the structure leaked. He heard howling outside, then saw a flash followed close by the stentorian cracking of thunder.

The lightning continued, growing brighter and more frequent by the minute. Rain dashed against the windows. It assailed the glass in thick waves and drummed on the exterior walls. Intermittent flares of pure white lit the sooty atmosphere and filled the interior much more brightly than his purpose desired. He determined to time Nature' reveals and move in its interstices.

Between the rising and falling wail outside, his ears began to decipher the muffled interior mumblings into two voices, though still indistinct and unintelligible. They seemed to be carried out of a hallway to his right. He swapped his knife to his other hand and made carefully for the source.

The two sconces lighting Thomas' reading failed within minutes of one another and could not be coaxed back to life. His fireplace moaned and belched hot sooty vapors back into the room. He tossed down his tinderbox and felt for the door, guided by the occasional glow of the storm, and went slowly down the wide stairway. The smoke was thick but seemed to abate as he descended.

In the great library, he found Geoffrey in a pool of uncertain light emitted from a candelabrum built to hold five tapers but tonight hosting only three. The flames capered erratically in the small gusts admitted through imperfections in the high windows. His lord glared down at a scrawny figure spread-eagled on the floor.

"Thomas! Come meet our guest," Geoffrey said.

Thomas waved aside a particularly thick wisp of smoke. The boy on the floor was young, his face shining with sweat. He scowled up at Thomas in defiance, squarely meeting his eyes.

Thomas suddenly could think of nothing but his son. He was out there somewhere. Was he as brave as this youth? Who would teach him to be a man? The training of his daughter did not bother him – she would grow up like her mother and aunt, fearless and deadly.

Geoffrey prodded his captive's thigh with the point of his boot. "This cur has caused our fireplaces to back, as you may have noticed, and I am sure he is involved in the problem with our lamps tonight."

"Who is he?"

"He will not say – yet," Geoffrey said. "He is part of a party which attacked me in the Carolinas, quite ineffectively. They managed only to shoot and kill one of their own men. Now they follow me here."

The storm shifted from a minor into a major key; the conductor gesturing frantically for more volume.

"I should have killed them all there and then," Geoffrey continued. "But I was preoccupied." He pointed down at Nat. "Do you still doubt this land is filled with mongrels who will never leave us in peace?"

Thomas said nothing and did not return his lord's gaze. The boy on the floor struggled against invisible restraints, his face determined and full of his terror at the same time.

Geoffrey produced an emerald flask the size of his fist and tapped the cork with one finger. "I have the solution to that problem."

Thomas looked up in alarm. "What?"

"Another bit of genius from the late Bakr ibn Mayyam. I did not wish to employ this one. There will be chaos and hysteria... but these people give us no choice." He held the flask up to eye level, displaying it to both members of his audience. "The contagion within corrupts those not protected by the water. You and I, Thomas, will feel nothing. These... things–" He pointed down at the boy. " –well, it is not pleasant. I had ibn Mayyam prove its efficacy before his payment. It – *digests* – the weak of flesh, but not entirely. Perhaps I should have let him perfect the formula before I made him drink it."

Thomas took a deep breath. This revelation would have once disturbed him profoundly, but he had over the centuries grown inured to Geoffrey's cruelty, accepting it as the right immemorial of the master of the lands to dispose of his possessions as he pleased.

Newman eased his head around the end of the wall separating him from the quivering light and opened his eyes wide to resolve as much of the scene as possible. Two shapes of men, and on the floor – his heart began to hammer. The slight figure could only be Nat. They had captured his charge.

He slid back out of their possible sight and listened to the two talk. For some time his mind would not make sense of the words – he had to fight back the nightmarish, incapacitating memory of lying on a wooden table unable to cry out as these same two voices sounded.

For several weeks as Newman lay healing from his illness and his immersion in the icy Hudson, Ruttee had sat beside his bed teaching him some useful tricks. One was a sure way to calm the mind. Newman called on this method now. He took one hand in the other and pressed hard on the palm while imagining he was singing Tempus Adest Floridum to the slowing tempo of his heart.

After several verses of the old spring song, he was level

enough to unsheathe another technique – the most important one, according to Ruttee. It was the Dibele's considered opinion the Giza were sensitive to the thoughts of others, and therefore an attacker who was free of thought might not be detected. The Major separated his hands and relaxed all of his muscles, then began to imagine he was watching himself from above. *I become a formless mass, like the smoke itself, absent from this body. I hide layered on the ceiling, thin and innocuous and silent. Like the air I drift on the slow current.*

October 15, 1781
The Holy Land

One of us must survive to tell of this bravery. Proctor squatted beside the nearest cannon, which lay on the ground, its muzzle elevated slightly. All their cannons had been dismounted and now mixed in the sandy earth with the corpses of Janissaries who had faithfully and recklessly defended them.

He seized up – he could not remember what was in the box or how it was to be deployed. Then he had the memory of Franklin, laboriously down on one cranky knee in the slush coating de Chaumont's garden, driving the metal spike.

The grounding must be well into the earth.

Proctor reached into the excelsior and searched with his fingertips until he felt the long cold nail. He yanked it out and pushed the tip into the dirt. Franklin had used a hammer to set it. Proctor reached for a nearby rock and smashed down on the metal.

Fasten the chain.

Again into the fluffy wooden shavings to draw out a thin brass chain looped again and again – it was long enough to use as a sounding line. This had an eye on one end, which he pressed down on the spike.

He could not help it – he had to glance up. Bin and Ward had drawn the creature away and were keeping a fair distance from it while taking slow turns firing. The Marathas were warmed to their task and supported them with intermittent but steady musketry. The creature still stumbled, trying to shake off the effects of Bin's creations, but Proctor could not see that any actual damage had been done. He knew the supply of the special shot was limited. He had to complete this assembly before it ran out.

He fixed the other end of the chain to a screw on the butt of the wooden sabot. *When the powder ignites*, Franklin had said, *the shock will break a membrane. The components will mix.*

Proctor had nodded understanding without possessing any.

The substances inside will react to generate an energy counter to that in the water – and let us pray – in the being to whom the water belongs and from which it must derive.

And the chain? A rope would not serve?

The conducting nature of the brass will lead the excess energy from the conflict between the two – which must be unbalanced, as we have no way of knowing the quantity for which we must allow – harmlessly into the ground.

Proctor recalled the last detail and the confidence with which the old man – who would not be present – had pronounced the word *harmlessly*. He reached into the box once more. This time he took out a small rectangular leather case opening to a pair of spectacles and put them on.

The creature had stopped its retreat and was stalking Bin and Ward. The two darted in opposite directions as an opportune cluster of shot from the Indians distracted the being momentarily from pursuit. Instead it turned its huge head to the group of Maratha, who loosed a collective shriek and scrambled away. Seen through the spectacles, the creature moved continuously. Proctor lowered his head and looked over the glass – this image stuttered and jerked.

The cannon at his feet had been loaded but not discharged. There was no time to draw the shell, so Proctor slid the sabot into the muzzle and cast about until he saw a ram lying nearby. He fetched it and stuffed Franklin's invention down as far as it could go. The chain disappeared into the dark breech like a rope into a well to where the sabot rested on top of the existing canister. *It will have to work double shotted.*

He went to the breech and tried to move it with his arms so it would bear on the creature, then he sat down and tried to push against it with his feet. The massive cannon would not budge. He jumped up and tried to use the other end of the ram as a lever, but the stick was not designed to survive this angle of applied force and broke cleanly.

Proctor glanced up in anguish and saw Bin had noted his efforts. Bin began to pick up his spent pistols and throw them at the creature. He yelled, "Hold!" at Ward, who was just taking aim. Bin had one last pistol. He sprinted toward the being in a wide arc. He fired at its face, then veered and slowed as he approached the field of Proctor's cannon.

The creature grimaced and came after Bin.

Proctor realized what the man was doing and scrambled to his feet. He scanned the ground around the cannon, then around the one closest by, finally seeing a thin wisp of smoke rising from slow match. He dashed to fetch it. On his way back to the cannon he saw the fall had knocked the powder from the touchhole. He stopped abruptly and spun in a full circle. There was no powder bag anywhere close by. He slapped his hand on his empty holster and cursed Tayar Dogantez to the depths of Hell.

He groaned as if in pain. The cannon had spun on its fall – the touchhole axis pointed below the horizontal instead of straight up. Even if he had powder, it would not stay in the shallow depression at such an angle.

Songay Bin slowed, stopping carefully on a spot he seemed to have chosen on the unmarked ground. He stood twenty paces off, directly in front Proctor's muzzle, anxiously eyeing the approaching creature. He turned to face Proctor, and they locked eyes for an instant.

Proctor wanted to scream at his friend to run. He had no way to fire the cannon. Franklin's weapon was useless after all. They were doomed, the old statesman's genius wasted on their incompetence.

Proctor rubbed his right hand nervously on the left forearm of his uniform jacket. The wool had trapped so much of the splintery excelsior that it grated against his skin.

I am packing it in excelsior, Franklin had said. *It is the best cushion. I wish it were not such a fire hazard.*

He guffawed like a lunatic. In an instant, he scraped together enough of the wood shavings to roll between his palms into a thin strand and pushed this into the touch hole, rasping it in and out until he saw the far end emerge coated in a fine black dust. He turned his creation around, pushed it back in, and brought the slow match to the exposed bit.

The creature launched itself. Proctor could see it through his spectacles, but Bin appeared to lose sight of the thing. It had gone clear. Proctor screamed, "Get down!", and the Dibele dove to the ground with his arms covering his head. The being landed on him.

Proctor stepped back. His improvised fuse spat and hissed, making a small billow of white smoke and partially obscuring the horrible scene. He could do no more – their fate was in the hands of God and Benjamin Franklin.

A spark reached home, and the cannon exploded. Captain Moses Proctor flew through the strange pinkish sky, thinking it was the most beautiful sunrise he had ever seen.

October 15, 1781
York County, Virginia

The squall raced down the broad flat river valley. It spat drops of rain that beat against them like buckshot and gathered grit and splinters into swift abrasive tornadoes. Caroline and the sergeant both lifted hands to shield their faces from the assault. Lighting struck somewhere very close, and the thunder rolled physically over them. The ground shook violently, pressing up on their feet and actually bouncing them and all loose items around them into the air for an instant. Night sky flamed an odd pink – Caroline wondered for an instant if fireworks were part of Washington's plan. She lurched to her right trying to regain her balance and heard the sergeant's boots sliding on the straw-strewn ground.

But the private was unaffected. He stood slumping, as if he were a clockwork mechanism whose spring had run down. His head fell back; his mouth fell open. He gaped unblinking up into the storm, still gripping the trigger.

Caroline flinched at an unearthly howl, high and terrific. The redheaded woman flew into her field of vision and launched herself at the private. Before the two collided, Caroline flung one arm behind her, knocking the barrel of the musket aside, and dove in the other direction. She snatched up her pistol – waiting each instant for the close explosion of the sergeant's gun – but when her roll took her back to her knees she saw only his back as he sprang out of the barn.

She fired both barrels, but his stride did not alter. She tossed her discharged weapon aside in frustration and turned to the private, who lay inert on his back. The camp wife knelt on top of him, panting, the rain streaming from her shining hair. She grabbed the tin box and pulled it free of its charge. The fuse ripped loose, soggy powder dripping harmlessly.

Caroline ran over and took up the private's musket. It had been fitted with its bayonet, as was the custom of the guards, which gave her a flash of satisfaction. She reversed it and plunged the tip down into the golem's left eye. He convulsed once – then he was still. Blood fountained from the puncture. Caroline released the stock and bolted after the sergeant.

The raw horror of a wail pierced her as she was poised to jump over the stubs of barn siding. She glanced back and saw the frantic woman cradling her baby. The fragile infant in its sling had been crushed in the attack.

The wife of a lowly enlisted man had overheard the unbelievable and without hesitation had put two lives in mortal peril to save a man she probably had never even met. And now the baby sprawled naked, unbreathing and pale.

Caroline quivered, desperate to be on the chase, yet unable to tear herself from the scene. The woman cried out again and kissed the tiny corpse.

The bead scorched the skin between Caroline's breasts. She put a hand to it and felt its hard form as the woman rocked with grief. Other Dibele thought the water itself evil, but she believed that though the fluid possessed palpable power it was ultimately a human who bore the responsibility of its use. Thus it always had been her comfort to keep a drop against such time she might herself be fading from this earth.

She ripped the necklace off as she bolted back to the sobbing woman and bit the wax off the top of the phial. The redhead clutched her babe with terrible strength − it took Caroline a moment to pry the limp body from her arms. She knelt, put the still form on its back, and upended the phial between the child's parted blue lips. Some detached part of her mind was calm enough to note it was a girl.

Almost immediately the baby began to choke and cough. It drew in a wheezy breath and began to cry. Caroline thrust it back at her bewildered mother and raced out of the barn.

October 15, 1781
Hudson River Valley, New York

"The troublesome General deserves our special attention," Geoffrey said, "but all the rest have earned this pestilence. It will be a new land, Thomas, free of all the stinking vermin, ready to be repopulated with our faithful servants."

Geoffrey shook his deadly little jug. "This travels by water and by air. From hand to hand. Brother to brother, father to son−"

A hand emerged from the darkness behind and clamped over his mouth. The knife flashed at Geoffrey's throat, but in the next instant the old knight merely bent slightly at the knees, and when he straightened – without seeming effort – the attacker spun high in the air and dropped.

The back of Newman's head slammed against the floor. Bursts of color, a sensation almost forgotten, filled his wretched eyes, and he floundered. His knife was gone. He tried to reach out and search for it, but his arms were stuck where they had landed. His legs were numb; his tailbone radiated stabs of pain. His throat filled with the beginnings of vomit, from the nauseous blow and the realization he had failed. The monster had defeated them – and it was Jeptha's fault once more.

Nat noted all this from the corner of an eye, for he had fixed his whole attention on one thing. The Major's assult had dislodged from Geoffrey's locks a single white hair. This snowy line drifted down in the candlelight, swinging to and fro, Nat intently tracking the journey until it went beyond the ability of his head to rotate and landed somewhere above his shoulder.

"I knew you would be about," Geoffrey said triumphantly. "The demonstration could not be started without you." He gripped the cork. "It is time to start clearing out the dead wood."

Thomas took one step, his hand going for the hilt of his small sword, but Geoffrey merely turned his face and Thomas froze. His fingers gripped air, and he remembered he was unarmed.

"You have stopped taking the water," Geoffrey said. "It has left you weak and altogether too sentimental. When we are done here you will begin it again."

Thomas opened his mouth but could not produce sound. He flexed his shoulders – he was caught in an invisible web, unable to prevent this abomination. Unable to save his wives and his children.

Geoffrey staggered. An invisible blow to the abdomen took his breath. Thomas felt it too, as if one of the rolling claps of the enraged storm above had erupted within the room. The suddenly liquefied floor bounced with waves, and both men lurched. An unlikely pink glow filled the sky outside, persistent and seemingly above the clouds, unlike the instantaneous brilliance of the bolts which continued nearer the earth.

Nat felt his limbs slip free. He flipped onto his side and searched the floor. The hair lay like a silver thread on black tapestry. He pinched it up with one hand while with the other pulling the grigri from inside his shirt. Opening the top, he stuffed the hair inside – and felt a tingling dread. He looked up. Geoffrey was glaring at the tiny leather pouch with a scowl of concentrated hatred.

The old knight steadied himself, raised the container of pestilence, and began to draw the cork.

He pulled at it once, then again. He glanced down at Nat, slightly puzzled and mightily annoyed, then returned his full energies to removing the suddenly obstinate stopper.

Thomas stumbled to the side, his body disengaged from Geoffrey's grip, and he clattered into an armor suit. He pushed the empty souvenir out of his way and grabbed one of the crossed broadaxes hanging from the wall. With both hands he heaved it far behind his back and swung it forward.

Geoffrey wrenched at the damn cork, his face screwed into a rictus of frustration, and just managed to lift his head in time to see the glinting edge of the axe blade as it sped toward his nose.

The steel bit into skull, the speed and heft of the weapon carrying it deep into the Lord of Emberton's brain. His head snapped back as Thomas let go of the handle, and the body collapsed to the floor, spraying a pinwheel of gore and blood. The green bottle skittered away into a corner, its cork still firm.

Newman, dripping with the dead man's fluids, sprang to his feet and drew a pistol. He made out the shape of Nat rising to his knees.

Thomas looked first at the boy and then at the man who was sighting on him down the pistol barrel with his horrible milky eyes. Outside the storm intensified. The lightning was closer now, the thunder coincident with the light and vibrating every stone in the building. An intense blue-white pulse froze them all in a static image – Geoffrey dead, Nat amazed, Newman crouching, Thomas exhausted.

"Once we were knights," Thomas said quietly. He took two quick steps and smashed through a window. Glass shards and wood splinters exploded into the room on a whipcrack of wind, forcing the Major and Nat to twist away from the shrapnel.

Nat wiped the water and debris from his face and ran to the hole. He thrust his head out into the howling tempest, his eyes narrowed to slits, but could make out nothing but streaming rain and the empty river far below.

October 15, 1781
York County, Virginia

There were few officers in front of the headquarters. Most there were enlisted men – couriers in tight groups gossiping over the background of pounding artillery. Next to them was a line of horses, lightly restrained in preparation for quick dispatch. Caroline sprinted out of the dark, skirting the circle of light cast by a lone lantern hanging near the General's tent, and in a single motion unwrapped the reins of a bay roan stallion and hopped into a stirrup. By the time her bottom hit the saddle her mount was tearing head down into the night, chased by the wild yells of the astonished men.

The muscular horse reminded her of the near-feral Arabians the Dibele used in training. This one, a veteran of war, was not spooked by the jangling discord of the marching troops she thundered past or the impact of the larger British shells rocking the ground. The night was close to perfect black, the moon a mere white fingernail, but she knew where she needed to go from an earlier survey taken high in a tree. The land around Yorktown was a flat plain leading down to the river, with only minor rises scattered about. The defending

British had turned two high spots near the town into redoubts bristling with sharpened tree trunks. Behind the Continental lines, half a mile inland, was another longish elevated knob. Washington would be atop that point observing the two assaults. Geoffrey's man must be on his way there to kill the General. No longer so spectacularly, perhaps, but she was sure the villain had another method of death in reserve.

Rider and horse jumped narrow creeks, dodged through stands of trees, and bolted across fields and meadows while above and to the east the slow ascension and decline of sparking points against the black sky marked the battle of the big guns. The shells thumped as they were launched and boomed as they exploded, but her stallion did not hesitate. She heard shouts as passing soldiers marked her color. Another hazard – the ranks knew the British position was a haven for escaped slaves, slaves who often knew much valuable information about the Continental army. She made herself as flat against the horse's back as fear could shrink her.

The horse recognized the trench first and swerved to the right. Caroline tilted precariously at the unexpected change and was pushed far out of the saddle, saved from plummeting off only by her fierce grip on the short reins. Ahead of her she just made out another rider pounding in the same direction, a white plume on his helmet like a beacon in the gloom.

The sergeant was on the other side of the trench. Caroline swore and jerked the reins sharply. She had been lucky. Her stolen horse was faster than the sergeant's mount. She beseeched the spirits she had chosen a jumper. The big stallion did not disappoint, but folded its ears back and sprang into the night without a pause.

The landing shook Caroline down hard onto the stiff saddle. Her legs were not long enough for her feet to remain in the stirrups, so her legs could not help absorb the impact. She squeezed with her knees and grabbed the mane with both hands and just managed to avoid slipping off as her horse instinctively raced after the other.

But the sergeant had noticed her, despite all the deafening

noise of cannon fire and explosions and howling, and as she drew near he lifted a saber and began to slash backwards at her. His first blow struck against the neck of her horse and opened a long gash in his hide, the deadly edge cutting a rein and then sliding sideways and catching Caroline's arm above the wrist. Odd – the blow was not at all painful, though it had sliced loose a large curling flap of skin. She clutched at the remaining rein with both hands, blood running down one arm and making her grip slippery and tenuous.

Her horse felt the gash and backed a half stride, putting her just out of the sergeant's reach. She realized only then she was unarmed, while the sergeant had his blade and a musket.

The two horses galloped along the lip of a rare straight section of the zigzagging trench. Caroline heard a sharp cry from her right, then felt the heat of a gun discharged at point blank range. Something punched her calf, and her stallion stumbled. One rear leg missed its next step, twisting the animal to the left. It slammed into the hindquarters of the horse in front, and both animals plunged straight ahead, writhing like hooked fish, into the trench.

Caroline lost her grip and shot into the air. She tried to rotate, to present her back to the fall, but still she smacked sideways against the hard earth wall of the trench and rolled to the bottom. She heard her horse collide with something metallic that clanged as the bells of ten churches accompanying the terrified screams of the poor beast.

She tried to stand, but a bone in her calf broke with a sickening crack. She dropped to her knees, gasping in pain, and squirmed forward in the trench, past her thrashing horse. She patted it in apology and rolled away from one flailing hoof. A little ways on was the sergeant's mount, unmoving, its neck at a horrible angle, its eyes bulging and empty.

She felt desperately around for a weapon as she crawled but found only a tree root abandoned in the construction. She grabbed this crooked bludgeon and continued forward, the pain filling her sight with explosions of grainy color. She heard nothing but hammering – pulsating layers of cannon and the throbbing in her body singing together in an agonizing chorus.

The explosion of a shell above lit the ditch for an instant, and she saw a man in blue standing over her, his arm raised. She yelped a wordless expression of anger and jumped up on her sound leg, excitement washing all the pain from the other, and parried with her flimsy root.

The blow never came. The figure did not move. In the flash of another shell, she saw the sergeant had landed against a section of abatis abandoned in the rush, and the spears of green wood had ripped entirely through his body and out the front of his uniform. One dripping red point extended from his mouth like an obscene tongue. His wide eyes stared past her, unfocussed and yet amazed.

She hopped backwards and sagged against the trench wall. The pain began to reestablish its dominion. It was going to be bad. She closed her eyes, fury depleted, exhaustion taking control.

The sound of cheers brought her back. The cannon fire had stopped, and nearby and in the distance men shouted huzzahs and bellowed in triumph. She straightened and looked over the lip of the trench. Ahead of her was a mound, and on the top of the mound the pitifully inadequate light of the slivered moon momentarily waxed. A beam of cool ivory shot down and penetrated the smoky haze of battle and of night. Illuminated at the peak was a tall man, a stern-faced figure who surveyed the grounds about him – at the gathering of officers near and the clusters of troops farther off – then lifted his hat to wave salute at the taking of the redoubts.

October 17, 1781
The Holy Land

He had had always treasured the traditions of Daskara Hafiz. He was proud to be a Guardian, one of the chosen. But today Ghazi ibn Abbas wished one ancient ritual had been discarded. Today he wore the breast straps of his dead brother, and the leather strips weighed on him like stone, reminding him every second of his sin.

Men who fell in defense of the village – and by extension, of the Pillar – were wrapped in their ceremonial robes and buried in the sands with their weapons. Other possessions were distributed among their relatives and incorporated into battle gear that the spirit of the deceased might fight on. Ghazi and his two surviving brothers each wore parts of the outfit the women had stripped from Ahmed's corpse. He wondered if his brothers were as burdened by theirs.

He would not ask – it was an unmanly topic. Besides, the Guardians had not talked much these past few days. He knew they burned with the same excited fusion of anger and shame and apprehension that was torturing him. He could see it in their faces, in the way they would not meet his eyes, even in the way their horses shied and pranced nervously as if they sensed the turmoil of their masters.

There had been no gold. The men had been tricked. After three days of fruitless searching, a vicious sandstorm scattered them across miles of desert, and they limped back to Daskara Hafiz to find the men they had left to watch over the village and valley murdered and the wives and children of both living and dead keening entreaties to the Giza Mashujaa for revenge.

The elders convened; the facts were examined. A military force had lured the Guardians out and destroyed them. These desecrators were now in the unguarded valley. There was no doubt these trespassers had also been responsible for the gold deception. To avenge the murders of their brothers – and to seek the forgiveness of the Giza – the criminals would have to die. Their corpses would be broken into a thousand pieces and left for the scavengers of the desert so their spirits would never know rest.

Assuming, of course, the Dark Warriors had not already dealt with the offenders. Ghazi prayed that they lived, that he would be given the chance to prove his fitness and loyalty to the Giza. He looked up and down the line. Forty-eight men had mounted, including the oldest elder. Enough to annihilate the intruders even if the men had not been energized by their almost unbearable guilt.

The enemy would not be given an honorable chance to fight – as they had given none to Ahmed and the others. The warriors perched invisibly on high ground above the lone pass to the valley. Concealed paths led down to either side of a narrow part of the gorge. When the thieves wandered between those two jaws, the trap would be sprung.

Riders had gone into the valley earlier and returned with the news that their prey was preparing to travel. Now the men waited patiently under the hot sun for the second scouts, the most careful and cautious of their village, who had crept close to the approaching enemy to count their number, evaluate their progress, and return unseen to the trap so their fellows would be well prepared.

Ghazi heard murmurs from the warriors on the far end of the line, then he heard the thudding of hoofs on hard ground. Two sets, coming in a hurry. The frantic riders burst into the trap and passed through as fast as they could induce their horses to gallop under a vigorous whip. They did not stop to report; they did not take any care to veil their haste or their presence.

The warriors concealed above were too disciplined to call out, but they glanced at one another in concern. The men kept to cover but began to inch toward the valley side, standing in their stirrups to get a peek of what had driven two of their most reliable number to flee in abject panic.

A twisting column of dust soiled the pale blue horizon, and under the plume they could make out men and animals. Riders, marchers, wagons. Yes, there were cannon, but the cannon were still hitched to their wagons and would be of no use in the quick business to follow. The number was a concern, but sharper-eyed warriors determined many of the enemy were bandaged; arms in slings and heads wrapped in bloody cloth. They would fire in haste when surprised and be dead before they could reload.

The enemy vanguard was a mounted troop. The first horseman rode two lengths in front of the others and carried a long pole with some kind of standard at the top. Ghazi smiled. That would make a famous trophy, displayed at the center of the village to remind themselves of this day of glorious retribution.

The enemy drew closer, and Ghazi heard some of his fellows gasp and cry out in disbelief. What was this? He rose up as high as he could stretch and remained there until his eyes too resolved the image and he absorbed the horrible truth.

Moses shifted the heavy, unwieldy staff yet again. His horse paced cautiously, but still the butt slipped from the improvised holster on the front of his saddle at every other step. It was probably the lubrication of the blood running down the wooden staff and trickling over his crusted hand.

The copious sweat did not help. He was drenched, though the dazzlingly bright day was cool. The closer he came to exiting the valley the more he questioned his tactic, and the anxiety heated him from the inside like a furnace.

He squinted into the sun to make sure his prize faced the right way and smiled wryly. Faced. He would remember and use the jest – if he lived through this next hour or so.

The Maratha sparked Proctor's idea when they had to a man shivered in horror and turned away from the find. A French private had caught sight of a hand in the rubble and called his fellows to dig it free. They found it attached to much of a torso and, most notably, the rather well-preserved head of the late Tower occupant. Moses observed the commotion, noted the intense emotions the scowling face of the deceased drew forth from every man, and then quietly called a conference.

The allies began discussing strategies to make their exit from the valley almost as soon as they recovered their senses from the incredible sight of the creature's destruction. Many of them had been not a stone's throw from the being when

Franklin's shell slammed home and exploded in a vast roaring belch of fire that blinded every eye. The sun itself had gone dark and a pink haze coated the heavens. As their vision slowly repaired, they saw in the fading afterimage only Songay Bin, coated with hot metal and steaming slime and smoldering traces of powder. The Dibele groaned and moved; he was burned and slashed and broken in several places. But unbelievably, alive.

After the dead had been buried and the wounded patched, the survivors pondered the mundane matter of escaping. The men of Daskara Hafiz would be coming for them soon, or more likely, be waiting in ambush.

Moses figured the allies could fight their way out, but their escape would be bloody. He was tired of blood. Ward had, in proper naval tradition, delivered the butcher's bill with his own bandaged hands once he had tallied the graves and surveyed the injured. Moses read the list of the dead – names all too familiar to him now, men he had come to know and respect – Maratha, Turks, French. *And one contentious American sailor.* But that name was not on this list.

He called for a volunteer possessing a sharp sword, a sure hand, and a lack of superstitious unease at the task. A bitter French private had stepped forward and taken some pleasure in separating the head from its neck. Moses claimed the longest pike in their possession and fixed it crudely to his saddle. He then lowered it to where the French soldier, with a chilling burst of hysterical laughter, skewered the head onto the point. Their gory prize plain in sight, the allies were ready for the worst, and departed the battlefield with all weapons primed, cannons loaded with canister, and the slow match already smoking.

The walls narrowed, and Moses felt nauseous with anxiety. It was so damnably quiet. He motioned for the two remaining cannons to halt and deploy to cover their front. The horses behind seemed to tiptoe. The wagons creaked softly, the chains tinkled, even the recalcitrant camels shuffled but raised no dust.

Then a queer sound came over all – a deep liquid puffing and catching. The allies scanned the dappled sandstone walls. Someone was crying!

Moses Proctor would remember the sight for the rest of his life. Of all the improbable scenes in his recent adventures, this was the one he would tell most often to his children and grandchildren, who would pass the tale down as long as there were Proctors to sit in front of fires.

One by one and then two by two and then in groups the fierce, hard warriors of Daskara Hafiz urged their horses up to the lip of their perch to look down on the unseeing visage of their beloved Giza as it passed beneath them. Tears flowed freely down their faces; they let their weapons slip from their shaking hands and fall to the ground. Some heads drooped, chin on chest, in abject sorrow, but every brimming eye remained on the grisly trophy until it had passed out of the valley and out of their sight.

February 17, 1782
Nafase Dibele, Central Africa

It was oddly still. Caroline scanned her home as it came into view. At this time of day there should be women gathered at the water's edge gossiping, children splashing and fishing, men fussing with their landed flatboats. The boats were there, but no villagers of any age or sex.

Caroline glanced at the man poling the craft to the shore. His eyes were wide with apprehension. He could feel it too, and he touched only long enough to let her hop off before pushing energetically back into the current.

She dropped her bag on the shore and limped past the nearest huts. Once away from the river noise she could hear soft sounds – voices in low rhythms tinged with sadness. She increased her pace, though the muscle and bone in her leg throbbed painfully.

Her mother sat on the floor of her hut dressed in blue mourning robes, crying. She turned her face up as Caroline entered, but it was not clear she recognized her daughter.

Caroline knelt and embraced her. "Maza – what is wrong?"

Her mother rubbed tears on Caroline's blouse. "The Father...".

Caroline felt suddenly ice-cold. "Dead?"

Her mother nodded against her breast. Caroline held her mother for several minutes, her own mind totally blank, then said, "Where is Nikima?"

"Hunting."

Hunting? Her brother was training to be a Watcher. Watchers did not hunt. Perhaps they were off at shooting practice, and her mother in her distress was confused. In any case, the woman was too distraught to question, so Caroline kissed her and told her she would be back soon.

She shuffled as quickly as she could wield her cane to a hut on the edge of the community. A bachelor's house, smaller and in need of some upkeep, the lot of a traveling Watcher. Songay Bin stepped onto the small porch. He was more gaunt than she remembered. Fresh scars still healing striped his cheek and chest.

"Oh!" she cried. "What happened?"

He watched her faltering approach, favoring one leg and leaning heavily on her cane. "What happened to *you*, cousin?"

They embraced. "It seems we have stories to tell one another," Caroline said.

A ragged voice called from inside the hut, "Not without me!"

Caroline went inside. On a cot in the front room Ruttee lay with one leg elevated. He put up a hand in greeting, and Caroline gasped. Two of his fingers were missing, raw stubs in their place.

"You first," she said.

Ruttee pulled his hand down and contemplated the lost

digits, nodding. Caroline came near and took the hand in hers, caressing it lightly as he told her about his deception of the guardian warriors.

"They were not pleased when I could not find the gold. At sundown they beat me and then took off one of my fingers, promising to do the same each day until they found their treasure." He laughed. "But their plan was deeply flawed. I would have been dead after the sixth of those beatings — leaving me still with fingers but them with no gold."

Caroline shook her head. Her old friend had always been slim, though strongly muscled. Now he resembled loose black sticks inserted into clothes. His hand, or what was left of it, felt like bones wrapped in thin hide.

"Fortunately, on the third day a mighty sandstorm blew up. It was so ferocious it dispersed the searchers, and I was able to slip off my mount and bury myself in the sand. I lay there for a long time, my fingers safe. But after a day or so I did not have the strength to rise. I managed to uncover my head, and that is all I remember."

Songay Bin put a flat hand horizontally against Ruttee's ear, showing her the how much had protruded. "Captain Proctor and I," he said, "persuaded one of the guardians to lead us to where they had last seen their captive. It was a minor miracle we found him. The storm had rearranged the land, and Ruttee's thick gourd was just another bump in the dunes."

"The same ones who cut off his fingers helped you find him?"

Bin nodded. "They became quite cooperative when we showed them a Giza's head on a pike."

Caroline stared at him open-mouthed. Ruttee laughed. "Call for some pito, cousins. We have a long evening ahead."

The next day they climbed to the ruins. Songay Bin heaved Ruttee over his shoulder for the journey, and his thanks for this kindness was his burden complaining of the view the whole way.

They sat together on one of the high rocks and gazed out

over the village, the river, and the jungle surrounding them.

"What now?" Caroline said at last, voicing their common thought. "If there are no more Giza, is there any need for Dibele?"

Bin frowned. "We are a small tribe. We could join with the Luba, or perhaps the Mongo."

Ruttee sighed. "I do not need any more scars. You know they will insist we take their marks."

"And I like my lips the way they are," Caroline said.

"Without the Father's powers and his reputation the Dibele are minnows," Bin said. "Traveling the world has spoiled us."

There was a long silence, then Ruttee whispered, "I do not think we can stay here."

Caroline looked down at Nafase Dibele, at the hut where she had grown up and where her mother and natural father lived, at the hut where her grandmother lived. She could not see but knew well the clearing in the jungle where her Dibele ancestors lay under the soil. Her eyes stung, but she would not make tears in front of these cousins. "Where shall we go?"

Bin pointed to the horizon and swept his finger along a wide swath. "We have been many places. Let us pick our favorite. All Dibele who wish to follow us can come. Let the rest cut their skin and join with the Luba."

"And how shall we feed ourselves when we arrive at this wonderful destination?" asked Caroline.

"We are Dibele. We will use our wits."

"So," Ruttee asked them, "will it be Spain? Or Paris? Or Istanbul?... Or New Jersey?"

April 28, 1782
Bari, Kingdom of Naples

The boatman tried Greek, which Moses did not recognize. It was understandable – the man had taken him off

355

a ship flying an Athenian pennant. Moses attempted a few words in Turkish. The man shook his head as he rowed.

"Parlez-vous–" Moses began, and the man interrupted him with a torrent of happy French, some of which Proctor was able to follow.

"Is this your first landing in Bari?" The man spoke loudly over the splashing of his rapid oars. "Do you have accommodations? I have a brother who owns a café – near the basilica holding the bones of the blessed Saint Nicholas – who will give you a special rate on one of his rooms upstairs. Do you know our Saint? Nicholas is the patron saint of sailors as well as repentant thieves – not that there is any difference except for the repenting–"

I shall stop in the basilica and light a candle begging the indulgence of Nicholas. For my sailing and my theft.

The boat placed him on the town's main key, where he shouldered his pack and picked up his case and started walking as the boatman's travelogue followed him.

"You see the church up there! To your left! To your left! Ask at the Strada San Marco for the house of Piccinno!..." The man's voice faded into the early morning bustle of seaport commerce as Proctor picked his way among barrels of fish and stacks of nets and other hazards to pedestrians.

It took him a good hour to find someone who spoke French and could also answer his question. This was not Piccinno but an elderly native taking the sun in a plaza on the far side of Nick's reliquary. Patiently smoking a tarry clay pipe, he assured Moses it was common knowledge in Bari. He even drew a map on the dusty stones which Moses did his best to memorize, though the man was confident all the traveler needed to do was keep asking which way and how far.

By his estimation of noon he was five miles north of Bari. The coastline was flat and sloped gently down to the sea. He walked past bright green vineyards and orchards thick with olive trees. Round stone houses with sharply pitched thatched roofs housed the caretakers of the plantings. The stones were white washed, the sun reflecting hard from their alabaster perfection.

Finally he came to a stout iron fence surrounding a stretch of manicured garden of ornamental shrubs and lush flowering bushes and other impractical and inedible vegetation. In the middle of the plantings rose a formidable stone mansion. He called to one of the servants, a lank dusky man digging under a tree. The man shook off his dirt like a dog rids itself of water and trotted to the house with Moses' request.

The Countess Mergasova received him in a cavernous room facing the sea. Her emaciated, waxen body was protected from the sun by translucent curtains, but the doors and windows stood open to allow the salty breeze.

He kissed her hand and was silently dismayed at how cold it felt on his lips. He had sought her over the past few weeks, first being turned away at her Kiev home and directed to seek her in Budapest, where he was told she had been there but then removed to Graz, and in that quaint locale the natives pointed south to the Adriatic. A Russian general shared two bottles of vodka with him in Zadar, slapped him on the back, and roared she was certainly in Athens, which she loved for the ruins. Athens was empty, but a full-bearded fat priest of the Greek school confided her party had shipped in toto to Bari.

It was optimistic of him to interpret her flights as signals of health. Once he touched her flesh, though, he knew she was trying to elude her mortality. She looked at ease – perhaps she had finally realized death was upon her and sailed where she sailed, a bulky fur that could not simply be left behind.

"Captain," she said softly, "I trust you are well."

"I am, my Lady," he said. "And even more now that I am returned to the presence of your beauty."

She smiled. "I love your lies. Please stay and tell me more. I might use them to drive out the truths."

He bowed.

"You have been adventuring." Her eyes were still sharp. She examined the back of his hand, where a broad scar showed abnormally pink under his tan. "I sense an exciting tale in each new mark."

"I am at your service to recite them all."

"Truly?" She was serious. "You have no duty calling you away?"

"None. The conflict sputters out."

"I am told your nation has won great victories. I congratulate you."

He bowed again. "Shall we travel across the ocean and view the things I once promised to show you?"

She tried to keep her countenance flippant, but he saw the flash of dismay before she could scrub it off. She bent her still-graceful lips to make a reply, then apparently changed her mind. She wriggled her fingers, and a manservant in a stiff cream jacket bent close to hear her orders. He left the room and soon returned carrying a silver bucket containing a fat amber bottle capped by a cork in a cage of twisted wires.

"Prosecco Superiore," she said. "I have come to love it as much as Champagne."

Moses lifted the bottle and motioned with his head to the servant, who, seeing nothing more than his mistress comfortable in the company of an old friend, backed out of the room.

The Countess gazed out onto the brilliant blue sea as her breath rattled horribly through fluids in her throat. She coughed, trying to keep the act dainty, but it came on her like an attack. Moses saw a flash of red on her handkerchief as she wiped her lips, though she tried to palm the cloth without him seeing it, which reminded him of one of Scudman's prestidigitations.

He would tell her about Scudman's tricks and his bravery and about how the unlikely company of allies had scoured the desert and battled some kind of creature in which he still could barely believe, much less identify. The village of Daskara Hafiz, the cannonade which brought down the Tower – she deserved the whole odyssey and would get as much as she could stand to hear. First, however, he needed to act.

The turnover pressed into his side. From its home in a

snug well-fastened vest pocket it dented his ribs comfortingly. He extracted it. It was much like a wee lead pastry, a round of soft metal doubled over and crimped fast by hammering around the meeting edges in quite the same way he had watched the Janissary women encapsulate meat or beans or vegetables in dense dough.

The creature's pyrotechnic exit had left the surviving allies stunned. Some wandered about slowly, amazed to be alive, or lay where they had fallen. It was quite a long time before a anguished shout drew the ambulatory into the exposed grotto. Moses limped into the sunless space, glancing upwards as he passed under the shattered wall of the Tower. It seemed to him it must collapse soon, that entering here was madness. But they were one and all – even those bleeding and battered – in no fear of anything worse happening today.

Two of the Dibele knelt by what remained of the Father. He had been crushed and rendered almost in two by the stamp of the being's clawed feet. Moses knew in one glance what the Children had realized. The damage was far too cruel to be put right by any amount of the water.

Lieutenant Lefevre balanced on the lip of the creature's bath, calling and pointing down to where the crack had widened. Water gushed out and ran into the earth. Moses grabbed at the rock and pulled himself up far enough to peer down into the emptying crypt. The walls were irregular, as if hacked out of the stone in haste, and on each wall sprouted patches of crystals, dark purple with mirrored facets reflecting thousands of tiny images of the Frenchman.

Moses heard dismay behind him. He dropped back down onto a pile of broken ceiling and watched as Yildirim crawled through the fleeting pool of water, trying to catch some of it in an ivory flask. The man whimpered as he pushed the open neck of his container against the crack and then down into the loose stones. Moses hoped he would be able to catch enough to satisfy his Sultan.

Then Moses saw a regular shape in the draining water and

had an epiphany. He jumped down beside Yildirim, cast about for a flat space and a small rock to fit his hand, and picked up the ball. It had already been partially flattened by striking against the crypt. He set it down and began to hammer it flat.

Songay Bin, bruised and crusted with huge spots of his own blood, appeared over them as Moses knelt crimping the edges. He expected the Dibele to chastise them for mucking about in the essence of evil and command them to pour the vile fluid out. But Bin just sighed.

"It will not be the same," he said.

Moses finished his seal and held the product in his closed hand, feeling somehow ashamed and common.

"The creature is dead," Bin continued through gritted teeth. He scraped a gooey paste of blood and sand from one crooked arm where the sharp white end of a bone jutted through his skin. He grimaced in pain even as he watched Yildirim, who was digging down with his hands in search of the fleeing moisture. "The source of power is removed."

Yildirim looked up in terror. Moses felt a surge of pity for him. Bin must have as well, for he quickly said, "I think it will retain the vital force for some time. How long that will be, no one knows."

Yildirim nodded and jumped up, stoppering his flask. Moses expected him to sprint for the opening and keep running until he had delivered the container to the Sultan, but Yildirim just stood pressing the bottle to his bosom and gaping around the destroyed chamber where the fabulous creature had slept since time immemorial.

Moses twisted the cork. It came free of the neck with a satisfying pop, and the wine gushed a rope of minute bubbles as clear as water. The air filled with cherries and honey. He poured two glasses, tall flutes perfect for accentuating the sparkles, leaving one just shy.

He raised his crude turnover and bit hard along the seal, the taste of lead causing his body to vibrate, the memory of muscles recalling this familiar prelude to loading and firing –

his hands could almost feel a musket. *Not today*, he thought. Into the gnarled opening of his lead pouch he coaxed several drops of the happy beverage, shook the metal carefully, and dripped the solution back into the glass.

He held this transparent chalice up against the brilliance of the columns outside. Had the improvised seal even held all this time? How long had it been since the cavern? Bin had said the power would fade; yet Bin could only guess. Perhaps the water had been mere water even as he had been packaging it, and this whole chase had been for nothing, and nothing would come of this visit except his misery as he sat by her deathbed.

But there was something. He held his own glass alongside to compare. Somehow not the same. He brought the first glass close to his face – and smiled. In the center of each perfect sphere rushing to the surface he could just see a dot of violet, a glowing pinprick.

She accepted her drink. "To the United States," she whispered. "And safe passage on your journey."

Moses Proctor touched his glass most delicately against hers. "To the United States. And safe passage on *our* journey."

October 22, 1783
Dijon, France

The Cathédrale Saint-Bénigne de Dijon stood between Franklin and the morning sun, its shadow blocking what little warmth the young day held. He was on the far side of a modest boulevard empty but for a shabby horse tied to a stair railing in front of the church and a dead dog sprawled in the middle.

Dijon, the enthusiastic coachman had told him, was home to no fewer than nine cathedrals, but Franklin knew from experience every chapel with two rooms and a belfry advertised itself as a cathedral to draw the tourists past its collection box.

When he was younger he had spent his times in England

and France eagerly visiting legendary houses of The Almighty. The first score or so he had undertaken to study in great detail, often recording observations and drawing sketches in his notebook. He wanted to analyze each one and skin it with his imagination down to its bones and the very pit from which it rose. How the underpinnings were placed to support the soaring elements, how the architect had planned out the open spaces against the solid and how the orientation to the compass influenced their relative disposition. By the second score he was beginning to notice more the mistakes where human and material insufficiencies cropped up. And lately, on those occasions when he was kidnapped by well-meaning Frenchmen and obliged by good manners and diplomacy to view some shrine to a sanctified martyr nobody outside of ten kilometers from the altar knew, he could mentally destroy the building in half a minute and resurrect it in five, much improved in structure and beauty.

Perhaps I will take up architecture. Christopher Wren was a layman, self-taught. He lived to ninety-one. Plenty of time.

The final resting place of the sainted Msr. Bénigne was unimpressive. It brought to Franklin's mind a paving stone stood on end and inexpertly decorated – slab-sided, angled where art demanded curves, plain walls where there should be ornamentation, topped by an incongruous round house. It was unwelcoming and unfriendly. Perhaps its other sides were more remarkable, but he was not going to find out.

Inside the cathedral it felt colder than outdoors. Franklin pulled his heavy coat up more tightly under his chin. In the tunnel of a nave a handful of Dijonians were taking the mass. One of them turned from the priest's drone to the intrusion and frowned at Franklin's failure to remove his hat, a round-crowned wide-brimmed black topper that made the wearer appear much like a Catholic official in his saturno. The hat rode hard on Franklin's brow, but he made no move to shed it. He nodded to the statue of Jesus and moved to the side of the nave, taking care not to tap his thick walking stick against the slab stones of the floor.

Between small chapel spaces which shot off at right angles from the axis of the nave were several wooden doors. Franklin, confident from his long study of the construction of these things, selected one and went to open it. Behind was a shallow archive of brooms from various centuries. He pursed his lips and consoled himself: a pithy proverb might be made of this, but some other time. He quickly and quietly shut this door and reconsidered.

The third door he attempted opened onto descending stone steps. He stepped inside and closed the thick wood behind him, droning Latin instantly attenuated to incomprehensible mumbling. Now his heavy walking stick showed its value as he probed down to find the next step. There was light here, squeezing in from slits in the foundation, but not enough to make his footing confident.

At the bottom of the stairs, more light came from hidden windows. The space was formed by rough columns joining in amateurish, irregular arches. Hasty work, Franklin noted. Was this crew less skilled or was this the part more ancient than the rest of the place? He saw neither central structure that might hold bones nor any mark on the floor suggesting they were buried. Many cathedrals had crypts built into the foundation walls – simple display spaces. The actual volume occupied by your average saint's remains was oddly small.

The burial place of Bénigne was different. At the end of the vault stood a wide marble table, and behind that another wooden door marked with a cross. Did the clergy perform a Mass for the dead down here? Franklin visualized such a service and silently declared it suitably unnerving. Attending a gathering in this spectral space would raise hackles on even the most fervent nonbeliever and drive any unrepentant sinner to the confessional.

He bypassed the table and pushed on the cross. The door had no visible handle and no hint of an operating mechanism, but one touch and it swung open on greased hinges, quiet and fast.

The pistol came out of the blackness in the hand of a

hooded figure. "Welcome, Ambassador."

Franklin took a step back, and the man advanced the same distance toward him.

"I shan't bother to ask how you found me. The wretched French are enamored of you and no doubt eagerly share their intelligence. They are a nation of gossipers and old women."

Franklin recovered enough to make a brief bow. "How shall I name you, sir?"

"I am Guy of Poitou, once a Crusader of the Holy Land in the service of His Holiness Frederick the Second. A knight and warrior for his Lord Jesus, who now cowers in the corners downstairs like a cockroach. Address me as you please."

"Very well, Guy of Poitou, I must point out that Dijon in Latin means 'the sacred fountain'."

Guy laughed. The sound was dry and not very sincere. "I congratulate you on the conclusion of your treaty. Even we lowly insects receive the tidings of the day eventually. A great accomplishment." He paused, then said, "How old are you?"

"Seventy-seven, or so I am told."

"I have lived five and a half centuries. There is no one to tell *me* that – as no mortal has kept pace. If you were to live so long perhaps you could make a name for yourself."

"Why did you not let them kill me in the alley that night?" Franklin was suddenly enraged. He lifted his walking stick and jabbed it down, hard. "Why create my savior?"

"So you enjoyed my little trick?" Guy nodded. "I found her in Monaco. She lay in her own waste waiting for death. Cleaned and refreshed with a trick or two, she was transformed into a creature most pleasurable."

Franklin's face was hard but he did not speak.

"We did not want you to be a martyr, to provide inspiration from the grave. We required you only to lose your fervor for politics. A demonstration to dishearten the rebels – their most dedicated man had moved on to his next fancy."

"You flatter me...and expand my influence beyond reason."

"I do not think so. Lack of passion is like an illness,

spread by mouth and inflamed by self-interest. You should have infected the whole of your little nation."

"Ah – the nation you wanted."

"The continent we should have had."

"You are welcome to come over and obtain a plot."

"Do not make sport with me. You destroyed the Tower. The water is gone. I felt it. One day the earth seemed to shake. I heard a thundering, but the sky was clear – save for a pulsing light I felt in my guts. No one about me even looked up. I knew the being was awake. I could feel the water throbbing in my veins. Then – nothing. You had killed the root of its power."

"I freely confess to it."

"So tell me – before you die – was it a demon or an angel?"

"Why do you care?"

"If I have been nurtured by the essence of an angel these centuries my mind will be more at ease."

"Alas, it was ruined beyond examination. My agents could not tell," Franklin said.

Guy turned a bit, just enough so the faint light showed his face. *His flesh is deteriorating. It must be some time since he has had a taste.*

"Then my interest in this conversation has come to an end." The muzzle centered on Franklin's heart. Guy hesitated and tilted his head, a dog just catching a scent.

He has taken it, Franklin thought, and said quickly, "But this might be." He took a pewter flask out of his pocket and pulled the stopper. A faint quivering beam of blue came out, like dancing smoke. "Your brother Ordulf had no more use for it."

Guy put out a hand. Franklin shrugged and gave it over. "Shall we call our mutual debts cancelled?" he asked.

The knight said nothing, but smiled – and pulled the trigger.

Franklin saw the finger tighten and just had time to tip his head down as if wondering where the ball would strike. The

365

flintlock sparked, and the muzzle flash lit the cellar through a billowing gray cloud of smoke. The ball slammed into his chest. Layers of cloth erupted – a crater ejected threads and woven shards, and Franklin fell back. His body bounced once and then lay inert on the stones. His walking stick remained upright, its sharp end jammed into a wide joint.

Guy stood over the corpse and lifted the flask up as if proposing a toast. "You should have drunk this and sailed home," he gloated. "Your reputation for cleverness is apparently undeserved." Franklin's round hat touched his foot. Guy flicked it away with a kick. It rolled true, not folding as mere felt ought, and struck the leg of the stone table with a dull clang.

Guy frowned as he studied the hat.

Franklin's eyes opened. The two men stared at each other for an instant, then Franklin gripped Guy's ankle. Something bit into the flesh. Guy grunted in alarm and pulled at his belt, his fingers working to find purchase on a knife handle. He noticed a metallic line running from his ankle to the walking stick – and the walking stick was... humming? Guy at last extracted his knife and lifted it high.

The walking stick erupted with an aura of pulsing ruby light, the glow shimmering also around a line running to his ankle. Guy checked his knife thrust as he tried to balance. It felt like a powerful hand was hauling him into the earth.

A crimson glow flew up his leg and enveloped his body. The knife clattered from his hand, and he wheezed. The hood fell from his head as he clutched at his chest.

Franklin watched as the same corruption that had consumed his beloved embraced Guy and wrenched him physically and spectacularly back through stolen time. But Guy had farther to fall – five and a half centuries. Guy's skin turned translucent, then clear as still water, and Franklin saw the old knight's muscles, his sinews, his tendons, his bones, then in a rush his brains and blood – each layer of the man releasing long-stored energy back into the grounding wire and into the earth. What was left of Guy howled thinly and collapsed straight to the floor.

Franklin sat up slowly, grimacing. At least two ribs broken, he estimated. Carefully pulling back the several layers of heavy cloth holding fast his overlapping iron plates, he noted the healthy dent the ball had made. The design seemed to be sound. The armored hat, too loose in the crisis, was more of a risk. That concept would have to be refined. Perhaps a chinstrap.

He pulled himself laboriously to his feet and looked down, panting in pain, on the empty robe and desiccated mass of gnarled dark tissue, and remembered his lovely Madame. He sighed – and instantly regretted the action as rib bones ground their shattered ends together.

The flask lay on its side. He decided against bending over for it and reached cautiously out for his walking stick. It was warm to his touch, the series of miniature Leyden compartments he had constructed within it having fully discharged. Franklin worked it free of the earth.

The water slowly gurgled out of the flask. It pooled atop stone on its way to the dirt between, a fluid tinged with cardinal and violet and cobalt, the colors flashing in turns at the edges. Franklin held the walking stick in the air above the flask for a beat, watching this phenomenon and postulating several testable hypotheses, then shook his head and used the stick to fully upend the vessel. The last of the water rushed out into the earth and was gone.

www.ingramcontent.com/pod-product-compliance
Lightning Source LLC
Chambersburg PA
CBHW072113250626
47159CB00007B/2427